A House
Like a Lotus

ALSO BY MADELEINE L'ENGLE

The Small Rain (1945)

Ilsa (1946)

And Both Were Young (1949)

A Winter's Love (1957)

Meet the Austins (1960)

A Wrinkle in Time (1962)

The Moon by Night (1963)

The Twenty-four Days Before Christmas (1964)

The Arm of the Starfish (1965)

Camilla (1965)

The Love Letters (1966)

The Journey with Jonah (1967)

The Young Unicorns (1968)

Dance in the Desert (1969)

Lines Scribbled on an Envelope (1969)

The Other Side of the Sun (1971)

A Circle of Quiet (1972)

A Wind in the Door (1973)

The Summer of the Great-grandmother (1974)

Dragons in the Waters (1976)

The Irrational Season (1977)

A House Like a Lotus

Madeleine L'Engle

SQUARE
FISH

Farrar Straus Giroux
New York, NY

SQUARE
FISH
An Imprint of Macmillan

ISBN 978-0-312-54798-1

Library of Congress catalog card number: 84-48471

Originally published in the United States by Farrar Straus Giroux
First Square Fish Edition: February 2012
Square Fish logo designed by Filomena Tuosto
macteenbooks.com

10 9 8 7 6 5 4 3 2 1

LEXILE: 790L

For Robert Lescher

One

Constitution Square. Athens. Late September.

I am sitting here with a new notebook and an old heart.

Probably I'll laugh at that sentence in a few years, but it is serious right now. My sense of humor is at a low ebb.

I'm alone (accidentally) in Greece, and instead of enjoying being alone, which is a rare occurrence, since I have six younger siblings, I am feeling idiotically forlorn. Not because I'm alone but because nothing has gone as planned. What I would like to do is go back to my room in the hotel and curl up on my bed, with my knees up to my chin, like a fetus, and cry.

Do unborn babies cry?

My parents are both scientists and for a moment I am caught up in wondering about fetuses and tears. I'll ask them when I get home.

The sun is warm in Constitution Square, not really hot, but at home, on Benne Seed Island, there's always a sea breeze. Late September in South Carolina is summer, as it is in Greece, but here the air is still and the sun beats down on me without the salt wind to cool it off. The heat wraps itself around my body. And my body, like everything else, is suddenly strange to me.

What do I even look like? I'm not quite sure. Too tall, too thin, not rounded enough for nearly seventeen, red hair. What I look like to myself in my mind's eye, or in the mirror, is considerably less than what I look like in the portrait which now hangs over the piano in the living room of our house on the beach. It's been there for maybe a couple of months.

Nevertheless, it was a thousand years ago that Max said, 'I'd like to paint you in a seashell, emerging from the sea, taking nothing from the ocean but giving some of it back to everyone who puts an ear to the shell.'

That's Max. That, as well as everything else.

I've ordered coffee, because you have to be eating or drinking something in order to sit out here in the Square. The Greek coffee is thick and strong and sweet, with at least a quarter of the cup filled with gritty dregs.

I noticed some kids at a table near mine, drinking beer, and I heard the girl say that she had come to stop in at American Express to see if her parents had sent her check. "It keeps me out of their hair, while they're deciding who to marry next." And the guy with her said, "Mine would like me to come home and go to college, but they keep sending me money, anyhow."

There was another kid at the next table who was also listening to them. He had black hair and pale skin and he looked up and met my eyes, raised one silky black brow, and went back to the book he was reading. If I'd been feeling kindly toward the human race I'd have gone over and talked to him.

A group of kids, male, definitely unwashed, so maybe their checks were late in coming, looked at me but didn't come over. Maybe I was too washed. And I didn't have on jeans. Maybe I didn't even look American. But I had this weird feeling that I'd like someone to come up to me and say, "Hey, what's your name?" And I could then answer, "Polly O'Keefe," because all that had been happening to me had the effect of making me not sure who, in fact, I was.

Polly. You're Polly, and you're going to be quite all right, because that's how you've been brought up. You can manage it, Polly. Just try.

I'd left Benne Seed the day before at 5 a.m., South Carolina time, which, with the seven-hour time difference, was something like seventeen hours ago. No wonder I had jet lag. My parents had come with me, by Daddy's cutter to the mainland, by car to Charleston, by plane to New York and JFK airport. Airports get more chaotic daily. There are fewer planes, fewer ground personnel, more noise, longer lines, incomprehensible loudspeakers, short tempers, frazzled nerves.

But I got my seat assignment without too much difficulty, watched my suitcase disappear on the moving belt, and went back to my parents.

My father put his hands on my shoulders. 'This will be a maturing experience for you.'

Of course. Sure. I needed to mature, slow developer that I am.

Mother said, 'You'll have a wonderful time with Sandy and Rhea, and they'll be waiting for you at the airport, so don't worry.'

'I'm not worried.' Sandy is one of my mother's brothers, and my favorite uncle, and Rhea is his wife, and she's pretty terrific, too. I'd be with them for a week, and then fly to Cyprus, to be a general girl Friday and gofer at a conference in a village called Osia Theola. I've done more traveling than most American kids, but this time, for the first time, I'd be alone, on my own, nobody holding my hand, once I left Athens.

Athens, my parents kept telling me, was going to be fun, since Rhea was born on the isle of Crete and had friends and relatives all over mainland Greece and most of the islands. Sandy and Rhea were both international lawyers and traveled a lot, and being with them was as safe as being with my parents.

Why hadn't I learned that nothing is safe?

'Write us lots of postcards,' Mother said.

'I will,' I promised. 'Lots.'

I wanted to get away from my parents, to be on my own, and yet I wanted to reach out and hold on, all at the same time.

'You'll be fine,' Daddy said.

'Sure.'

'Take care of yourself,' Mother said. 'Be happy.' Underneath her words I could almost hear her saying, 'Don't be frightened. I wish I could go with you. I wish you were a little girl again.'

But she didn't say it.

And I'm not. Not anymore. Maybe I'd like to be. But I'm not.

My family knew that something had gone wrong, that something had happened, but they didn't know what, and they respected my right not to tell them until

I was ready, or not to tell them at all. Only my Uncle Sandy knew, because Max had called him to come, and he'd flown down to Charleston from Washington. This was nothing unusual. Sandy, with or without Rhea, drops in whenever he gets a chance, popping over to the island en route to or from somewhere, just to say hello to the family.

Fortunately, I'm the oldest of our large family, including our cousin Kate, who's fourteen, living with us and going to school with us on the mainland. So no one person comes in for too much attention.

Mother put her arm around me and kissed me and there were questions in her eyes, but she didn't ask them. Flights were being called over the blurred loudspeaker. Other people were hugging and saying goodbye.

'I think that's my flight number—' I said.

Daddy gave me a hug and a kiss, too, and I turned away from them and put my shoulder bag on the moving conveyor belt that took it through the X-ray machine. I walked through the X-ray area, retrieved my bag, slung it over my shoulder, and walked on.

On the plane I went quickly to my window seat and strapped myself in. The big craft was only a little over half full, and nobody sat beside me, and that was fine with me. I wanted to read, to be alone, not to make small talk. I leaned back and listened to the announcements, which were given first in Greek, then in English. A stewardess came by with a clipboard, checking off names.

'O'Keefe. Polly O'Keefe. P-o-double l-y.' My passport has my whole name, Polyhymnia. My parents should have known better. I've learned that it's best if I spell my nickname with two l's. Poly tends to be pronounced as though it rhymes with pole. I'm tall and skinny like a pole, but even so I might get called Roly Poly. So it's Polly, two *l*'s.

Another stewardess passed a tray of champagne. Without thinking, I took a glass. Sipped. Why did I take champagne when I didn't even want it? Not because I don't like champagne; not because I'm legally under age; but because of Max. Max and champagne, too much champagne.

At first, champagne was an icon of the world of art for me, of painting and music and poetry, with ideas fizzing even more brightly than the dry and sparkling wine. Then it was too much champagne and a mouth tasting like metal. Then it was dead bubbles, and emptiness.

I drank the champagne, anyhow. If you have a large family, you learn that if you take a helping of something, you finish it. Not that that was intended to apply to champagne, it was just an inbred habit with me. When another stewardess came by to refill my glass I said, "No, thank you."

A plane is outside ordinary time, ordinary space. High up above the clouds, I was flying away from everything that had happened, not trying to escape it, or deny it, but simply being in a place that had no connection with chronology or geography. All I could see out the window was clouds. No earth. Nothing familiar. I ate the meal which the stewardess brought around, without tasting it. I watched the movie, without seeing it. About halfway through, I surprised myself by falling asleep and sleeping till the cabin lights were turned on, and first orange juice and then breakfast were brought around. All through the cabin, people yawned and headed for the johns, and there are not enough johns, since most of the men use them for shaving.

Window shades were raised, so that sunlight flooded the cabin. While I was eating breakfast I kept peering out the window, looking down at great wild mountains. Albania, the pilot told us: rugged, dark, stony, with little sign of habitation or even vegetation.

A dark and bloody country, Max had said.

Then we flew over the Greek islands, darkly green against brilliant blue. Cyprus. After Athens, I would be going to Cyprus.

I had a sense of homecoming, because this was Europe, and although we've been on Benne Seed Island for five years, Europe still seems like home to me. Especially Portugal, and a small island off the south coast called Gaea, where the little kids were born, and where we lived till I was thirteen.

Then we moved back to the United States, to Benne Seed Island. Daddy's a marine biologist, so islands are good places for his work, and Mother helps him, doing anything that involves higher math or equations.

Being brought up on an isolated island is not good preparation for American public schools. Right from the beginning, I didn't fit in. The girls all wore large quantities of makeup and talked about boys and thought I was weird, and maybe I am. Some of the teachers liked me because I'm quick and caught up on schoolwork without any trouble, and some of them didn't like me for the same reason. I don't have a Southern accent— why should I?—so people thought I was snobby.

The best thing about school is getting to it. We all pile into a largish rowboat with an outboard motor, and running it is my responsibility. I suppose Xan's taking over while I'm away. Anyhow, we take the boat to the mainland, tie it to the dock with chain and padlock around the motor. We walk half a mile to the school bus, and then it's a half-hour bus ride. And then I get through the day, and it's bearable because I like learning things. When we lived in Portugal, there was no school on Gaea, and we were much too far from the mainland to go to school there, so our parents taught us, and learning was fun. Exciting. At school in Cowpertown, nobody seemed to care about learning anything, and the teachers cared mostly about how you scored on the big tests. I knew I had to do well on the tests, but I enjoy tests; our parents always made them seem like games. So I did well on them, and I knew that was important, because I will need to get a good scholarship at a good college. Our parents have made us understand the importance of a good education.

Seven kids to educate! Are they crazy? Sandy and Dennys will probably help, if necessary. Even so . . .

Charles, next in line after me, will undoubtedly get a good scholarship. He knows more about marine biology than a lot of college graduates. He's tall—we're a tall family—and his red hair isn't as bright as mine.

Charles and I were the only ones to get the recessive red-hair gene. The others are various shades of ordinary browns.

Alexander is next, after Charles, named after Uncle Sandy, and called Xan to avoid confusion, since Sandy and Rhea come to Benne Seed so often. Xan is tall—of course—but last year he shot up, so that now he's taller than I am. It's a lot easier to boss around a little brother who's shorter than you are than one who looks over the top of your head, is a basketball star at school, is handsome, and adored by girls. We got along better when he was my *little* brother. He and Kate team up against the rest of us, especially me. Kate is beautiful and brown-haired and popular.

After Xan is Den, named after Uncle Dennys. He's twelve, and most of the time we get along just fine. But every once in a while he tries to be as old as Xan, and then there's trouble. At least for me.

Then come the little kids, Peggy, Johnny, and Rosy. Because I'm the oldest, I've always helped out a lot, playing with them, reading to them, giving them baths. They're still young enough to do what I tell them, and to look up to me, and to accept me just as I am. And I feel more like myself when I'm playing on the beach with the little kids than I do when I'm at school, where everybody thinks I'm peculiar.

Under normal circumstances I would have been delighted to get away from the family and from school for a month. Mother tries not to put too much responsibility on me, and everybody has jobs, but if Mother's in the lab helping Daddy work out an equation, then I'm in charge, and believe me, all these brethren and sistren have about decided me on celibacy.

The plane plunged through a bank of clouds and the stewardess called over the loudspeaker that we were all to fasten seat belts and put seats and tray tables in upright position for the descent into Athens. I kept blowing my nose to clear my ears as the pressure changed. With a minimum of bumps, we rolled along the runway. Athens.

I joined the throng leaving the plane, like animals rushing to get off the ark.

I followed the others to baggage claim and managed to get my suitcase from the carousel by shouldering my way through the crowd. As I lugged the heavy bag toward the long counters for customs, I heard loudspeakers calling names, and hoped I might hear mine, but nobody called for Polly O'Keefe.

The customs woman peered into my shoulder bag; she could have taken it, as far as I was concerned. But I couldn't refuse the bag, which Max sent over from Beau Allaire, without someone in the family noticing and making a crisis over it. It was gorgeous, with pockets and zippers and pads and pens, and if anybody else had given it to me I'd have been ecstatic.

The customs woman pulled out one of my notebooks and glanced at it. What I wrote was obviously not in the Greek alphabet, so she couldn't have got much out of it. She handed it back to me with a scowl, put a chalk mark on my suitcase, and waved me on.

I went through the doors, looking at all the people milling about, looking for Uncle Sandy and Aunt Rhea to be visible above the crowd. I saw a tall man with a curly blond beard and started to run toward him, but he was with a woman with red hair out of a bottle (why would anybody deliberately want that color hair?), and when I looked at his face he wasn't like Sandy at all.

Aunt Rhea has black hair, shiny as a bird's wing, long and lustrous. I have my hair cut short so there'll be as little of it to show as possible. Daddy says it will turn dark, as his has done, the warm color of an Irish setter. I hope so.

Where were my uncle and aunt? I'd expected them to be right there, in the forefront of the crowd. I kept looking, moving through groups of people greeting, hugging, kissing, weeping. I even went out to the place where taxis and buses were waiting. They weren't there, either. Back into the airport. If I was certain of anything in an uncertain world, it was that Sandy and Rhea would be right there, arms outstretched to welcome me.

And they weren't. I mean, I simply had to accept that they were not there. And I wasn't as sophisticated a traveler as I'd fooled myself into thinking I was. Someone else had always been with me before, doing the right things about passports, changing money, arranging transportation. I'd gone through passport control with no problem, but now what?

I looked at the various signs, but although I'd learned the Greek alphabet, my mind had gone blank. I could say thank you, *epharisto*, and please, *parakalo*. *Kalamos* means pen, and *mathetes* means student, and I'd gone over, several times, the phrase book for travelers Max had given me. I'm good at languages. I speak Portuguese and Spanish, and a good bit of French and German. I even know some Russian, but right now that was more of a liability than an asset, because when I looked at the airport signs I confused the Russian and Greek alphabets.

I walked more slowly, thought I saw Sandy and Rhea, started to run, then slowed down again in disappointment. It seemed the airport was full of big, blond-bearded men, and tall, black-haired women. At last I came upon a large board, white with pinned-up messages, and I read them slowly. Greek names, French, German, English, Chinese, Arabic names. Finally, P. O'Keefe.

I took the message off the board and made myself put the pin back in before opening it. My fingers were trembling.

DELAYED WILL CALL HOTEL SANDY RHEA

They had not abandoned me. Something had happened, but they had not forgotten me. I held the message in my hand and looked around the airport, where people were still milling about.

Well, I didn't need someone to hold my hand, keep the tickets, tell me what to do. I found a place where I could get one of my traveler's checks cashed into Greek money, and then got a bus which would take me to the hotel.

It was the King George Hotel, and Max had told me that it was old-fashioned and comfortable and where she stayed. If Max stayed there, then it was expensive as well as pleasant, and that made me uncomfortable. I wouldn't have minded my father paying for it, though marine biologists aren't likely to be rolling in wealth. I wouldn't even have minded Sandy and Rhea paying for it, because I knew Rhea had inherited pots of money. But it was Max. This whole trip was because of Max.

It was in August that Max had said to me, 'Polly, I had a letter today from a friend of mine, Kumar Krhishna Ghose. Would you like to go to Cyprus?'

Non sequiturs were not uncommon with Max, whose thoughts ranged from subject to subject with lightning-like rapidity.

We were sitting on the screened verandah of her big Greek revival house, Beau Allaire. The ceiling fan was whirring; the sound of waves rolled through all our words. 'Sure,' I said. 'But what's Cyprus got to do with your Indian friend?'

'Krhis is going to coordinate a conference there in late September. The delegates will be from all the underdeveloped and developing countries except those behind the Iron Curtain—Zimbabwe, New Guinea, Baki, Kenya, Brazil, Thailand, to name a few. They're highly motivated people who want to learn everything they can about writing, about literature, and then take what they've learned back to their own countries.'

I looked curiously at Max, but said nothing.

'The conference is being held in Osia Theola in Cyprus. Osia, as you may know, is the Greek word for holy, or blessed. Theola means, I believe, Divine Speech. We can check it with Rhea. In any case, a woman named Theola went to Cyprus early in the Christian era and saw a vision in a cave. The church that was built over the cave and the village around it are named after her, Osia Theola.'

I was evidently supposed to say something. 'That's a pretty name.'

At last Max, laughing, took pity on me. 'My friend Krhis is going to need someone to run errands, do simple paperwork, be a general slave. I've offered you. Would you like that?'

Would I! 'Sure, if it's all right with my parents.'

'I don't think they'd want you to miss that kind of opportunity. Your mother can do without you for once. I'll speak to your school principal if necessary and tell him what an incredible educational advantage three weeks on Osia Theola will be. It won't be glamorous, Polly. You'll have to do all the scut work, but you're used to that at home, and I think it would be good experience for you. I've already called Krhis and he'd like to have you.'

Just like that. Three weeks at Osia Theola in Cyprus. That's how it happened. That's the kind of thing Max could do. Now that I thought about it, it seemed likely that Max had paid for my plane fare, too.

The week in Athens, before the conference, was something Max said I shouldn't miss, and my parents agreed. I had never been to Greece, and they were happy for me to have the opportunity.

We were all less happy about it by the time I left Benne Seed than when the plan was first talked about, Max enthusiastically showing us brochures of Athens and Osia Theola, the museums, the Acropolis. Those last weeks before I flew to Athens, my parents looked at each other when I came into a room as though they'd been talking about me, but they didn't say anything, and neither did I.

And now I was on a bus, sitting next to a family who were talking loudly in furious syllables. The man wore a red fez, so I assumed they were Turkish, and Turkish is a language I've never even attempted. During the drive I began to feel waves of loneliness, like nausea, until I was certain the hotel wouldn't have a reservation for me, and what then? I certainly wasn't going to call South Carolina and ask someone to come rescue me.

But I was welcomed, personally, by the manager, and given a message which said the same thing as the one at the airport.

I liked the hotel, which reminded me a little of hotels in Lisbon. But I felt very alone. I followed the bellman to my room. He opened the door, put my bag down on the rack, flung open doors to closets, to a big bathroom, opened floor-length windows to the balcony.

"Acropolis," he said, pointing to the high hill with its ancient, decaying buildings, and I caught my breath at the beauty. Sounds of the present came in, contradicting the view: bus brakes, taxi horns, the wail of a siren.

I stood looking around, first at the view, then at the room, which was comfortably European, with yellow walls, a brass bed, a stained carpet, and an enormous bouquet of mixed flowers on a low table in front of the sofa.

After a moment I realized that I'd forgotten the bellman and that he was waiting, so I dug in my purse for what I hoped was the right amount of money, put it in his hand, saying, "*Epharisto.*"

He checked what I'd given him, smiled at me in approval, said, "*Parakalo,*" and left, closing the door gently behind him.

The sunlight flooded in from the balcony, warming me. Despite the heat, I felt an odd kind of cold, like numbness from shock. I unpacked, spreading out notebooks and paperbacks on the coffee table to establish my territorial imperative. No photographs. Not of anybody.

Whenever I stepped out of the direct sunlight, the inner cold returned. And a dull drowsiness. Although I had slept more on the plane than I had expected, it was a long time since I'd actually stretched out on a bed. The early-afternoon sun was streaming across the balcony and into my room, but my internal time clock told me I was tired and wanted to go to bed.

Max had suggested that I get on Greek time as soon as possible. 'Take a nap when you get to the hotel, but not a long one. Here.' And I was handed a small travel alarm. 'I won't be needing this anymore, and it weighs hardly anything. Sleep for a couple of hours after you arrive, and then go to bed on Greek time. It'll be easier in the long run.'

I didn't want Max's alarm clock, and I didn't want Max's advice, no matter how excellent. If it hadn't been for the telephone, I'd have gone right out, defiantly, and wandered around Athens. But I couldn't do anything until I'd heard from Sandy and Rhea.

'Do you still love me?' Sandy had asked.

'Of course I do.'

'It was I who introduced you to Max.'

'I know,' I had said.

It all seemed a very long time ago. And yet it was right here in the present. I had crossed an ocean and still I couldn't get away from it.

The sunlight fell on the bed. I stretched out in its warmth, lying on my side so that I could see the Acropolis. I looked across twentieth-century Athens, across hundreds of years to a world long gone. To the people who lived way back when the Parthenon was built, who worshipped the goddess Athena, what had happened to me wouldn't be very cosmic. To the other people in the hotel, also maybe looking out their windows from the present to the past, it wouldn't seem very important, either.

'It's all right.' Sandy had his arms about me. 'You have to go all the way through your feelings before you can come out on the other side. But don't stay where you are, Polly. Move on.'

There was a knock on the door, and I realized I had been hearing Sandy's voice in a half dream. I sat up.

"Who is it?"

"Some fruit, and a letter for Miss O'Keefe."

I opened the door to a young uniformed man who bore a large basket of fruit, which he put down on the dresser. "With the compliments of the manager." He handed me an envelope. "We neglected to give you this when you arrived."

"*Epharisto*." I shut the door on him and ripped open the envelope. One page, in the familiar, strong, dark handwriting. "Polly, my child, take this week in Athens in the spirit in which it is given. Forgive me and love me. Max."

I crumpled up the letter. Flung it at the wastepaper basket. The phone jangled across my thoughts.

It was Sandy, sounding as close as when he called at home, ringing South Carolina from Washington.

"Polly, you're there!"

"Sandy, where are you? What happened?"

"Still in Washington. An emergency. Sorry, Pol, but in my line of work you know these things do happen."

His work has more to it than meets the eye. He and Rhea don't just work with big corporations and their international deals. It's top-secret kind of stuff, but I know it has something to do with seeing that under-developed nations don't get ripped off, and when tensions rise in the Middle East or South America or Africa they're often sent there to ease things. Rhea and Mother are close friends, and I have a hunch she tells Mother a good bit, but the most I've ever got out of Mother was an ambiguous 'They're on the side of the angels.'

I said to Sandy, "I know these things happen, but are you going to come?"

"Of course we're coming. I'll be dug out by Monday night, with Rhea's help, and we've changed our flight to Tuesday. We should be with you in plenty of time for dinner, three days from now. Will you be all right?"

"Sure," I said without much conviction. But Sandy always makes me feel that I can manage anything, and I didn't want to let him down. "Do Mother and Daddy know?"

"Do you want them to?" he asked. It was a challenge.

I accepted it. "No. They might worry." Funny. We've been given a lot of independence in many ways, we've had more experience than a lot of kids, and yet we're also in some ways very overprotected. They *would* worry.

"Do you have enough money?" he asked.

"Max gave me three hundred dollars in traveler's checks. Daddy gave me two hundred. I'm rolling in wealth."

"Good. Don't blow it all the first day. But make a reservation on the roof restaurant of your hotel tonight, and just sign for your dinner. There's a superb view."

"There's a superb view from my room," I said. "I can see the Parthenon."

"Good. Max is an old friend of the manager. I knew you'd get one of the best rooms."

"It's very European and comfortable. Sandy, it's got to be expensive."

"Forget it," he said briskly. "It's peanuts to Max. Check with the concierge and get yourself a ticket for a bus tour or two and see the sights. Don't waste these days till Rhea and I join you."

"I won't. I'm not a waster, you know that."

"That's my Pol. You all right?"

"I'm fine," I said, which meant, I accept your challenge, Sandy. I'll be fine in Athens on my own. I'm not a child.

"See you Tuesday," he said. "I love you, Polly."

"I love you, too. See you."

When we hung up, I lay down on the bed, fighting the tears which Sandy's voice had brought rushing to my eyes. Sandy believes that things have meaning, that there are no coincidences, so I had to suppose there was some meaning to his being detained in Washington. Maybe it was to knock my pride down, to remind me that I might have seen a good bit of the world but I'd never been completely on my own before.

I went into the bathroom and took a hot, soaky bath; wrapped myself in two large, thick towels and sat at the open window to dry and look at the view. In the distance the Acropolis and the bright stones of the Parthenon were dazzling. In the foreground were the streets of Athens, with tropical trees which reminded me of home.

When I was dry I put on a cool cotton skirt and top and looked at my watch, which I'd changed to Greek time on the plane. Just after 2 p.m. I went to the balcony again to set myself in time and space.

The great city was spread out before me. And I wondered: What do the old gods, the heroes in the *Iliad* and the *Odyssey*, think of the cars and buses and gas-and-oil-smelling streets of today, or the modern hi-rise buildings going down to the harbor and stretching up the mountainsides? Piraeus, the port, and Athens are one vast city. In the days of Homer, what did all this look like? Were there great plains between the city and the harbor?

I went down to the lobby and made a reservation for dinner on the roof. The restaurant didn't open till eight, and the concierge looked at me as though he thought I was gauche when I asked for an eight o'clock reservation, so I put on my most aloof look and told him that I had jet lag and wanted to get to bed at a reasonable hour, which, after all, was true. Then I checked on Sandy and Rhea's reservation, and of course they'd already taken care of changing it. I asked about tours, but there were so many I decided I was too tired to choose until I'd had a good night's sleep, and I just went out of the hotel and across to Constitution Square.

I passed three evzones. Rhea had talked about them— Greek soldiers still dressed in the same colorful costumes they wore in Turkish times, white-skirted tunics with vivid splashes of red. They were marching briskly along, looking ferocious, and suddenly I had a police-state kind of feeling. But all around me everybody was bustling, hardly turning to stare, and I heard a lot of American accents and saw women in pants, which I should have thought would be too hot in this weather, and men with cigars—the ugly Americans Max had talked about. We didn't see that many Americans when we lived on Gaea, but we were in Lisbon often enough for me to have to face the fact that we aren't very much loved. Most of the shops around Constitution Square seemed to be entirely for the benefit of American tourists, junky gift shops, phony icons, sleazy clothes, and pictures of American credit cards on the glass fronts of the doors. One souvenir shop had a sign reading, "Welcome, Hadassah," and was recommended by some Jewish Association. I wouldn't have been surprised to find a shop window with a commendation by the Pope, or another by the World Council of Churches. I didn't like it. But that was judgmental of me. I still didn't like it.

Most of the Americans seemed to be clustered in the cafés on the sidewalks across from the Square. There was one big café which appeared to be used exclusively by kids my age, or not that much older, all dressed exactly alike in jeans, with backpacks which were dumped on the ground by their tables. In the Square itself, where I went to sit, there were some Americans, but also many Greeks, relaxing and drinking coffee and reading papers.

The light was the way Sandy and Rhea had described it, blue and gold, alive with color. I'd thought they were just rhapsodizing, and that nothing could beat the blue and gold of south Portugal and Gaea, but this was really different, more dazzling, with a quality of brilliant clarity, so that I could almost see Apollo driving the chariot of the sun across the sky. And in this light I could believe in Pallas Athena, could see her eyes, the same blinding blue of the sky.

Max said my eyes were that color, and that's unusual in carrottops.

Max was, theologically, heterodox. Religion, Max said, is divisive, and went on to cite the horrors going on between Christians and Moslems in the Middle East, between Hindus and Buddhists in Sri Lanka, between Protestants and Catholics in Ireland. If we could forget religion, Max said, and remember God, we might have a more reasonable world.

Max liked reading aloud, and had read to me from books written in the very early days of Christianity, works by Gregory of Nyssa and Basil the Great and Clement of Alexandria, because their world was like ours, changing rapidly, with the Roman Empire falling apart around them.

'Listen to this,' Max said one winter night when we were eating supper in front of the library fire and the northeast wind was beating against Beau Allaire. 'Clement of Alexandria:

Now the fables have grown old in your hands, and Zeus is no longer a serpent, no longer a swan, nor an eagle, nor a furious lover.

Isn't that superb?'

I turned away from Max in my mind. No more furious lovers. I was no Semele.

Max's house, Beau Allaire, is built of soft pink brick and surrounded by three-story white verandahs, a house built for shade and breeze. It is at the far end of Benne Seed Island from our house, just past Mulletville, which used to be a functional fishing village till a developer came in and started an expensive housing development, now that islands are becoming status symbols. It's a cocktail-partying place, cheek by jowl with what's left of the original village. There's a causeway from Mulletville to the mainland, and a school bus comes to take the development kids to Cowpertown—those who don't go off to boarding school. Beau Allaire is set on a hundred acres, but even so, Max is not happy about the development on what used to be an almost private island.

Between Mulletville and our house are two privately owned plantations and a state wildlife preserve, so we're moderately isolated. Benne Seed is shaped like a crescent moon, the Mulletville and Beau Allaire point of the moon much closer to the mainland than our point. Our house and Beau Allaire are in all ways at opposite points of the compass. Beau Allaire is a great house, often photographed for books on Southern architecture. Our house was once a motel, but Benne Seed is really not a tourist-type island, or we wouldn't be there. There's a tricky undertow, and swimming isn't safe unless you know the waters well.

Mother and Daddy rebuilt the falling-down motel, dividing the rooms so each of us kids would have our own bedroom and there'd be a few extra for the uncles and aunts and other visitors. Mother and Daddy's bedroom was what had originally been the office and lobby, with a big screen porch off it, facing the ocean. Our rooms were off on either side, and the ocean side was all screens in summer, with enormous storm windows for winter. There were two wings, one for Daddy's labs, with cases of starfish and lizards and squid and various kinds of octopuses and a medium-size computer for Mother; the other had a big long living room, a big dining room, and a good kitchen. The wings made a kind of court, where we had swings for the little kids, and a picnic table under an ancient water oak. The wood of the house was weathered, so that it was a soft, silvery grey, and behind it were great, jungly trees, full of Spanish moss and mockingbirds. We were fairly high up on the dunes, so there was a long wooden ramp which led down to the beach. It was comfortable and informal.

Beau Allaire was formal. The Greek revival columns rising up the three full stories emphasized the height of the ceilings. It was by far the most elegant of the three plantation houses, and the best kept up. The other two were owned by Northerners who were seldom there and probably used them as tax write-offs. Max has always had several yard men, and a couple living over the garage to take care of things and clean the silver—and everything else of course, but there is a great quantity of silver. All the doorknobs, for instance, are silver. 'They come from my mama,' Max said, 'and I treasure them.'

There are Waterford chandeliers and candelabra, and paintings by Max, and also by Picasso and Pissarro and even a Piero. And portraits. Southerners do seem to have a great many portraits, and Max had more than most.

But, until last Christmastime, Beau Allaire was no more than a name to us.

Early winter was miserable, cold and rainy and dank. In Cowpertown it seemed as though the sun never shone, and the fluorescent lights at school glared. Nobody turned on any strobe lights for me. And I certainly didn't have that inner luminosity Max saw in the portrait of me in the seashell, a luminosity which Max brought out in me. December was grey day after grey day, with fog rolling in from the sea, so bad that Daddy wouldn't let us take the boat to Cowpertown but drove us the fifteen or so miles to Mulletville to take the school bus from there, and we hated that.

And then Sandy and Rhea came for Christmas, and Uncle Dennys and Aunt Lucy, bringing Charles with them. It was wonderful having Charles home for three weeks. He's by far my closest sibling. But when Uncle Dennys and Aunt Lucy decided that Kate needed to live with a family and stop being an only child for a few years, they suggested that Charles go to Boston as a sort of exchange, partly because they didn't want to be completely without children, and partly because Charles is a scientist, or will be, and the science department at Cowpertown High leaves a great deal to be desired.

It was our turn to have everybody for Christmas. One of the good things about being back in the United States is getting together for holidays. Almost all of us. Daddy's parents are dead, and his family is pretty well scattered. But there are Mother's parents, who are also scientists. Our grandfather is an astrophysicist, and our grandmother a microbiologist. Then there're Sandy and Rhea. And Dennys and Lucy. Dennys and Sandy are twins, and very close. Mother's youngest brother, the one Charles is named after, is off somewhere on some kind of secret mission, we don't know where. Anyhow, when the larger family is gathered together, it makes for a full house. This past year our grandparents didn't come, because our grandfather was just getting over pneumonia. We missed them, but it was a lot of people, in any case.

The morning after everybody arrived, Sandy and I were alone in the kitchen, because Daddy had taken everybody else out in his cutter to show them around the island. Sandy and I warmed our toes at the fire and had one last cup of cocoa made from some special chocolate he and Rhea'd picked up in Holland.

The phone rang, and I answered it. 'Sandy, for you.'

'Me? Who on earth would be calling me here? I told Washington under no circumstances . . .' he muttered as he took the phone. '*Max!*' His voice boomed out with pleasure.

When he finished talking (I washed the dishes to give him privacy), he rubbed his blond beard and smiled. 'Polly, I'd like you to meet a friend of mine. I think you'd get on.'

Sandy knew things at school were not going well for me. He'd pumped me thoroughly, and it was not easy for me to keep anything from my favorite uncle. 'Who? Where?'

'A painter. A very good painter. And not far from here, at the other end of the Island, Beau Allaire. Want to drive over with me?'

I'd go anywhere with Sandy. 'Sure. Now?'

'Anything else on your social calendar?'

Coming from Xan, that would have been snide. From Sandy it was okay. 'I didn't know anybody was living at Beau Allaire.'

'Max has been back only a few weeks. I want to find out what on earth has brought Max to Beau Allaire.'

We drove through the stark December day. We never have snow on Benne Seed, but winter can be raw.

'Max's family built the hospital in Cowpertown,' Sandy said. 'It's named for Max's sister, Minerva Allaire Horne, who died young and beautiful. But I suppose you know all about that.'

I shook my head. 'No. Only that it was given by a family with pots of money and Daddy says it's an unusually good hospital for a place like Cowpertown. He knows some of the doctors there. And he and Mother were saying it was too bad nobody lived in Beau Allaire.'

'Max has had it kept up. The land is rented for cotton. And there are gardeners and two old-time Southern faithful retainers, Nettie and Ovid, like characters out of a movie. Max usually comes for a week or so each winter, but Beau Allaire hasn't really been lived in for years. Max said she was staying all winter. Wonder why.'

'She?'

'Maximiliana Sebastiane Horne. The parents gave both daughters absurdly romantic names. Minerva Allaire—Allaire was the mother's name and the plantation came from her—was always known as M.A., and Maximiliana Sebastiane is called Max, or Maxa, or sometimes Metaxa. Metaxa is a rather powerful Greek brandy, and it's not a bad name for her.'

We drove up a long driveway of crushed shells, lined with great oaks leaning their upper branches over the drive till they touched and made a green tunnel. The car crunched over the broken shells. As we drew near, I saw the graceful lines of a verandah, and Sandy pointed out the beautiful fanlight over the door. 'And eleven chimneys, count them. The architect was well aware of the dampness that can seep into an island house.'

We got out of the car and started toward the door just as a sports car pulled up behind us. Out of it emerged a tall woman wearing a dark green velvet cape lined with some kind of soft, light fur, with the hood partway up over midnight-black hair. Her light grey eyes were large and rimmed darkly with what I later learned was kohl.

'Good enough for Isak Dinesen, good enough for me.'

Isak Dinesen was a Danish writer who used to be famous, and Max said that the wheel would turn and she'd come into her own again.

Now Max held her arms out, wide, and so did Sandy, and they ran and embraced each other. It was theatrical, but it was also real, and I envied the freedom that allowed them to be so uninhibited. I stood watching their pleasure in each other, feeling that I shouldn't have come in old jeans and a yellow sweater that was too small for me.

After a moment Sandy and the woman broke apart, and he introduced me. 'Max, this is Polly O'Keefe, my sister's firstborn. Pol, this is Maximiliana Sebastiane Horne.'

I held out my hand. 'Hello, Mrs. Horne.'

She took my hands in hers, and from her hands I realized that she was older than I'd thought. 'Max, please, or Maxa. I'm not Mrs. Horne. My husband was Davin Tomassi, but I had already made a start as a painter when we married and he wanted me to keep my own name.'

He *was*. So she was a widow.

'Come in, come in, don't stand out here in the cold.' She opened the heavy front door, which creaked. 'I'll have to get this oiled,' she said, leading us into a large hall.

Sandy took my elbow. 'Look at this hall, Pol, it's an architectural gem, with a groin-vaulted plaster ceiling and beautifully proportioned woodwork.'

It was gorgeous, with the walls papered a color I later learned was Pompeian red.

Max opened another door, to a long, high library, the kind of room we'd love to build onto our house, where we've long ago run out of book space. But this wasn't a beach-house room. It was so high-ceilinged that there was a ladder which could be moved along a wooden rail so the books on the top shelves could be reached. There was a fireplace with a wood fire burning, though the room still smelled and felt damp. The mantelpiece was Georgian and beautiful, and over it was a portrait, in a heavy gold frame, of a young woman with black hair, wearing a low-cut ivory gown. She was so lovely it made you draw in your breath, and I assumed it was Max when she was young.

Max took off her cloak and flung it over a mahogany and red-velvet sofa, then went to the wall near the fireplace and pulled on a long, embroidered piece of cloth. A bellpull. I'd read about bellpulls, and when our TV worked I'd seen them in plays with Victorian settings, but this was the first one I'd seen in real life.

I studied the portrait again, and Max said, 'My sister, Minerva Allaire. M.A. was truly beautiful.' She perched on a low chair with a hassock covered in petit point. She wore narrow black pants and a black cashmere cardigan over a white, softly ruffled blouse. And yet, while I knew she was quite old, older than my parents, she did not seem old, because a tremendous, sunny energy emanated from her.

There was a knock on the door and a woman came in, a woman who somehow went with the house and the bellpull. She was stocky and had grey-brown hair, short and crisply curly. She bowed elaborately. 'Madame rang?'

Max laughed. 'Don't be dour, Ursula. It's damp and cold and this house hasn't been lived in for thousands of years.'

'Madame would like some consommé?' the woman suggested.

'Consommé with a good dollop of sherry,' Max agreed. 'And some of Nettie's benne biscuits.'

Sandy asked, 'Max still bullying you, Urs?'

The woman smiled, and the heaviness in her face lightened. 'What would Max be like if she didn't bully us all?'

'Ursula, this is my niece, Polly O'Keefe. Pol, this is Dr. Heschel.'

I'd thought she was some kind of servant, a housekeeper.

She shook hands with me, a good, firm clasp. Her fingers were long and delicate and tapered, but very strong. 'I'm glad to meet you, Polly. Your Uncle Dennys and I are colleagues.'

Well, then, she had to be a neurosurgeon. I took another look.

Sandy said, 'The world of neurosurgery is small. Dennys and I, as usual, both have connections with Max and Ursula. Davin Tomassi was a colleague of mine. So, separately, we've known Max and Urs for a long time. We'll have a terrific reunion.'

Dr. Heschel asked eagerly, 'Dennys is here, too?'

'The whole kit and caboodle of us. I don't know if the name rang a bell with you, Urs, but Polly's father is the O'Keefe who's done such amazing work with regeneration. His lab is now full of squid and octopuses. I suppose I have to take it on faith that their neurological system resembles ours.'

Dr. Heschel flung out her arms. 'Good Lord, when we left New York and came to Benne Seed I thought we were coming to the wilderness, and here is not only Dennys but a scientist I've long wanted to meet. Before I get overexcited, I'd better get out to the kitchen and see about that consommé.'

'We'll have a party,' Max said as the doctor went out. 'We'll bring Beau Allaire back to life with a real party.'

Sandy and Max talked about mutual friends all over the world until a frail old black man came in, carrying a silver tray which looked much too heavy for him. He wore rather shiny black trousers and a white coat. He put the tray on a marble-topped table in front of a long sofa, looked at Max with loving concern, and left.

Dr. Heschel sat in front of the tray and handed out cups of consommé in translucent china. I thanked her for mine.

'Call her Ursula,' Max ordered. 'She gets enough doctor-this and doctor-that in New York. People treat neurosurgeons as though they were gods. And many of them fall for it.'

Dr. Heschel—Ursula—responded mildly: 'Your iconoclasm takes care of that.'

'Are you on vacation, Urs?' Sandy asked her.

'Leave of absence.' And, as though to forestall further questioning, she added, 'I was overdue a sabbatical. I'm glad to see you still have your beard, Sandy.'

'I grow tired of it,' he said, 'but it's the best way to tell Dennys and me apart. We still look very much alike. Max, show Polly some of your paintings.'

Max shrugged, so that her thin shoulder blades showed sharply under the cashmere. It looked to me as though she needed a doctor handy, though an internist would likely have been more help than a neurosurgeon.

'Most of my best stuff is in museums or private collections,' Max said. 'Contrary to opinion, I do have to earn a living. M.A.'s untimely death caused my father to start a hospital in her memory, and that's where the money went. Not that I begrudge it.'

Sandy gave a snort and turned it into a sneeze.

'You ran through a good bit on your own.' Dr. Heschel —Ursula—smiled.

'True, and I enjoyed it. But now I have to work for the finer things of life.' She looked at both of them and burst into laughter. 'Like many filthy-rich people, I tend to cry poor.' She smiled at me. 'Never believe people who tell you they have no money, Polly. People who don't have it seldom mention the fact. People who do, tend to be embarrassed about it, and so deny it, especially in front of someone like Sandy, who spends his life fighting the big international megacorps. Come on, and I'll show you some of my work.'

'Don't forget the painting of Rio Harbor,' Ursula said.

'First I want to show her my self-portrait.' Max drained her cup and put it back on the tray. 'Come on.'

I followed her into the big hall and up a curving staircase and then into a room which was as large as the library.

There was a huge, carved four-poster bed, with a sofa across the foot. I turned and saw another high fireplace, with a large, white fur rug in front of it, and I could imagine Max, in black, lying on the white rug and staring into the fire. The fire was laid, and there was a copper bucket of fat pine beside it. The far end of the room had a big desk, a chaise longue, some comfortable chairs upholstered in smoky-rose velvet. A long wall of French windows opened onto the verandah and the ocean view.

On the wall over the desk was a portrait. I knew it was Max because she'd said so. She was as young in this picture, or almost, as the girl in the portrait in the library, and they did look very alike, with the same dark hair and light grey eyes and alabaster skin. Max was thinner than M.A., and she was looking down at something she held in one hand. A skull.

It reminded me of etchings of medieval philosophers in their studies, with skulls on their desks and maybe a skeleton in the corner, contemplating life and death. It was a beautiful painting. A shaft of light touched the skull, and the shape of bone was clean and pure.

'I was a morbid young woman in many ways, Polly, and felt it would do me no harm to cast a cool eye on my own mortality. It did keep me from wasting time as I might otherwise have done. I've had an interesting life, and I've had my fair share of vicissitudes, but it hasn't been dull and it hasn't been wasted. What are you going to do with yourself when you finish your schooling?' She sat on the foot of the chaise longue.

'I don't know,' I said.

'Where do your interests lie?'

'Almost everywhere. That can be a real problem. I'm interested in archaeology and anthropology and literature and the theatre. I pick up languages easily. I'm not a scientist, like my parents.'

'But you're intelligent.'

'Oh, yes. But I haven't found my focus.'

'You've got a couple of years,' Max said. 'When the time comes, you'll find it.' She got up. 'Come, I'll show you the picture that Urs likes.' On the way she pointed out some of the other pictures. A Hogarth. A de Chirico sketch. A Van Gogh. 'Fortunately, the Islanders don't know how valuable they are—just Maxa's junk. Even with Nettie and Ovid living over the garage, we aren't immune to burglars. If I'm short of cash, I sell one of the pictures. I do have very extravagant tastes.'

The painting of Max was what is called representa-
tional. The one of the harbor at Rio was expressionist, I
think, with vivid colors which looked one way straight
on and another if you glanced sidewise.

'Why isn't this in a museum?' I was awed by it.

'Because I won't let it go,' Max said. 'I have to keep a
few things. Urs wants to buy it, and if I sold it to anyone
it would be to her.' She looked at the painting. 'She'll
get it soon enough.'

We went back out into the hall, and as we started
down the stairs I saw something on the landing I hadn't
noticed on the way up, a wood carving on a marble
pedestal, of a man, with his head thrown back in laughter and delight.

'That's the Laughing Christ of Baki.' Max paused. 'I
had a reproduction made. The original is life-size and
gives the effect of pure joy. It's probably nearly ten
thousand years old.'

'The Laughing Christ?'

'The Bakians simply assumed, when the missionaries
told them about the Son of God, that it was their statue,
which had never before had a name. Anthropology is
one of my hobbies, Polly. Someday I'll show you the
sketch books I've made on my travels. This statue is one
of my most favorite possessions.'

'I love it,' I said, 'I absolutely love it.'

We went on downstairs and back to the library, and
Max had another cup of consommé, complaining that
Nettie hadn't put enough sherry in it. 'She disapproves.
Nettie and Ovid are growing old, and I'd like to get
someone to help them, but they won't hear of it. Urs
likes to cook, and Nettie and Ovid come in after dinner
and do the washing up, and they bring us our breakfast.
Nettie is a firm believer in a good breakfast, grits and

fried tomatoes and eggs and anything else she thinks she can get me to eat.'

'You could do with a few more pounds,' Sandy said.

Max sat on a low chair and stretched her legs out to the fire. 'So you and Rhea are here for Christmas, Sandy? How can you take all those children?'

'Very happily,' Sandy said. 'We'd hoped to have children of our own, but that didn't happen to be possible.'

'Oh, God, Sandy, I'm sorry.' Max put her hands to her mouth.

'It's probably just as well in our line of work,' he said. 'We have to travel too much of the time. And with all our nephews and nieces, we don't do too badly.'

I'd wondered about Sandy and Rhea not having kids of their own.

He looked at his watch. 'We'd better go, Pol.'

Max put her hand very lightly on my shoulder. 'Come back and see me, little one, and we'll talk about anthropology.'

'All right,' I mumbled. But I knew I wouldn't. Not unless Max called me. And she did.

But not until she and Ursula had joined the throng for Christmas. As soon as Mother and Daddy heard that Max and Ursula were at Beau Allaire, and about the connections with Sandy and Dennys, they invited them for Christmas.

'Max won't come,' Sandy said.

But she called and accepted the invitation. 'So Urs will have someone to talk neurosurgery with.'

'Granted,' my Uncle Dennys said, 'Ursula Heschel has overworked ever since I've known her, but it still seems atypical of her and Max to come here in the dead of winter. In the spring when the azaleas are out, yes, but not in December.'

'It's quiet,' Mother said.

'True, it's quiet. But I'm the one who's the researcher. Ursula's a superb surgeon.'

'You're right, Dennys,' Sandy said. 'There's something odd about it.'

Christmas was cold and clear and perfect. The sun glinted off the Atlantic. We had fires going in both the living and dining rooms. The little kids played outside with their new toys, so the rest of us could have some reasonable conversation indoors. Dennys, Urs, and Daddy talked about the mysteries of the brain, and Daddy took them off to the lab. It does seem weird to me that the octopus and the human being share so much of the neurological system.

Max, Mother, Rhea, and Lucy talked about the state of the world, which as usual was precarious, and about the state of American education, which was deplorable.

'Kate is getting an education just living in this zoo,' Aunt Lucy said while we were gathered in the kitchen basting the turkey and doing various last-minute things.

Kate was nibbling the candied grapefruit peel we'd made a few days before. 'Cowpertown High's okay. I'm learning plenty.'

'And going to all the dances?' Aunt Lucy asked.

'Enough,' Kate said. She could have said 'all.' Kate always had half a dozen boys after her whenever there was a dance, and I knew that Mother and Daddy felt responsible for her and worried about whichever boy was driving and whether or not booze or joints had been sneaked in. But Kate had sense enough not to drive home with anyone who was stoned, and she had already called twice to ask someone to come for her. Though we didn't tell Lucy and Dennys.

If Mother and Daddy worried about Kate being popular and successful, they worried about me being alone too much. It was okay. I didn't want to go. Kate loves parties and dances and barbecues, and she gets bored if she doesn't have a lot to do. Not me.

We'd put all the extensions in the table. Max had brought over an enormous damask banquet cloth, and with candles and oil lamps lit and the Christmas tree lights sparkling, it looked beautiful. The little kids all behaved reasonably well, and no one threw up. It was a good Christmas.

And then Max and Ursula asked us for New Year's Eve—the grownups, plus Charles and me.

Charles had grown taller, though he wasn't quite as tall as Xan, but he was still my special brother Charles who understood me better than anyone else. We spent hours up in our favorite old live-oak tree, talking, catching up. I was going to miss him abysmally when he went back to Boston; in my eyes, Kate was not at all a fair exchange for Charles. But at least Charles was still here for New Year's Eve, and Beau Allaire was a perfect place for a party.

All the verandahs were full of light as we drove up, and the great columns gleamed. Nettie and Ovid passed hot hors d'oeuvres, and there was lots of conversation and laughter. We played charades. Sandy and I were the best at pantomime, and Mother and Max were best at guessing, but we all threw ourselves into the game and had a lot of fun.

As all the clocks began to chime midnight, Ovid opened a magnum of champagne, and after a toast we all put our arms about each other's waist, standing in a circle, and sang *Auld Lang Syne*. When we were through, Ursula put an arm around Max, tenderly, protectively. And I thought I would like to be protected like that.

Sitting in Constitution Square, being warmed by the sun, I did not want to think about Max. But that was not very intelligent of me. What I needed to do was to think about Max objectively, not subjectively. I'm enough of a scientist's daughter to know that nothing can be thought about completely objectively. We all bring our own subjective bias to whatever we think about, but we have to recognize what our bias is, so that we will be able to think as objectively as possible.

Daddy had said that he could not even study his lab creatures totally objectively, because to observe something is to change it.

That was certainly true. Max had observed me. And changed me.

I had finished two cups of the thick, sweet coffee, and that was more than enough. I put my pen and journal back in the shoulder bag, crossed the street to the hotel, went up to my room, and napped. It seemed that all I wanted was sleep, and not just because of jet lag. Sleep is healing, Sandy said, and when I woke up, I did feel better. I had one foot in Athens and the present, and although the other foot was still across the Atlantic and dragging in the past, at least Max had made me aware of how complex we can be, so it did not surprise me to be in both worlds simultaneously.

The problem was that I could not comprehend the vast span of Max's complexity. My parents are, as human beings go, complex, but also moderately consistent. I can count on them. And the bad people I've met have been so bad that I could count on them being bad, which does simplify things. But shouldn't I have learned that life is neither consistent nor simple? Why did it surprise me?

I looked at the travel alarm I'd put on the bed table. Nearly eight. Just time to dress and go up to the roof for dinner. I took a book so I wouldn't be lonely. I love to eat and read, but in a family like ours I don't often have the opportunity—only if I'm sick enough to stay in bed, which doesn't happen often, and when it does, I'm usually too miserable to read.

Sometimes, when I went over to Beau Allaire, Max and I ate together, with books open beside us on the table, and didn't talk, unless one of us wanted to read something to the other. We usually ate in the screened part of the back verandah, rather than in the formal, oval dining room. A breezeway went from the screened porch to the kitchen, which was slightly separated from the rest of the house, in the old Southern manner.

'Pol, listen to this,' Max said. 'It's by a physicist, A. J. Wheeler. He says: "Nothing is more important about the quantum principle than this, that it destroys the concept of the world as 'sitting out there,' with the observer safely separated from it by a 20-centimeter slab of plate glass. Even to observe so minuscule an object as an electron, we must shatter the glass." ' She made a movement with her hand as though breaking through glass, and her face was bright with interest as she looked up from the book, blinking silver eyes against the light of the candles in the hurricane globes. 'We cannot separate ourselves from anything in the universe. Not from other creatures. Not from each other.'

But I had put the glass up between Max and me, erected a barrier, so that we could no longer touch each other.

I got up to the restaurant at two minutes before eight, and the doors were just opening. I was the only person there, though people did begin to trickle in after a few minutes. It was a beautiful, open-air restaurant, with lots of plants, and candles on all the tables. I had a waiter who spoke good English, so I didn't try to practice my Greek. He was concerned that I was all alone, so I told him about Uncle Sandy and Aunt Rhea and that they would be with me on Tuesday.

This seemed to reassure him, and he began explaining the menu to me, and I didn't think it would be polite for me to tell him that I had a Greek aunt and was used to Greek food. Anyhow, I liked his taking care of me, and he was a kind of surrogate uncle for an hour or so.

Two couples came in and were seated at tables between me and the view of the Acropolis, and I think one man thought I was staring at him when all I was trying to do was see the Parthenon.

Dinner tasted good, really good. And that in itself was a big improvement. I ordered fruit and cheese, and my waiter told me that if I lingered over dessert and coffee I'd see, if not hear, the *son et lumière* show at the Acropolis.

I ate slices of pear with Brie, a French rather than a Greek dessert. I don't have a sweet tooth and I'm not fond of baklava or any of the other pastries dripping with syrup. Spreading the soft Brie on a crisp slice of pear, I felt a presence behind me, thought it was the waiter, and turned.

It was the black-haired kid who'd raised his eyebrow at me while we were sitting in Constitution Square. And he was tall. Taller than I.

"Hi, Red," he said.

If Sandy and Rhea had been with me as planned, I'd have ignored him. Though likely if I'd been with Sandy and Rhea he wouldn't have spoken. I intensely dislike being called Red.

"Saw you walk over to the King George from the Square this afternoon," he said. "I'm Zachary Gray, from California. You *are* American, aren't you?"

"Yes." Did I really want to talk to this guy?

"May I sit down?"

"Feel free." I still wasn't sure.

"What's your name, and where're you from?" he asked. He was really spectacular-looking, with black eyes and long black lashes. I envied him those lashes, though I'm happy with my own eyes. Kate would have fallen all over him.

I didn't exactly want to fall over him, but I decided I did want him to sit down. "I'm Polly O'Keefe, and I've come from an island partway between Savannah, Georgia, and Charleston, South Carolina."

"You don't have a Southern accent. Almost English."

"Middle Atlantic," I corrected him. "I spent a lot of my childhood in Portugal." Max's accent was softly Southern, not jarringly, just a gentle, musical rhythm.

"So, what're you doing all by your lonesome in Athens? Are your parents with you?"

"My parents are home on Benne Seed Island. I'm here for a week, and then I'm going to Cyprus. What're *you* doing here?"

"Just bumming around. I'm taking a year off from college to wander around Europe and get some culture."

He didn't look like the typical American backpacker. He looked like money, lots of money.

The waiter came over and Zachary greeted him. "Hello, Aristeides. This young lady's a friend of mine."

"Yes?"

I almost told Aristeides I'd never seen him before in my life, but I shut my mouth on the words. I was lonely. And being picked up by a desirable young man was a new experience.

Zachary ordered a bottle of retsina. "It's a white wine, soaked over resin. It tastes like the Delphic Oracle."

Rhea looks down her nose at retsina.

But Zachary went on: "There are other Greek wines which are much better; I just happen to like it. Aristeides, by the way, means someone who is inflexibly just."

"You speak Greek?" I asked.

"A few words and phrases. You pick it up."

A waiter's name which means 'inflexibly just' would be fine to set down in that journal I was supposed to be keeping for school. "How do you happen to know Aristeides?"

"I like good food and pleasant places to eat it in. And Athens is my favorite city. I infinitely prefer it to Paris or London or Rome. How come you're going off to Cyprus right at the beginning of the school year? You don't look like a dropout."

"I'm not. It's an educational trip. I'm going to be a gofer at a conference in Osia Theola."

"How'd you get chosen for the job?"

"I'm not afraid of hard work."

Zachary said, "Your parents must trust you, to let you

come this way all alone and stay all by yourself at a hotel in Athens."

"They do trust me," I said. I didn't think it necessary to say they had no idea I was all alone in Athens.

"So where's this place on Cyprus?" he asked.

"Osia Theola. It's a small village with a conference center in what used to be a monastery."

"Maybe we'll have a chance to get better acquainted before you go. I decided when I spotted you this afternoon that you were someone I wanted to know."

How to respond to this? Kate would have known exactly the right thing to say. I didn't.

"I'm glad your parents put you in the King George. You'll be safe here." His tone was condescending. "What's on your agenda for tomorrow?"

I replied firmly, "I'm going on a bus tour." I didn't want this Zachary taking too much for granted.

"No, no, not a bus tour," Zachary said. "They're the pits. You're coming with me." He sounded very sure of himself. "I just happen to be free for the next couple of days, and I'll give you the million-dollar tour."

Aristeides brought the wine and two glasses and looked at me questioningly.

"No, thank you," I said to him. "Not after I spent all last night on a plane and my internal clock is all mixed up."

Zachary started to protest, so I added, "I'm underage, anyhow," and Aristeides nodded at me and took my glass away, then poured some for Zachary, who held the glass out to me. "Take a sip at least."

Because of Rhea's taste in wines, I'd never had retsina. Maybe my tastes are low, but I liked it; it made me think of pine forests, and Diana walking through fallen needles, her bow slung over her shoulder.

Aristeides moved away to serve another table, and Zachary looked at me over the rim of his glass. Zachary really was in Athens on his own, while my being by myself was because of some kind of crisis in Sandy and Rhea's work. And I was suddenly grateful that my parents cared enough about me so that I was not like this Zachary, or the other kids checking in at American Express for their money while their parents did whatever parents do who just want their kids out of their hair.

"How old *are* you?" Zachary asked.

"Nearly seventeen."

He leaned toward me. "It's hard to tell by looking at you. I'd have thought you were older, except that your blue eyes are a child's."

"I'm not a child."

"Thank God. Tell me about this Benne Seed Island where you live. It sounds as though it's out in the boonies."

"Beene Seed makes the boonies look metropolitan," I said. "But isolation is good for Daddy's work."

"What does he do?"

"He's a marine biologist," I said briefly. We've learned never to talk about Daddy's experiments, because they're in an incredibly sensitive area and in the wrong hands could be disastrous. But Zachary seemed to expect me to say something more, so I added, "My father needs a lot of solitude for experiments that take a long time to show any definitive results."

"Isn't that hard on you? How do you feel about all that solitude?"

I shrugged. "I have six younger brothers and sisters, so it isn't all that solitary."

He nearly swooned. "Seven kids! What got into your parents? You Catholic or something?"

I shook my head. Sometimes I wondered myself what had got into my parents. It seemed to me that when we were living on Gaea they felt they had to repopulate the island all by themselves so we'd have people to play with.

Who, of all of us, would I send back? Not even Xan, who's the one who rubs me like sandpaper.

From my seat I still had a good view, despite the middle-aged man who thought I was looking at him, and suddenly the walls of the Acropolis were lit by soft, moving lights, shifting from pale rose to green to blue. "Look," I said.

Zachary turned around in his chair, and back. "It's pretty vulgar." (Rhea would have agreed with him there.) "But I'll take you tomorrow night if you like."

Again, I didn't know what to say. Yes? Kate says boys don't like it if you're too eager. The only person I'd ever dated was Renny, and I'm not sure having pizza with Renny even qualified as a date. He was an intern, and I was a kid who listened to him talk.

I pushed the thought of Renny away. If I was going to go out with Zachary the next day, I ought to know something more about him. "When you finish getting culture and go back to college, where are you going? What are you planning to be?"

"One at a time," he said. "I'm going back to UCLA, and I'll be studying law. My pa's a corporate lawyer, and I mean a multinational corporate lawyer, with his finger in pies on every continent."

As I thought: money. I watched the lights shimmer on the hillside and then blink off.

"I'm taking this year off to find out what I really want. I'll tell you what I want right now. I want to spend tomorrow with you."

With me. This extremely gorgeous-looking young man wanted to spend the day with me. It sounded a lot better than going on a bus tour with a lot of people I didn't know. I wasn't sure I trusted Zachary. But I didn't have any reason to trust a lot of strangers on a bus, either.

"Here we are, both on our own"—Zachary reached across the table and lightly touched the tips of his fingers to mine—"and I think we can have a good time together."

Not only had I not mentioned to Zachary that my parents had no idea I was on my own, I also did not tell him about Sandy and Rhea.

He went on. "When I saw you in the Square this afternoon you reminded me of a wild pony, ready to shy off if anybody frightened you. You still have that look, as though you might suddenly leap up from your chair and vanish. You're sophisticated enough to be eating alone on the roof of the King George and yet you have an innocence I haven't seen in anyone your age in I don't know how long."

For want of anything better to say, I murmured, "I've lived on islands most of my life."

"I was expecting to take off for Corfu tomorrow, but I'd much rather stay here and show you around. I'll rent a car so we can go off into the countryside."

I was flattered. I suspected my cheeks were pink. Kate collects male animals as I collect specimens for Daddy, going out in the boat to get squid or whatever he needs. Nobody anywhere near my age had ever wanted to spend a day with me before. "That sounds like fun. But I think right now I'd better go to bed and get a good night's sleep if I'm to be awake for you tomorrow."

"I'll take you to your room," he said.

"No. Thanks. I'll go myself."

"Don't you trust me?"

I shook my head. "It isn't you."

"You *are* a wild little animal," he said. "I'm not a wolf."

I stood up. "What time shall we meet tomorrow?"

"Ten okay?"

"Sure."

"I'll pick you up. What's your room number?"

"I'll meet you in the lobby."

"Okay, okay, pretty Pol, I suppose you have every right to be suspicious of some guy who's just picked you up. I'm staying at the Hilton, by the way, because it has a better view. Wait till you see it. Lobby of the King George. Ten a.m. tomorrow."

"I look forward to it," I said. I was glad I'd already signed for my meal, so I could just walk away, without looking back.

The view from my room at night was as beautiful as it had been in the full sunshine, although the *son et lumière* show was long over. I looked at the ancient stones and wondered what all those centuries did to our own troubled time—put it in more cosmic perspective perhaps? But even if the Acropolis speaks of the pettiness and brevity of our mortal lives, while our lives are going on they matter.

The ancient stones seemed lit from within. Sometimes I think the past has its own radiance. I turned from the balcony, switched on the lights, and ordered my breakfast for the next morning, hanging the breakfast chit on the outside of the door. Breakfast in the room was my Uncle Sandy's suggestion. He and Rhea like to keep their mornings quiet when they're traveling, and I thought I might like that, too—continental breakfast, *café au lait* and croissants, and a book. It sounded good to me.

The bed had been turned down while I was at dinner, and it looked so comfortable that I got undressed right away and climbed in, pushing the pillows up behind me, dutifully writing in the journal for school. Most certainly the day in Athens had not been in the least what I had expected. No Sandy and Rhea; instead, a boy called Zachary. That was not the kind of thing to write down. I thought for a moment, then described the view from my room and mentioned Aristeides, the inflexibly just, to prove that travel is truly educational.

And then the phone rang.

I was not entirely surprised to have it be my Uncle Dennys calling from Boston. Sandy and Dennys have the special closeness of twins.

All Dennys wanted to know was that I was okay, that I wasn't lonely or frightened. He and Sandy use the long-distance phone as though it were local. They both feel that it's very important to keep in touch. And I suppose they can both afford it. Nevertheless, it awes me. He asked, "What are your plans for tomorrow?"

"I'm going sightseeing."

"All alone?"

"No, I met this guy from California who knows a lot about Athens, and he's going to show me around."

"Are you sure he's okay?"

"Who can be sure about anyone? I can take care of myself."

"Sure you can, Pol, but be careful."

"I'll be careful. Don't worry."

"Sorry Sandy got held up, but maybe it'll be good for you to have this time on your own."

"Don't tell Mother and Daddy—"

"Never fear. Sandy's already made me promise. Strikes me he's being more protective of them than he is of you."

"He just wants me to grow up," I said.

"You will. You already are, in many ways." We said goodbye, and I felt warmed by Dennys's call. Sandy had promised me that what Max had called him about wouldn't go any further, he wouldn't tell anyone, even his twin. And I knew he hadn't.

When I put the phone down I looked at my school journal and decided I was too tired to write any more. I slid down in bed and turned out the light. It was cool enough, with the balcony windows open to the night breeze, for me to snuggle under the covers. I plummeted into sleep, and slept deep down dark for a couple of hours, and then woke up and felt myself floating to the surface. At first I thought I was in my familiar bed at home. But I heard street noises instead of the surf rolling and the wind in the palmettos. I was alone in a hotel in Athens. Sandy and Rhea were still in Washington, but Zachary Gray was not far away in the Hilton. Amazing.

What time was it at home? Never mind. I'd better get body and mind on Greek time. I leaned on my elbow and peered at the travel alarm. Midnight. I lay down. Wrapped the covers about me. Too hot. Pushed them down. Too cold. Slipped into half sleep. Half dream.

Renny.

Queron Renier.

(With a name like Queron, who wouldn't be called Renny?)

Like Zachary, Renny was tall, taller than I. Most of the kids at Cowpertown High were shorter. Zachary was sophisticated and exotic. Renny was serious and nice-

looking in a completely unspectacular way. His light
brown hair bleached in the summer from sun and salt
water. His grey-blue eyes peered behind thick lenses in
heavy frames. In the dream he was standing beside me
on the open verandah at Beau Allaire, wearing his white
doctor's coat, with his stethoscope dangling out of his
pocket, looking like a young doctor on TV. He said, 'An
intern's life is hell,' the way he had said it to me at least
a dozen times, but in a tone of voice that belied his
words. Renny loved being an intern. He loved the hospital and everything about it. When I first met him I
assumed that he was at the M. A. Horne Hospital because it was the only place he could get. Renny is from
Charleston, and there are bigger hospitals in Charleston.
There are bigger hospitals in Savannah and Jackson-
ville. Or Richmond or Baltimore.

In the dream he sat on the white rail of the verandah.
'You watch out for this guy who's picked you up. I don't
trust him.'

'I can handle him,' I said.

'You're much too sure of yourself, Polyhymnia
O'Keefe. Pride goeth before a fall.'

'I'm not really sure of myself,' I said. 'It's just a front.'
It was. I'm sure of myself as far as my brain is concerned. I've got a good one, thanks to my genetic background. But in every other area of life I'm insecure. I can
talk easily and comfortably with adults, but not with
kids my own age.

'Watch it,' Renny said, his voice echoing in the dream.
'Watch it . . . watch it . . .'

His warning woke me and brought me back from
Beau Allaire to my bed in the King George. I was hot,
so I got up and went out onto the balcony, and the night
sky was that extraordinary blue which was deep behind

the stars. Greek blue. Blue and gold by day; blue and silver by night. I wondered how much human nature had actually changed in the thousands of years since the Acropolis was built, and if all that had happened to me was so extraordinary after all.

I'd seen Renny every week or so during the past winter and summer. Going out with him for barbecue or pizza on his rare free evenings, and listening to him talk about tropical medicine, was a good antidote to not being asked to a dance at the Cowpertown High School, but that's all it meant, until a couple of weeks ago.

Renny was still an antidote, but for something far more cataclysmic than not being asked to a dance, or watching my cousin Kate go off with a bunch of kids, usually including Xan, while I stayed home. Kate is everything Mother and Daddy would have liked me to be. She's not short, but she's shorter than I am, and when she goes to a dance she doesn't loom over the boys. And she's beautiful, full and beautiful. I'm no longer the same measurement all round; I have reasonable curves both in front and behind, which is a big improvement over the pole I used to be, but Kate has pheromones which draw boys to her like honey. I wasn't exactly jealous of Kate; I didn't even want to change places with her; I was just wistful.

The light on the Acropolis was different now than it had been earlier, a deeper, darker blue, with many of the city lights extinguished around it, though not all. Cities never go completely to sleep. While they are alive, that is. I stood looking at the pearly light on the stone until I was chilly. Then I went back to bed. Edges of dawn were outlining the windows as I slid into sleep. I didn't wake up till there was a knock on the door.

Breakfast. I was wide awake in an instant. Breakfast

in Athens. I grabbed my bathrobe and rushed to open the door. A nice young waiter who looked like pictures of Greek statues carried in a breakfast tray which he took out to the balcony. There was a pot of coffee, a pitcher of hot milk, a dish with croissants and toast, jam, honey, and butter.

When we lived on Gaea and school was whenever Mother and Daddy decided we should start lessons, breakfast was unhurried, too. We fixed trays and ate in our rooms and emerged into the day when we felt like it, some of us getting up at dawn, some not till seven or even eight. But at Benne Seed we were on a schedule; we had to get to the mainland in time for that school bus. So, though Mother set breakfast out and we were free to get our own and eat it whenever we liked, we couldn't help bumping into each other. If Mother and Daddy could have gone on teaching us I might have loved Benne Seed as much as I loved Gaea. It was Cowpertown and the high school which depressed me. The island itself was home.

So breakfast alone in Athens reminded me of breakfast on Gaea, though it was much more elegant. I thanked the waiter in Greek which was, if not flawless, at least understandable, and he beamed at me. "*Parakalo*," he said, and then he pointed to the Acropolis with the morning light bringing the stones to life, gabbled at me in Greek, beamed again, and left.

The telephone rang, jolting me. I went back to the room and answered, and why was I surprised when it was Zachary Gray?

"I just wanted to make sure we were getting together today."

He was worried about *me* backing out? "Of course."

"Have you had breakfast?"

"I'm having it right now, out on the balcony, enjoying the view."

"We'll have lunch together somewhere, then, though I want you to see the view from my balcony first. Can you be in your lobby at ten sharp?"

I looked at my watch. It was just after eight. "Sure. See you at ten."

The sun was so bright as it slanted across the balcony that I hitched my chair back into the shadows so I could see to read without being half blinded. The croissants were crumbly and delicious, and the *café au lait* was good, much better than the sweet thick stuff. Instead of reverting to childhood, having breakfast alone in Greece as we used to do in Portugal, I suddenly felt very grown-up. Absurd. Why did it take being alone in Athens to make me feel mature enough to look at human nature and feel part of it? Not better. Not worse. Just part.

I was reading a book Sandy had given me, about Epidaurus, where he was planning to take me. There's a magnificent theatre there, though we were going to be too late in the season to see any plays. And there were holy precincts in Epidaurus where, back in the high days of Greek civilization, people were brought to be healed, some with physical ailments, some with mental ones. There were really interesting things in the book. The snake pit, for instance. Those snakes in the pit where really sick mental patients were put weren't just snakes, which would have been enough to send them out of their minds for good; they were snakes with a strong electric charge. So it was, you might say, the first electric-shock treatment, and probably no more inhuman than any kind of electric-shock treatment. I wondered what Renny would think of it.

The brilliant sun dazzling off the stones of the buildings and onto my stretched-out legs and arms was a shock treatment in its own way. My spirits lifted, and I took the last bit of apricot jam and licked it off the spoon.

The sun tingled against my legs, which had a good tan from summer. Unlike a lot of redheads, I do tan, as long as I'm careful and do it slowly. I also have long, straight toes, probably because I've worn sandals or gone barefoot most of my life. Feet are usually not the prettiest part of the body, but my feet were one of the things I could feel pleased about.

In Epidaurus, before sick people could go into the sacred precincts for healing, they had to stay outside the gates to pray, to be purged of bad feelings, anger, resentment, lack of forgiveness. Only then could they go in to the priests.

I looked at the words: *anger, resentment, lack of forgiveness*, and in the brilliant light the letters seemed to wriggle on the page like little snakes. I needed that purging. Nobody could get rid of all those bad feelings but me, myself. The warmth of the sun on the balcony, and those words leaping off the page at me, had made me see that much. Or maybe it was getting away from everything and everybody so I could see it in perspective.

'You'll like Krhis Ghose,' Max had said, showing me a snapshot of a thin man who looked something like Nehru. We were up on the second-floor verandah outside her bedroom, where she had comfortable Chinese wicker furniture, and the breeze from the ocean, plus the ceiling fan, plus mosquito coils, kept the insects to a minimum.

'Is he a Hindu or a Moslem?'

Max fanned herself slowly with an old-fashioned palm-leaf fan. 'A Christian. One who actually *is* one. A person of total integrity. Why we get along so well I'm not sure, but I count him among my closest friends.'

'How did you meet?'

'In Bombay. Much against my will, I was dragged to a lecture Krhis was giving on the connection between religious intolerance and land boundaries. And instead of being bored, I was fascinated, and we went out with him afterwards and talked all night. He's come through hell. Saw his wife and child shot. God, they do keep shooting each other in that part of the world. But he's come out on the other side, somehow or other. Without bitterness.'

You could not go into the sacred precincts in Epidaurus with bitterness in your soul. Inner and outer illnesses were seen as part of each other, and both patient and priest participated in the healing. The Greeks understood psychosomatic, or holistic, medicine long before they were heard of in the West, where we've tended to separate and overspecialize. In Epidaurus, healing was an art, rather than a science.

Sandy and Dennys say it's an art for Daddy, too, and that's why he's had such remarkable results in his experiments on regeneration.

Ursula Heschel was fascinated by Daddy's work, and when she and Max came over for dinner, she and Daddy always spent time together in the lab. Xan and I both helped in the lab, feeding the animals, cleaning the tanks, and I had to wash down the floor with a hose once a day. Max was interested and intelligent, but Ursula was the one who truly understood. She and Daddy really hit it off.

Once in January, Daddy and Ursula went to Florida to a lab there specializing in the nervous system of the octopus. In February they went together to Baltimore, where Daddy was giving a paper at Johns Hopkins. They had lots in common.

Xan said once, 'It's a good thing Ursula Heschel is much too old for Dad.'

'What are you talking about?'

'They sure like each other. Kate's noticed it. But Mother doesn't seem jealous.'

'They're just friends. There isn't any reason to be jealous.'

And indeed Mother, rather than being jealous, often suggested asking Max and Ursula to dinner.

But if Urs, as it were, belonged to Daddy, Max belonged to me. And my parents encouraged the friendship. Mother said, 'I expect too much of you, Polly. The oldest always gets too much responsibility foisted on her. I should know. Of course you can go over to Beau Allaire this afternoon.'

If the car wasn't free I'd go to Beau Allaire right from school, taking the bus from Cowpertown to Mulletville and walking over from there, and then later on, Mother would come for me, or Urs would drive me home.

Max had called and asked me for tea early in January. The uncles had left, Charles had gone back to Boston with Dennys and Lucy, and Kate had stayed with us. The house was back to its normal population. School had started again and was as stultifying as ever, and I was glad to be going over to Beau Allaire, but a little shy, driving over by myself. I'd got my license on my sixteenth birthday. One of the good things about Cowpertown High was the driver's-ed course, though Mother and Daddy said that driver's ed and similar courses were one reason why the science department was nearly non-existent, and why no languages were offered.

As I climbed the steps to the front entrance to Beau Allaire, Max flung open the door and welcomed me in. Nettie and Ovid were setting out tea in the library. I didn't see Ursula.

'Urs went into Charleston on a consultation,' Max explained. 'They don't have a neurological service at M. A. Horne, more's the pity. It would keep Urs busy. Dennys introduced her to the chief of neurology at Mercy Hospital and one would have thought Dennys had given him pure gold. In a sense, he did. People flock to New York to see Ursula. They'll flock to Charleston just for a consult. *Maintenant*.' She spoke to me in French. 'Did you bring your homework with you as I suggested?'

I replied in Portuguese: 'It's here, in my canvas bag.'

'Not Portuguese,' Max said. 'That *was* Portuguese, wasn't it?'

'Yes, and it's the language I speak best,' I answered in German.

She laughed. 'I concede. You're good at languages. Let me see some of your schoolwork.'

I pulled out my English notebook. On the bus from school to the Cowpertown dock, I'd written a sketch of the natives on Gaea, comparing them with the Indians we'd met when Daddy took Charles and me with him for a month when he was doing research in Venezuela.

'That's good, Polly,' Max said, to my surprise. 'You really give a flavor of the people you're writing about, but you haven't fallen for the Noble Savage trap. You look at them with a realistic eye. Where did you get your gift for writing?'

'I didn't know I had one. Daddy used to write when he was young, and Mother says he should go over his journals and have some of them published. But he's too busy.'

'If he's that good, he should make time,' Max said. She began leafing through my English notebook. 'You use imagery well. That's a good snow metaphor, *soft flowers that perished before they reached the ground.* Where have you seen snow?'

'Sometimes it snowed in Lisbon. And we've seen snow when we've stayed with our grandparents in New England.'

'Good. I didn't think you could have written that if you hadn't seen it. Does your English teacher appreciate you?'

'She gives me B's. She thinks I'm showing off when I write about Lisbon and other places we've been.'

'Are you?'

'No. When she wants a description of a place, I have to write about places I know.'

'True. But I can see that it might seem like showing off to your English teacher. What's her name?'

'Miss Zeloski.'

'Hardly a good South Carolina name. Who are your favorite poets?'

Sandy and Rhea often give me poetry for Christmas. This year it was a small volume of seventeenth-century writers. I loved it. 'There's someone called Vaughan, I think. I love the way he *relishes* words.'

'And Miss Zeloski?'

'If anything rhymes, Miss Zeloski says it's old-fashioned. She likes poetry that—that obfuscates.'

Max leaned back on the sofa and laughed. 'And I suppose she likes all that garbage full of genital imagery?'

'Not at Cowpertown High. The PTA has its eye out for obscenity.'

'*Go and catch a falling star,*' Max said. '*Get with child a mandrake root.*'

'She doesn't like John Donne. I think he scares her.'

'Too real?'

'That's not what she calls it. But yes. I think she's afraid of reality. So if the poetry doesn't mean anything, she doesn't have to cope with it.'

Max climbed up on the library ladder and pulled a book off one of the top shelves and read a few lines. 'e. e. cummings.'

'I love him,' I said. 'Sandy and Rhea gave me one of his books for my birthday a few years ago.'

'Not cool enough for your Miss Z.?'

'Too cool.'

Max climbed down from the ladder, and refilled my cup. It was a special tea, smoky, and we drank it without anything in it. I liked it. I liked Max. I liked talking with her. At home, everybody (except my parents) was younger than I, and our conversations were limited. And at school I didn't have any real friends. It wasn't that I was actively unpopular, I just didn't have anyone special to talk to. Mostly I felt I was walking through the scene, saying my lines reasonably well, but not being really in the show. At school I tried to play the role that was expected of me, as best I could. With Max, I was myself.

She laughed at me gently. 'What a snob you are, Polly.'

'Me?' I was startled.

'Why not? It's obvious that school bores you, and that there's nobody to challenge you, teacher or student.'

'A lot of the kids are bright.'

She cut me off. 'Go ahead and be a snob. I'm a snob. If you didn't interest me I wouldn't give you the time of day. Being a snob isn't necessarily a bad thing. It can mean being unwilling to walk blindly through life instead of living it fully. Being unwilling to lose a sense of wonder. Being alive is a marvelous, precarious mystery, and few people appreciate it. Go on being a snob, Polly, as long as it keeps your mind and heart alert. It doesn't mean that you can't appreciate people who are different from you, or have different interests.'

Max made me not only willing to be Polyhymnia O'Keefe but happy to be.

It was, oddly enough, through Max that I began seeing Renny. He called me early one evening late in January.

Xan shouted, 'Hey, Polly, it's for you. Some guy.'

I ambled to the phone. Sometimes kids in my class call me to ask about homework.

'Is this Polly O'Keefe?'

'Yes.'

'You don't know me. I'm Queron Renier, and I'm a distant cousin of a friend of yours, Simon Renier, the one who's staying in Venezuela.'

'Well, hello,' I said. 'It's nice to hear from you.'

'I'm an intern at the M. A. Horne Hospital in Cowpertown, and I thought maybe we could get together.'

Interns usually move in sometime in early July. This

was January. 'Well, sure.' I didn't sound wildly enthusiastic.

'I haven't called before because I'm basically a shy guy. But I was talking with an outpatient who's a friend of yours. I guess she saw I was lonely, and somehow or other I mentioned that I'd heard of you through Simon but I hadn't felt free to call—'

'Who was it?' I was curious now.

'A Mrs. Tomassi.'

It took me a moment to remember that Max's husband's name was Tomassi. 'Max!'

'I guess. She lives on Benne Seed at Beau Allaire—'

'What was she doing at the hospital?'

A pause. 'She was just in for some blood tests.'

I wanted to ask what for, but Daddy has talked to us often enough about confidentiality, and I knew that Renny wouldn't tell me.

He said, 'Well, could we get together sometime? Take in a movie in Cowpertown or something?'

'Sure.' I realized I wasn't being very hospitable. 'Would you like to come to dinner? Do you have anything on, your next evening off?'

'It's tomorrow,' he said. 'It's sort of short notice, but no, I don't have anything on.'

'Well, good. Come on over. Do you have access to a motorboat?'

'Nope.'

'Well, come by the causeway, then. It's a lot longer, but if you don't have a boat it's the only way. We're the far end of the island.'

'No problem.'

'About six?' I gave him directions, hung up, and then double-checked with Mother.

'Of course it's all right,' she said. I knew she was worried that I didn't bring friends home the way the others did.

Renny was nice. Everybody liked him. Kate made eyes at him, but fortunately she really was too young for him. Fourteen, after all. Anyhow, Renny and I got on well. He was almost as shy as I was, and I think he was grateful to have someone he could be purely platonic with. I mean, he hardly saw me as a sexpot. But he asked me to go out for something to eat, and see a movie, on his next free evening.

I saw Max the day after Renny came for dinner. She called me to come over after school, to do my homework at the long table in the library, and stay for an early supper.

Ursula was in the library, too, sitting in her favorite chair, deep in some medical journal.

'So how did you like my nice young intern?' Max asked.

'You described him,' I said. 'Nice.'

'Not exciting?'

'He just came over for dinner with the family. It was kind of a mob scene. But he was able to cope with it, and that says something.'

'Hm.'

'Max, why were you having blood tests?'

Ursula looked up from her journal but said nothing.

Max replied shortly, 'When one is my age, every time one sees a doctor, one has to have a million tests.'

'Why did you need to see a doctor?'

'When one is my age, it is prudent to have regular medical checkups.'

'Renny called you Mrs. Tomassi.'

'It was, after all, my husband's name.'

'You never use it.'

'Therefore it gives me a modicum of privacy, of which there is very little around here. And stop prying. It is not a quality I like.'

'Weren't you prying about Renny?' I countered.

'At my age, prying is permissible. Not at yours. Please treat me with the respect I deserve.'

Ursula put her journal down and stood up, stretching. 'I'm off to finish up in the kitchen.'

'Need any help?' I asked.

'No thanks, Pol. Nettie and Ovid already think I'm displacing them. I do try not to hurt their feelings, and I'm more than grateful to have them wash up. It's a dream of a kitchen, and cooking has always been therapy for me.'

At Beau Allaire it wasn't always easy to remember that Urs was at the top of her profession. She seemed to enjoy acting the housekeeper.

'I take outrageous advantage of Urs,' Max said, as the doctor shut the library door. 'But she doesn't have to let me.'

'Well, she loves you.'

'So, are you going to see Renny again?'

'Yup.'

'When?'

'He's not on call on Thursday. We're getting together.'

'He's coming to the Island for dinner again?'

'No. I'm going out with him.'

This seemed to please Max. And that surprised me. Max did not strike me as the matchmaking type.

Ursula came in with a decanter of sherry and said she'd fixed a good French peasant stew for dinner and it could sit on the back of the stove till we were ready. 'Like Nettie and Ovid, I tend to ignore the electric stove and use the old wood-and-coal one. I suppose I'll be grateful for the electric stove come summer.' She poured a small glass of sherry for Max, half glasses for herself and for me, and put the crystal stopper back in the decanter. 'You're good to spend so much time with us, Polly.'

'Good! You've rescued me! You've no idea how lonely I've been.'

'I do,' Max said. 'I grew up at Beau Allaire. I, too, went to school in Cowpertown. You were probably luckier on your Portuguese island, where you were the only Americans, the only Europeans, really, and had to make your own company.'

I nodded. 'I was lots less lonely than I am here. It's not the island—I love Benne Seed.'

'Too bad you and Kate don't hit it off better. M.A. and I made life under the Spanish moss bearable for each other.'

'Kate and Xan are the ones who get along. And Kate's wildly popular at school.'

'You're not?' Ursula's voice was gentle.

'I think the other kids think I'm weird.'

'You're brighter than they are,' Max said, 'and that's threatening.'

'A couple of guys in my grade killed a tortoise the other day,' I said, feeling sick all over again. 'I mean deliberately, and I could have killed them. I wanted to, it was awful, but then I realized that the tortoise was already half dead so it was better to let them finish the job, and everybody laughed because I was making such a case of it.'

'Kate and Xan, too?' Ursula asked.

'They weren't there. Xan would have stopped them.'

Ursula spoke reassuringly. 'Don't worry, Polly. You'll have friends, too, even if you have to wait till you get to college and meet more people. You're friend material, and once you have friends you'll keep them for life.'

Renny had borrowed a motorboat from one of the doctors, which saved us nearly an hour. He took me to a Greek restaurant, Petros', near the dock, which shared a run-down sort of boardwalk with a seafood restaurant.

Renny and I sat in a booth and he told me about his special field, tropical medicine, especially in South America.

That surprised me. I looked at Renny sitting across from me, and there was something solid about him. His blue-grey eyes behind the thick lenses were amused. 'I inherited the Renier myopia,' he said. He'd have been good casting for a young doctor on a soap opera. If I'd been asked to guess what he was going to specialize in, I'd have said orthopedics, or maybe general surgery.

No. South American amoebas and parasites.

'What about India?' I asked, because I've always wanted to go to India. 'Aren't there vast quantities of amoebas and parasites there?'

'Yes, but I'm particularly interested in some parasites which are found largely in South America. They get into the bloodstream, and—to try to simplify a long procedure—eventually invade the heart.'

'Doesn't sound nice.'

'Isn't. The parasite Trypanosoma enters the body usually through the bite of an insect. There are two types of Trypanosoma problems I'm interested in—Chagas' disease and Netson's. Netson's disease is even more lethal than Chagas', particularly to someone with no immunities. When it gets to the heart, ultimately it kills, and thus far we don't have any successful treatment. More important than treatment is finding a means of prevention.'

'Hey. Is there any of this disease around here?'

'No, no, don't worry. So far, it's found almost exclusively in South America. None indigenous to North America.'

Behind Renny was a large poster of the Acropolis, the Parthenon prominent. Despite the Greek decor, the menu was Italian. But I had no idea, that first pizza with Renny, that I'd ever be going to Greece.

'So how come you're interning at M. A. Horne in Cowpertown if you're so interested in South American diseases?'

'Because Bart Netson's on the staff of M. A. Horne. He's my immediate boss.'

When I looked totally surprised, he grinned. 'I have the feeling you suspected that M. A. Horne was at the bottom of my list when I applied to hospitals.'

I could feel myself flushing. I had once again jumped to conclusions. I had judged Renny quickly and unfairly. 'Offhand, a small general hospital off the beaten track doesn't sound like a number-one choice. I didn't know about this Netson or his disease. Why is *he* at M. A. Horne?'

Renny laughed, a nice, hearty laugh. 'He was born in Charleston but spent most of his childhood in Argentina because his father was in foreign service. He came back to Charleston to medical school and married an Allaire. He spends a couple of months each year in South America doing research. He's published a lot of good material, probably the best in the field of tropical medicine, and it's prestigious for M. A. Horne to have him. They're heavily enough endowed to give him pretty much whatever he wants.'

'So he's a sort of cousin of Max's?'

'Has to be. Her mother was an Allaire.' He cut two more slices of pizza and put one, dripping cheese, on my plate. 'Polly? If I go on riding my hobbyhorse, we'll miss the movie.'

'That's okay. I'd rather talk.'

He looked eager. 'Sure?'

'Sure. I'm interested. I wouldn't think you'd have many patients coming into M. A. Horne with South American diseases.'

'You'd be surprised.' He took a large bite of pizza and a swig of milk. 'With the continuing flood of refugees from South American countries, some of them coming in via Cuba and Florida and filtering up through Georgia, we get quite a few. And because of Bart Netson, their problem is recognized more quickly than in other places. For instance, a mild case of conjunctivitis plus a fluctuating fever isn't usually equated with a parasite.'

'Conjunctivitis? You mean pinkeye?'

'The vector—the biting insect—often bites the face at the mucocutaneous junction—'

'Translate.'

'The lip, or the outer canthus of the eye.'

'How'd you get involved?' It did seem an odd choice for a perfect Southern-gentleman type like Queron Renier.

'I spent a couple of summers working in a clinic in Santiago. Eventually, I want to go back.'

'Like a missionary?'

He shook his head. 'To do research. A lot of good medicine has, in fact, come from medical missionaries who give their lives to help people nobody else gives a hoot about—millions of people worn down and living half lives.'

'So how'd you get to Chile and this clinic?'

He looked over my head at one of the Greek posters. 'I met a girl from Santiago while I was in college. Jacinta was over here taking pre-med courses and stayed on for medical school. It was through her I got the summer jobs in Chile.'

'You were in love with her?' He nodded. 'And vice versa?'

A shadow crossed his face. 'To some extent. But there wasn't any future for us.'

'Why not?'

'For one thing, Jacinta was Roman Catholic.'

'Would that really matter?'

'To her, yes. And she came from a big Chilean family, and she was engaged to someone there. They still arrange marriages.'

'She sounds like an independent type. Why'd she accept it?'

'Who knows? Maybe she liked the guy. Maybe he had enough money for her clinic.'

'And you don't want me to ask you any more questions about her.'

'It's okay,' Renny said. 'I've pretty well got her out of my system.'

'But you're still into tropical medicine.'

'Yeah. I guess I'm grateful to her for that. I really am fascinated by it.'

And he was still bruised over the Chilean girl.

'Jacinta's interning in Louisiana,' he said. 'I might bump into her if I ever get back to Chile. But she'll be married by then. They make good baklava here. Want some?'

'Too sweet. You go ahead.'

After we finished eating, he drove back to the dock and we got into the motorboat. About halfway to the Island, he cut the motor and kissed me, which Kate had given me to understand was mandatory, whether the guy really liked you or not. I hoped that Renny liked me. He kissed nicely.

'I'm glad your friend made me call you,' he said.

That was Renny, and I liked him, as the older brother I'd always wanted, even if I got a little tired of tropical medicine. And maybe I was helpful to him in getting his Chilean girl out of his system.

The view of the Acropolis from the balcony at the King George was very like the poster at Petros' in Cowpertown. I took longer over breakfast than I'd expected, looking out at the view, reading bits from the book on Epidaurus (Sandy would expect me to have done my homework), relaxing in the warm morning sunlight.

So I had to dress in a hurry to get down to the lobby by ten. Not difficult. I don't have a large wardrobe to choose from, unlike Kate, who could barely get all her clothes plus herself into her room at Benne Seed. Well, Kate's an Only, and if I had that many clothes I'd have a terrible time deciding what to wear.

I put on a blue-and-white seersucker dress and my sandals and was ready when Zachary pulled up in a diesel taxi with flames coming out the tail pipe. I remember thinking the car was on fire when I first saw a diesel taxi in Lisbon.

I felt simultaneously warm with excitement and frozen with shyness as I sat by this extremely handsome young man on the drive to the Hilton. Zachary did the talking, so I didn't have to worry about what to say. "And listen, Red"—as we drew up to the Hilton—"uh—Pol—about coming up to my room—it's perfectly okay—I mean, I'm not going to try anything or anything like that. So just relax."

His room was on the eleventh floor of the Hilton, "in the best curve of the building," he told me as we went up in a very swift elevator. He led me through his room and right out onto the balcony, and I caught my breath in awe and delight. He had a view not only of the strange, flat-topped hill with the Parthenon but also a wide vista of the harbor at Piraeus, with the Aegean Sea to the left. And there was a high, stony mountain rising out of cypress trees, topped with a stone belfry, and then a large, white building, probably a monastery. It was far more spectacular than the view from the King George, or the poster at Petros'.

I had let my breath out in what was almost shock at the vast sweep of gloriousness. He gave me a proprietary smile. "Told you it would wow you."

It did. But the funny thing was that despite the staggering magnificence of the view, I liked my old hotel better than the Hilton.

As though reading my thoughts, Zachary waved toward the room. "The decor is pure Hilton, and a Hilton is a Hilton is a Hilton. However, my pa has connections, and the view redeems it. And the bathroom is European, black marble, with a tub made for people who prefer baths to showers."

"Like me," I said.

"I can't start the day without a shower. Okay, what now?"

"The Acropolis, please, if you haven't been there too many times."

"The Acropolis, pretty Pol, can't be visited too many times. We'll just grab a cab."

"Can't we walk?"

"We could, if we had nothing else to do all day. I want to drive out in the country with you, and then come back to Athens, and maybe go to the Plaka to one of my favorite small tavernas." He was planning to be with me the whole day. I felt a thrill of pleasure ripple over me. I glanced at him out of the corner of my eye. He was just as gorgeous as I thought, and at least two inches taller than I.

It was a glorious end-of-summer day. Despite Zachary's chatter about the terrible pollution which was destroying the Parthenon and other ancient sites, and which gave him allergies, to me the air was clear and crisp and invigorating. It would be romanticizing to say it was like Gaea, because Gaea had as much fog and dampness as any other island, but it was like Gaea as I remembered it.

Zachary insisted on paying the entrance fee for both of us, and I was not happy about this. I didn't want to be beholden to some guy I had just met who came from the world of megabucks. I pulled out my Greek money and my booklet of traveler's checks, but he brushed me aside and got our tickets and I couldn't very well armwrestle him in the middle of the throng. I followed him through the gates, along with a lot of other tourists. Many were bunched together in groups, with guides herding them like sheep.

Zachary pointed to a cluster of Japanese tourists slung with cameras. He nudged me. "They say that Japanese tourists really aren't pushy. They just get behind a German." He laughed, then said, "Or don't you approve of ethnic jokes?" Just at that moment we saw a big, red-faced man in lederhosen pushing his way through the crowd.

"See?" Zachary said. But the man opened his mouth and called to someone, and he spoke in pure middle-American. "Ouch." Zachary made a face. "Corn belt. What does he think he's trying to prove? No wonder most of the world hates us. Come on, Pol. If you think there's a mob today, you should see it in midseason." He took me by the hand.

I pulled back, looking at the scaffolding partly concealing a beautiful building. "Not so fast."

He stopped. "Okay, listen, this is really interesting. They're literally inoculating the stone with antibiotics to try to slow down decay. The Caryatids—you know what Caryatids are?"

Max had seen to it that I would not come to Greece unprepared. "Female forms, sort of like columns, holding up a roof."

I think Zachary was slightly annoyed that I knew about Caryatids. (Kate had said to me, 'Listen, Polly, guys don't like it if they think you know more than they do.' 'I *do* know more than they do.' 'You don't need to show it.') "Okay, then," Zachary said, "they're trying to restore the Caryatids which hold up the Erechtheion. That's what all the scaffolding is for. And that's why the Parthenon is roped off, because all those tourists' feet were wearing down the marble. Okay, Red, c'mon. The Theseum is one of my favorites. What gets me is knowing that all this beauty was destroyed not so much by the erosion of time, and normal wear and tear, as by war, and greed, and man's stupidity. It really makes me more anti-war than some of the more obvious things, like nuclear stockpiling. Lots of these fallen columns were destroyed by people scavenging for metal."

"What for?"

"Guns. Cannons."

I shuddered. "You mean they really destroyed gorgeous temples just to get a small quantity of metal?"

"That's exactly what I mean."

"And Lord Elgin, all those marbles he took—" I looked around. "I suppose he really thought he was saving them from the Turks, but shouldn't they be back now where they belong? At least those which didn't get lost when that ship sank?" Why don't you shut up, Polyhymnia. You're showing off how much you know again, reeling back the tape of what Max taught you.

Zachary knew I was showing off. But he was nice about it. "You've done your homework, haven't you? That's okay. Lots of Americans don't know anything about what they're gawking at, and don't really care. Like my pop. He has a fancy camera and takes hundreds of slides, and when he gets them home he can't even remember where he was when he took the pictures." He led me to a marble bench in the shade of an ancient olive tree. "Let's sit for a minute, and watch the crowd go by, okay? You know, Red—"

"Don't call me Red."

"Polly. You really intrigue me. You aren't like any girl I've ever met."

Was that good? He made it sound good.

"You said you're nearly seventeen—"

I nodded.

"I'd say you're nearly thirty and nearly twelve. And there's something virginal about you. Nice contrast to me. But don't worry. I won't do anything to hurt you. Trust me."

Did I trust this guy? I was not in a trusting frame of mind. But I didn't have to trust him to enjoy being with him.

❈

"Are you?" Zachary asked.

"Am I what?"

"A virgin."

I hesitated. She who hesitates is lost.

He gave me a long, scrutinizing look. "Still waters run deep, eh?"

I tried to recover myself. "That is not a question you should ask somebody you have just met. It is not an acceptable question."

He actually looked discomfited. "Sorry. Sometimes my curiosity gets the better of me. And you make me intensely curious, pretty Pol."

"I don't play around," I said. "Not ever."

"Sweetie, I never thought you did. Not for a minute. Whatever you did, and with whomever, would be totally serious." He touched my arm lightly. "I didn't mean to upset you. Shall we change the subject?"

"Please." I was trembling.

We got up and started to walk along again, brushed by tourists who were hurrying to catch up with their groups. If there was going to be any further conversation between us, he would have to start it. I wanted to tell him to take me back to the hotel, but my voice was lost somewhere deep down inside me.

After a while he spoke in a quiet, normal way. "The Parthenon is probably more beautiful to us today than it would have been when it was built, because now it's open to the Greek light that plays on the marble and brings it to life. In the old days, when it was complete, the main body of the building, the sanctuary that housed the goddess, was enclosed and had no windows, so the only light came from the doorway."

"Wait, please." I dug into my shoulder bag. "Let me

get some of this down, so I can write about it in the journal I have to take back to school."

"Now you sound like a little kid again. Why bother? Teacher'll spank you if you don't?"

"I said I'd do it." I opened the journal and made a couple of notes. My hand was steady.

"You might add," Zachary said, "that despite their brilliance, the Greeks were limited in their architecture, because they never discovered the arch. With the arch you can support lots more weight, and that's why the great cathedrals can be so spacious."

Writing furiously, I said, "You certainly know a lot."

"I'm not stupid. I got kicked out of several prep schools because I was bored. But if I'm interested in something, I learn about it. Okay, take your notes and then we'll go on. We can come back to the Acropolis another day. It's so overwhelming you can't take too much at a time."

I wrote down what Zachary had said, and I wondered about the Greeks and their gods. Why had they closed in the Parthenon, so that the goddess Athena had been hidden?

Zachary surprised me by picking up on my thoughts. "Odd, isn't it, Pol, how all the different civilizations want to box God in. The ancient Hebrews wanted to hide the Tabernacle in the Holy of Holies, so the ordinary people couldn't see it. Christians are just as bad. Peter wanted to put Jesus, Moses, and Elijah in a box on the Mount of Transfiguration."

We had come to another bench, and I sat down; it was not easy to write standing up, and the notes I had taken were an untidy scrawl.

"I'm an atheist, obviously," Zachary said.

I looked up at him. "For an atheist, you seem to know a lot about religion."

"That's why I'm an atheist."

Maybe it was because Zachary was older than the kids I went to school with that he did not seem to be afraid to talk about ideas. I was far more comfortable with ideas than with ordinary social conversation.

Athena was the Greek name for the goddess. The Romans called her Minerva. Max's sister was Minerva Allaire. This was the kind of conversation Max delighted in.

The sun was hot, the same sun which beat down on these stones and other people thousands of years ago.

"Penny, Pol," Zachary said.

"Oh—just wondering what it would be like to worship a goddess." Was that a Freudian question?

"You a feminist?"

"Liberation for all," I said. "The Greeks had a pantheon of gods of both sexes, didn't they?" I put the notebook in my bag. "Why am I suddenly famished?"

"Breakfast was a long time ago." Zachary took my hand to pull me up. "I've ordered the car for eleven. We'll drive to Delphi and have lunch at a xenia. Know what a xenia is?"

Sandy and Rhea and I would be staying at xenias. "Greek-run inns." ('You don't have to show off all the time,' Kate said.)

"Ever been in one?"

"I just arrived yesterday."

"Okay, c'mon, let's go."

The car was an old VW Bug, a bit cramped for our long legs.

"Sorry about this rattletrap," Zachary said. "It was all I could get at the last minute."

"We have a Land-Rover on Benne Seed." Daddy could drive it over the dunes, and it didn't get stuck in the sand the way an ordinary car would. "This is a lot less bumpy than that."

Zachary drove too fast. I buckled my seat belt tightly. I'd much rather have puttered along and looked at the countryside. But I kept my mouth closed.

Zachary was a new experience for me, and I didn't want to turn him off by saying the wrong thing. If he was intrigued by me, I was certainly intrigued by him. I couldn't figure out why he had picked me, out of all the kids in Constitution Square. But the fact that he had certainly did something for my ego.

I think I expected Delphi to be bigger and grander than it turned out to be. It's a small village on top of a mountain, facing a great valley and what appears to be a large lake but is actually part of the Bay of Corinth. We stopped at a small xenia set in the midst of gardens built on several levels, with the roofs of the lower levels planted with grass, trees, flowers, so that the xenia seemed part of the hillside. If Delphi was smaller than I'd expected, it was also lovelier, and the mountains were higher and grander. I was overwhelmed by the mountains.

The xenia served only one dish, a lemony chicken that was delicious. But again I felt tongue-tied.

"What's wrong, Red?"

"Polly."

"Polly. What's wrong?"

"Nothing."

"Come on. I know better than that. Someone's hurt you."

"You can hardly get to be my age without being hurt."

"You're a constant surprise to me. When I relax into

thinking of you as a child, you turn into a woman, wounded."

"Don't be romantic."

"Don't you want to talk to me?"

"Of course I want to talk to you. What've we been doing all day?"

"Chatting. Showing off how much we both know. With a few minor exceptions, we haven't been talking."

Well. He was more sensitive than I'd realized.

"So, shall we talk?"

Out of desperation, I asked, "Why don't *you* talk?"

"About what?"

"Well, why are you in Greece instead of college? It's not just for the culture."

"Little Miss Smarty-pants. No. It's not."

"So who wounded *you?*"

As though stalling for time, he signaled the waitress for the check. "I got dumped by a girl I liked, and I deserved to be dumped. As is my wont, I showed off, tried to prove what a big shot I am, and when she really needed me I let her down. I don't like accepting that about myself." Suddenly his face crumpled. Then he was back in control. "My self-image took a beating. Hey, Red, I don't talk about myself like this, not with anybody. What've you done to me?"

This time I didn't tell him not to call me Red.

He went on. "So it seemed wise to take some time off, to find out more about who I am, what I want to be."

"Have you been finding out?"

"No. As usual, I've been running away. It hit me a couple of days ago in Mykenos. I've been running so I wouldn't have to stop and look at myself. Do I want to be a lawyer, part of an enormous global corporation, like Pa? I always thought I did. Putting growth and profit over the interests of any nation. Multinationals are not accountable to anybody. That's Pa's world. Do I want to inherit it?"

It occurred to me that the world which Zachary stood to inherit was the world which Sandy and Rhea were devoting their lives to fight. Sandy and Rhea put the interests of human beings above the interests of corporations, and I knew they'd upset several global oligarchies.

"Do you want to inherit that world?" I asked.

"It's power," he said.

"Power corrupts."

"Well, Red, I don't know, I just don't know. It's easier to face your own weaknesses in a context of money and power than looking in the mirror in the morning while you're shaving. If you have enough money, and enough power, nothing else matters. Pa's never loved anything except money. He and Ma endured each other —she died a couple of years ago. The extent of their conversation was, 'I need another ice cube.' Or, 'Where shall we go for dinner?' I doubt if they ever slept together much after I was conceived. What about your parents? Do they still have sex?"

He'd revealed too much about himself, I thought, so he had to turn it on me. My voice was cool. "They sleep in the same bed. What they do in it is their own affair."

Zachary paid the bill, putting out what seemed to be a very small tip. "Let's get out of here and climb up to the stadium."

It was quite a climb, and Zachary got out of breath. If he was wandering around Europe finding out who he was and what he wanted to do, he must have been doing it in taxis and rented cars and expensive hotels. I felt sorry for him. But he also represented a world which was ruthless, where money mattered, and not people.

We'd had to leave Portugal because of that world, because of people coming to Gaea and trying to get hold of Daddy's work on regeneration and exploit it, long before it was safe. I liked Zachary, and not just because he liked me; there was just something about him that appealed to me. But I was also frightened by the world in which he'd grown up. Mixed feelings. As usual.

The stadium was impressive, with many of the original marble seats intact, carved right out of the hillside. We sat looking at the mountains looming above us, at the valley far below, caressed by the golden air. The land was very dry and bare-looking. There were a few trees, but very little grass, and that was parched and brown. But this was only part of a great cycle, Max had told me. In the winter the rains would come and the earth would be green again.

I didn't like it when Zachary asked me about my parents' sex life. I'm not like Rosy, of course. At four, Rosy still thinks of Mother as an extension of herself. I don't. But still, I want Mother to be Mother, Daddy to be Daddy.

Max, in a different way from Zachary, also separated my parents from me, seeing them with her clear grey eyes in a way that I had never seen them.

'Your mother's restless,' Max said, one rainy winter day when we were sitting in the library.

'Oh?' Mother, restless?

Max got up from the long sofa and put more fat wood on the fire. 'She's been a good mother to all of you, but it's beginning to wear on her. She's got a fine brain, and not enough chance to use it.'

'She helps Daddy a lot in the lab, does all the computer stuff.'

'Yes, she does, and that's a saving grace, but it's not her own thing.'

'She's going to finish her Ph.D. as soon as Rosy's in school.'

'Easier said than done. You do a great deal, too much, I think, but you'll be out of the nest soon. The boys aren't going to be that much help.'

'Everybody helps out,' I said. 'Everybody has chores.'

'Most of it still falls on your mother,' Max said. 'She's so tired and so restless she's ready to do a Gauguin and walk out on all of you.'

'But she won't—' The idea was preposterous.

'No. She won't. Your Uncle Sandy told me that your mother suffered as an adolescent because her own mother was beautiful and successful in the world of science—didn't she win a Nobel Prize?'

'Yes, for isolating farandolae within mitochondria.'

'Your mother felt insufficient because of your grandmother, and she didn't want the same thing to happen to you, to make you feel you had to compete. So she's held herself back, and it's beginning to tell. She *will* get to her own work, eventually, but eventually no doubt seems a long time away.'

I stared into the fire. Now that Max had pointed out that Mother was restless, I could see that it was true.

'Your mother is a truly mature human being, and they're rare. She's learned to live with herself as well as with your father, and believe me, your father's no easy person. He may be a genius, but single-minded scientists tend to let people down.'

'Daddy doesn't—'

She cut me off. 'Of course he does. We all do. You

won't grow up until you learn that all human beings betray each other and that we are going to be let down even by those we most trust. Especially by those we most trust.'

I didn't like this, but it had the ring of truth. And I didn't like that, either.

'If we put human beings on pedestals, their clay feet are going to give way and they are going to come crashing down, and unless we get out of the way, they'll crush us.'

And I didn't get out of the way.

I hardly heard Max. 'Your mother has the guts to stick it out on this godforsaken island with amazing grace. Your father's work is important, and it demands isolation and considerable secrecy, but it's hard on the rest of you.' She continued to squat by the fire, poking at the smoldering logs. The fat wood caught and its bright flames soared. Satisfied, Max sat back. 'Your parents have one thing going for them. They love each other.'

My response was again a reflex. 'Of course.'

Max turned from the fire and smiled at me, her loveliest smile. 'There's no "of course" about it. Lots of married people barely tolerate each other. People stay together because of the children, or for financial convenience. Divorce is expensive. But your parents love each other. They're lovers, and that's probably incomprehensible to you, but it's a wonderful thing indeed.' The fire was blazing brightly now, and she got up and sat next to me on the sofa. 'It worries your mother that Kate goes to all the school dances and you don't.'

I shrugged. The wind beat the rain across the verandah and against the library windows. 'I don't like disappointing her.'

Max put her arm around my shoulders. 'You don't disappoint her. She just doesn't want you to have the same kind of difficult adolescence that she did. But she weathered it. You will, too.'

'I suppose.'

'Polly, love, having it easy is no blessing. To my mind, it hinders maturing.'

Zachary and I climbed down from the stadium to the sacred precincts and the theatre. I wanted to be able to walk in awe, here where so many extraordinary mysteries had gone on thousands of years ago. It was here that people came to consult the Delphic Oracle in times of emergency. How lonely the Oracle must have been, speaking only in riddles, with no one to understand her except the priests, who may or may not have translated correctly what she was saying.

The guides were herding their groups like goats—sheep at the Acropolis; why did I think of them as goats in Delphi?—and shooting facts at them in German, English, French. The noise cut across the clarity of the air. Noise pollution is as destructive as any other.

If I focused on one of the guides I could translate what he was saying. But the facts were delivered with the boredom of repetition.

"Apollo was worshipped here," Zachary said, "and Dionysus. Light and dark, reason and fecundity, waxing and waning like the moon."

We were standing on a green knoll. Across the valley

were the great, dark mountains. The sky moved upward
into a vanishing vastness of blue.

"I'm an Apollo worshipper," Zachary said. "Or would
be if I lived in Greek times. Apollo, the god of reason."

"You strike me as being rather Dionysian," I said. The
name Dennys comes from Dionysus, but my Uncle
Dennys is both sober and reserved. Sandy says it's because Dennys spends his time with the unfathomable
mysteries of the human brain.

Zachary bowed. "Thank you. I take that as a compli-
ment. But I don't want you to think about philosophy.
I want you to pay attention to me."

"Even you can't compete with all this."

He took my hand. "*Avanti!* Let's go."

It was a good day. Confusing, but good. Zachary made
me feel I wasn't just a gawky, backward adolescent who
didn't even need a bra till I was fourteen, but that I was
mature, and attractive to him.

We went to the *son et lumière* show at the Acropolis,
which somehow had less magic close up than it had had
from the roof of the King George the night before. Then
to the Plaka for a late supper, a small place Zachary
had discovered that wasn't touristy. Good food and Greek
music and lots of laughter in the air. I decided that I
was meeting Sandy's challenge pretty well. *Very* well.

After the meal, we sipped small cups of the sweet
Greek coffee and I was sorry the day was almost over.

"Polly, I haven't had this good a time in ages. You
don't put any pressure on me. You take me as I am. Dare
I ask you to spend tomorrow with me?"

Dare *he*? I hadn't dared dream that he would. "Dare ahead."

"We'll do something fun. Take a drive. Have a picnic. I'll pick you up at ten again, okay?"

"Fine." What would I have been doing if Zachary hadn't picked me up? Going on that bus tour and feeling sorry for myself?

Max had once said, 'We cannot afford the luxury of self-pity.' Self-pity is destructive, I do know that. But Zachary made it very easy for me not to need the luxury.

In the taxi he leaned toward me and brushed his lips against mine, then kissed me, gently. "That's not your first kiss," he said.

No, but it was different. I was different.

He kissed me again. "Polly, I don't know what you're telling me."

"Good night," I said firmly as the taxi drew up in front of the hotel. "And thanks, Zachary. It's been a good day, a really good day."

Back in the room, I undressed and bathed and then wrapped myself in towels and sat at the desk, getting my journal for school finished for the day. How would Miss Zeloski translate what I had written? I wrote about what I had seen, but not that I had been with anybody.

Then I took a postcard from the stationery folder and wrote the family. Wrote a separate card to Charles. And to Renny.

There was one postcard left. Should I write Max and Ursula?

I shut the folder.

❀

Writing the journal for Miss Zeloski was as much fun as it was work. Even if I didn't tell her about being with Zachary in Delphi, I enjoyed writing about Apollo and Dionysus.

Max had shown me some sketchbooks she'd made in Greece. Line drawings not of the present but of the past —Semele and the swan; Jason being brought up by the centaur Chiron; Orpheus with his harp.

There were other notebooks I'd loved looking through, each one dealing with a special place and time. The Bushmen of southern Africa, a race of tiny people who had come, Max thought, originally from Egypt. The Schaghticoke Indians from the part of New England where my grandparents still live and where I was born. The nomads, or Numidians, of North Africa.

Max had not been familiar with Gaea, so I showed her some more pieces I'd written about the native Gaeans. I didn't go into anthropology, just wrote about the way they lived, accepting some things from the twentieth century, rejecting others. She liked my Gaean pieces, and so did I.

It was nevertheless a complete surprise the day she called and suggested I come over for supper, that she had something to show me.

'Let's go to the bedroom,' she said. 'I've a good fire going, and with the February northeaster blowing, it's the warmest room in the house. It can be colder on Benne Seed Island than in the Arctic.'

'Where's Urs?'

'Shopping on the mainland. Planning something special for supper.'

I paused on the landing, as usual, to look at the Laughing Christ. There was no way one could feel self-pity in front of that absolute joy. Even in laughter the face reflected a tolerance and forbearance that made me ashamed of my own tendency toward judgmentalness.

Max paused, too. 'I'm glad you like him.' We went on up the stairs. The long windows in Max's room that led out onto the verandah were closed, and though we could hear the wind sweeping around the house, the fire was comforting.

'What do you have to show me?' I asked.

She smiled at me, the firelight bringing out silver glints in her eyes, then moved slowly to her desk and got an envelope, which she handed to me. It was addressed to Polyhymnia O'Keefe, c/o Maximiliana S. Horne. It had come from a travel magazine, not an important one, but still a real magazine, and they had accepted one of my pieces on Gaea. I wouldn't get any money, but I'd get two complimentary copies of the magazine. I couldn't believe it.

Max laughed and took my hands and swung me around, and I saw an ice bucket on a stand near the fireplace. 'This calls for a celebration.' She put a napkin over the bottle and uncorked it gently. 'The idea that the champagne cork should pop up to the ceiling is insulting to good champagne.'

We lay on the rug in front of the fire, and after a while Ursula came in and joined us. She brought a bowl of shrimp which had been caught that afternoon, and some spicy sauce. It was lovely. One of the happiest times I'd ever known.

And I was happier at home, too. The fact that I hated school no longer seemed important. Max was my teacher,

as Mother and Daddy had been my teachers on Gaea.
And because I was learning, and felt happy about it, I
was more patient with the little kids. I helped get them
ready for bed without being prodded, read to them if
Mother was working with the computer in the lab. I let
Kate borrow my favorite necklace for one of the school
dances. Xan and I didn't spat as much as usual.

And at least a couple of times a week I did my homework over at Beau Allaire. When I'd finished with the
written stuff, Max would pull a book down from one of
the library shelves and have me read aloud to her. 'You're
going to have more than one option when you come to
choose a career. You have a lot of acting ability.'

'I'm too ugly.'

'You aren't ugly at all. You have the kind of face that
comes alive when you're speaking. Why would I want
to paint you if you were ugly? I'll take you over Kate,
any day.'

Max taught me to see the world around me with her
painter's eye. Now I noticed not only the loveliness of a
new moon seen through a fringe of Spanish moss, I saw
also the delicacy of a spider's web on the grass between
two tree roots, saw the little green lizard camouflaged
under a leaf. And this seeing the particular wonder of
the ordinary was reflected in what I wrote for school, but
if Miss Zeloski noticed it, she didn't particularly like it.
And Miss Zeloski was the one who gave the grades, and
I had to get good grades.

'Why?' Max demanded. 'One does not live by grades
alone.'

'I want to go to a good college, and I need to get a
scholarship. After all, there are seven of us to educate.
So grades matter.'

Max put the back of her hand to her forehead in a

swift gesture of apology. 'Of course. Stupid of me. Like most people who've never had to worry about money, I can be very dense. So. How do we win Miss Zeloski? Get her to give you A's instead of B's? What does Miss Zeloski *want*? That's the first question you have to ask. You don't have to compromise in order to please her. Find out what she's looking for, and then give her that in the very best way you possibly can.'

'I don't want to give Miss Zeloski anything.'

'You really dislike her, don't you?'

'She grades unfairly.'

'You are very opinionated, Polly. Part of becoming a mature woman is learning compassion.'

'I know I'm opinionated. I'm sorry.'

'Don't be sorry. Just think. You talk about being odd man out. How do you think Miss Z. feels?'

It took me a while to answer. 'Lonely.'

'And maybe insecure. And that may help explain why obscure poetry is comforting to her. I'll bet she loves footnotes and all the vines of the groves of academe. The next time she gives you a free writing assignment, give her a well-documented essay. It'll be good discipline for you.'

It was. Max made me see the fun of cross-referencing, of finding out, for instance, what was happening in the world of science when Montaigne was writing his essays, and what the lineup of nations was, and who was painting, and what was the popular music of the day. And it worked. Miss Zeloski didn't seem such a bore to me, and her nasal Southern accent didn't grate so, and she gave me A's.

Max taught me to understand that Miss Zeloski was far lonelier than I was. She taught me to see that some of the kids who drank and slept around were lost and groping for something they couldn't find. But she didn't have much patience with those who hunted down animals and birds. 'Sadism isn't limited to the rich and corrupt. One doesn't tolerate it even when it comes from ignorance and stupidity.' Then, 'Come out on the porch. I brought in a Cape jessamine bud this morning. It's blooming in a small crystal bowl and the air is full of its scent and the promise that spring is just around the corner.'

Through Max's eyes I saw more than I'd ever seen before.

One beautiful early-spring evening, Max and Ursula came to dinner. Daddy and Urs went to the lab, as usual. When dinner was ready, Mother sent me to call them. As I came to the screen door, I heard my name and stopped.

'You mustn't let Polly bother Max,' Daddy was saying. 'Polly has Max confused with God, and she'll give her no peace if Max goes on encouraging her.'

Ursula laughed, her warm, sane laugh. 'I dare say God gets no peace, either, and I'm sure he continues to give encouragement.'

'Max has certainly brought out the best in Polly.'

I realized I'd done enough eavesdropping, and banged on the door to call them in to dinner.

At dinner Kate and Xan were talking about tryouts for the school spring play, open to everybody in the high school. It was always a Shakespearean play, and this year was going to be *As You Like It*.

Xan said, 'They chose that because there are so many female parts. They never get enough guys.'

'Oh, come on, Xan,' Kate urged. 'If you try out, you'll get any part you want.'

'It'll interfere with tennis.'

'No, it won't,' Kate said. 'They schedule rehearsals so it doesn't interfere with anything.'

I knew she'd talk him into being in the play. And she'd probably be Rosalind.

Max asked, 'What are you going to try out for, Polly?'

I used Xan's ploy, which hadn't worked for Xan. 'I'll be practicing for swimming.'

'I told you,' Kate said, 'the rehearsals are during school hours. You could have one of the boys' parts if you want, Pol. They always have to use girls, too.'

I saw Max and Ursula look at Kate, then at each other.

Daddy said, 'I don't think Polly needs to limit herself to male roles.'

'Oh, I didn't mean—' Kate said. 'It's just that she's tall and they need tall girls to play men.'

I'd tried out for the play the year before, and had a walk-on. Even so, it was the most fun I'd had from school the whole year.

'Do you get a choice of whom you try out for?' Ursula asked.

Kate said, 'Well, you can ask.'

Xan said, 'I'll try out if Polly will.'

'Oh, sure,' I said. 'At least I can paint scenery.' I did not mention that I had no intention of trying out for the backstage crew; I was going to try out for Rosalind or Celia. Miss Zeloski did the casting.

❀

In March, Beau Allaire was brilliant with azaleas in great banks around the house. Max's gardener got extra help, and the grounds rivaled the great gardens in Charleston. The magnolia trees were heavy with waxen white blossoms. The camellias were exceptionally brilliant. All the long windows were open to the verandahs and the ocean breeze and the singing of the mockingbirds.

On the day of the tryouts I got home from school to find a normal kind of chaos. The little kids had friends over and were shouting out on the swings and slide. The lab door was shut, with an old hotel DO NOT DISTURB sign on it, which meant Mother was doing something tricky with equations on the computer and needed to concentrate.

I called Max. 'I have news.'

'Good?'

'Terrific.'

'Come on over and tell me. Urs is in Charleston and I was going to call you anyhow. You beat me to it.'

I didn't want to disturb Mother about the Land-Rover, but Xan said go ahead, he'd tell Mother as soon as the lab door was open again. So I headed for Beau Allaire, singing at the top of my lungs.

Max was out on the steps, waiting for me. 'So what's this big news?'

'I'm going to play Celia in *As You Like It*.'

She flung her arms wide, then gave me a big hug. Then pulled back. 'Who's playing Rosalind?'

'One of the seniors.'

'What about Kate?''

'A shepherdess.'

Max laughed. 'I'm delighted about Celia, absolutely delighted. She has some splendid lines. With the right director, Celia can be almost as good a role as Rosalind.'

She pulled me into the hall. 'Let's go up to my verandah. There's a lovely breeze.'

On the landing we paused to look at the statue of the Laughing Christ. 'He approves,' Max said. 'He thinks you're terrific.'

When we got out on the verandah I sat at the glass-topped table to get my homework out of the way. Max curled up on the cushioned wicker couch and read till I'd finished. When she saw me putting my books away, she said, 'Your parents have done a good job with you, Polly. And they've taught you something contrary to today's mores, that instant gratification is a snake in the grass.'

'What do you mean?' I zipped up my book bag.

'When you eat a meal, what do you eat first? What do you eat last?'

'I eat what I like least first, and save what I like best till last. Why?'

'Because people who eat the best first, and then likely can't finish the meal, are apt to be the same way with the rest of their lives. Fun first, work later, and the work seldom gets done.'

I giggled.

'What's funny?'

'A couple of years ago when we spent Christmas in New England with the grandparents, I was asked out to dinner with some friends who had a daughter my age, and they had turnips. Ugh. So I ate mine up, fast, so I could get rid of them and get to the rest of the dinner. And the mother saw me, and beamed at me, and said how wonderful it was that I liked her turnips so much, and before I could say anything, she gave me another great big helping. I was almost sick.'

Max laughed. 'Don't let it stop you from saving the

best. When you came in today you sat right down and did your homework, not putting it off till later.'

'Well, as you said. If I put it off, I won't get it done.'

'What about your classmates?'

I pondered briefly. 'Some do the work. Some don't.'

'How do *they* expect to live?'

'I don't think they think much about it. I think about it, but I haven't got anywhere.'

'You'll do all right, whatever you choose. Wait.' She disappeared into the bedroom and came back with a book.

'Listen to those mockingbirds,' she said. 'They sound right out of the Forest of Arden.' She riffled through the pages. 'Here. This is practically my favorite line in all of Shakespeare, and it's Celia's: *O wonderful, wonderful, and most wonderful! and yet again wonderful! and after that, out of all whooping!*'

'It's going to be fun.' I said. 'Rosalind has a line I love: *Do you not know I am a woman? when I think, I must speak.*'

'A bit chauvinist,' Max said.

'Maybe men ought to speak more than they do?' I suggested.

'Stay here,' Max said again, and disappeared once more, but instead of coming back with a book, as I'd expected, she came with a bottle of champagne. 'Nettie and Ovid have left some salad for us in the icebox,' she said.

We never got to it. We kept reading bits and pieces from *As You Like It*, and then some other plays, sad ones, funny ones. I'd never before realized just how alive Shakespeare is, how very present.

❁

When I got home I parked in the shed at the end of the lab wing. I felt tingly, and as though the ground was about a foot lower than it ought to be. I walked to the dunes and stood looking down at the water. Then I turned back to the house and heard the phone ring. It wouldn't be for me, so I didn't pay any attention. When I reached the lab, Daddy was standing in the doorway.

'Come on in the lab for a minute, Polly.'

I went in and sat on one of the high stools.

'I just answered the phone, and it was Max, very apologetic because she was afraid she'd given you too much champagne and shouldn't have let you drive home.'

I could feel that my cheeks were flushed. 'You always let us have a little wine when you have it.'

'There is such a thing as moderation. I'm grateful to Max for calling me, but surprised she let you drink so much.'

'We didn't have that much.' How much had we had? I had no idea. Max kept filling my glass before it was empty, and I certainly wasn't counting.

Daddy sat on the stool next to mine. On the high counter was a pad full of mathematical scribblings: Mother's writing. Daddy moved the pad away. 'Max was concerned enough to call to see that you were safely home.'

I felt deflated. And defensive.

'You're a minor, Polly, and you're not accustomed to drinking, and it's very easy to have too much without realizing it.'

'Please don't make a case out of it, Daddy. Max isn't in the habit of giving me too much to drink. We were celebrating.'

'Celebrating what?'

'I'm going to play Celia in *As You Like It*. It's a really good role.'

'That's wonderful news, honey. Just don't overcelebrate next time. Have you told Mother?'

'I haven't had a chance to tell Mother.'

'She's reading to the little ones. Why don't you go tell them? And send Xan out to me if you see him. He hasn't cleaned the lizard tanks.'

I cleaned my share of the tanks in the morning before school so I wouldn't have it hanging over me. Xan probably does a better job than I do, but he leaves it till last thing. He does it—I don't think he's forgotten more than once—but he puts it off.

'Okay. Daddy—'

'What, my dear?'

'I'm not drunk, really. It's as much excitement about getting a part in the play as anything. Xan's playing Jaques, by the way, but he couldn't care less.'

'And Kate?'

'She's one of the shepherdesses.'

'Is she disappointed?'

'Yes. But I didn't have even a walk-on when I was Kate's age.'

Daddy put his arm around me. 'We hoped that Kate would be a friend for you, a girl you could have fun with.'

'Kate's okay.'

He pulled me closer. 'Polly, you don't have to compete with Kate in any way. Not in looks, not in talent, not in school. I wouldn't have you be any different. You don't need to prove anything, to anybody. I truly don't have favorites among my children, but you are my first child, and very special. I love you.'

I returned his hug. 'You're special, too.' And I wished that there were more times when Daddy and I could have time alone.

Daddy and Ursula went to Charleston together the next week, and I think they talked about all that champagne, because there wasn't any more after that. At least when Ursula was there. And, as a matter of fact, the next time Max brought out champagne was the day after the production of *As You Like It*. The performance was in mid-April so as not to interfere with all the academic stuff that accumulates in the last semester.

As You Like It was a big success, and I even got my own curtain call, and everybody said what a pity it was to put in all that work for one performance. But it was worth it, at least for me.

Max called me over to celebrate. Ursula had been to see me play Celia but had flown to New York in the morning for some kind of big consultation. Max brought out a bottle of champagne, but we had only one glass each, and with it a lot of fried chicken which Nettie had fixed for us, and a big casserole of okra, onions, and tomatoes. I don't like okra, I think you have to be born to it, and I told Max I was eating it first to get it out of the way.

That weekend there was a school dance, and I went with the guy who played Orlando. Rosalind was going steady with another senior. We were to meet at the school, so I drove Xan and Kate. Xan was going stag, and he said he didn't trust Kate's date to bring her home.

If Daddy wanted me to have a warning about booze,

I got it. The girl who played Phebe got sick all over herself.

'Go help her clean up,' Xan said disgustedly. 'The kids she came with are all stoned, and so's Kate's so-called escort.'

Kate came and helped me.

Not that Cowpertown High is full of alcoholics and junkies. Just a few, like any other high school. But even a few is too many.

After we got Phebe moderately tidy, Xan and Kate wanted to go home. I was actually having a good time with some of the kids from the play, who seemed aware of my existence for the first time. The boy who played Oliver was dancing with me when Xan came over, followed by Kate, who was followed by half a dozen boys. I didn't want to leave, but I was the one with the driver's license. And maybe it was better to leave while I was doing well and wasn't what the Cowpertowners still call a wallflower.

We talked about the dance the next night at dinner, and I suppose it was a good and maybe unusual thing that we *could* talk with our parents.

'Pot is an ambition damper,' Xan said in his most dogmatic voice.

'You're right,' Daddy agreed. 'But on what do you base your conclusions?'

'The kids who use pot regularly aren't doing much, and they don't seem to care.'

Den put in, 'I'm pitching in the next game between Mulletville and Cowpertown. Y'all coming?'

Kate picked up on Xan's last remark. 'They didn't

learn their lines for *As You Like It*, and they simply dropped some of the light cues. The shepherdesses were practically in the dark.'

'Hey, you should see me do the double flip.' Johnny tried to get our attention.

Xan cut across his words. 'It hasn't helped the tennis team.'

'Any addiction's a bad thing,' Daddy agreed.

Peggy said loudly, 'We're going to have an addic sale at school.'

'Xan's addicted to tennis,' Den said.

'When do you think I'll be old enough to wear a bra?' Peggy shouted loudly enough so that she was finally heard.

'A long time, if you're anything like Polly,' Xan said, and went on, 'I don't want to be addicted to anything. I don't want some chemical to be in control of my body. Or mind.'

'A lot of kids are smoking,' Kate added. 'Not just pot. Cigarettes.'

'Yukh.' Den made a face. 'With all the pollution we have no choice about breathing, why add to it?'

'Smoking's gross,' Peggy said.

'More rice and gravy, please, *please*.' Rosy jogged Mother's arm.

'We can't do anything about acid rain,' Xan continued as though there had been no interruptions or interpolations, 'or red tides, but we don't have to put gunk into our lungs on purpose.'

Den grinned at me. 'Or does he mean on porpoise?'

At least Xan and Kate hadn't called me Puritan Pol.

Later, while we were brushing our teeth, Kate asked me, 'Have you ever tried pot?'

I shook my head. 'Minority me.'

'I don't like it. Don't worry, I haven't smoked here, it was last year in Boston. I hated it. You know what, I think it's more square to try pot than not to. I hope your parents don't think Cowpertown is unique. It's no worse than any place else.'

'I know,' I agreed.

'And at least we have swimming and crew almost all year round. And Shakespeare. You were really good, Pol.'

That was nice of Kate, and I thanked her. Playing Celia had done me no harm at school.

I was in my Celia costume, but I was not in the Forest of Arden the kids had made with branches of trees hung with Spanish moss. I doubt if there was Spanish moss in the real Forest of Arden, but it was a pretty set.

Renny was dressed in the forest-green costume Orlando had worn. I was dreaming. In Athens, I was dreaming of Renny, who led me under a tree which became enormous, looming up through the roof of the stage at the end of the school gym.

Why Renny, in Athens, two nights in a row?

Why not Renny?

I saw him maybe every other week. Sometimes we went to the movies, if anything decent was showing in Cowpertown. Usually we sat in our booth at Petros' and talked. The place smelled of cheese and tomatoes and a whiff of fish from the other restaurant on the dock. Renny went on and on about his pet South American diseases. He talked to me about medicine as though I could understand everything he said. He thought I was terrific as Celia, and he'd had to get someone to cover for him in order to come see the show. I liked the way he never put me down. I liked the way he kissed me, giving, rather than taking.

Sometimes he talked about his girl, Jacinta, in Chile. They'd really had a big thing going. Someone would have to do a lot of measuring up to get Renny's attention. Sometimes when he kissed me I understood that steady, sturdy Renny could unleash a lot of passion at the right moment, and with the right person. I was safe, because I was too young.

I wasn't too young with Max, and that's one reason I loved being with her. Chronology didn't enter into it. Max was as young as I was, and I was as old as Max. And when Ursula was there, I was treated as an equal.

I had emerged from my dream of Renny into that half-waking, half-sleeping state where thoughts are not really directed but shift around like the patterns in a kaleidoscope. I slid deeper into sleep, thinking to myself about the glory that was Greece and the grandeur that was Rome.

I woke to the glory that was Greece, about five minutes before breakfast was brought and set out on the balcony. It was another blue-and-gold day. I had a date with a young man who would set my cousin Kate reeling. I felt moderately reeling myself.

Zachary and I started off by going to the museum, because he said it was mandatory. There was far more than I could absorb in an hour, though it wasn't quite as overwhelming as the Prado in Madrid. Nevertheless, it was a city museum, and it would take days to see everything. There were some marvelous, very thin gold masks,

ancient, thousands and thousands of years old, and yet
they reminded me of faces in Modigliani paintings. We
saw the statue of the Diadumenus. He seemed to be tip-
toeing with life, even though parts of the statue were
missing.

Zachary kept checking his watch, and after exactly
one hour he said, "Okay, that's enough culture. Let's go."

"Where?"

The VW Bug was waiting for us, and as he opened
the door for me, he said, "A funny old place called
Osias Lukas."

"What's that?"

"It's an old monastery tucked into a cup in the hills,
and there are good picnic places nearby."

"Osias Lukas—Blessed Luke?"

"Yes. His chapel was built in the tenth century, I
think, and there are some nice icons. And the mosaics
have been well restored. It's a small enough place so you
can see it all and not get saturated. Osias Lukas was a
monk who, allegedly, was a healer."

Why do I dislike so intensely the skepticism, the self-
protectiveness, of *allegedly*? It's part of the legal jargon
Zachary was inheriting, but it still strikes me as a
cowardly word.

Max's attitude about theology makes more sense to me
than Zachary's dogmatic atheism. Max was always willing to take a metaphysical chance, Sandy said once; she
was an eager observer, tolerant of human foible, open to
the unexplainable, but nobody's fool.

We stopped at the entrance of Osias Lukas to buy postcards for me to send home. There was a comfortable
feeling to the cluster of buildings nestled against the
hills, protected from weather and the anger of the gods.
I wondered if people had truly been healed by Osias

Lukas. Ursula, who didn't talk about religion, agreed
with Daddy and Dennys that not only attitude but faith
had done almost unbelievable things in the way of healing. They were scientists, properly skeptical, but open.

I wondered if Osia Theola in Cyprus was going to be
anything like this protected place. Osia Theola, Max
had told me, was reported to have been given the divine
gift of truth after she had seen her vision. People still
came to her church to pray, to seek the truth.

'Superstitious, perhaps,' Max said, 'but if one should
go to the cave of Osia Theola to seek the truth, one would
need to be extremely brave.'

"Daydreaming?" Zachary asked me. We were standing in the chapel and I was looking at the fresco over
the altar without seeing it.

"I was just thinking Theola and Lukas might have
liked each other."

"They were nearly a thousand years apart," Zachary
said.

I thought I'd better not say that people like Lukas
and Theola probably weren't bound by chronology.

Suddenly we were surrounded by a group of Japanese
tourists, and Zachary said, "Come on, let's get out of
here. The Hilton has packed us a super picnic, and I
know a good spot."

We sat on a hillside overlooking water and sky. Zachary made me feel amazingly happy about myself.

Then he spoiled it by pulling me to him and kissing
me, much more of a kiss than I wanted. I pulled away.

"Why not?" he asked.

"We don't even know each other."

"So?"

"Getting to know people takes time."

"But we make music together. You like me, don't you?"

"Very much."

"And you told me you aren't a virgin."

I pulled further away. "I didn't say that."

"Your silence did. Or am I wrong? Are you a virgin?"

Silence was admission, but I could not speak. My throat was dry, my tongue tied.

He put one hand on my cheek and turned my face toward him. "Did it hurt you very much? Was the guy a bastard?"

I moved my head negatively against the pressure of his hand.

"Sweet Polly. Someone has hurt you, and you're putting a hard shell of protection about your wound. But unless you break the shell, the hurt can't be healed. And I'm speaking from very painful experience."

I nodded. Blinked. I would not cry. Would not.

"I won't do anything you don't want me to do," Zachary said. "You're beautiful, Polly."

Max had made me see that inner beauty was better than outer beauty, that it could, indeed, create outer beauty.

'You shone as Celia,' she said, 'in that depressing gym, on a dreadful stage, with appalling lighting. You had a radiance nobody else in the cast even approached.'

We were in her studio, which was a separate building to the north of the house, with the entire north wall made of glass. I was sitting for the portrait in the seashell.

'You have elegant bones. Tilt your head just slightly to your right. Beautiful slender wrists and ankles, like princesses in fairy tales. Bet Cousin Kate envies them.'

I didn't think Kate envied anything about me.

'Don't move,' Max said. 'What splendid eyes you have, like bits of fallen sky, and wide apart, always suggesting that you see things invisible to lesser mortals.'

Ursula, coming in with iced tea, heard her. 'Don't turn the child's head.'

Max paused, paintbrush in hand, a dab of paint on her nose. 'It can do with a little turning. She still underestimates herself.'

Ursula put the tea down and came to stand behind Max, looking over her shoulder at the painting, nodding approval.

Max said, 'Enough for today, or I'll start overpainting.'

Playing Celia and having my portrait painted were definitely doing something for my ego.

It was a beautiful painting when she finished. Even if I didn't recognize the Polly Max saw in the seashell, I knew that the painting was beautiful. Max brought it to my parents.

'It's a superb painting,' Daddy said, 'but we can't possibly accept something that valuable. It's much too great a gift.'

Max smiled calmly at his protestation. 'It's little enough. You O'Keefes have made a winter which could well have been the winter of my discontent into a stimulating and pleasant one.'

Daddy looked at her, a brief, diagnostic glance. 'It's a

beautiful picture, Maxa. We're more than grateful. Where shall we hang it?'

Well, it ended up in the living room, on the wall over the piano. We keep a light on by the piano because of the beach humidity, to keep it dry enough to stay in tune, so the portrait was well lit, and it dominated the room. The little kids said, 'Polly's eyes keep following us wherever we go.'

Xan and Den made rude remarks, which I did not take personally. Kate said, 'I don't know why nobody's ever painted a portrait of me.' She said it several times, once in front of Max, but Max simply smiled and said nothing.

About a week after the portrait was hung, we had the first really hot weather of the season, so that as soon as we came home from school we put on shorts and sandals. At dinner the little kids were wriggly, and the moment they'd finished eating, Mother said they could go out and play and she'd call them in for dessert.

As soon as they had gone outdoors, Xan asked, as though he had been waiting, 'Do you think it's good for Polly to spend so much time with those dykes?'

What?

Daddy paused with his fork halfway to his mouth, looking at Xan. 'Who're you talking about?'

Xan looked at Kate, and Kate looked at Xan.

Kate said, 'Well, some of the girls were talking to me at recess, and I didn't like what they said about Polly.'

'Kate, what are you talking about?' Daddy demanded.

Again Kate and Xan looked at each other. Xan said, as though sorry he'd started whatever it was he was starting, 'Some of the guys said Polly looked really pretty as Celia, with makeup on.'

'I don't wear makeup,' I said.

'Well, that's part of it,' Kate said. Kate didn't wear much makeup, but she wore some. I had no idea what she and Xan were looking at each other for. I asked, 'Why do you two keep looking at each other as though you had some secret?'

'It's no secret,' Xan said.

'What, then?'

Xan looked down at his plate. 'You do spend a lot of time over at Beau Allaire.'

'Why not?' I demanded. 'I'm welcome there. I'm happy there.'

Again Xan and Kate exchanged glances. 'Of course we know Polly isn't,' Kate said.

'Isn't what?' I demanded. 'I don't know what you're getting at.'

'Don't you?' Xan asked.

Daddy said, 'Xan, is this something you really want to talk about?'

Xan flushed a little. 'I'm sorry, but if Polly doesn't know people are talking, I think she ought to know.'

'Who's talking? About what?' And suddenly I didn't want to know.

'Some of the girls from Mulletville,' Kate said.

Xan went on, 'Mulletville's right near Beau Allaire and you're always there with Max and Ursula and everybody knows they're—'

'Shut up!'

Mother tried to calm things down. 'Xan and Kate, I'm surprised at you. What "everybody knows" is usually gossip, vicious gossip.'

'I know it's vicious,' Kate said. 'I hate it.'

'I don't like hearing glop about my sister,' Xan said.

'You punched that guy,' Kate said.

Den got into the fray. 'All you and your friends think about is sex and who has it with who, and who does what. It's sick.'

Daddy banged a knife against the table. 'This conversation has already gone too far. Xan, you know what we think about gossip, either listening to it or spreading it.'

'But, Dad, I thought you ought to know. Polly—'

'Stop him,' I said. 'How can you let him say vile things about our friends? They're your friends, too, aren't they?'

Daddy replied quietly, 'They are indeed our friends. Ursula Heschel is one of the finest people and one of the most brilliant surgeons I've known. You've always been interested in the brain, Xan. And your father's a neurosurgeon, Kate, and Ursula's friend.'

'And Max is one of Sandy's closest friends,' I cried. 'Sandy introduced us to them.'

'Sandy makes mistakes, like everybody else,' Xan snapped.

Den pushed away from the table. 'May I be excused? This conversation is gross.'

'Yes, go, Den, by all means,' Daddy said. When Den had left, he turned back to Xan and Kate. 'Do you think your Uncle Sandy would introduce Polly, or any of us, you two included, to people he didn't trust and respect?'

Kate and Xan looked down at their plates.

'Do you think Mother and I would have them here so often if they weren't our friends?'

'I'm really sorry,' Kate said. 'Xan and I talked about it, a lot, and we thought you ought to know what people—'

I interrupted. 'It's a good thing the little kids are outside. I'm glad they aren't hearing this garbage. Den was right to leave.'

Mother absentmindedly passed the salad to Daddy, who tossed it. 'Sandy knew we had a lot in common with Max and Ursula. That's what makes friendship. Like interests. Your father and Ursula have nourished each other this winter.'

'And Max has nourished me,' I said. 'She's made me believe in myself.'

'Sure, she flatters you,' Xan said, 'paints your portrait, swells your head—'

Daddy cut him off. 'Xan, are you feeling well?'

'I have a sore throat. What's that got to do with it?'

'After we finish eating, I'm going to take your temperature. And I would remind you that a morbid interest in people's sexual activities is as perverse as anything else.'

'We're sorry,' Kate said.

Mother added, perhaps trying to bring this ugly conversation back to normal dinner-table talk, 'Possibly the high divorce rate has something to do with a tendency to equate marriage with sex alone, instead of adding companionship and laughter.'

'Ursula and Max aren't married.'

'Alexander!' Daddy was getting really 'angry.

When Xan gets hold of a subject, he can't let go. 'Lesbianism does exist. I should think you'd be worried about Polly.'

We all spoke simultaneously. I said, 'Leave me out of it.'

Mother said, 'Xan, I think you're feverish.'

Kate said, 'We're just trying to protect Polly.'

Daddy said, his voice so quiet we had to stop talking in order to hear, 'Don't you have any faith in Polly? Or our ability to understand and to care? Of course lesbianism exists, and has since the beginning of history, and we have not always been compassionate. I thought it was now agreed that consenting adults were not to be persecuted, particularly if they keep their private lives private. We human beings are all in the enterprise of life together, and the journey isn't easy for any of us. Xan, come with me. I want to take your temperature. Polly, you can bring in dessert and call the others.'

Xan had a fever of 102°. He was coming down with a strep throat. He went to bed with penicillin instead of dessert.

'That explains it,' Daddy said. 'I'd better keep a close watch on the rest of you. Polly, will you come out to the lab with me, please?'

I followed him. He gazed into one of the starfish tanks, jotted something down on a chart, then sat on one of the high stools. 'I don't want you to be upset by what Xan and Kate said.'

I perched on the other stool, hooking my feet around the rungs. 'I am upset.'

'In this world, when two people of the same sex live together, assumptions are made, valid or not.'

'I hate the Mulletville girls. They think they're better than anybody else, and they love to put people down. They didn't like it that I got Celia in the play, and they didn't like it that I was good. None of them got anything but walk-ons.'

'You think they're getting back at you for succeeding?' Daddy asked.

'Sure. I've been the bottom of the pecking order. They don't want me to move up.'

'Polly, I don't want this to affect your friendship with Max and Ursula.'

'Don't worry. It won't. It hardly affects my feeling

for the Mulletville girls, either. It was already rock-bottom.'

Daddy hugged me and I burst into tears. 'It's your first encounter with this kind of nasty-mindedness, isn't it, Pol? Island living has kept all you kids more isolated than you should have been.'

'That's fine with me.' I reached for the box of tissues behind the Bunsen burner.

'No, Polly, you live in a world full of people of all kinds, and you're going to have to learn to get along with them.'

'I suppose.'

'And, Polly, I don't want you to worry about any gossip about you. You're a very normal sixteen-year-old.'

'Am I?'

'You are. You're brighter than a lot of your peers, you're physically a slow developer and intellectually a quick one.'

I said, 'I'm not a lesbian, Daddy, if you're worried that I'm worried about that.'

'Sure?'

'Sure.' I pressed my face against his firm, comfortable chest. 'But I wish we were back in Portugal.'

'We aren't. And even in Portugal, time would have passed; you'd still be in the difficult process of growing up.'

'I've got some history reading to finish,' I said. 'I'd better go do it.'

'All right, love. But don't let all of this get out of proportion. Put at least some of it down to strep throat.'

"Sure. Thanks, Daddy.'

Xan did not give me his strep throat, but he had planted an ugly seed, uglier than strep. Talking about Max and Ursula the way he had was a far cry from the remark Xan had made weeks ago, that it was a good thing Ursula was older than Daddy. That, at least, made a certain amount of sense.

But the seed was planted.

While we were little, Mother and Daddy were anything but permissive parents. The little ones don't get away with much. But once we get well into our teens— and that meant Xan and Charles and me, and Kate, while she was with us—they moved into a hands-off policy. If we hadn't learned from all they had tried to teach us when we were younger, it was too late.

And what we'd learned was as much from example as from anything they said. Our parents were responsible toward each other as well as toward us. What's more important, they loved each other. Max didn't need to tell me that. I knew it. It was solid rock under my feet. And love means that you don't dominate or manipulate or control.

Xan missed a few days of school. Den was the only one to catch anything from him, but Daddy was watching us all, and Den lost only a day. The rest of us were all right, as far as strep was concerned.

What Xan and Kate said shouldn't have made any difference. I should have thrown it away, forgotten it.

Or I should have asked Daddy when we were out in the lab together if he believed what they'd said about Max and Ursula. But I didn't ask him. And what's said is said. Xan's and Kate's words were like pebbles thrown into the water, with ripples spreading out and out . . .

It kept niggling at the back of my mind.

I didn't want to think about sex. The male population of Cowpertown High was still in intellectual nursery school. Renny didn't want me to be anything but a kid sister to him. Who else was there?

Friday night I couldn't sleep. Finally I got up and went into the kitchen to make myself something warm to drink. We'd put away the winter blankets, and the night was cool. Mother was already there, in her nightgown, waiting for the kettle to boil.

'I'm making herb tea,' she said. 'Want some?'

'I'd love some,' I said, 'as long as it's not camomile.'

'I don't like camomile either, unless I have a very queasy stomach.'

'My stomach's queasy,' I said, 'but I still don't want camomile.'

'Why is your stomach queasy, honey?'

'What Xan said.'

'What, that Xan said? Xan says a lot.'

'Xan and Kate. About Max and Ursula.'

Mother got two cups from the kitchen dresser and fixed our tea. 'I hoped Daddy'd relieved your mind about that.'

'It keeps coming back.'

She handed me a steaming cup, and we sat at the kitchen table. The windows were partly open and the steady murmur of the ocean came in, and the wind moved through the palmettos, rattling them like paper.

Mother slid one of the windows closed. 'Xan and Kate are both fourteen. At that age, children tend to have a high interest in sexual activity, because they're just discovering themselves as sexual human beings. Their interests do widen after a while, as yours have.'

'When I was fourteen, I hardly knew lesbianism existed, and I wasn't particularly interested.'

'You and Xan are very different people. You and Kate, too. For one thing, if you'd heard upsetting gossip at school, you'd have come to your father or me privately. You wouldn't have brought it up as dinner-table conversation.'

'Xan thinks anything's okay for dinner-table conversation.'

'That's partly our fault. We encourage you to talk about what's on your minds. You've always been interested in an unusually wide variety of topics. What do you and Max talk about?'

'Philosophy. Anthropology. Lately she's been on a binge of reading the pre-Platonic philosophers. She says they were the precursers of the physicists who study quantum mechanics.'

'Shouldn't that tell you something?'

'Tell me what?'

'Where your interests lie. And Max's.'

I couldn't hold the question back any longer. 'Mother, do you think Max *is* a lesbian?'

Mother sighed and sipped at her tea. Outside, a bird sang a brief cadenza and was silent. 'The point I thought I was making is that what's important to you about Max is her interest in ideas. She's someone who appreciates and encourages the ideas you have. You might not have tried out for Celia if it weren't for Max.'

I couldn't leave it alone. Maybe I'm more like Xan than I realized. 'But if she *is* a lesbian, wouldn't that worry you and Daddy—I mean, that I'm over at Beau Allaire so often?'

Mother sighed again. She looked tired. Daddy had been off to Tallahassee with Ursula. Mother had stayed home with us kids. Daddy had been promising her a few nights in Charleston, to go to the Dock Street Theatre, to the Spoleto Festival, but there hadn't seemed to be time. Or money. Charleston may not be New York, but theatre tickets aren't cheap anywhere. The neuro-surgeon Dennys had introduced Ursula to, who also knew Daddy, had offered his guesthouse, which put it in the realm of possibility. It just hadn't happened. Daddy traveled around, to medical meetings, and Mother stayed home.

'Polly,' she said, 'there are a great many areas in which Daddy and I simply have to trust you kids. We have to trust that how Charles lives his life while he's in Boston is consistent with the values we've tried to instill in all of you, just as Dennys and Lucy have to trust Kate while she's with us. When Kate and Xan—and you—go to a school dance, we have to trust you not to give in to peer pressure and experiment with alcohol or with drugs you know to be harmful and addictive. We've been grateful and perhaps a little relieved when Kate has called us to come get her, rather than drive home with someone who's been drinking, and I suspect Dennys and Lucy feel the responsibility for Charles as strongly as we do for Kate.'

'Kate's got good sense.'

'And so do you. And that's why we trust you; and we trust Max and Ursula not to do or say anything that would harm you. Has our trust been justified?'

'Yes.' I nodded agreement. This was how Mother and Daddy thought. This was how they behaved.

'If they were pulling you away from other people, then we'd think that was not a good influence. But you've been happier in school, haven't you?'

'Yes.'

'You've been asked to be in the chorus, haven't you?'

'Yes.' I did not tell her that the teacher who taught chorus went into ecstasies because she said I had 'the pure voice of a boy soprano.'

'You're getting more phone calls from your classmates. Things are generally easier for you.'

'Yes.' I'd hardly realized it consciously, but it was true. Except for those snobs from Mulletville.

Mother continued. 'Trusting people is risky, Polly, we are aware of that. Trust gets broken. But when I think of Max and Ursula, I don't feel particularly curious about their sex lives, one way or another. They're opening a world of ideas for you, ideas you're not likely to bump into at Cowpertown High. I'm sorrier than I can say that there's been ugly gossip from the Mulletville girls and that the gossip has touched you. You're young to bump into this kind of gratuitous viciousness, but it hits us all sooner or later. I've had to sit out a good bit of gossip about your father and female colleagues.'

'But it wasn't true!'

'No, it wasn't true, Polly. That's the point I'm making. If you can, try to forget Xan and Kate's fourteen-year-old gossip.'

Now I sighed. 'I'll try. But I wish they'd kept their big mouths shut.'

'So do I, Polly, so do I.'

❀

She had not told me whether or not she thought Max was a lesbian. But perhaps that was part of the point she was making.

April, turning into May, was Benne Seed's most gorgeous weather. We had a few summer-hot days, but mostly it was sunny and breezy and the air smelled of flowers and the sky was full of birdsong. Kate made a tape of a mockingbird to take home.

Daddy and Ursula drove down to Florida again, overnight. Daddy was to give a paper on new developments in his experiments with octopuses, with Ursula giving another paper about how it could be applied to neurosurgery on human beings. I found myself wishing that Xan was still concerned about Daddy and Ursula.

Max called when I got home from school, as she almost always did when Ursula was away. I drove over; Urs and Daddy had taken Ursula's car; a Land-Rover's not great for long distances. And suddenly, when I was about halfway to Beau Allaire, the fog rolled in from the ocean, and the outlines of the trees were blurred, and the birds stopped singing. There was a damp hush all over the island. Turning on the headlights just made visibility worse, and the fog lights didn't help much. I slowed down to a crawl, and was grateful to arrive safely at Beau Allaire. We went right up to Max's room, which is always the pleasantest place when the wind swings to the northeast. When the sun is out on the Island, it's warm, even in winter. When the sun is hidden by fog, it feels cold, even if the thermometer reads 80°.

We were sipping tea when Mother called, to make

sure I'd arrived safely and to say that the visibility at
our end of the island was nil. She agreed without hesitation when Max suggested I spend the night and go to
school in the morning on the bus with the kids from
Mulletville.

That was the only part I didn't like. I looked into the
fire so Max wouldn't see my face.

But she saw something. 'Your mother's confidence in
me means more than I can say. But—'

'But what?' I asked, still looking away from her.

'For some reason you're not happy about going to
school with the Mulletville contingent.'

'They're all snobs, and anyhow, I'm needed at home
to handle the boat.'

'And you don't want the students from Mulletville to
know you spent the night here.' Her voice was flat.

'If the fog lifts, I'll get up early. Anyhow, I have to
get the car home—Mother didn't think of that.'

'What she was thinking of was your safety. When
your father and Ursula get back, Urs can drop him off
here and he can drive your Rover home.' I didn't say
anything, but I turned to look at her, and her eyes were
bleak, the color of ice, and the shadows under them
seemed to darken. 'I hope this isn't going to compromise
you any more than you've already been compromised.'

I stared back at the fire. 'I don't care.'

I could hear Max draw in her breath, let it out in a
long sigh. 'It's taken a long time for gossip to reach you,
hasn't it? I expected it to raise its ugly head long before
this.'

'Gossip is gossip. Mother and Daddy take a dim view
of it. The girls from Mulletville are the bitchiest group
at school.'

Max sighed again, and I turned once more to look at

her, lean and elegant, stretched out on her side, leaning on one elbow. 'I'd hoped this conversation wouldn't be necessary. Urs said it would be, sooner or later, since the world considers personal privacy a thing of the past. Have you noticed how, whenever there's a tragedy, the TV cameras rush to the bereaved to take pictures, totally immune to human suffering?'

'Well—our TV doesn't work—but I know what you mean.'

'And I'm avoiding what I need to say. You're pure of heart, Polyhymnia, but most of the world isn't. I wish Urs were here. She could talk about it more sanely than I, so that it wouldn't hurt you. We—Ursula and I—have been lovers for over thirty years.'

I stared down at the white fur of the rug. If Max wanted to avoid this conversation, so did I.

'When people think of homosexuals they usually think of—Ursula and I have had a long and faithful love.'

In my ears I heard Xan's words about two dykes. It didn't fit Max and Ursula. Neither did the words I heard at school, gays and faggots and queers.

'I love you, Polly, love you like my daughter. And you love me, too, in all your amazing innocence.'

There was a long pause. I hoped the conversation was over. But Max went on. 'Ursula'—she paused again—'Ursula is the way she is. She's competed in a man's world, in a man's field. There are not many women neurosurgeons. As for me—'

—I don't want to know, I thought. —Keep this kind of thing in the closet where it belongs. That's what doors are for. It doesn't have anything to do with me.

'We'd better go downstairs,' Max said. 'I asked Nettie and Ovid to set the table on the verandah.'

I followed her. Instead of going directly out to the

verandah, she paused at the oval dining room, switching on an enormous Waterford chandelier which sparkled like drops of water from the ocean.

Mother and Daddy have eaten in the oval dining room at Beau Allaire. When I ate with Max and Ursula, it was supper, not dinner—sometimes if it was chilly, on trays in the library, or sometimes on the big marble-topped table in the kitchen. Ursula kneaded dough on that table, and the kitchen usually held the fragrance of baking bread.

'Nettie, really!' Max exclaimed, and I saw that two places had been set at the mahogany table, which, like the room, was oval.

As though she had been called, Nettie came in through the swing door which led to the breezeway and the kitchen. 'Verandah's too damp, Miss Maxa. Table's wet. Fog's thick.'

'Fine, Nettie,' Max said. 'You're quite right. We'll eat here.' She sat at the head of the table and pointed to the portrait over the long sideboard, a portrait of a man, middle-aged or more, stern and dignified, with white hair and mustache, a nose which was a caricature of Max's, and a smile which made me uncomfortable.

Ovid came in and lit the candles on the table and in the sconces on the wall.

'My papa.' Max nodded at the portrait and her smile matched the smile on her father's face. I felt cold, chillier than the dampness the fog brought in.

'Looks like him,' Max said. 'Spitting image, as they say. It's not a bad piece of work. One has to admire the artist's perception which transcends the stiffness of his technique. What do you think?'

I couldn't very well say, 'His smile gives me the creeps.' I said, 'He looks rather formidable.'

'Formidable? Oh, he was.'

Nettie and Ovid came in with silver dishes, cold sliced chicken, hot spoon bread, served us, and withdrew.

Max said, 'When my sister and I were little, we used to think God looked like Papa, and I suspect he fostered the idea. Papa liked being God. You don't make as much money as Papa did without a God complex. Beau Allaire belonged to Mama, and Papa got a job in the family bank. He was a big frog in a little pond, but he made the money not only to keep up Beau Allaire but to build a hospital. And he had no hesitation in shoving people aside if they got in his way. After all, isn't God supposed to do whatever he wants?'

That wasn't the way I thought of God. Or the way I thought Max thought of God.

She took her fork and spread spoon bread around on her plate. 'I wonder if God ever feels guilt? The M. A. Horne Hospital is Papa's big guilt offering. Urs sees God as a benevolent physician. That's a better image than mine. The only way I can get rid of the false image of Papa as God is to think of the marvels of creation. The theory now is that everything in the universe, all of the galaxies, all of the quanta, everything comes from something as small as the nucleus of an atom. Think of that, of that tiny speck, invisible to the naked eye, opening up like a flower, to become clouds of hydrogen dust, and then stars, and solar systems. That softly opening flower —I visualize a lotus—is a more viable image of God for me than anything else. I keep the portrait of Papa to remind me that God is *not* like him.'

I liked the image of the gently opening lotus. I didn't like the man in the portrait.

Ovid came in with a bottle of wine in a napkin and poured a glass for Max. 'This will help your appetite,

Miss Maxa. You need Nettie's good spoon bread.' Then he put a very small amount in my glass and filled it up with water. My talk with Daddy was still clear in my mind. That was plenty for me.

'M.A. and I were only eleven months apart, and were more like twins than just sisters. Not that we didn't think for ourselves, but there wasn't anything we couldn't tell each other. She was the younger, and when we were four or five years old our mother died—she had a weak heart—and that made us closer than ever. Mama's portrait is the middle of the three across from you.'

I looked at the three gold-framed portraits. The middle, and largest, was of a fragile-looking woman, almost beautiful, but too washed-out to make it. She was not vivid like Max, or translucent, like M.A. in the portrait in the library. 'She looks pretty. But tired.'

Max laughed, not a happy laugh. 'Papa was a tiring man. Our maternal grandfather, our Allaire grandfather, must have been equally tiring. Poor Mama. Her name was Submit, and her two sisters, in the portraits on either side of her, were Patience and Hope. Which gives you an idea of the frame of mind of our Allaire grandmother. Mama's calling us Minerva Allaire and Maximiliana Sebastiane may have been her way of getting even. She died before we had much chance to know her, but she was affectionate and gentle.'

Ovid came to take away our plates, checking that Max had eaten most of her meal. Nettie followed him with salad, delicate greens from the Beau Allaire greenhouse.

'Keeping this enormous house with inadequate help killed Mama. I have one wing completely closed off, but while Papa was alive, all the rooms had to be ready at a moment's notice. Papa did not make his business deals on the golf course, he made them here in the oval dining room, over port.' She paused. 'The portrait's uncannily like him. I don't think the artist realized how accurate he was.'

We sat in silence for a while. Then she said, 'I'm not really a portraitist, but every once in a while there's someone I know I must paint—like you. Ursula's never allowed me to paint her, but she can't stop me from making sketches.'

Nettie came in, bearing *crème brûlée*, which she put in front of Max, beaming. When she went back to the kitchen, Max laughed, a nice laugh this time. 'Nettie feels she must compete with Urs. Bless Urs. She has to make godlike decisions all the time, but she has more genuine humility than anyone I've known. She picks up her scalpel and she holds life and death in her hands. No wonder she comes home from the hospital and bakes bread and creates casseroles and listens to Pachelbel and Vivaldi.' She served me a luscious dish of *crème brûlée*. 'Bless Nettie, too. I'm far better served than I deserve.'

When we had finished dessert, Max suggested we go upstairs again. The fire had died down, and she rebuilt it, then sat on the rug, head on her knees, watching the fat pine take flame. 'As soon as we were old enough, M.A. and I became Papa's hostesses. After Mama died, he got a good housekeeper, but M.A. and I sat with him in the dining room every night, were with him when he entertained business guests. I think it was expected that eventually we would marry from the guest list. Money tends to marry money. And when Papa snapped his fingers, we did whatever he wanted us to do. He wasn't beyond hitting us if we didn't obey promptly. M.A. was deathly afraid of him. I suppose I was, too, but I pretended I wasn't. I talked back to him, and he liked that. One didn't show fear in front of Papa.'

Something in Max willed me to turn from the fire and look into her eyes, grey, like the fog, the silver glints dimmed. She spoke in a low, chill voice. 'Papa was a lecherous old roué. It killed my mother. But she submitted, poor darling, until her heart gave out, living with a man completely unprincipled. He killed M.A., too. He hated women, I think, but he wanted them. All of them. One night when I was away, he . . . She got away from him and ran out into the rain, and died of pneumonia. And anguish. I will never forgive him.'

I shuddered. The fog seemed to be creeping into the room. It did not seem like May.

'Sorry, Polly, darling Polly. Hate is a totally destructive emotion, I know that. But I hate him. I hope you will never have cause to hate anyone as I hate Papa. I would like to forgive him, but I don't know how.'

I stole another look at her. Her eyes burned, and I thought she had fever.

'It's extraordinary how I can hate Papa—and at the same time acknowledge that in my youth I wasn't unlike him, completely indiscriminate in my affairs after my marriage broke up. What I did had little connection with love. And then I met Ursula. Blessed Ursula, who loved me and healed me. We have been good for each other. Nourishing. As your parents nourish each other.'

Max comparing herself and Ursula to my parents? Was that possible?

'Sandy trusted me enough to bring you over to me. I value that trust. I want never to hurt you. And I already have, haven't I? Or vicious gossip has. People are assuming that because you are very dear to me, you are like me. The world being the way it is, they'd assume it even if I was straight as a pin.'

'Never mind,' I said clumsily. 'They're stupid.' I

thought of the girls from Mulletville who thought they were better than anybody else. To put themselves up, they had to put other people down.

Max said, 'I love you as I would have loved the daughter I couldn't have. You don't need a mother, you have a fine one. But every adolescent needs someone to talk to, someone to whom she is not biologically bound, and I serve that purpose. We are alike in our interests, you and I, but not in our ways of expressing our sexuality.' She looked straight into my eyes. 'Don't be confused about yourself. You're not a lesbian. I know.'

I suppose, looking back on it, that it was brave, maybe even noble, of Max to tell me all this.

She took a long brass wand and blew into the fire. The flames soared. She put the wand back, speaking as though to herself. 'Bad hearts run in the Allaire family. Mama. M.A. My little—' She broke off. 'I have a heart as strong as an ox. What irony.'

I didn't understand the irony.

A sudden crash of thunder cut across my thoughts. Almost daily thunderstorms are part of summer on Benne Seed Island. Five minutes of lightning and thunder and rain and the air would be cleared. This sudden storm would dissipate the fog.

'Your father and Urs are friends, Polly. I don't know whether or not they've talked about this, because it isn't within the context of their interests, but I suspect your father knows.'

I suspected that both my parents knew. That they knew before Xan and Kate brought it up at dinner.

Max said, 'I asked Ovid to light the fire in the green guest room to cut the damp. We'll just wait till this storm is over.' She took a soft wool blanket from the chaise longue and tucked it around me. I was overwhelmed by great waves of sleep, a reaction of shock from what Max had told me.

'Little one,' she said softly. 'Let it go. You don't have to bear it with me. It's over. You have a terrifying ability to enter into the experience of others, that's why you're such a good little actress. You feel things too deeply to bear them unless you can get them out of yourself through some form of art.'

I closed my eyes and her words drifted away with the smoke.

When I woke up, it seemed that a light was shining in my eyes. The fog had cleared, and the moonlight was coming through the windows. By its ancient light Max was looking at me, her eyes as bright and savage as a gull's.

But her voice was gentle. 'Time for bed.'

I staggered to my feet and followed her to the green guest room. The fire had died down to a glow, but it had taken the damp away, and the breeze coming in from the window was summery. I slipped into bed, and Max tucked the covers about me. I drifted back into sleep.

In the morning I got up early, drank a glass of milk, drove the length of the Island to our house, and took the boat across the water to Cowpertown and the school bus.

Stubbly grass was prickling against my cheek, and a hand moved gently across my hair. I opened my eyes and looked up at Zachary.

"Have a nice nap?"

I sat up and pushed my fingers through my hair. "I guess I'm not quite over jet lag yet. Sandy says it takes a day for each hour."

"Sandy? Who's Sandy?" he asked suspiciously.

"My uncle. He and Aunt Rhea are coming into Athens tomorrow, late afternoon, I think."

"Are you going to ditch me for them?"

"We do have plans . . ."

"Will you at least spend the day with me, Sleeping Beauty?"

I probably looked a mess, with grass marks on my cheek and my hair sticking out in all directions, and here he was asking me to spend another day with him. "I'd love to spend the day with you."

"You cried out in your sleep," Zachary said. "Listen, about whoever it was who hurt you, remember I've been hurt, too. It's not a nice feeling. It takes the already shaky ego and shrivels it, like putting a match to a plastic bag. I'm not pushing you, Polly, but it really might help if you talked about it."

I shook my head. "Thanks, Zach, I don't want to talk about it till I have it all sorted out."

"Sometimes talking helps sort things out."

"I'm not ready. You talk if you want to. I'm sorry you got hurt. I do care."

"You do, don't you? Thanks, Pol, but I'm a selfish bastard and I deserved anything I got. I lived by sophomoric mores, Number One all the way. In my world, love affairs were taken with incredible seriousness, which ought to mean at least an expectation of permanence."

"Doesn't it?"

"Ha. Totally serious can mean a few days, and then along comes someone over the horizon who has more money or more prestige, and whoops, musical chairs, change partners. You know how, at cocktail parties, the person you're talking to is looking over your shoulder, in case there's somebody more important to talk to?"

I didn't. I'd never been to a cocktail party.

"In my world they're looking over your shoulder while they're making love, and it's musical chairs again." He sounded bitter.

"Are you talking from experience?" I asked.

"Pretty Pol, in experience I am old enough to be your grandfather." He put his head down on my lap, and I ran my fingers through his silky black hair. Another first for me. I was amazed at how natural it seemed.

"You're lucky, Red," he said. "My parents don't know anything about trust. They never trusted each other, and they never trusted me. And I've never trusted them. And your parents trust you, enough to let you come to Greece all alone, not because they want to get rid of you, but because they trust you. I mean, that's pretty incredible."

Even though my parents didn't know I was in Greece all alone, their trust in me, and in the rest of us, was indeed pretty incredible. And that trust had been betrayed, and I hoped they'd never have to know the extent to which it had been betrayed. Part of growing up, I was discovering, was learning that you did not have to tell your parents everything.

Did Mother and Daddy carry trusting us to an extreme?

What choice did they have? The three little ones were the only ones young enough to be monitored twenty-four hours a day. Den was in junior high, the rest of us in high school. We did have curfews, and if there was a valid reason we couldn't make them, they trusted us to phone. When Xan and Kate were late, twice, without calling, they were given a 10 p.m. curfew for the month, which meant no going to Cowpertown after school hours. From their point of view, that was only an inch away from capital punishment. They complained the entire time, but they kept the curfew.

If I'm a slow developer, Kate's a rapid one. I knew that she'd gone a lot further with boys than I had, not that I'd had much chance, and that this concerned Mother and Daddy. And sometimes Xan seems older, as well as taller, than I. But how much did Mother and Daddy know about string-bean Xan? He was already six three, and good-looking, and a little arrogant, and he brought home straight A's and was star of the basketball team and president of his class. But did they know him?

And how much did they really know about me? When I went out with Renny, Mother and Daddy knew what our plans were, whether we were going to drive, whether Renny had borrowed a boat. They probably suspected that Renny kissed me good night. Did they trust us blindly?

How could Max ever trust anybody again, after what her father did? And yet she trusted.

And I knew that there wasn't any other way to live. You simply cannot go around sniffing suspiciously at everyone and everything, expecting the worst. At least, Mother and Daddy couldn't. And, by gene and precept, neither could I.

'People are trustworthy only by virtue of being trusted,' Daddy had once said.

Having your parents trust you is a pretty heavy burden.

On the other hand, I trusted my parents.

"What're you thinking?" Zachary asked.

"Oh, trusting people. Letting them down."

Zachary patted my thigh. "I can't imagine you letting anybody down."

I ran my fingers through his hair again. "You don't know me very well." The thought flashed across my mind that I had let Max down. I pushed it away.

Zachary yawned. "We'd better be getting back to town. I've made reservations on the roof of the Hilton. We'll have drinks outside first, and I've reserved a window table. The view is better than the food, though the food's not bad. Rather bland, to please unexperimental Americans. You can even get a hamburger." He eased out of my lap, stood up, held out his hand to me, then took one finger and touched my cheek. "So soft," he murmured. With the tip of his finger he circled my eyes, then leaned toward me and kissed me.

I pulled away, and started toward the car.

"What's the matter?" he asked. "You know our chemistry's explosive."

"Chemistry's not enough."

"Why not?" I didn't answer. "If you gave in once, why not now, when you know things are really fizzing between us?"

"I said," clenching my jaw, "chemistry's not enough." I picked up the picnic basket and put it in the car.

Zachary ran after me. "Hey, wait up. Was I being offensive?"

"You might call it that."

"Well, listen, Pol, hey, listen, I'm really sorry. Okay?"

"Okay." I still sounded pretty chilly.

"You're going to have dinner with me tonight? I'll be good. Promise. Okay? I've never met anyone like you, and I've learned, honest I have, it's a mistake for me to think you're going to react like anyone else. I don't want you to. I like you the way you are. So you will have dinner?"

"Sure. Dinner will be fine."

I'd never had anyone pleading to have dinner with me before. If I needed affirmation, Zachary was providing it.

The view from the roof garden of the Hilton was as spectacular as the view from Zachary's balcony. I ordered lemonade, and Zachary had a Metaxa sour.

Metaxa. Urs often called Max that.

"Have a sip?" Zachary asked.

I shook my head.

"Polly, I'll see you tomorrow?"

He was saying it, and I still didn't quite believe it, that he really wanted to be with me three days in a row. "I'd love to."

"And after tomorrow, what? Am I ever going to see you again?"

"Who knows? It's a small world."

"I'd like to be friends with you forever. I want to know there's something permanent in human relations."

I sipped my lemonade. "I'm not sure there is."

He signaled the waiter for two more drinks. "I'm the one who's the cynic, not you. What about your parents? They sound pretty permanent to me."

"As things go in this life, I guess they are."

"And that's what you're looking for?"

"Ultimately. But not for a long time. I have to get through college and figure out how to earn my living."

"And you're going to wear your chastity belt all that time?"

"I don't know," I said. "If I've learned nothing else, I've learned that you never know what's going to happen. But right now, tonight, in Athens, I'm wearing my chastity belt." I thought I'd better be firm about that, for myself as much as for Zachary.

The maître d'hotel summoned us then, and took us to our table. After we'd ordered, Zachary said, "I wish I knew who he was, this guy who hurt you so much. He's made you put your armor on so there isn't even a chink. Why are you rejecting me?"

"I'm not rejecting you. We've just met, and already we're friends. I could have been very lonely, and you've been wonderful."

He smiled at me across the table. "If you ever take off that chastity belt, Polly, it'll be for real."

He walked me back to the King George and kissed me gently just before I got in the elevator. I took another long, hot bath, to help me unwind. Got into bed and read. I realized that I missed the family, even Xan.

He had come into my room one night while I was reading in bed, knocking first, which is a tradition. Our rooms are our own.

'Yah?' I didn't sound very welcoming.

He stuck his head in the door. 'I'm sorry about the other night.' He was so tall that he almost had to bend down to get in the door. His wrists and ankles showed past his pajama sleeves and legs, and he was skinny, because of having shot up so quickly.

'What other night?'

'You know. What Kate and I said about the Mulletville kids and stuff. About Max and Ursula and you. I'm really sorry.'

'Okay.' But it wasn't okay, and I didn't sound or feel

gracious. Maybe eventually Max would have told me all that she'd told me, but it mightn't have hurt so much.

'I hate those Mulletville kids,' Xan said. 'It's not *fair*.'

He sounded so vehement that he reminded me of my little sister Peggy, who frequently stamped and said, 'It isn't *fair*,' and Mother would reply, 'We never told you life was fair.' 'But it *ought* to be,' Peggy would insist.

Max had said once, 'The young have an appalling sense of justice. Compassion doesn't come till much later.'

Was I looking for justice without compassion? I'm not even sure what justice would be. If the milk has soured, there's no way to make it sweet again.

Now I said to Xan, 'Since when did you expect things to be fair?'

He hovered in the doorway. 'Can I come in?'

'Sure.' I closed my book, a finger in it to mark the place, to give him a hint that I didn't want him to stay long.

'I had a long talk with Dad.'

'Did you?'

'In the first place, I shouldn't have listened to the Mulletville kids. In listening to them, I was encouraging them.'

I shrugged. 'I listen to gossip, too.'

'About me?'

'People don't gossip much about you.'

He sat on the foot of my bed. Because I'm the oldest, I have the room farthest from the main part of the house and Mother and Daddy's room. I have a combination desk/chest of drawers. A chair. A closet for my clothes. And a view of the ocean through an enormous chinaberry tree, which is a favorite of redbirds.

Xan said, 'Dad told me that Ursula is very highly

thought of, and he feels privileged to be her friend, and Max's.' He looked at me and added, 'At least all this has taught me something.'

'What?'

'I used to think of lesbians as being different from other women, kind of freakish. I didn't think they were like other people, like Ursula Heschel doing a good job. I mean, being a neurosurgeon is tough.'

And Ursula managed it without playing God. She came home and baked bread. And took care of Max.

Xan said, 'We do gossip and bitch at school about things we really don't know about. I'm as bad as Kate. What I want to say is, I'm really sorry we brought it up. Being sick was no excuse.'

'Forget it,' I said.

Xan stood up. 'It's hard to keep your head on straight in a world like this.'

'You're right,' I agreed. 'It's not easy.'

'You're not still mad at me?'

'No.'

On the whole, I thought, Xan kept his head on straighter than I did. I decided I'd write him a postcard all his own, not just a family one.

I woke up in the night hearing sirens. Greek sirens. I do not like sirens, anywhere. They mean police and fire and violence. They made me feel very alone in a hotel in a strange city. I comforted myself with the thought that Sandy and Rhea would be with me in time for dinner, and it might be a good idea if I made a reservation for a table at the roof restaurant.

Zachary and I were going to meet in the morning,

drive out in the country again, and take the ferry ride from Itea, at the foot of Mount Parnassus, to Aegea, and wouldn't be back till late afternoon. Was it because I was seeing Zachary in a new country, with home far behind me, that we had come to know each other so quickly? It took weeks and weeks of seeing Renny before we could talk the way Zachary and I had talked in only two days. I had mixed emotions. In a way I would almost be glad to say goodbye to him when Sandy and Rhea came, because he did have a powerful effect on me, and it scared me. And at the same time it would be a wrench to leave someone forever who had appeared when I really needed rescuing.

Zachary knew that I expected Sandy and Rhea, but not that I'd expected them to be at the airport to meet me, that these days alone in Athens were not part of anybody's plan. If I still believed in guardian angels, I'd suspect it had all been prearranged for my benefit.

Max sometimes talked about the delicate balance between a prearranged pattern for the universe and human free will. 'Sometimes our freedom comes in the way we accept things over which we have no control, things which may cause us great pain and even death.'

I didn't understand then that she was talking about herself. We were sitting on the verandah, overlooking the ocean. The wisteria vines were in bloom, the blossoms moving from pale lavender to deep dark purple. Pungent scents from flowers and herbs wafted toward us.

She changed the subject. 'I wonder how long Benne

Seed will be the kind of lovely island it is now? If the other two plantations should ever be sold, there'd be more developments like Mulletville, only bigger.'

'I'd hate it,' I said. 'Daddy'd hate it. He'd have to look for another island.'

'I don't think it'll happen for a while. Spring and early summer, before the long heat sets in, are as lovely here as any place in the world. I'm not sure why I love Beau Allaire. I was never happy here. M.A. and I came out in Charleston, but most of the time Charleston seems as far from Benne Seed as New York. And I've spent far too much of my life on that asphalt island. Maybe that's why I love to come here. But I'd die of loneliness, intellectual loneliness, if I had to live on Benne Seed for long.'

The idea that Max might not stay on the Island was horrible, but why had I ever thought her return to Beau Allaire was permanent? I remembered Sandy and Dennys questioning her coming, thinking there was something odd about it. But I felt that I, too, would die of loneliness without Max to talk to. 'You're not leaving, are you?' When she did not reply, I asked, 'Is Ursula's sabbatical over?'

Max looked down at her hands, lightly folded, pale against her dark dress. 'No, Polly. And no, I am not going back to New York.'

During the normal pattern of Max and Ursula's year, Urs took August off and they traveled abroad together. In the winter, Max went off by herself to paint, to check on Beau Allaire, to get away from the city.

'And,' she added, 'from Ursula. We're both dominant personalities, and people who love each other need to be apart periodically. I have my own studio on Fifty-seventh Street, but even a city as big as New York can be too small. And I enjoy travel more than Urs does. Even though it's getting daily more difficult, and one expects planes to be late, connections to be missed, trains to stop for hours instead of minutes, I still love it. Two years ago I spent a month in Antarctica. I nearly got frostbite on my aristocratic nose, but I was totally fascinated by that wild, cold world. I wanted to bring Urs back a penguin, but only if I could bring back a square mile of its environment.'

For a while I was embarrassed when Max talked about Urs, but she was so matter-of-fact that it stopped bothering me. She talked about Urs as anyone would about a good friend. Slowly I began to forget Xan and Kate's gossip, even to forget what Max had told me. As Mother had pointed out, it was not where Max's and my interests lay.

Mother and Daddy seemed to take it for granted that I might go over to Beau Allaire a couple of times a week. I got my chores in the lab done in the early morning, helped with the little ones as much as possible, once a week stripped the beds and put the sheets through the washing machine. What time was left, apart from school, was my own.

Max and Ursula came across the Island to have dinner with us every few weeks. And if Xan and Kate heard any more gossip, they didn't say anything. Sometimes I wondered about Max's husband, Davin Tomassi, and why they'd married, and what had happened. I asked Mother one day when we were taking sheets off the line, smelling of ocean and sky.

'I don't know much about it,' Mother said. 'I gather Max and Davin remained very good friends, and kept in touch until he died. Max is a very complex human being. A very fine one.'

The phone rang. In the middle of the night, in the King George Hotel in Athens. Groggily, fearfully, I reached for it, heard a thick male voice asking for Katerina, got an apology for disturbing me. I'd have been furious if I hadn't been half awake, anyhow. Even so, it scared me. Phone calls in the middle of the night aren't usually good news.

I'd thought it might be about Max.

❀

One warm May afternoon I was over at Beau Allaire. Ursula and I had gone for a swim. Max said she didn't feel up to it and I thought Ursula's glance was anxious.

But the two of us had a fine swim. We knew the tides and undertows and so were able to go out beyond the breakers. When we got back to the house, Max was on the verandah, curled up in the wicker swing, a pile of her old sketchbooks beside her, one open in her lap.

Ursula picked up a sketchbook Max had filled when they were on safari, shooting with cameras, not guns. Ursula had the camera, Max the sketchbook, and had filled it with pictures of wildebeests, honey badgers, lions, elephants, giraffes.

'Get dressed,' Max said sharply. 'I don't want sand and salt water all over my sketchbooks.' Then she smiled at us, her special, slow smile which made me feel—oh, not just that Max was fond of me, but that being Polyhymnia O'Keefe, just as I was, with red hair and legs that were too long for me, was an all right thing to be.

I changed in the green guest room, which was beginning to be 'Polly's room,' and went back to the verandah. Urs was in the kitchen, 'doing something elegant with chicken and fresh dill,' Max told me.

I picked up another African sketchbook, this one filled with people rather than animals, pencil drawings of Africans doing tribal dances. Pygmies. Bushmen. Matabeles.

Another sketchbook. From Asia. More odd dances, people wearing masks, leaping about fires. 'What's it about?' I asked.

'Aggression,' Max said. 'Getting rid of it legitimately. We don't, nowadays, we sophisticated peoples. As society evolved, we began to repress the destructive, aggressive instincts we needed to acquire back when we were living in caves and trees and had to protect ourselves from wild animals—or wild people. What do you do about your own anger?'

'I chop wood,' I said. 'That's the good old-fashioned way of getting it out of your system, but it works.'

Max pointed to a pen-and-ink sketch of naked people dancing. They had long legs, and long slender necks, and Max had given them a wild rhythm. 'They're acting out their feral feelings in a way which doesn't endanger society. Kids in inner cities, or even places like Cowpertown, don't have any legitimate way of working out their aggressions. Not too many of them—in the South, at least—chop wood.'

'Benne Seed gets mighty cold, and we use a lot of wood. I can split a cord as well as Xan.'

'Even the old scapegoat'—Max riffled through the pages —'was a useful device whereby people could dump their sins onto the animal, and not be crushed under a burden of neurotic guilt.' She put down the sketchbook, picked up a pad, and began sketching me. 'If I had it to do

again, I'd be an anthropologist. Who is it who said the
proper study of mankind is man?' I didn't know the
answer, and she went on, 'We all have our own burdens
of neurotic guilt. Sketching helps me get rid of mine.'

I reached for another sketchbook. It was filled with
watercolor paintings of brilliant, jungly-looking birds,
flashing color in deep-green forests, and then more people, wearing masks and dancing.

To my surprise, Max grabbed the sketchbook. 'I don't
like those paintings.'

'Where were you when you did them?' I asked, not
understanding why she was so vehement.

'Ecuador.'

Ecuador. In South America. 'Were you in the jungle?'

'For a while.' She pulled out another sketchbook.
'Now look at these sketches, Polly. It's from my last
China trip.'

'When were you in Ecuador?' I persisted.

'Last year. Look, here's the Great Wall of China. It's
almost unbelievable, even when you're looking right at
it.'

I looked, not at Max's drawings of the Wall, but at
Max herself, her pallor, her thinness. And the pieces of
the puzzle suddenly fitted together. This was why Max
had come home to Beau Allaire, why Ursula was on leave
of absence from her hospital in New York.

If I'd seen Urs alone, I'd have asked her if my guess
was right, but there wasn't a moment. Once Urs called
to us that dinner was ready, the three of us were together
the whole time, and then they both waved me off when
I left for home. I wished the Land-Rover hadn't been
available, so I could have asked Urs to drive me.

As soon as I got back, I checked in, and then went out
to the lab and called from the phone there, called the

hospital in Cowpertown and left a message for Renny to call me. I'd never done that before.

I took the hose and sluiced down the cement floor of the lab, so I'd be there to grab the phone when it rang. I was cleaning one of the tanks when he called.

'What's up, Polly?'

I perched on one of the high stools; the telephone was on the wall above a shelf full of beakers and jars and a lot of lab paraphernalia. 'Max was in Ecuador last year. Has she got one of your awful parasites?'

A pause. Then, 'Thousands of Americans go to South America every year.'

'Max was in the jungle, not on a cruise ship.'

Renny was silent.

'Listen, I know all about doctors' confidentiality, but you've talked to me a lot about your field, and unless you tell me I'm wrong, I'm going to assume that Max got infected while she was in South America, and this thing is going to kill her. Is killing her.'

Renny said, 'Polly.' And then, 'Look, I can't talk on the phone. Where are you?'

'In the lab. There's no one around.'

'Pol, I can't talk about it at all. You know that.'

'Then it's true. Okay, I know I'm not next of kin, I have no legal right to ask. But Max is my friend. She matters to me.'

Renny sounded very far away. 'If Mrs. Tomassi wanted you to know, she'd tell you.'

'That's telling me. Thanks.'

'What are you going to do with it?'

'Nothing. You're right. If Max wanted me to know, she'd tell me herself. But I want to talk to you, please. Not about Max. You've talked to me plenty about vectors, and parasites circulating in the blood of the host in Trypanosomal form.'

'You know too much about too many things,' Renny said.

'You don't have to talk to me about Max. Just talk to me about Netson and his research.'

'I suppose I owe you that much. It's all my fault that you guessed. I'm not on call tomorrow evening.'

He'd borrowed a boat, so we went to Petros' as usual. Renny had brought an article by his boss in the *New England Journal of Medicine*, and I skimmed it, then went back to read more slowly. Clinically, the patient experiences a recurrent fever. The Trypanosomal organisms go through some kind of change, but eventually they get back in the bloodstream and invade the heart. In the case of people like Max (though we never mentioned her name) who have no immunities whatsoever, severe heart disease develops. Even with people who have lived for generations in areas where the disease is endemic, about ten percent of the population end up with congestive heart failure, and sudden cardiac arrest is common.

'How did Max find out she had Netson's?' I handed him back the *New England Journal*. Renny began leafing through it, not answering.

I felt angry and frustrated, and at the same time I respected his attitude. I spoke slowly, quietly. 'You don't have to tell me. I can figure it out. Max is no fool, and Ursula is a doctor, even if tropical medicine isn't her field. But she must have heard of these diseases, and Max is an omnivorous reader. If she had a bite on the eyelid, followed by conjunctivitis while she was in Ecuador, she'd have suspected. One of the foremost specialists in tropical diseases is her cousin, on the staff of M. A. Horne, which was started with her father's money. Ironic, isn't it?'

Renny looked at me over the magazine, but said nothing.

I went on. 'So it would be a logical thing for her to come home to confirm a diagnosis she and Ursula already suspected, and to stay here, because Dr. Netson's in Cowpertown, and Beau Allaire is home. And Ursula's on leave of absence, to be with Max until—' My voice broke, and I looked at Renny. He did not contradict me, so I knew I was right, if not specifically, at least generally. For a moment a wave of nausea broke over me. I fought it back. 'Isn't there any treatment?'

'Nothing satisfactory.' Renny spoke reluctantly. 'We're trying primaquine in the dosage suitable for malaria. And there's a nitrofurazone derivative that shows promise. But if there's organ damage, it's irreversible, at least at present.'

'What about a heart transplant?' I suggested.

'They're chancy, at best, and contraindicated in Netson's. Polly, I've told you more than I should.'

'You haven't said a word about Max. You've just talked to me about a disease in which you're particularly interested. If Max weren't involved, you could have said everything you've said to me, and it wouldn't have hurt. That's the difference.'

His voice was heavy. 'She's a special lady. A real lady, and there aren't many around nowadays. I truly admire her. I wish there were something I could do for her. You're lucky to have her for a friend.'

'Yes. I know.'

We didn't finish our pizza. Petros came and asked us

if anything was wrong with it, and we assured him it was fine, but he wanted to make us another, on the house, and finally I convinced him I didn't feel well.

Renny asked him for the check. 'Polly, sweet. I'm sorry.'

'I know.'

'For all the breaks we've been getting in medicine, there's still a lot we can't do anything about.'

My voice was brittle. 'Nobody ever promised us life was going to be safe. Everybody dies, sooner or later.'

'Would you want not to?' Renny asked. 'To go on in a body growing older and older, forever? Even if we could keep the body in reasonable shape, would you want to live forever?'

'Yes,' I said, and then, 'No. Forever would be crippling. One would never have to do anything, because one could always do it tomorrow.' *One could*—I'd picked that up from Max, as so much else. 'But not extinction. I can't imagine Max being annihilated.'

Renny didn't say anything, and I didn't want him to, because he's an intern, and I knew what he'd say. At least I'm older than Renny in that way. He can take on faith that there are mitochondria and farandolae, and that there are quarks and quanta, even though they can't be seen. Well, so can I. My parents are scientists, after all. But I can also take on faith that Max is too alive to be extinguished by anything as—as banal as death.

Renny paid for the pizza. 'Polly—'

I looked at him.

'Can you keep . . . what you've guessed . . . to yourself?'

'I'll try. If I don't see Max for a couple of days, maybe I'll get it all into some kind of perspective. I'm not very good about hiding things from people I care about.' Max had guessed immediately that I'd heard gossip about her and Urs. But this was different. I'd have to keep her from knowing that I knew.

We drove to the dock and jumped into the small motorboat. Halfway to Benne Seed, Renny cut the motor as usual, but instead of kissing we looked up at the stars.

'In the life span of a star,' I said, 'our lives are less than a flicker, whether we live for ten years or a hundred.'

'In the life span of the universe,' Renny said, 'that life of a star is less than a flicker.' And then he kissed me. And I wanted him to. Just as it was beginning to build, he broke off. 'Time to take you home.'

Heavy with unwanted knowledge, I went to my room, saying that I had a lot of reading to do for school. Which was true. Exams were coming up, and I had to do well.

And my room was full of Max. The little crystal bird she'd given me for the opening of *As You Like It* was on my desk, by the window, where it caught and refracted the light sparkling off the ocean. Over my desk chair was flung a Fair Isle sweater Max had loaned me one early spring night when it had grown unexpectedly chilly, and then told me to keep because she didn't need it anymore. On my bed table were books she'd taken down from the library shelves at Beau Allaire and given me to read.

Now that I knew all that I knew, I couldn't understand why it had taken me so long to realize just why it was that Max had come home to Beau Allaire.

But I learned that I was capable of keeping a secret.
Max and Ursula did not know that I knew.

In the King George Hotel in Athens I woke up with
tears on my cheeks, and the sound of the redbird in the
chinaberry tree in my ears. The sound faded into the
night noises of a city, and I knew that I had been crying
about Max. Suddenly I heard a soft rain spattering on
the balcony floor, and a cool breeze came in. And I went
back to sleep.

In the morning the sky was even more brilliantly blue
and gold than it had been, with no heat haze, and a cool
breeze.

Zachary called while I was having breakfast, the Fair
Isle cardigan over my shoulders. He explained that we'd
need to make an early start if I wanted to be back in
time for dinner with Sandy and Rhea. "Can you be in
the lobby at nine?"

"Sure, why not?"

"Leave a message for your uncle and aunt, that you
may not be back when they arrive. When are they getting in, by the way?"

"I'm not sure. Uncle Sandy just said in plenty of time
for dinner."

"Okay, then, he doesn't expect you to hang around.
I'll have you back at the King George in good time to
bathe and change. Just leave them a message."

"Will do." Sandy would certainly not want me to
hang around.

"That was quite a downpour we had during the
night," Zachary said. "Did it wake you?"

"I heard it." It was mixed up in my mind with the

redbird in the chinaberry tree and my conversation with Renny. "But now we've got the most glorious day of all." I had carried my coffee cup from the balcony to the telephone in the bedroom, and took a swallow. It was cooling off. "See you at nine."

The air was dry and warm when we started off in the VW Bug, which was beginning to seem like a familiar friend. Zachary'd brought another picnic basket, not from the Hilton this time, he said, but very Greek: cold spinach pie, feta cheese, wrinkly dark olives, taramasalata, cucumber dip.

"And I got them to make me some fresh lemonade at the Hilton. I don't suppose you want to greet your uncle and aunt with wine on your breath."

"I'm not much of a drinker," I told him.

"There's a difference between having an occasional glass of wine and being an alcoholic."

"Of course. But I'm still a minor, in case you've forgotten, and I've seen enough of the results of the abuse of alcohol to be very wary of it."

He looked at me with open curiosity. "Not your parents?"

"Heavens—no!"

"Who?"

I didn't say Max. It was a while before I realized that sometimes she drank too much. She frequently switched from wine to bourbon. 'It's good for elderly hearts,' she said.

I asked Renny if it was all right for her to drink bourbon, and he said that to an extent Max was right, that a moderate amount of whiskey actually dilated the arteries. And he added that it was a painkiller. He gave me another of Netson's articles to read, this one way over my head, but I gathered that in the last months of the disease there is a good deal of acute pain, and the damaged heart muscle will not tolerate ordinary pain-killers.

One evening when Max and I were alone at Beau Allaire she talked to me about her husband. We were sitting at the table out on the verandah, and she was sipping bourbon. Only the slight flush to her cheeks made me realize that she was drinking more than usual, but there was nothing ugly about it.

'I married Davin Tomassi in good faith,' she said. 'I wanted family life, wanted children, and I thought Davin and I could make it. He was the gentlest man I have ever known, and occasionally he could get through all my blocks and inhibitions, but not often. God knows it wasn't Davin's fault there was no miracle. He was infinitely patient. And when I got pregnant—oh, God, how we rejoiced. But the baby was born with the Allaire weak heart, and lived only a few days. After that—it was apparent things weren't going to work out for us as husband and wife. That was my worst time, after I left Davin. I fell apart in the ugliest possible way. Then I met Urs. And was able to be friends with Davin again. I will always love Davin, in my fashion, and be grateful to him.' She put her hands to her cheeks, and her fingers trembled. 'I think I want you to go home now, Polly. I'm tired.'

I left. It had been almost as hard for Max to tell me about her marriage as it had been for her to tell me about her father and M.A. I wondered when she was going to tell me that she was dying.

The next time I was at Beau Allaire, Ursula was there, and I managed a few minutes with her in the kitchen (Max didn't give us much time alone, basically because

Max didn't want to be alone). 'Urs, I don't mean to pry, and I know Max doesn't want to talk about it, and nobody told me, I mean Renny didn't say anything, but I guessed—'

Ursula turned from the stone sink. 'Did you? I thought you might have. How much do you know?'

'That Max has Netson's disease, and that there's no cure.'

Ursula wiped her hands carefully. 'Oh, Polly child, this is a lot for you to handle, and you're in too deep now for you to turn your back on Max and withdraw.'

Withdrawing had not occurred to me. 'Can't anything be done to help her?' I knew the answer, but Ursula was older and more experienced than Renny.

'Not much. When Bart Netson confirmed the diagnosis I don't think she realized how much she was going to have to endure. With some people it's just a slow wearing down of energy, and then quick heart failure. It's being much slower with Max; she's very strong. The pain is bad, and getting worse. I'm grateful to you, child, for all you do to help Max. You're both friend and daughter to her. Did she tell you that she and Davin had a little girl?'

'Yes.'

'That was a devastating blow to Maxa, seeing what appeared to be a perfect infant, and then watching it wilt and die. You're Max's child, Polly, the child she couldn't have, and that's an enormous burden to put on a sixteen-year-old. What have we done to you, Max and I?'

'You've made me alive,' I said quickly.

'I worry about you.' She turned back to the stone sink. 'I hope we're not—I hope we're not destructive to you.'

'Constructive,' I said quickly. 'Sandy brought me to Beau Allaire to meet you, just me, remember? He wouldn't have, if he hadn't known I needed you and Max.'

'Bless you.' Ursula refilled the kettle and put it back on the stove. 'Bless Sandy. Dennys, too. They're good friends.'

Mother went to Charleston with Ursula, at last, to go to the Spoleto festival in the afternoon while Urs was consulting at Mercy Hospital, and then go out to dinner, and back to the festival in the evening. She came back glowing.

The following week Max said, 'It's your turn, Pol. Urs has to go back to Charleston to see Ormsby—there are times I could kill your Uncle Dennys for offering Urs to him—but Urs needs the stimulation, so I'm simultaneously grateful. There's an interesting play on at the Dock Street Theatre in the evening.'

'When?'

'Tomorrow. We've already cleared it with your parents. Urs will be getting her hair trimmed, so we'll kill two birds with one stone and get yours styled.'

'You're not coming?' Of course she wasn't coming. She wasn't up to it, and I knew it.

'Not this time. You go with Urs and have fun.'

Ursula and I stayed in the Ormsbys' guesthouse, which was a separate building behind the house and had been the kitchen in the old days. There was a comfortable sitting room overlooking the garden, a bedroom with twin beds, a bathroom, and a tiny kitchenette, so the guests could be self-sufficient. The furniture was antique and beautiful—Mrs. Ormsby was an interior decorator—and there was air-conditioning.

We said hello to Mrs. Ormsby, who was welcoming and chatty and asked about Daddy and then Uncle Dennys, and talked about getting Mother into Charleston more often, and wouldn't Ursula be interested in serving on some committees? 'And how is Maximiliana doing?' she asked, a tentative note coming into her voice.

'As well as can be expected.' Ursula's tone was carefully noncommittal.

'I wish we could help, my dear,' Mrs. Ormsby said.

Suddenly and for the first time I realized that Ursula was bearing Max's death on her own shoulders, bearing it for Max as well as for herself. And I had a faint glimmer of what that death was going to mean to Ursula. Max had said that they had been together for over thirty years. That was longer than Mother and Daddy had been married. How would either of my parents feel if they were watching the other die? I couldn't quite conceive it. Now, as I watched and heard Ursula being courteous and contained, some of her pain became real to me.

Mrs. Ormsby, returning to her social, light voice, told us there was iced tea in the fridge, and a bottle of white wine.

We thanked her and then went to the hairdresser, chic and undoubtedly exorbitantly expensive. I felt a little odd, having my hair styled. Kate's chestnut hair is curly, and even when she nibbles at it with the nail scissors, it looks just right. If I hack at mine with the nail scissors, it looks exactly as though I've hacked at it with the nail scissors. Mother usually cuts it.

'Cut it short, please,' I said to the stylist, 'as short as possible.'

'Why so short?' he asked.

'It's an awful color, and the shorter it is, the less of it.'

'If I could make up a dye the color of your hair, half

my ladies would come flocking. You have a beautiful neck. We will show off your neck to the best advantage.'

(Kate's reaction when I came home was, 'Golly, Polly!'

Xan said, 'Gosh, Pol, what'd they do? You look almost pretty!'

'She *is* pretty,' Mother said.

Max simply made me turn round and round, looking at me critically from every angle, nodding with satisfaction.)

I could hardly believe it myself. When the stylist was through with me, my straight hair actually lay in soft curves, capping my head.

Ursula's hair looked nice, too. 'Max found Dominic for me,' she said. 'If Max didn't see to it that I go to a good stylist, she knows I wouldn't bother. After all, a surgeon's hair is frequently concealed under a green surgical cap.'

When we left the hairdresser, Ursula went to the hospital and I went to the art gallery, where there was an interesting exhibition of women painters: Rosa Bonheur, Berthe Morisot, Georgia O'Keeffe. O'Keeffe. Hm. Two *f*'s. I liked the way it looked. My parents had not objected when I put the extra *l* in Polly, but I doubted if they'd let me get away with putting an extra *f* in O'Keefe.

I'd gone back to the cottage to change, and was delayed by Mrs. Ormsby, so I was a few minutes late and Ursula was waiting for me. She was evidently known by the people who ran the restaurant, and the waiter was smiling and respectful. 'We have the *moules marinières* that you like, Dr. Heschel.'

'Splendid, François. I think you'll like the way they prepare them here, Polly.'

'Fine.'

She did not order wine. We had Vichy water. 'This place is small enough to be personal, and I've got in the habit of eating here when I'm in Charleston. Did you have a good afternoon?'

'Terrific. It's ages since I've been in an art gallery.'

'Sometime I'm going to take a real sabbatical. But it's been good for me to keep my hand in during all these months. Norris Ormsby called me in today on an interesting and tragic case, a young woman in her thirties who has had a series of brain tumors. Benign, in her case, is a mockery. After her first surgery, some nerves were cut, and her face was irrevocably distorted, her mouth twisted, one eye partly closed. A few days ago another tumor was removed, and several more smaller ones were discovered. I agreed with the decision not to do further surgery. She said that she is looking with her mind's eye at the tumors, willing them to shrink, *see*ing them shrink. And she quoted Benjamin Franklin to me: *Those things that hurt, instruct.* An extraordinary woman. A holy woman. She looks at her devastated face in the mirror and, she says, she still does not recognize herself. But there is no bitterness in her. She sails, and as soon as she gets out of the hospital she plans to sail, solo, to Bermuda. At sea, what she looks like is a matter of complete indifference. My patients teach me, Polly. Old Ben knew what he was talking about, and it's completely counter to general thinking today, where we're taught to avoid pain and seek pleasure. Pain needs to be moved through, not avoided.'

Ursula was referring to her own pain, I thought. And Max's. And mine.

'Why is hurting part of growing up?' I demanded.

'It's part of being human. I've been watching you move through it with amazingly mature compassion.

You've been the best medicine Max could have. Well, child, it's a good thing the play is a comedy. This is more than enough heaviness.'

We spent two hours in the theatre laughing our heads off. Then back to the guest cottage. Ursula went into the main house to have a drink with the Ormsbys, and I got ready for bed, and read until she came in. She took a quick shower, and then got into the other twin bed, blowing me a kiss. 'Sleep well, child. I've enjoyed our time together.'

'Me, too. It's been wonderful.'

'We'll have a bite of breakfast at seven, and then drive back to the Island before the heat of the day. Sleep well.'

'You, too. Thank you. Thanks, Urs.'

Urs wasn't Max. But she was still pretty special.

"Who?" Zachary asked as we drove toward Mount Parnassus.

"Who what?" I asked stupidly.

"Who's abused alcohol, to make you so uptight about it?"

"Zachary, I go to high school, okay? Occasionally I get invited to dances. Kids sneak in booze and drink themselves silly. You have no idea how much time I spend holding kids' heads while they whoops, or mopping them up afterwards if they don't make it to the john. It's enough to make me join the WCTU."

"What on earth is the WCTU?"

I giggled. "The Women's Christian Temperance Union."

He didn't think it was funny. "Your parents aren't teetotalers, are they?"

"No. But they're moderate."

"Anything good can be abused. I know that from very personal experience. But I've learned that I am capable of temperance, and temperance means moderation, not abstinence."

"Okay, okay, I'm not arguing with you. Moderation in all things, as the immoderate Greeks said."

It was from Max that I'd heard about the Greeks talking about being moderate. It was, she said, because temperamentally they were totally immoderate. Starting a war over Helen of Troy is hardly moderate. The vast quantity of gods and goddesses isn't very moderate, either.

We'd talked comfortably over a cup of tea, Ursula making cucumber sandwiches for us, and then I sat at the table on the verandah, and did my homework, while Ursula sat in the white wicker swing, reading a medical journal, and Max sketched. When I was through—it wasn't a heavy-homework night—I left my books and papers on the table and went to stand by Max, looking down at her sketchbook. A sketch of me. One of Ursula. Several sketches of hands.

'Polly—'

Something in her tone of voice made me stop.

'Urs tells me that you know.'

Ursula let the magazine slip off her lap onto the floor, but did not bend down to pick it up. The swing creaked noisily from its hooks in the ceiling.

'Yes, Max, I know.'

'Because of Renny, I suppose—'

'He never talked about you—'

'No, he wouldn't. He just talks about tropical diseases ad infinitum. And you're no fool. Dear, square Renny. I'm glad he's assisting Cousin Bart. Glad you have him for a friend. I'd hoped to spare you, Polly, at least a little longer.'

'No, no, I'd rather—' I started, and trailed off inadequately.

'Not many people have the privilege of being given time to prepare for death. I can't say that I'm ready to die—I'm still *in media res* and I have things I'd like to paint . . . things I'd like to do—but I'm beyond the denial and the rage. I don't like the pain.'

'Oh, Max—' I looked helplessly at Ursula.

Urs glanced at Max, rose, picked up the journal, and dropped it in the swing. 'I'm off to the kitchen. Come and join me in a few minutes, Polly.'

'Little one,' Max said. 'There are worse things than dying. Losing one's sense of compassion, for instance; being inured to suffering. Losing the wonder and the sadness of it all. That's a worse death than the death of the body.'

I was silent. Trying to push back the dark lump of tears rising in my throat.

'I don't know how long I have left,' Max said. 'Bart doesn't know. I'm strong as an ox. My heart is not going to stop beating easily. But it's been an immensely interesting journey, this life, and I've been given the child of my heart to rejoice me at the end.'

She stood, pushing up from her seat with her hands, and I was in her arms, tears streaming down my cheeks. She wiped them with her long fingers. 'Dear, loving little Pol. But it's better this way, isn't it? Out in the open?'

I nodded, pushing my fingers in my pocket to look

for Kleenex. She put a handkerchief in my hand. 'Max, I don't want to go to Cyprus.'

'Nonsense.' Her voice was brusque. 'I am not going to allow my plans for the education of Polyhymnia O'Keefe to be disrupted.'

I wanted to ask, 'Will you be here when I come back?' I mumbled, 'I still don't want to go.'

She smiled at me. 'You'll go, Polly, if only for me. You won't disappoint me. Now. Go help Ursula. And let's have a merry meal. I've had a rich life, Polly, and I'm grateful indeed.' She gave me a gentle hug, then a small shove, and I went out to the kitchen.

I could ask Urs what I couldn't ask Max. 'Urs, if I go to Cyprus, will Max be . . . will Max be alive when I get back?'

'I can't answer that, child. I don't know. There are no tidy answers to Netson's. But things aren't going to get better.'

'I don't want to go.'

'You must. You know that. Part of growing up is learning to do things you don't want to do.' She looked at me gravely. 'Child, I promised Norris Ormsby I'd go back to Charleston next week. Just this once more. I've made it clear that it's the last time. Max won't ask you to stay with her, now that she knows that you know. She won't want to burden you. But I'm going to ask you to come stay with her overnight. Are you up to it?'

'Yes,' I said.

'It's a lot to ask of you. I know that.'

'You don't need to ask. I want to be here.'

'You're a strong child, Polly.'

—It's all a front, I wanted to say, but I didn't. And I didn't mind when Ursula called me child. I'd have hated it from anyone else.

She handed me a plate of cold chicken and ham. 'I hope you're not going to regret these months since Sandy brought you over to Beau Allaire as his Christmas present to Max and me.'

'Never!' I cried. 'I've learned more in these past months than I've ever learned in school. I could never regret them.'

'Never' is a long word.

"Am I never going to see you again, after I take you back to the hotel this afternoon?" Zachary asked.

"It's been wonderful being with you," I said. "I've had a marvelous time. I'll write you postcards from Cyprus."

"I want more than postcards. You really do something special for me, Polly, you really do. Do you honestly enjoy being with me?"

"I wouldn't be with you if I didn't." Zachary evidently didn't even suspect that I was anything but a social success in Cowpertown and that having a young man after me was a totally new experience.

"Mount Parnassus isn't that far beyond Delphi, O goddess mine," he said, "but I won't trace any of our route. Did you do your homework?"

"Sure." In my mind's eye I saw Max sitting with me on the verandah swing, showing me pictures and sketches, got a whiff of her perfume, of Beau Allaire's flowers in the spring. "Mount Parnassus is sacred to Dionysus, and the Thyiads held their Bacchic revels on one of the summits."

"I'd like to have a Bacchic revel with you." He took

one hand off the steering wheel and pulled me close to him. I must have stiffened. "Relax, pretty Pol. I'm not going to hurt you."

I did relax during the ferry ride. We stood on deck and the light of sun on water was so brilliant it was almost blinding. The sea was choppy, white-capped, with a high wind which dried the spray as fast as it blew up at us. To our right was a barren coast of stony mountains, with only a little scrubby-looking vegetation on the lower slopes. I wondered if it had been greener for the Dionysian revels; I could hardly imagine them on hard, bare stone.

The sea got choppier and choppier as we approached land, and the sky more lowering. "It rained last night," Zachary said. "I forbid it to rain today."

But as we got back in the Bug to drive off the ferry, big raindrops splattered against the windshield. Zachary swore. Then, "There's a place nearby where we can have a glass of tea and see what the weather's going to do."

The small restaurant he took me to was right on the shore, and we could watch the rain making pockmarks on the water. The waiter seemed sorrowful but not surprised when Zachary asked for tea and nothing else, and while we were drinking it the skies opened and dumped quantities of water, and then, abruptly, stopped.

"I have a rug for us to sit on," Zachary said. "I think we can drive on and have our picnic." The sun was out, and the wet flagstones outside the restaurant were steaming.

The wind was still strong, and it was a wild, warm, early afternoon of swiftly shifting clouds which went well with the grandeur of the scenery. Zachary drove to a grove of ancient pines, from which we had a view of a crumbling temple, the stone shining and golden in the post-storm sunshine.

Zachary spread a rug over the rusty needles, and we ate comfortably, protected by the trees, which swayed in the wind, sounding almost like surf. Zachary popped a wrinkled little olive into his mouth, and then lay down, looking up at the blue sky through the green needles of the pines, a high, burning blue with golden glints.

I looked at one of the crumbling columns. "It's so old—"

"And gone," Zachary said, putting his dark head in my lap. "As our own civilization will soon be gone. It's a never-ending cycle of rise and fall, rise and fall. Except that there's a good possibility we'll end it." He spat out the olive seed. "With the new microtechnology, there'll be less than a fifteen-second lapse between the pressing of the button and the falling of the bombs. All those bomb shelters people have built, my pa among them, will be useless. There won't be time to get to them. When it happens, it'll happen without warning."

I pushed his head off my lap. "Shut up."

"Ow." He rubbed his head and put it back on my lap. "It might happen now, in the next few seconds. A light so bright we'd be blinded, and heat so intense we'd be incinerated before we realized what had happened. It wouldn't be a bad way to go, here, with you."

I pushed at his head again, but he didn't move. It's one thing to contemplate one's mortality realistically, another to wallow in melodrama. It was almost as though this strange young man was deliberately inviting disaster.

"Don't be an ostrich," he said, "hiding your head in the sand."

"I'm as realistic as you are, but it doesn't do any

good to dwell on the horror. Nobody wants it, and it doesn't have to happen."

"Give a child matches, and sooner or later he'll light one."

"We had an essay contest, not just our school, but the whole state, on how to prevent nuclear warfare, and I wish the President of the United States would listen to the kids."

"Did you win?" Zachary asked.

"I was a finalist. At least I was able to speak my piece. And we have to live as though there's going to be a world for us to live in."

"What's the point of making plans?"

I countered, "What's the point of *not* making plans?"

"We're at the end of our civilization, let's face it."

"Oh, Zach." Absently I began to run my fingers through his hair. "Think of all the groups who decided they knew exactly when the end of the world was coming, because of the lineup of planets, or some verse from Revelation, and dressed up in sheets to wait on some mountaintop for Judgment Day. Or had big Doomsday parties. And refusing to live, because it wasn't worth it when the end of the world was so close, and even selling their property—and then, when the world didn't end at the predicted moment, there they were."

"I'm not selling my property," Zachary said. "You needn't worry about that. Just in case, I'll hang on to what I have."

"You can't take it with you."

"I'll keep it till the last second. I've got five thousand dollars in traveler's checks with me right now."

I did not like this aspect of Zachary. I'm realistic enough to know the possibilities for the future, but there are some positive ones, too, as I reminded Zachary.

There are people like Sandy and Rhea whose work is about diametrically opposite to Zachary's father's, though I didn't mention that. A lot of doctors are refusing to take part in emergency medical-disaster planning, making it clear that it's unethical to delude people into false beliefs that there are any realistic mechanisms of survival after an atomic war. More and more people are rising up against nuclear stockpiling. At home. Abroad. We don't have to blow up the planet.

Max said once, 'We do make things happen by what we think, so think positively, Polly, not negatively. When you think you are beautiful, you are beautiful. If you believe in yourself, you will do well in your life's work, whether you choose acting or writing or science.'

It was a warm summer evening and we were out on the verandah upstairs, off Max's room, watching night fall. The sky over the ocean was rosy with afterglow, which Max said was more subtle than the sunset. The ceiling fan was whirring gently. In the purply sky above the soft rose at the horizon a star came out, pulsing softly so that it was more like the thought of a star than a star, and then there it was, followed by more and more stars.

Max pointed to the sky. 'The macrocosm. Stars beyond countless stars. Galaxies beyond galaxies. If our universe is finite, as many astrophysicists believe, there may be as many universes as there are galaxies, floating like tiny bubbles in the vastness of space.'

'Tiny bubbles?'

I was sitting on a low stool at Max's feet, and she reached out her fingers and massaged the back of my neck gently. That's where I get tired when I write a lot, and I'd just finished my last long paper of the year for Miss Zeloski.

'The last time Urs and I were at your house, Rosy and Johnny were blowing bubbles, lovely little iridescent orbs floating in the breeze. And when one thinks of the macrocosm, and then the microcosm, size makes no never-mind, as Nettie would say.' She laughed gently. 'Is a galaxy bigger than a quark? I lean more and more on the total interdependence of all creation. If we should be so foolish as to blow this planet to bits, it would have reper-cussions not only in our own solar system but in distant galaxies. Or even distant universes. And if anyone dies—a tree, a planet, a human being—all of creation is shaken.'

How different that was from Zachary. Frightening, but in a completely different way, because it gave every-thing meaning.

'Never think what you do doesn't matter,' Max said. 'No one is too insignificant to make a difference. When-ever you get the chance, choose life. But I don't need to tell you that. You choose life with every gesture you make. That's the first thing in you that appealed to me. You are naked with life.'

And wasn't that what drew me to Max, that abundant sense of life?—pointing out to me the fierce underside of a moth clinging to the screen; fireflies like a fallen galaxy on the dunes in front of our house; the incredible, pulsing life of the stars blooming in the night sky, seeming to cling to the Spanish moss on the old oaks.

I looked at the crumbling golden columns near Zach-ary's picnic spot, the chipped pediments, and thought that Max would see in them not the death of a civiliza-tion but the life. I got up and walked slowly toward the temple, and Zachary followed me.

He dropped his doom talk. "When am I going to see you again?"

"Uncle Sandy has plans to take me to various places for the rest of the week, and then I'm off to Cyprus."

"I like Cyprus. I'll come see you there."

"No, please, Zachary. I'm there to do a job, and I'm not going to have time for anything else."

"How long is this job?"

"Three weeks." We'd reached the temple, and I sat on the still-damp stone of a pediment with a lotus-leaf design. Did the Greeks think of the lotus as flowering into an entire universe?

Zachary counted off on his fingers. "Three weeks, okay, I may go to Turkey for a while, then. How're you getting home after the conference?"

"Cyprus Airlines to Athens, then on to JFK in New York, and then to Charleston."

"You change planes in Athens?"

"Of course."

"How long do you have between planes?"

"Nearly three hours."

"I'll meet you at the airport, then, and we can have a bite together and a chance to catch up. When we get back to the hotel, write me down your flight numbers."

"Okay, that would be fun." I tried not to let on just how thrilled I was that he didn't want to drop me when Sandy and Rhea arrived.

He touched my nose, then my lips with his finger. "I can't imagine anything nicer than fun with you, Polly. You're like a bottle of champagne just waiting to be uncorked. Or don't you like that analogy?" I had turned away, and he pulled me back. "I didn't mean to hurt you, sweet Pol. Since you haven't told me anything, I can't help blundering." He pressed my face against his shoulder, gently.

It was nearly seven when we got back to the hotel. Zachary insisted that I give him the Cyprus Airlines flight number, so I let him into my room just long enough to check my ticket and write down the information for him. He was looking around the room, and I'm sure it gave him the impression the O'Keefes are a lot richer than we are. But I didn't explain.

He kissed me goodbye, and electricity vibrated through me. But we don't have to act out everything we feel. I'd learned that much.

"I've got to call Uncle Sandy's room. Thanks, Zach. These have been good days for me. Really good. Thanks."

"Believe me, the pleasure was mine. And this is not goodbye, Pol, you're not going to be able to get rid of me this easily."

I hoped he would be at the airport to meet me at the end of my three weeks in Cyprus. But I thought I'd better not count on it.

I rang Sandy and Rhea's room, and he answered. "Polly! We arrived about an hour ago and got your message. Glad you were off doing something. Been having a good time?" There was both question and challenge in his voice.

"Yes. I have. I met a guy from California—did Uncle Dennys tell you?"

"He mentioned it."

"I've been off sightseeing and doing things with him."

"Not too much, I hope?"

I laughed. "No fault of his, but no, not too much."

"My, you sound grown up."

"It's about time," I said. "I hope it's all right that I went ahead and made a reservation for dinner on the roof at nine. I thought that might be easiest for you—"

"It's just right," he said. "Rhea's napping, but I'll wake her up in time. See you at the restaurant."

I soaked in a warm bath. Zachary had been an escape route in many ways. I could forget that Sandy was likely to ask me questions. Some of the questions had no answers. But there were other ones which I was going to have to respond to, and I wasn't ready. I felt as though a splinter of ice had lodged deep in my heart. While I was with Zachary I was able to forget it, but now it was there, chilling me.

I stayed in the tub as long as possible, but it didn't thaw anything. Then I dressed in the one dressy thing I'd brought with me, a soft, floaty geometric print of mauves and blues and lavenders, which softened my angles and brought out the blue of my eyes and made my hair look less orange. Rhea had given it to me for Christmas, and I'd worn it for the New Year's Eve party at Beau Allaire, and for Zachary when we went to the Hilton for dinner. Rhea knew how to buy clothes which were just right for me.

At nine sharp, I was standing in front of the elevator, and when I got to the roof, Sandy and Rhea were waiting. I hugged them, rubbing my face against Sandy's soft golden beard, smelling Rhea's familiar, exotic scent, embraced by them both. For a fleeting moment Rhea reminded me of Max. They both had black hair. They were both tall. They both had fine bones. They knew how to dress. But that was it. Max's eyes were silver, and Rhea's like dark pansies. Max was thin, and Rhea was slender. Max vibrated like a plucked harp, and Rhea was serenely quiet. Max, with her acute awareness of life, was dying, and Rhea still had her life ahead of her.

We were shown to a table with a good view, one of Aristeides' tables. He greeted me like an old friend, and I introduced him to Sandy and Rhea.

"You seem to have made yourself very much at home," Sandy said.

Rhea smiled at me approvingly. "We're proud of you for managing on your own so well. Of course we knew you would."

Sandy and Aristeides spent quite a while discussing the merits of various dishes, and when Rhea said something in Greek Aristeides was delighted, repeated everything in Greek, rattled off a list of wines, and approved of Rhea's choice. It was not retsina.

During dinner, Sandy and Rhea told me that after they had visited some of Rhea's relatives they'd been invited to tour the islands on a friend's yacht, and then they had a job to do. They didn't tell me what or where, but I was used to secrets. A lot of Daddy's research was secret, too.

Rhea and Sandy were even more cosmopolitan than Max, and I was only Polly, the island girl, but I was completely at ease with them.

Zachary came with the after-dinner coffee, appearing at Sandy's elbow and introducing himself.

"I thought you might like to see who it is who's been escorting Polly these past few days." He looked handsome in dark pants and blazer and a white shirt.

Rhea invited him to sit down, and I could see they thought I'd done pretty well, until Zachary mentioned his father's corporation, and something in Sandy's eyes clicked, like the shutter of a camera. Then he switched the conversation to my job in Osia Theola, and the tension evaporated, and we talked comfortably. Zachary flattered Rhea without being obvious, and was politely deferential to Sandy. He shook hands with them as we parted, kissed me on the cheek, and said, "Be seeing you, Pol," and left us.

Sandy laughed slightly. "Your young man doesn't suffer for lack of funds."

Rhea spoke gently. "You can't blame him for his father."

"True. I'm glad you had a good time with him, Polly."

Sandy had rented a car big enough for the three of us and our luggage. As I left my room and my balcony I felt a sudden pang of homesickness for this place where I had been for only a few days.

Sandy came to my room to see if I needed anything. "Set?"

"I think so. The flowers are pretty well wilted, but I've put the rest of the fruit in a plastic bag—I thought we might want it while we're driving."

"Good thought." He sat down on the sofa. "I talked with your parents last night." Sandy and Dennys must have astronomical phone bills, but still I was surprised. "Everyone's fine, and I gave them a good report on you. They haven't heard from you yet, it's too soon."

"I've written every day, at least a postcard."

"They're aware that mail takes at least a week or ten days. Should I have phoned when you could talk with them?"

I shook my head, slowly.

"And I talked with Ursula and Max. We could call again, if you like, so you could talk."

I shook my head again, bent to pick up my shoulder bag.

"Max is weaker, Urs says, and in a good bit of pain." It was more a question than a statement.

I slung the bag over my shoulder. We'd had all the big conversations on Benne Seed. I had nothing to add.

Sandy went to the door. "Someone will be up for your bag in a moment. We'll meet you in the lobby." His voice was even, not condemning, not judging.

"Okay." I sat down to wait. I didn't want to leave. I wanted to be going somewhere with Zachary. I'd been devastated when Sandy and Rhea were not at the airport to meet me. Now I'd be delighted if they were delayed for another week.

A knock on my door. Time to go.

Rhea insisted that I sit in front with Sandy since she was so familiar with the countryside. I told them what Zachary and I had done, where we'd gone, and they approved.

"He wasn't very thorough. One hour in the museum. And I'll have to go back to Delphi, and Osias Lukas. It's all so overwhelming—there's far more than I can manage to see in a week."

"And you don't want to get saturated," Sandy said. "Just a sip here, a taste there, and you'll know what you want to drink of more deeply the next time. And there'll be a next time, Polly, maybe not for the next few years, but you have travel in your blood, and Greece will draw you back. Now, my loves, my plan for today is this. We'll stop in Corinth for lunch and a little sightseeing, and go on to Nauplion for the night. Then tomorrow we'll push on to Epidaurus. We'll spend a good part of the day there, and then we'll have to head back to Athens to get you on your plane to Cyprus."

"We'll stick to a fairly easy pace," Rhea added. "Sandy and I are in the mood to putter along, enjoy things without pressure. All right?"

"Fine. Absolutely anything's fine. Charleston is the farthest I've been from Benne Seed in years, and I've missed Europe."

Rhea leaned over the seat. "Have you read Robinson Jeffers's play about Medea?"

"Max had me read it, along with a lot of Aeschylus and Sophocles."

"How did you get along with all that classicism?"

"With Max's help, pretty well." I didn't want to talk about Max, but with Rhea and Sandy it was impossible not to.

Sandy and Rhea were much more thorough sightseers than Zachary. "If we want to plummet Polly back thousands of years," Sandy said, "Mycenae's the place."

It was. As we drove steadily uphill, the sky clouded over, and as we approached Mycenae, the wild grey of the sky seemed to go with the stark and ancient magnificence. Max had shown me her sketchbooks of Greece, but they hadn't prepared me for the reality. She'd taken me through a good bit of Sophocles, some of which I thought was absolutely fantastic and some of which was boring, and I knew that the Acropolis of Mycenae was the setting for his plays.

We parked the car and walked through the stone gates

at the top of the mountain. Sandy grasped my arm. "Do you realize, Pol, that these are the gates through which Agamemnon and Orestes walked? Come on, I'll show you the place which is thought to be where Clytemnestra murdered Agamemnon in his bath. You'll read Sophocles differently after this."

I reached for his hand. "Why are human beings so violent?"

"We can be tender, too," he said, "and we can laugh at ourselves. Didn't Max give you any comedies to read?"

"I think we just didn't get to them."

"Perhaps she thought they were too bawdy?" Rhea suggested.

Sandy laughed. "I doubt that. Max is committed to opening Polly's eyes."

But Max's plans for the education of Polyhymnia O'Keefe had been interrupted before we got to the comedies.

In the xenia in Nauplion, Sandy and Rhea had a large corner room, facing the Bay of Argos. From their balcony we could see a Venetian fortress. My room, next to theirs, overlooked the water, and the sound of wind and waves was the sound of home, but wilder, because here the sea beat against rock, not sand. But it was still the familiar music of waves, and I slept.

I was in a small boat in the wide stretch of water between Cowpertown and Benne Seed Island. The waves were high and the boat was rocking, but I wasn't afraid. I held a baby in my arms, a tiny little rosy thing, but it wasn't Rosy, or any of my younger siblings. It had no clothes on, and I held it close to keep it warm. Above us a seagull flew.

And then something seemed to be hitting at the wooden sides of the boat, and I looked over to see what it was—

—And Sandy was knocking on my door in the xenia in Nauplion and calling, "Wake up, sleepyhead. Come and have breakfast with Rhea and me on our balcony."

"Be right there," I called.

But I dressed slowly, still partly in the dream, which had been strangely beautiful. Bending down to fasten my sandal strap, I remembered, with somewhat the same windswept clarity as in the dream, that last evening with Max, when we sat drinking lemonade before dinner and she had talked about her baby again. Her little girl had been born in the same month that I had, and just the day before, though a lot of years earlier. Max's voice as she said this was cool and calm, with the barest hint of sadness. Birds were chirping sleepily in the oaks, and the rolling of the breakers was hushed. The air was heavy with humidity, and heat lightning flickered around us. But Max seemed relaxed, and the pain lines which were permanently etched in her forehead seemed less deep than usual, and her grey eyes were not shadowed.

She put her hand gently over mine as she said that sometimes when one gives something up completely, as she'd given up the thought of ever having another child, then God gives one another chance, and God had done that for her, in me.

And she said that, said God.

So that was what the dream was about, I thought, and perhaps it had come to me because I went to sleep with the sound of the sea in my ears. But why was I holding the baby?

'Dreams are messages,' Max said. 'But don't get faddy about them. Take them seriously, but not earnestly. It can be a form of self-indulgence if you overdo it.' Nettie came and refilled our glasses. I think Nettie was always delighted when Ursula was away, but Nettie also loved Max, and knew that Max needed Ursula.

When Nettie had withdrawn to the kitchen quarters, Max said, 'Don't be sorry for me, Polly. I've had a good life. I'm not a great painter, but I'm a good one, and I've had more than my fair share of success. I have few regrets. Not many people can say that.' We were silent for a while, listening to the evening sounds around us. A tiny lizard skittered up the screen. Summer insects were making their double-bass rumblings. 'There isn't anything that happens that can't teach us something,' she said, 'that can't be turned into something positive. One can't undo what's been done, but one can use it creatively.' She looked at me and her eyes were sea-silver. 'I'm glad I had the experience of having a baby. I wouldn't undo it, have it not have happened. The only thing is to accept, and let the scar heal. Scar tissue is the strongest tissue in the body. Did you know that?'

'No.'

'So I shouldn't be surprised if it's the strongest part of the soul.'

Perhaps, when the ice thawed, the scars on my soul would heal.

But had Max's? Once again I thought of the portrait

of her father, of the smile on his face which gave me chills. Did healed scars ever break open again? Get adhesions? Could one get adhesions on the soul?

I fastened the second sandal strap and went to join Sandy and Rhea on their balcony, where wind from the sea blew the white tablecloth so that it flapped like a sail.

The theatre in Epidaurus was impressive all right, great stone seats built into the mountain. It must have seated tens of thousands. Rhea and I climbed to the top row to test the acoustics, and Sandy stood in the center of the stage and recited "The Walrus and the Carpenter." We'd thought we were the only people there, till a group of kids rose up from the seats and began applauding. They drifted off, and Rhea and I climbed down and took the stage. She recited a passage from *Antigone*, in Greek, which made me shiver. I didn't understand more than a few words, but the Greek rolled out in glorious syllables.

"Your turn, Polly," she said.

Uncle Sandy called down, "Do one of your speeches from *As You Like It*."

"Oh, do," Rhea urged. "We were so sorry we couldn't be there for the performance. Only one performance for all that work!"

"It was worth it," I said. "Okay, here goes." I stepped to the exact center of the stage, where the acoustics were supposed to be perfect. I chose a speech early in the play, where Rosalind is about to be banished by Celia's father, who was just about as nasty as Max's father. But Celia stands up to him, defending Rosalind. She reminds

him that after he had taken the dukedom and banished
Rosalind's father

> *I did not then entreat to have her stay;*
> *It was your pleasure and your own remorse.*
> *I was too young that time to value her;*
> *But now I know her: if she be a traitor,*
> *Why so am I; we still have slept together;*
> *And wheresoe'er we went, like Juno's swans,*
> *Still we went coupled and inseparable.*

Sandy and Rhea applauded, and Rhea said, "That was
superb, Polly. If I'm ever in need of a defender, I'll take
you."

Sandy said, "The Elizabethans understood friendship.
This pusillanimous age seems afraid of it. You can have
sex with someone without commitment, but not friendship. You were excellent, Pol. Have you thought of acting
as a career?"

"I've thought of it. Max says I read aloud well, but I
doubt if I'd have a dream of making it on Broadway. Or
even at the Dock Street."

"You made friendship real again. Did any of the kids
misinterpret?"

"Of course. The Mulletville girls. Miss Zeloski talked
about affluence going along with intellectual depriva-
tion. I think she was pretty upset that it was the kids
with affluent backgrounds who made the nastiest cracks."
I did not add that the cracks were particularly nasty
because of Max, though they never actually mentioned
her name.

"In a world where pleasure rules, people tend to be
underdeveloped in every other way. Your Miss Zeloski
sounds like a good teacher."

"She is," I said, "though it took me a while to realize it."

"Let's go on to the sacred precincts," Sandy suggested. "There's a lesson in compassion."

"It's a sort of B.C. Lourdes," Rhea explained, "dedicated to the god Aesculapius."

"I gave Polly a book about it." Sandy galloped down the high marble stairs as agilely as Xan.

When we got to the sacred precincts, we stopped talking. We saw dormitories for sick people, saw the special baths in which they were given healing waters. In the museum we saw ancient surgical instruments, and Sandy remarked that some of them were like those in Dennys's office.

When we left the museum he said, "They knew a lot about psychology, those old Greeks. One of their medicines for healing was comedy. The patients sat just where we were, and on the stage the best actors of the day played comedies—Euripides, and other less well known playwrights. They were exceedingly bawdy—Shakespeare would have been right at home—and exceedingly funny, and laughter does have healing qualities."

"Miss Zeloski said that Shakespeare was bawdy, but never dirty."

"True." Rhea nodded. "The Greeks were way ahead of the present world in many ways. I'm proud of my ancestry." I thought I saw Sandy give her a look, a signal. She went on, "I'm rather tired and I think I'll just sit and rest for half an hour. Then it'll be time for lunch. You two go on."

"You all right?" Sandy sounded concerned, so maybe it wasn't a signal after all.

"I take longer to get over jet lag than you do. I'm fine, and I'll be famished for lunch."

"Okay, Pol?" Sandy asked.

"Sure." We wandered along the path together. I was glad there weren't many other tourists that morning, because the ancient stones, even the air we breathed, filled me with awe.

We stood near the site of the snake pit. "You read the book on Epidaurus I gave you?" Sandy asked.

"I finished it last night."

"A patient couldn't get through the outer gates until all bitterness and self-pity and anger were gone. The belief was that healing wasn't possible until the spirit was cleansed. I think you're better, Polly, but not all the way. Am I right?"

I nodded.

"What are you holding on to? What can't you let go?"

I turned away from him.

He followed me.

"Zachary said I'd put a hard shell around myself."

"That's more perspicacious than I'd given him credit for. Hardness doesn't become you."

"I know."

"I'm not asking you to forget, Polly, because you're never going to forget. What you have to do is remember, with compassion, and forgive."

My voice trembled. "Uncle Sandy, I don't like having a piece of ice stuck in my heart. It hurts!"

"Sit here in the sun," he said, "and let it thaw. I'll be back for you in a few minutes. I'm going to see how Rhea's doing."

He was leaving me for Rhea just as Ursula had left me—

Stop it, Polyhymnia O'Keefe. That's plain self-pity, self-indulgent self-pity. None of that.

I sat where Sandy had left me, on an uncomfortable

stone bench. I closed my eyes, and a vision of the dream from the night before came back to me, unbidden. I was in the boat, protecting the baby, and the seagull flew over us.

And the seagull was Max.

Ursula had called Daddy to tell him she was going to Charleston for one last consultation with Dr. Ormsby, and asked if I could go over to Beau Allaire to stay with Max. Nettie and Ovid roomed over the garage, and it was not a good idea for Max to be completely alone. Ursula would be back as early as possible on Saturday.

'Do you want to go?' Daddy asked me. We were in the lab, and it was September-hot; sometimes it seems September is the hottest month of all. Daddy wore shorts and a white T-shirt. I had on shorts, too, and a halter top, and I'd just scrubbed down the floor and cleaned my tanks.

'Max shouldn't be alone.' I looked at him. I'd talked with him about Max, and he'd treated me as an intelligent adult. I didn't want him to treat me as a child now.

He didn't. 'I've talked with Dr. Netson, and he doesn't expect any radical problem in the immediate future. But this disease is unpredictable, so if Max should show any kind of alarming symptoms, call him at once. Or call Renny. And of course, call me.'

'Okay, but you don't think there will—'

'No, Pol, I don't think so. Your mother and I are very fond of Max and Ursula, and I'm glad we can help, even a little. Max has given you a lot, in self-confidence particularly.'

Daddy was sitting in an old leather chair that was too battered, even, for our house. I perched on the sagging arm. 'Daddy, people are so complicated!'

'That hasn't just occurred to you, has it, Pol?'

'No. But Max and Ursula seem particularly complicated.'

'In a way, they are. But, you know, I prefer their kind of complication to some of the cocktail-partying, wife-swapping, promiscuous lives of some of the people in Cowpertown.'

'And Mulletville.'

'Yes. Many of them are on third or fourth marriages. Love has to be worked at, and that's not popular nowadays.'

'I'm glad you and Mother don't worry about being popular.'

'We do work at our marriage. And it's worth it.'

'And I'm glad you trust me,' I said.

'Over the years, you've proven yourself to be trustworthy.'

'I hope I'll never let you down.'

He pulled me onto his knees. 'You will,' he said gently. 'It's human nature. We all let each other down. I may be putting too much responsibility on you, in allowing you to go over to Beau Allaire to stay with a very ill woman.'

'I want to go.'

'I know you do, and I'm glad you do. Your mother and I have always given you a great deal of responsibility, and you're a very capable young woman. Just remember, call me if there's even the slightest sense of emergency.'

'All right.'

But I didn't get a chance to call.

On Friday I piloted everybody home in the boat, then

packed my overnight bag. Mother was going to drive me
to Beau Allaire because Daddy had some kind of meeting to go to and would need the Land-Rover.

'Just call on Saturday morning when you're ready,
and I'll be over.'

'Urs said she might be able to bring me home.'

'Whichever. Just remember, it's no trouble for me.'

She dropped me outside the house, waited till Ovid
opened the door, waved, and drove off.

Ovid led me through the house and onto the back
verandah. The ceiling fans were whirring, but the air
was oppressive.

Max held out her hands in greeting. 'Heavy electrical
storms forecast, with possible damaging winds. I lost a
great oak in the last storm, and I don't want to lose any
more. Nettie has fixed a cold meal for us and left it in
the fridge. She and Ovid feel the heat, and I told them
to take the evening off. We'll leave the dishes in the
sink and they'll take care of them in the morning.'

We watched Ovid retreating toward the kitchen, a
slight figure in his dark pants and white coat, and cottony
hair. Then I regarded Max and was grateful that the
pain lines were not deep.

Ovid came back in to refill the pitcher of lemonade,
then said good night to us and left. I wondered if he and
Nettie knew how ill Max really was.

She took a long drink and put her glass down. 'Do
you believe in the soul, Polly?' Max never hesitated to
ask cosmic questions out of the blue.

'Yes.' I thought maybe she'd turn her scorn on me,
but she didn't.

'So, what is it, this thing called soul?'

This scarred thing, full of adhesions. 'It's—it's your
you and my *me*.'

'What do you mean by that?'

'It's what makes us *us*, different from anybody else in the world.'

'Like snowflakes? You have seen snow, haven't you—yes, of course you have. All those trillions of snowflakes, each one different from the other?'

'More than snowflakes. The soul isn't—ephemeral.'

'A separate entity from the body?'

I shook my head. 'I think it's part. It's the part that—well, in your painting of the harbor at Rio, it's the part which made you know what paint to use, which brush, how to make it alive.'

Max looked at the silver pitcher, sparkling with drops, as though it were a crystal ball. 'So it's us, at our highest and least self-conscious.'

'That's sort of what I mean.'

'The amazing thing is that one's soul, or whatever one calls it, is strongest when one is least aware. That's when the soul is most aware. We get in our own way, and that diminishes our souls.' She pushed up from her chair and headed toward the table, which was already set with silver and china. 'Be an angel and bring the food out to the verandah.'

We ate comfortably together. Max had a book with her and began leafing through it, looking for something. 'There's a passage our conversation reminds me of . . .'

'What?'

'In the Upanishads—a series of Sanskrit works which are part of the Veda. Here it is, Pol, listen: *In this body, in this town of Spirit, there is a little house shaped like a lotus, and in that house there is a little space. There is as much in that little space within the heart as there is in the whole world outside.* Maybe that little space is the reality of your *you* and my *me*?'

'Could I copy that?' I asked.

'Of course. I've been watching that little space within your heart enlarging all year as more and more ideas are absorbed into it. Some people close their doors and lock them so that nothing can come in, and the space cannot hold anything as long as the heart clutches in self-protection or lust or greed. But if we're not afraid, that little space can be so large that one could put a whole universe in it and still have room for more.' She stopped and her hand went up and pressed against her chest, and I could see pain dimming the silver in her eyes.

'Get me some whiskey. Quickly.'

I ran into the house and into the dining room, turning on the lights. The Waterford chandelier sparkled into bloom. I hurried to the sideboard and got the decanter of bourbon, with its silver label, turned out the light, ran back to the verandah, and poured Max a good tot.

She drank it in a gulp, so quickly that she almost choked, then sighed and put the glass down. 'It works, and quickly. I'm sorry, Pol, I don't like you to see me in pain.'

I reached across the glass top of the table and put my hand on hers. It was hot and dry. Mine was cold.

'Don't be afraid, little one. I'm all right. These episodes are bad, but they don't last.' She reached for the decanter and poured herself some more.

'You're sure I shouldn't call—'

'Polly. I'm all right. There's nothing anyone can do. Don't fret. The pain's much better.'

I took our plates out to the kitchen, rinsed them, and left them in the sink for Nettie and Ovid. I thought that maybe I should try to call Daddy, and then decided that it would make her angry. When I got back to the verandah, dark was falling. The long evenings of summer were behind us. Night was closing in early, though the shadows of evening still held the humid heat of the day.

Max was leaning back in her chair, and there was just enough light for me to see that the look of pain had eased. She took a sip of bourbon and put her glass down. 'It leaves me tired,' she said. 'Let's sit here for a while and watch the stars.'

I sat across from her, glancing at the unlit candles in their hurricane globes. 'Do you want any light?'

'No. Even candle flame adds to the heat. Look, there's a star.'

The wind was rising, but it was not a cooling wind. The gentle whirring of the paddle fan, the slow rolling of the waves across the sand, the chirring of locusts, were hot, summer sounds. A seagull screamed.

'Another star,' Max said. 'All the galaxies, the billions of galaxies—the possibility of billions of island universes —floating like bubbles in a great spacious sea—'

'There's the Big Dipper,' I said, relaxing a little.

'The Great Bear,' Max said. 'I talk about the unimportance of size, the microcosm as immense as the macrocosm—but then I think of Beau Allaire sitting on a small island on an insignificant planet—how can God keep track of it all? Do you think God really does count the hairs of our heads?'

'Yes.'

'Why?'

'I don't know why. It's just what I think.'

'At least you don't give me glib answers. If human beings can program computers to count astronomical figures, why should God do less? If there isn't a God who cares about our living and dying, then it's all an echoing joke. I don't want my life to be a bad joke, so I have to believe that God does care. That there is a someone who began everything, and who loves and cares.' She shivered. 'Funny, how intense heat can make one break out in gooseflesh, just like cold. Let's go up to my room. It's cooler there. Why don't you get ready for bed, and I will, too.'

We paused on the landing, as always, to look at the statue of the Laughing Christ. The light touched the joyous face, and there was compassion in the eyes.

While I was changing in the green guest room, thunder began to rumble in the distance. The air was so thick with humidity you could squeeze it. The sky flickered faintly with electricity.

Max's nightgown was ivory satin, so lovely it could have been worn as an evening dress. She sat on the white rug, her hands about her knees. A Chinese screen was in front of the fireplace, gold background with flowers and herons painted on it.

'You've grown over the summer,' Max said. 'You're going to be tall.'

My old seersucker nightgown was too short. 'Not too tall, I hope.'

'You come from a tall family, and you carry it well. Don't ever slump. That just makes one look taller. Hold your head high, like royalty.'

The light from one of the lamps glinted off the decanter of bourbon and onto Max's glass, half full of amber liquid. I hoped that she knew how much she should drink. Then I noticed a bottle of champagne. 'I really don't need anything,' I said awkwardly. 'There's more lemonade if I get thirsty.'

'I've already uncorked the champagne,' Max said. 'Hold out your glass.'

I picked up the tall fluted glass which was on the hearth in front of the Chinese screen, held it out, and she poured. I thought her hand was a little unsteady, and I was concerned.

Why should I worry about that decanter of bourbon, or that maybe Max was drinking too much? If she was dying and it eased the pain, what difference did it make?

But it did. It did make a difference. This was not the Max I knew, the Max who made me believe there were wide worlds open for Polyhymnia O'Keefe.

Thunder again. Low. Menacing.

'To you,' Max said, her voice slurring. 'To all that you can be.' Some of her whiskey spilled on the rug.

I wanted to throw it at the Chinese screen. This could not be Max, this woman with her hand clutching the decanter of bourbon.

She poured herself more. Her eyes were too bright, her cheeks too flushed.

Lightning flashed again, brightening the flowers on the screen. 'That's too close,' Max said as the thunder rose. We could hear the wind whipping the trees. 'I'm afraid, oh, little one, I'm so afraid . . .'

Not of the thunderstorm.

'Afraid of the dark. Afraid of nothingness. Of being alone. Of not being.'

This was naked, primordial fear. I wanted to call Daddy, but what would I say? Max is drinking too much and she's afraid of dying?

Lightning again, but this time there were several seconds before the thunder. 'Are you afraid?' Max whispered.

'No. I don't mind thunderstorms as long as I'm not alone.'

A slow wave of thunder rolled over her response. 'I need an affir'—her words slurred—'an affirmation. An affirmation of being.' She picked up her glass. I glanced at the decanter and saw that it was half empty.

Oh, Max, I wailed silently, I wish you wouldn't.

She bent toward me, whispering, 'Oh, my little Polly, it's all so short—no more than the blink of an eye. Why are you afraid of Max? Why?'

Her breath was heavy with whiskey. Her words were thick. I was afraid. I didn't know what to do, how to stop her. How to make her be Max again.

In the next flash of lightning she stood up, and in the long satin gown she seemed seven feet tall, and she was swaying, so drunk she couldn't walk. And then she fell . . .

I rolled out of the way. She reached for me, and she was sobbing.

I scrambled to my feet. Ran. I heard her coming after me. I turned at the landing, rushed down the stairs, heard her unsteady feet, then a crash, and turned to see that she had knocked over the statue.

I ran on, panting, past the dining room, slipped in my bare feet on the polished floor, and almost fell. I reached out to steady myself, and my hand hit the light switch, and the crystal chandelier bloomed with light, and the light touched the smile on the face of the portrait of Max's father.

'Pa!' she screamed out, staggering toward me, carrying the statue. 'Damn you! Damn you! I'm just like you, damn you!'

I pushed open the heavy front door and burst out into the pelting rain.

I ran up the long drive, hardly realizing I had on only my nightgown. The crushed shells hurt my feet but did not slow me down. My nightgown was drenched and clung to my body. I felt a sharp pain in my foot. Rain streamed from my hair and into my eyes, so that the headlights of an approaching car were nearly on me before I saw them, and heard the shells crunching under the tires, and veered to the side of the road.

Brakes were slammed on. The car stopped. A window was opened and someone looked out. 'Polly!'

It was Ursula.

'Something told me—' She flung open the door. 'Get in, child.'

Ursula would take care of everything.

I stumbled into the car.

'Child, what happened?'

'Max is drunk—oh, Urs, she's—drunk—and I got away from her and ran. She . . . she ran after me, she knocked over the statue of the Laughing . . . and the light came on and hit the portrait of her father, and . . .' I babbled on, hardly knowing what I was saying.

'Oh, Max,' Ursula said. 'Oh, Max.' She started the car again and drove up to the house. 'Wait here, child.' She ran indoors. I heard her calling, 'Max! Max, dear, it's Urs. Where are you?' And the door slammed on her words.

Two

I n the morning, before time to take me to the airport for my plane to Cyprus, Sandy came into my room. Once again he suggested that I might want to call the United States. "Phoning anywhere from Cyprus isn't easy." He didn't say, 'Do you want to call the family?' or 'Do you want to call Max?' and I think he was leaving all options open.

I just said, "No, thanks." And then, because I felt that I was being ungrateful and ungracious, I said, "I think it's time I cut the umbilical cord."

"From your family?" he asked. "Or from Max?"

I fumbled in my suitcase, refolding a blouse.

"I should have realized," Sandy said, "how young and vulnerable you are. You're so mature in some ways it's easy to forget how inexperienced you are in human relationships. You idolized Max, and that is always the prelude to disaster."

—I speak five languages, I thought irrelevantly, and it doesn't make any difference at all.

He put his hand over mine. "The toppling of your

goddess was nothing I could have conceived of, and I do not in any way condone what happened. But it was an aberration, a terrible one, and it was nothing that had anything to do with the Max I have known for twenty years."

I shut the suitcase, clicking the latches.

"Do you know, Polly, can you guess, what it must have cost Max to call me, to tell me what happened, what she did? The fact that she could do that tells me just how much she loves you, not in any erotic way, but as her child."

I heard, and I didn't hear. I rolled up the cardigan, the Fair Isle cardigan I'd brought in case it turned chilly, and put it in the shoulder bag.

"Your parents do not know what happened, because you didn't tell them, and that speaks well."

For me? For my parents? For Max?

"I think you will be able to forgive what happened, Polly. I'm not sure they would be able to. And they would blame themselves."

"They didn't have anything to do with it."

"I know that. But your parents wouldn't." He paused, looking at me. "Ursula says that Max has stopped drinking entirely, except for what Urs gives her for pain, and she doesn't want that but Netson has ordered it. I realize that nothing can take back what happened, what Max did. But would you want never to have known her?"

"I don't know."

"Perhaps where I hold Max most at fault is in letting you worship her. But you are a contained person, Polly, and I doubt if Max realized the extent of your adoration. Maybe you didn't, either."

I nodded, mutely.

"You're all right, Polly." He rubbed his hand over his beard. "Nearly ready?"

"Yes. Thank you, Sandy. I've loved these days with you and Rhea. Thank you."

"No thanks needed. You are very dear to us." He pulled me to him, kissed my hair. "Have you been keeping that journal for school?"

"Every day. I try to describe things, not only the ancient sites, but little things, like the men with braziers standing on the street corners in Athens selling roasted corn. That surprised me. I think of corn as being only American."

"We bring our worlds with us when we travel, we Americans." He gave me his rough, Uncle Sandy hug. "You bring the scent of ocean and camellias."

"That's nice. Thank you."

"And that young man, Zachary, who seems so taken with you, brings the smell of money and power. To the Zacharies of this world, Turkey, Pakistan, Kuwait are interchangeable. They exist only for their banks and insurance companies and megabucks. When money is your only concern, there isn't any difference between Zaire and Chicago."

"Hey," I protested, "you and Rhea don't even know Zachary. He's just like all the other kids who hang around Constitution Square."

"With his father's corporation behind him? Don't be naïve, Polly. I'm glad you had him to escort you around till we got here. I think he was good for you in many ways, but I'm just as glad you're never going to see him again."

"Wait a minute!" I said. "You saw him just that once. I spent three days with him. He's my friend." But

I remembered, too, Zachary's saying that even if he expected the world to end he'd hold on to his property. "He's complicated. Sure, he has lots of money, but there's more to him than that."

"You're willing to let Zachary Gray be complicated?"

"Of course."

"But not Max?" Sandy looked at me, a long, slow look from under those bushy blond eyebrows. I turned away from him and picked up my suitcase.

I kissed Rhea goodbye, and Sandy drove me to the airport. I was very glad he was with me. I didn't know about the airport tax of sixty drachmas, and I'd deliberately used up all my drachmas because in Cyprus I'd be using Cypriot pounds. Sandy paid the tax and then helped me get a traveler's check cashed into Cypriot money.

"Have a good time in Cyprus. Don't work too hard. Have fun."

I waved after him, and then there was a great shoving getting on the bus that whizzed across the airfield to the plane; then everybody jostled to get off, and then pushed to get up the steps to the plane—no jetway for the small plane to Larnaca. There was no attempt at queuing, and lots of people simply jammed their way into the line. A small amount of consideration was given to very old women and those with infants.

Finally I got onto the plane and into my seat, next to two Greek women. The hostess gave us landing cards to fill out, and the two women told me, with a lot of signs, that they did not know how to fill out their cards. So I did it for them. I had to put down their ages, and I was astonished to find out they were a great deal younger than they looked. The older, one of the grandmothers people made way for, was exactly Mother's age. With white hair pulled into a knot on top of her head, and wrinkles around her eyes and mouth, she looked old enough to be Mother's mother. Mother's hair is still chestnut brown, and she swims a lot, and her body is strong and supple. It was a vivid contrast.

In filling out their landing cards, I learned that they lived in England and were coming home to Cyprus for a visit. They spoke only a few words of English, and they did not know how to read or write. They beamed and nodded their thanks, and then began talking together in Greek as I filled out my own landing card.

Larnaca was a comparatively small, quiet airport, though no Greek-speaking public place is really quiet. So I was grateful indeed to see a man who looked like Nehru waiting for me. He introduced himself, told me to call him Krhis, took my suitcase, and led me to a battered old Bentley. At home it would have been snobbishly chic. Here, it was just functional.

"I'm glad your plane was a few minutes late," Krhis said. "I had a flat tire on my way in. This old wagon's not going to hold up forever. It's good to have you with us, Polly. The rest of the staff is already at the Center. Virginia Porcher and I have been here for a week, both resting and planning. And now we will all—the staff— have three days together before the delegates arrive. Did you lunch on the plane?"

"Yes. Thanks."

"Was it edible?"

"More than. There was something I thought was turkey which turned out to be smoked fish and it was really good."

He turned slightly and smiled at me. "You do not mind, then, eating the foods of the country you are in?"

I smiled back. "Not all Americans insist on hamburgers."

"Yes. Maxa told me you were a cosmopolitan young woman. Dear Maxa. How is she?"

I had a moment to think while he maneuvered the car around a donkey cart. If Max had not told Krhis anything was wrong, obviously she didn't want him to know. I said, carefully, "She hasn't been very well this winter. That's why she's been staying at Beau Allaire."

With a loud honking, a smelly bus provided another diversion as it forced Krhis over to the side of the road and roared past. He said, "Maxa tells me you have a gift for languages."

"Oh, I love languages." Now I could be freely enthusiastic. "I speak Portuguese, because we used to live in Portugal, and I speak Spanish and French and a bit of German, and Gaean, which probably won't be much use to you, but it was the language of the natives on the island off the south coast of Portugal where Daddy had his lab."

Again the slight turn, the gentle smile. "But Portuguese and Spanish will be helpful. We'll have a delegate from Angola, where many people still speak Portuguese. And another from Brazil. And two or three are from the Spanish-speaking countries of South America. However, all the delegates must have some facility with English, as it will be our common language."

He drove down a dusty road lined with tired-looking trees. It was as hot as Cowpertown in midsummer. Krhis said, "We won't see much of Larnaca today. It's on a salt lake as well as the ocean, and suffers from having the new superimposed on the old without much thought. Luxury hotels are sprouting like mushrooms."

What I saw of Larnaca looked rather barren. There were a few expensive-looking villas, a big oil refinery, and then we drove through several sizable villages, with low white houses surrounded by flowers and surmounted by dark panels for solar heating. We passed several working windmills, too. An island like Cyprus has both sun and wind, and the villages were making good use of them.

"You are the oldest of several children?" Krhis asked.

"Seven," I said. "We're old-fashioned and unfashionable."

"And you help?"

"We all do."

"But, as Max pointed out, the oldest bears the brunt of the work. She is very fond of you." He paused. "It is too bad she was not able to have children of her own."

I looked down at my hands, still summer-tan. "Yes. She— she—" Did he know about the lost little baby? "She wanted children."

"And now she has you. That is good. I had hoped she might be able to come with you. She would love Osia Theola—and our varied and various delegates. She has a great gift with people, does she not?"

I murmured agreement.

"With Max there are no barriers of race or culture. Or age. You are her friend as well as her child."

I did not reply, but leaned back against the seat and closed my eyes.

The humid heat and the rhythm of the car eased my thoughts, and I was dozing when Krhis said, "We are here." I opened my eyes as we drove through gates of golden stone, and we were at the Conference Center.

It was much bigger than Osias Lukas, not nestled in a cup in the hill, but perched on the side of the mountain. We entered a great, dusty courtyard surrounded by a cloister. There was a two-story building, a tallish rectangle forming part of the wall to our right, with arched doors and windows with eyebrow-like carvings over them. Krhis drew up in front of it.

"Now that the village is becoming a resort, the monastery grounds are not as quiet as they used to be. Tourists come to see the church and the fountain house and tend to wander all over."

I sat up and looked around at the gracious arches of the cloister, with glimmers of sun on sea sparkling in the distance.

Krhis continued, "It is a delight to us that the village church is within the monastery grounds—see, just ahead of us, the tall bell tower? You will see weddings and funerals and baptisms. The village is still small enough so that its life goes on, as it has done for centuries, and we who come here for conferences are, as it were, tourist attractions for the villagers. We'll be a strange group, but Osia Theolians are friendly and welcoming. Ah, here comes Norine." His face lit up.

A young Chinese woman, tiny and delicate, came hurrying to greet us, shook my hand with a firm grip, insisted on getting my suitcase out of the trunk while I stood awkwardly by, towering over her.

"Norine Fong Mar, Polly O'Keefe," Krhis introduced us. "Norine is one of my colleagues in London and is associate director of this conference."

"I am from Hong Kong," Norine said, "but lately I've spent more time in England than at home. Follow me." She set off at a rapid pace.

I hoisted the shoulder bag and followed her across the

dusty compound, almost having to run to keep up, despite my much longer legs. We went past the church and then veered to our left, to the center of the grounds, where there was a small octagonal stone building with open, arched sides and a domed roof.

"The fountain house," Norine said. "Very old. The only new building in the Center is the Guest House, and it is in the old style and doesn't stick out like a sore thumb." We went along a narrow path with roses blooming on either side, and the air smelled of roses and salt wind. The only roses on Benne Seed Island were at Beau Allaire, and grew there because the gardener was constantly watering and tending them.

Norine headed for a long, white building with a red-tiled roof, the blinding white of the stucco walls muted by flowering vines. Bougainvillea I recognized, and oleander; but the other flowers were new to me. It was much hotter on Cyprus than it had been in Greece, and I could feel sweat trickling down my legs. I'm used to heat; even so, it was *hot*.

Norine beckoned me imperiously, and I hurried to catch up. She opened a door leading to a long corridor. Over her shoulder she said, "Your roommate is from Zimbabwe. She's the youngest of the women delegates, and we thought you'd enjoy each other. But you'll have the room to yourself for these next few days." She spoke with a crisp English accent, more fluently than Krhis, whose words came slowly, thoughtfully. She was dressed in a denim skirt and white shirt and exuded efficiency.

She opened the next-to-last door on the left, which led into a pleasant room with twin beds, two desks with shelves for books, and two narrow chests of drawers. It was what I imagined a college dorm would be like, except for the dim bars of light on the floor, filtering through the closed shutters, which spoke of the tropics.

Norine heaved my bag onto one of the beds, then opened the shutters. The windows were already wide open, and I followed her onto a balcony which looked across terraced gardens to the Mediterranean Sea. It was different from Greece, but equally glorious.

"You like it?"

"It's absolutely lovely!"

She beamed at me, then glanced into the room. "See, you have been sent coals to Newcastle."

Not understanding, I looked into the room and saw a vase of hothouse flowers on the desk by the window. A small white envelope was clipped to one of the stems. I opened it and pulled out a card, and read: JUST SO YOU WON'T FORGET ME. ZACHARY.

I could feel myself blushing. Nobody had ever sent me flowers before; the ones at the King George had come from the management and didn't count. I put my face down to sniff them to hide my hot cheeks.

Norine laughed. "It seems that someone likes you. I may call you Polyhymnia? You will call me Norine?"

"I'd love to call you Norine, but call me Polly, please, Polly with two *l*'s."

"But Polyhymnia is a Greek name and she was one of the Muses—"

"I know, but plain Polly takes a lot less explaining."

"As you like." She sounded disappointed. "Since you are here first, you will have the choice of bed, desk, chest. You would like the window side?"

It was hardly a question. Fortunately, I *would* like the window side. "Thank you."

She looked down at the beds, which were unmade, showing mattresses with grey-and-white ticking. A bed pad, sheets, pillowcase, towel, facecloth, were in a neat pile in the center of each bed. "It will be very helpful,

Polly, if you will make the beds. Most of the delegates will have been traveling for many hours and will be very tired."

I can't say that making beds is my favorite job in the world, but I'm certainly used to it. I've done it often enough at home, particularly before the little kids were old enough to do their own. "Of course, I'll be glad to," I said.

Norine handed me a key on a leather thong. "This is the master key. We keep the rooms locked, because sometimes the tourists come snooping around, not realizing that this is a dormitory. They are not dangerous, only a nuisance, particularly those who go in for topless bathing. It upsets the villagers." I nodded. "If you are tired, don't try to make all the beds this afternoon. Just a few. You can finish tomorrow, or the next day. We are sorry it is so unseasonably hot. This heat wave began today. We hope it will break before the delegates arrive." She pulled open a desk drawer, and there was a box of matches and a mosquito coil. Norine started to explain, but I told her that I knew all about mosquito coils. Even with screens everywhere, the little kids are constantly running in and out, so we have to use mosquito coils a lot.

"Okeydokey, that is good. You can help me explain them to the delegates. This heat has brought the insects out, the night ones especially. Even with the coil, you will have to pull the shutters to at night." She snapped on a fan that was on the inner desk. "It helps a little. When you are in your room, you can leave the door open for cross-drafts. Now I go for my siesta. The staff will have a meeting at five o'clock this afternoon, before the evening meal. I will come for you to show you the way."

"Thank you."

As briskly as she had come in, she left, and I could hear her clip-clopping along the tile floor of the long corridor.

I moved back to the desk with the bouquet of flowers from a florist. Even if Norine was right, and sending flowers to a flower-filled place like Osia Theola was coals to Newcastle, I was thrilled with them. I checked to see that they had enough water, and moved the vase so that they would not get the direct heat of the sun. Then I looked around the room. There was an open closet near the entrance, and on the shelf above it were grey wool blankets. I doubted that we'd need them, unless the weather changed radically. There were four wire hangers on the rod, and I was glad Max had told me to bring hangers of my own. 'You'll have plenty at the King George, but not in Osia Theola unless I'm very much mistaken.'

The sun was streaming into the room from the balcony, which ran the length of the building, with high, stucco dividers between each room for privacy. There were two folding canvas chairs leaning against the wall, and I opened one and stretched out. I looked appreciatively at the view, across terraces planted with vegetables and vines, and windmills turning in the breeze; and then my gaze traveled on to the sparkling of the sea below. It was too hot to stay out in the sun for long, so I went back into the room, sniffed the fragrance of Zachary's flowers, and then unpacked, putting my notebook on the desk nearest the window; my books on the shelf; my underclothes in one of the chests of drawers; hanging my clothes in my half of the closet, leaving the four wire hangers for my roommate from Zimbabwe.

Once I was completely unpacked, I made up the two beds in my room. Then I took the master key and went into the hall, and opened the door of the room next to mine. It was stiflingly hot. I opened the windows while I made the beds. By the time I had done that room, and two others down the hall, I was dripping with sweat. I decided that in this heat four rooms, eight beds, were enough for a while. I felt suddenly very lonely, and at the same time I was grateful that I was going to have these first few days in the room by myself. I've never had a roommate. Mother says there are so many of us it's important that we each have our own room, even if it's no more than a cubicle.

I opened my notebook and started to describe the room and the view, to paint in words the Conference Center of sun-gilded stone and ancient buildings. Since the notebook was for school, I didn't mention Zachary's flowers.

I wrote about Krhis, Kumar Krhishna Ghose, with his gentle tan face with the long lines moving down from his eyes, and the smile that belied the sadness. Why wouldn't he be sad? seeing his family shot and killed. He hadn't pushed me to talk on the drive from Larnaca, and the silences between us had been good silences.

I described Norine Fong Mar, from Hong Kong, tiny and bossy. Krhis wasn't bossy at all, so perhaps he needed an assistant who was. Krhis was quiet; there was no static. Norine had considerable static. She was not calm inside, like Krhis. I wasn't, either.

Miss Zeloski, I thought, was going to enjoy my notebook. And if it hadn't been for Max, Miss Zeloski and I would never have become friends.

I shut the notebook. I was as hot as though I were at home. My fingers were making smudges on the paper. I went back to the balcony. There were no screens, just the long windows and the wooden shutters. I pulled the deck chair into the shade of the divider and stretched out. The light breeze from the sea, and the moving air from the fan in the room, met and blew across me. I slid into sleep.

The breeze from the Mediterranean blew over me, blew through the window of the car in which I was sitting. No. Not the Mediterranean breeze, but a stronger wind from the Atlantic, spattering me with raindrops as I sat huddled in Ursula Heschel's car, parked outside Beau Allaire. I sat there in the humid hothouse of the car and waited. What else could I do? It was still pouring, although the electrical storm had passed over. I couldn't walk very far—I noticed blood and saw that I'd cut my foot on a broken shell, a deep, ragged gash. All I had on was a too-small, very wet nightgown.

I felt tired as though I had been running for hours. A wave of sleep washed over me, and I gave in to it, as into death.

Ursula woke me. 'Polly. Child. You'd better come in.'
I didn't want to wake up.
'Polly. Come.'
'I want to go home.'
'No,' Ursula said.
'Please. I want to go home.'
'I can't take you this way. Your nightgown is soaked. Your parents are expecting you to spend the night here.'
'No.'
'Polly, child, I know that you are shocked and horrified by what happened. I am, too.'

I couldn't hear Ursula's shock, or any but my own. 'Please take me home.'

Ursula got in the driver's side of the car and sat beside me but did not touch me. 'Child, I'm sorrier than I can say for what Max—'

A funny little mewling noise came out of me, but no words.

'Poor child. Poor little one.' Ursula lifted one hand as though to pet me, then drew back. 'It wasn't Max doing any of—of what she did. It was pain and alcohol and fear . . .' I didn't answer, and there was a long silence. Finally Ursula spoke in a low voice. 'Max, unlike the true alcoholic, will not sleep it off and forget what happened. She will remember everything. I wish she *could* forget. I wish you could.'

I looked at her.

'Come.' Ursula spoke with her authoritarian doctor's voice.

I followed her in. I didn't see Max.

'What's wrong with your foot?'

I looked down, and there was blood on the soft green of the Chinese rug. 'I cut it, on a shell, I think.'

Ursula took me into the kitchen, washed my foot, and bandaged it. Warmed some milk. I took a sip and nearly threw up.

'I'm going to give you a mild sedative,' she said.

'No—Daddy—'

'I agree with your father. I do not use a sedative unless I consider it absolutely necessary. You *must* get some sleep.'

I don't remember how we got from the kitchen to the green guest room. It was as though fog had rolled in from the ocean and obliterated everything.

'I've brought you a nightgown,' Ursula said, and

helped me into it, much simpler than Max's satin one, but more elegant than my old seersucker.

Did she kiss me good night? I don't think she touched me. The sedative must have been working. Everything was blurred. I thought I heard someone crying, but I wasn't sure whether the sound came from me or from Max.

I closed my eyes.

Saw Max running after me with the Laughing Christ cradled like a baby in her arms, saw the statue fall, crashing, down an endless flight of stairs—

My scream woke me.

A woman came hurrying toward me from the path which ran just below the balconies. "Hoy! What's wrong?"

I looked at her in confusion as she jumped up onto the balcony. "I think I had a nightmare."

"This heat is enough to give you one. You're Polly O'Keefe, aren't you? I'm Virginia Porcher." She pronounced it the French way, Por-shay.

"Oh—Mrs. Porcher—I love your writing—"

"Not Mrs. Porcher. Virginia. Or Vee, as most people call me. We're all on a first-name basis here. You'll understand why when you hear the last names of some of the delegates—they make me understand why most people pronounce my last name as though it were the back porch. Simplify, simplify. And I understand you prefer being called Polly to Polyhymnia?"

I smiled at her. "Wouldn't you?"

"I think you could probably carry Polyhymnia, but

I sympathize. Polly. Krhis tells me you'll be helping me with the writing workshop, among your many other chores."

"Yes, anything I can do to help, anything at all."

"I expect there'll be a good deal. I hope this heat breaks. It's not at all seasonable. It's usually pleasantly warm during the day, and cool at night, by late September. Weather all over the world seems to be changing drastically. Why don't you come along to my room? Since I'm a workshop leader, I have the privilege of a room to myself. Krhis will have a folder for you at the staff meeting, but I thought you might like a preview of the schedule." She was chatting away, giving me time to wake up, to move out of the horror of the nightmare.

Virginia Bowen Porcher, one of my favorite writers, who wrote novels about people who were flawed but with whom you could identify, dealing with all aspects of the human being, the dark as well as the light, but never leaving you in a pit of despair. And in the simplest possible words and images she wrote poems which seemed almost light on the surface, and then, when you backed away from them, the fact that they were neither light nor simple kicked you in the teeth. Max compared Porcher's work to Mozart. When I told Miss Zeloski that Virginia Porcher was leading a workshop, that in itself was enough to get Miss Zeloski to urge the principal to let me take the month away from school.

And here Virginia Porcher was asking me to call her by her first name, and looking—well! Now that I had recovered enough from the nightmare to look at her, I saw that she had red hair. Not blatantly red like mine; it was much more subtle. But still, it was red. She had green eyes, really green, as my eyes are really blue. She wore a full cotton skirt with a tiny millefiori print, and a peasant blouse.

Meeting one of your favorite writers in the world can be scary. It's so easy to be let down. But I felt elated. I liked her, liked her as well as admired her. And she had red hair.

Her room was almost identical to mine. One of the twin beds was covered with books and papers. "My filing system." She picked up a blue folder, opened it, and handed it to me, and I looked at the typed schedule. Three workshops in the morning, with an hour before lunch for swimming. An hour for lunch, an hour for rest, and three more workshops in the afternoon. The evening meal. An evening program. A full schedule, indeed. The writing workshop was the first one of the day, at nine in the morning.

"This weather knocks out swimming at noon." Virginia Porcher sat on her bed, indicating the desk chair for me. "It's a twenty-minute walk to the sea, and it's much too hot under the broiling noonday sun. I've been taking my swim at bedtime, but Krhis won't be able to come with me now that the staff is all here. He'll have his hands full. This is a glorious place for a conference, isn't it?"

I nodded, looking around the room. On one of the desks was a picture of a man with dark hair and a kind, sensitive face. He must be her husband. He looked like the right kind of person to be married to one of my favorite writers.

"My sister-in-law, who's holding the fort at home, asked, 'Why Cyprus?' and I told her it's more or less a mean point geographically for the delegates. But, also, if the conference were being held in—say, Detroit—I wouldn't have accepted the invitation to lead a workshop. Krhis says you've had a week in and around Athens?"

"Yes. The *Iliad* and the *Odyssey*—all the Greek myths —everything means much more to me than it did. I'm overawed."

"That's a good reaction. So am I. No matter how many times I come to Greece or the islands, I'm swept out of the limited world of technocracy and into the wildness of gods and goddesses and centaurs and nymphs. We'll have a full moon this weekend and you'll understand anew why the moon has so often been an object of worship. The moon goddess, beneficent while she is waxing, harsh while she is waning. Astarte fascinates me. She was a Syrian goddess, but her worship spread to Greece. Aphrodite is, I guess, her Greek counterpart, though she isn't as much associated with the moon. So. How is Ursula Heschel?"

That startled me. "Fine, I guess. You know her?"

"I'm one of her more remarkable miracles. I had an aneurism which would have been inoperable before microsurgery, and even with all science now knows, it was a risky business. It was a long surgical procedure, and a very long recovery, and Ursula and I became friends. And then, of course, I met Max. And through Urs and Max I met Krhis Ghose when he was in New York. A conference like this tends to be very small-worldy. You're here because of Max, aren't you?"

"Yes." Beneficent while waxing, harsh while waning.

"How old are you?"

"Nearly seventeen. I'm a slow developer."

Virginia Porcher stretched out long, suntanned legs, wriggling her toes under the sandal straps. "I was, too. Still am. Some people say that we slow developers end up going further than the quick-flowering ones."

I nodded. I hoped she was right.

"Are you interested in writing?"

"I don't think so. I enjoy it, but I'm not passionate about it. I like acting, really a lot, but I know it's an awfully chancy field. What I'm best at is languages, but I don't want to be a teacher, and I don't think I want to be a simultaneous translator at the UN because I'm an island girl."

"Manhattan's an island."

"Oh. I guess I mean small islands with low-density population."

She laughed, a nice, warm laugh, not at all *at* me. "You still have time. Sometimes it's not an advantage to have too many talents." She reached down to scratch a bite on her leg. "Watch out for the bugs here. They're not bad during the day, but they're monstrous at night, and they love American blood."

"I'm pretty used to bugs," I said. "Benne Seed Island's off South Carolina—so I'm used to heat, too."

"You'll find"—she nodded—"when the delegates arrive that you'll be spending these next weeks with people who have experienced a great deal of life under conditions where personal freedom as we know it is hardly even a dream. When I fuss because the bathwater here is tepid, it chastens me when I remember that some of the delegates don't even have indoor plumbing. This dormitory building is going to seem wildly luxurious to most of them." She stood up. "I've got work to do now before we meet at five. By the way, a word of warning."

I paused by the door. "The tap water here is quite saline, and you won't be able to drink much of it. And this heat that clamped down on us today isn't supposed to let up for a while. There's a little shop outside the monastery gates and up the hill where you can buy sodas. And if you have any other questions, trivial or cosmic, don't hesitate to ask me."

"Thanks," I said, still feeling too shy about calling Virginia Bowen Porcher by her first name to call her anything. "Thanks a lot."

I took the master key and made up the beds in three more rooms. Even though I opened the windows, I was still streaming with sweat, so I went back to my room and sat at the desk to record meeting Virginia Bowen Porcher in my journal for Miss Zeloski.

For Miss Zeloski? Max. Even though Max would never read it, the journal was also for Max.

Because of Max's insight into someone she'd never even met, I was able to see Miss Zeloski as someone who hadn't had many breaks in life, someone who'd wanted a family, and children, and instead lived alone. Or, as I found out when Max prodded me, not alone but with an elderly father she supported and cared for. She was intelligent, and she'd probably have been a good college English teacher, but here she was, stuck in Cowpertown because of her father, teaching a lot of kids who weren't particularly interested in all she had to give. I hadn't been, until Max opened my eyes. I'd been as bad as the rest.

Here, in Osia Theola, I was on my own, making up my own mind about the people I was meeting, and learning that making up my own mind, just me, Polly, wasn't even possible. As I tried to describe Virginia Porcher to Miss Zeloski, I was seeing not only through my own eyes but through Max's, and through Miss

Zeloski's. And that was all right, too, because it gave an added dimension to what I was writing.

Left completely to myself, how much would I have noticed beyond the fact that Virginia Porcher had red hair? Would I have seen the kindness with which she drew me out of the nightmare?

But I didn't write about the nightmare, the Laughing Christ falling, falling.

I described the papers on Virginia Porcher's bed, and the small typewriter on the desk, with a pile of manuscripts beside it. I wished I'd dared ask her if she was working on a new novel.

I told Miss Zeloski she probably was, and that what struck me most was how natural she was, not a bit a prima donna, but as simple as her own work. As deceptively simple?

Norine Fong Mar called for me a little before five, as promised. "Okeydokey, time to go." She wore, now, a long yellow cotton print dress with a Chinese collar, the skirt slit, with braid at the sides, and looked far more exotic than when I had first met her.

The meeting was in the golden stone building by the monastery gates. We gathered in a sizable room on the second floor, where Krhis was already sitting by a table, with Virginia Porcher next to him. She smiled at me and patted the chair by hers.

"Vee tells me the two of you had a good talk," Krhis said.

"Yes. She showed me the schedule and helped fill me in." She had done far more than that, but I was em-

barrassed to say, "She was wonderful." Could I let her
be wonderful, and human, too?

"Good." On the table by him was a pile of blue folders,
and Norine handed me one.

"Here you are. One of our delegates is already here,
Omio Heno from Baki. There are only two days a week
when he can fly out, so he will be with us this weekend."

"I'm not sure where Baki is," I said.

Krhis answered, "It's one of those numerous islands
north of Australia. It used to belong to Australia, and
there are still many Britishers there in supervisory posi-
tions. Omio is in his mid-twenties, and very talented."

Norine added, "His English is considerably better than
that of many of the delegates, and he devours books as
we send them to him. He works in adult education, not
an easy job, as the level of literacy is still very low on
Baki."

Virginia Porcher suggested, "Perhaps the Australians
wanted to keep it low. Educate them, and they'll cause
trouble?"

Krhis smiled, shaking his head. "That's too facile.
However, Omio got into considerable difficulty all round
when he insisted that the native women be allowed to
learn to read and write. He ran into walls of prejudice,
but he finally got his coeducational classes. When Omio
sees something as right, he won't stop till he gets it. He's
quite a lad." He paused as we heard heavy footsteps,
and a large, dark-skinned woman came in. Krhis and
Norine rose to greet her, and she kissed them both, then
came to shake hands with Virginia Porcher and me.

Krhis introduced us. "Milcah Adah Xenda is our
storytelling expert. Millie, Vee is our writing-workshop
leader."

The large woman—wide, rather than tall—smiled.

"Yes, I know Mrs. Porcher's work." She spoke with an accent which was partly guttural, partly French. I couldn't place it. "We're lucky to have you."

"Thanks, I'm lucky to be here. And I'm Vee, please."

"At home in Cameroon, in the college where I teach, I'm called M.A.," Milcah Adah Xenda said. "Krhis calls me Millie, and I like that."

"Millie, then," Virginia Porcher said.

M.A. How ironic. I was glad we were going to call her Millie. I did not need to be reminded of Minerva Allaire.

Milcah Adah's handclasp was firm and dry, despite the heat. When she sat down, the chair creaked under her, but she exuded calm and comfort. She wore a loose cotton shift, and space shoes.

"Polly is going to help Vee in her workshop," Krhis said, "be with Norine in the office, and do all kinds of odd jobs. If you need special errands run, that's one of the things Polly is here for."

"I'm not much for running myself." Millie bathed me with her smile, which was not a quick flash but a slow spreading of appreciation.

I decided that I'd be happy to run anywhere for Milcah Adah Xenda, and that I would like to be young enough to climb in her lap. The fact that she came from Cameroon explained her accent; Cameroon used to be French. I liked her voice, which had a deep quality to it, like the night sky at home at Benne Seed when it is warm and the stars are blurred.

We heard more feet on the stairs, and two people came into the room. One was a woman, black, though a darker, more purply black than Millie, and tall, much taller than I am. She wore a loose robe of brown with a pattern in rust and black, and a turban, which made her seem even taller than she was, and she looked formidable.

Behind her came a man who surprised me simply because he looked so ordinary, like my father, or my uncles, or anybody I might meet at home. He had brownish hair with a touch of mahogany, not red, just warm, and nice eyes; they reminded me of Sandy's.

Krhis made the introductions. The immensely tall woman was Bashemath Odega and she came from Kenya. It was easy to think of Milcah Adah as Millie; but I couldn't conceive of giving Bashemath any kind of nickname.

Millie said, glancing at her folder, "You're the expert in childhood education?"

"That sounds very impressive," Bashemath said. "It's what I teach, and what I care about."

"And this is Frank Rowan," Krhis continued. "He's the publisher of a small educational press in Istanbul, and he will give the delegates hints on starting their own presses—difficult, but not impossible."

Bashemath Odega and Frank Rowan evidently knew each other, because Bashemath said, "We're running a small independent press, thanks to Frank. We're constantly on the edge of bankruptcy, but that's not Frank's fault." Her voice was deep, more guttural than Millie's.

Krhis introduced me as a colleague, not just a kid who'd been given a chance to be a gofer. Everybody was on a first-name basis, as Virginia Porcher had said, and I understood I'd have to get over my hesitancy. Would I ever feel really comfortable calling Virginia Porcher Vee? But already I felt so close to her that Mrs. or Madame Porcher sounded not only formal but unfriendly.

Krhis called the meeting to order. I liked him. I trusted

him, though I tried to remind myself that trusting people is dangerous. I watched him, with his coffee-colored skin and dark, grieving eyes, but no self-pity in the lines that moved downward, and I knew that Max loved him, and that he loved Max, and that there was a lot about human relations I didn't understand, and that maybe I was going to have to move through a lot of time before I was going to be able to understand.

Millie kept wiping her face with a large handkerchief. Bashemath fanned herself regally, with an odd-looking fan of ivory and feathers. Frank Rowan kept pushing his spectacles back up his nose, a gesture which reminded me of nearsighted Renny. If it had not been for the sea breeze coming in the arched windows, the heat would have been unbearable. The walls of the room were the same sun-soaked stone that was found almost everywhere in the old part of the monastery grounds.

Krhis discussed the schedule and explained that he would like us all to be at all the workshops, to encourage and support the delegates. "Your presence is important to the morale of the group." Then he smiled and told us that it was nearly time for supper, and that there would be fresh lemonade in the cloister while we waited for the meal.

Norine whispered to me, "Wait just a minute, Polly. I'd like to take you down to the office and show you how to use the mimeo machine. Vee and Bashemath both have some things they'd like you to run off."

Krhis and Millie went out together, followed by Virginia Porcher. Bashemath turned to Frank and I heard her mutter in a dark whisper, "If Krhis throws one of his ecumenical religious services, he can count me out. I'm here for early-childhood education. Period."

I couldn't hear Frank's murmured response because

Norine was buzzing, "Fresh lemonade is even more of a treat here than wine. It's not the lemons—there are plenty of those—but the bottled water which is an expensive luxury." Then she called to Frank and Bashemath, "Be careful of the steps, okeydokey? They've been worn down through the centuries, and they're slanting and slippery."

"Right-o," Frank called back, and I noticed that he was limping.

I followed Norine down the steps and into the office, which was a small room on the first floor.

"Do you know how to type?" she asked.

"I'm slow, but I can do it if I take enough time."

"Have you ever typed a stencil?" She handed me a sheet of purply, carbon-like paper.

"No. We have a photocopy machine at school."

"You Americans take for granted a lot of luxuries the rest of the world can't even contemplate. When you type a stencil you have to be careful, because you can't correct mistakes. Here's some stuff Vee would like to hand around to the delegates. You don't have to run it off now. There isn't time before dinner. Tomorrow morning, okeydokey?"

"Sure." Then I asked, "Why does Frank limp?"

"He lost a leg a few years ago. He and his wife were taking their children to the United States so they could go to high school there, and as they were driving to New York to fly back to Turkey, they were in a terrible automobile accident, and his wife was killed, and Frank lost a leg."

"How awful."

"Funny games fate plays," Norine said. "Frank's spent most of his life in the tinderbox of the Middle East, but tragedy hits him when it's least expected, in the safe

United States. His children are in college now. The eldest graduates next year."

So Frank was probably a little older than my parents —but I'm not good about chronology.

Norine showed me how to work the mimeo machine, once I'd done the stencil. "How are you coming on the beds?" she asked me.

"I've done quite a few."

"The staff members have already done theirs, of course. You can tell the staff rooms because the names are on the doors." She pulled a tissue from a box on her desk and wiped her forehead. "Lemonade?"

"I'm ready," I said. I was parched. I followed her out of the hotbox of the office. Across the compound a breeze was blowing from the sea.

In the cloister a table was covered with a blue-and-white cloth. It was on the Mediterranean side of the long walkway, where open arches gave onto vistas of the village and the sea. A young man stood by a small table on which there was a large pitcher and a tray of glasses.

"I bear refreshment for your thirst on this island, which is welcoming us as warmly as my island of Baki. I am Omio Heno." His voice was warm and rhythmic, his speech slightly overprecise. He poured me some lemonade.

Omio turned to me. "Krhis wrote me you would be here, all the way from the United States, and so young."

Don't rub it in, I thought. I took the glass he handed me. "I'm nearly seventeen." He looked very young himself. Mid-twenties, Krhis had said. Like Renny.

He smiled, showing perfect white teeth. His skin was so dark that it was a surprise when light brought out copper glints. His palms were pale pink, and so were the soles of his feet, showing a rim of pink between foot and sandal. His hair was fine and black, curling softly. He moved like a dancer, and Norine (who was to become my great source of information) told me later that one of the special pleasures I had to look forward to was Omio performing some of the traditional Bakian dances.

"And blue eyes so beautiful," he said, "like the first blue of sky after sunrise on a fine day."

I could feel the telltale blush. I had been given more cause to blush since I flew to Athens than in all the time on Benne Seed Island and at Cowpertown High. "Thank you." And then, "How long did it take you to get here?"

His smile widened into even more brightness. It was the kind of smile some people might have used to show off, but with Omio it seemed pure, spontaneous delight. Now he burst into a laugh and pointed at his wristwatch. "Time got changed on me so many times, lo back, lo forth, I don't know how long it has taken. A jeep, a bus, a train, four planes, two buses, and here I am."

I smiled back. "You speak very good English."

"I spent a year in London working with Krhis. I was given a scholarship and lo, I learned more than in the rest of my life, though we have many English-speaking people on Baki, more, almost, than Bakians. I learned also in London that I do not like English weather and that Baki is my home, and although we Bakians are thought of as primitive, we also have old wisdom. I work hard to teach people to read, to write, and most importantly to think, so that we will know how to hold on to the old wisdom, and not let it degenerate into superstition. I am writing down the stories of my people, how the world began and is held up on the spout of a great whale."

"I'd love to see what you've written."

His smile shone again. "One day, then, I will show

you." (When we know each other a little better, I thought the 'one day' meant.)

Krhis called us to the table and we stood around it holding hands the way we do at home. Holding hands around the table is the best way to keep the little kids quiet, but there's more to it than that, and I liked holding Virginia Porcher's hand on my right, Omio's on my left.

Krhis suggested, "*Saranam?*"

I did not know what he meant, and evidently neither did Virginia Porcher, but the others lifted up their voices to sing in beautiful harmony.

> *Receive our thanks for night and day,*
> *For food and shelter, rest and play,*
> *Be here our guest, and with us stay,*
> *Saranam, saranam, saranam.*

It was beautiful. Two Cypriote women standing in the background beamed and nodded appreciation.

We pulled out our chairs and sat down. There was a big pitcher of water on the table, and another of red wine. Krhis poured some of the wine into his glass, then filled it with water. "I'm afraid the wine is rather rough, and the water is salty. Mixed together, they are quite potable." He took out a large white handkerchief and patted his brow, although he did not look hot. "This is an unusual heat wave. And I have become acclimated to England."

Omio smiled at him. "In England I froze, lo, into the very marrow. This is like home."

Norine passed around a basket of bread. "You may find this a little sour, but it is baked fresh every day and is very good. They do not serve butter except at break-

fast, okeydokey?" She indicated two small dishes. "This
spread is made from olives, and this from cucumber.
Very good on the bread." She nodded at me, and I helped
myself and passed the dishes to Virginia Porcher. Vee.
I would have to start thinking of her as Vee.

A platter of what looked like onion rings was passed
around. "It is octopus," Norine explained. "It is a little
rubbery, but quite tasty."

One of the Cypriote women passed the platter to Virginia—Vee—who helped herself. "*Epharisto*, Tullia."

Fortunately I'd eaten octopus before, though not at
home. I watched Millie take a tentative taste and try
not to make a grimace. Frank Rowan, living in Istanbul,
was obviously used to it, and helped himself lavishly.

Bashemath took a middle-sized helping and looked
gravely at me. Why should eating octopus be worse
than eating shrimp or any other kind of fish? As I ate
mine, I thought of Ursula and Daddy and Dennys, and
their mutual interest in the octopus because of its nervous system.

The sour bread was good, and so was the bowl of
salad Tullia brought us. I drank half a glass of mixed
wine and water. For dessert we had fruit.

"This is simple, typical Cypriote fare," Krhis said,
"but to me it is enjoyable."

After Tullia and her younger helper ("Her name is
Sophonisba," Virginia Porcher whispered to me) had
cleared the table, refusing to let us help, Krhis suggested
that we stay out in the cloister to catch the breezes.
"And we should teach Vee and Polly some of our songs.
We will do a lot of singing together, and many of the
delegates will look to you to help them with songs they
are not familiar with."

"*Saranam*," Omio said, and turned his smile on me.

"It is an Indian song Krhis brought to us, but we have made many of our own verses."

"Sing a verse through for us," Krhis suggested.

With no self-consciousness Omio lifted up his voice.

> *For this small earth of sea and land,*
> *For this small space on which we stand,*
> *For those we touch with heart and hand,*
> *Saranam, saranam, saranam.*

He sang it until we all had memorized the words and the melody, and then dropped his voice to a rich bass accompaniment. Millie lifted hers in a descant. It was piercingly, painfully beautiful.

Almost too beautiful. I ached with unshed tears. Bashemath said suddenly, "Here's one we all know, and it will be good for all of us to hear it in the various languages of the delegates." I wasn't quite sure what I expected, but I was totally surprised when in her smoky voice she sang *Silent Night* in Masai. She sounded both tender and formidable. When she had finished, she bowed to Frank Rowan.

"I'll sing it in Turkish," Frank said. Although the words were foreign, he still sounded very American. Then he bowed to Norine. The familiar words sounded strange in Chinese, pitched rather higher than we were accustomed to, and with a gentleness I had not felt before in Norine.

Then came Omio, with his voice like black velvet, the Bakian words coming out softly, like an ancient lullaby. It was amazing how different the same song could sound. I'd been bored with *Silent Night* from over-exposure, so that I could no longer even hear it, and suddenly, in this hot late September night in a cloister in

Osia Theola, with the breeze barely stirring, it was alive and new.

I listened to Omio sing and felt tears come to my eyes, and looked at Vee and she was blowing her nose. I wondered what memories the familiar carol brought to her, and to the others of the staff. What was Christmas like in Kenya? Cameroon? For me, the familiar melody brought back Mother baking Christmas cookies with all of us, even the littlest ones, helping (hindering) her, and the smell of turkey and stuffing, and childhood, when my parents were Olympian and their love could solve all problems and keep us safe, and there was nothing on earth I couldn't talk to them about.

I looked around the circle of people; faces were unguarded, and when I saw Millie put her hands over her face, I turned away quickly, feeling that I was violating her privacy, and my glance fell on Frank Rowan and his eyes were bright with tears, and I turned away again, wondering if he was remembering Christmas when his children were little and his wife was alive. I looked at Norine, who sat with her hands tightly clenched in her lap, her eyes closed, no longer the efficient leader, but a woman with her own memories, her own griefs. I had not lived long enough to have learned the coming to terms with life which I felt from these people, but I thought of New Year's Eve at Beau Allaire when everything had been as shining and beautiful as the Christmas tree, and we had sung carols and played charades, and champagne was sparkling and didn't hurt anyone—but now I hurt, and I couldn't get out on the other side of that hurt.

Vee said (and was it *Silent Night* that was helping me to think of her as Vee?), "Polly, can you sing it in German?"

I nodded, and started, "*Stille nacht, heilige nacht,*" and while I was singing, there were no memories, nothing but the song for these people who were already becoming close to me.

Krhis said, when I was through, "Sing it in French, Vee. Millie, you'll use one of the native dialects?"

Millie nodded, and Vee sang in French.

When she was through, Millie lifted her voice in her clear soprano, as easily and joyously as a bird. Everybody had sung at least reasonably well; nobody flatted, or swooped, or sang nasally, but Millie's voice was extraordinary, and we were mesmerized. She sang with a complete lack of self-consciousness.

I had thought I had the tears well under control. But the pure effortlessness of Millie's singing made me choke up, and tears slipped down my cheeks. I got up quietly and went to one of the open arches and stood looking at moonlight making a wide path on the sea, then jumped down from the high sill to the sand below, walking along until I came to an ancient-looking tree shadowing the remnants of a wall. I stepped into its darkness and sobbed.

An arm came around my shoulders, and I was drawn to a lean, masculine body, smelling a musky, pungent smell. It was Omio.

"I'm sorry—I'm sorry—" I gasped.

"It is all right. Lo, many of us have brought wounds with us, and Millie's singing opened them and brought healing tears. Do you have a handkerchief?"

Omio's presence stilled the storm of tears. I dug in my pocket and found a tattered piece of Kleenex. "I'm sorry—"

"It is all right. Norine has provided punch and macaroons, and we'd better go back before we are missed."

When we got back to the cloister, everybody was drinking punch from tiny paper cups and munching macaroons. Nobody mentioned my absence.

Krhis asked, "You like to sing, Polly? Does your family enjoy it?"

"We love it. We used to sing more when we were all littler and had less homework, but when there are nine people in a family, singing is something everybody can do."

Norine said, "You have a nice voice, Polly. While we are working in the office tomorrow, we can do some singing as well."

Vee announced that she was going for a swim, and did anybody want to come?

"Sorry," Frank said. "The walk's a bit much for my inanimate leg."

"Not tonight for me, Vee," Krhis said. "Now you will find other swimming partners. But I beg all of you, and ask you to emphasize it to the delegates, do not go alone. There are strong tides and undertows. But the water is refreshing, and the walk at night will not be too hot."

Only Omio and I wanted to go. I was used to all kinds of undertows, and I felt sticky, and the idea of a swim at night in the Mediterranean was enticing. It had grown dark while we were singing, the sudden, subtropical dark I was used to on Benne Seed. Vee said, "Krhis is right that we should stick together. Polly and I live next door to each other, at the far end of the dormitory building. Let's meet just outside, at the laundry umbrella, and I'll show you the way."

Omio told us that he was on the second floor, and he'd be ready in two minutes.

"Make it ten," Vee said.

It didn't take me more than a couple of minutes to

get into my suit, so I went out the back door of the building and walked toward the laundry umbrella, which was like an empty tree, with one pair of bathing trunks (probably Krhis's) hanging like a single leaf. When everybody arrived, it would fill up.

As I stepped toward it, my foot slid out of my thong and I stepped on a pebble. A sudden pain shot up my leg.

Just as the sharpness of a broken shell sliced into my foot, as I was running away from Beau Allaire.

I did not see Max in the morning after Ursula bound my cut foot and made me spend the night at Beau Allaire. I woke around five, dressed, and slipped out of the house. But I no longer wanted to go home.

It was cool, before the sun was up; little webs of dew sparkled on the grass, which was kept green by constant sprinkling. I walked slowly down the drive because my cut foot hurt, and because the crushed shells crunched noisily. Ursula, I knew, got up early, so I walked carefully, as though that would keep her from looking out a window and seeing me. I was fleetingly grateful that her window, like Max's, faced the ocean, and not the front of the house with the gardens and the long curving drive. And even if Nettie and Ovid were already in the kitchen, that, too, faced the water.

The drive wound around until the house was no longer visible. It seemed miles until I got to the road with its smoother surface. I turned and headed toward Mulletville and the causeway. How was I ever going to make it with my cut foot? Periodically I stopped and sat at the side of the road until I had the energy to move on.

I did not want anybody in Mulletville to see me, but only the fishermen would be up, and they wouldn't care. The development people would all still be in bed.

I heard a car behind me and stepped to the side of the road. The car slowed down and someone called out, 'Hey, hon, want a ride? Look as if you could use one.'

It was a boy from Mulletville who went to Cowpertown High, called Straw because of his sun-bleached hair and his stubby, almost-white lashes. He went with a rough crowd, kids who smoked and drank a lot. Why on earth was he up and out so early? He was older than I was; I think he'd had to repeat a couple of years. I'd never had much to do with him, and didn't want to see him now, and I hoped he wouldn't recognize me. But he did.

'Hey, aren't you Kate's sister?'

'Kate's my cousin,' I said.

'So what's your name, Kate's cousin?'

'Polly.'

'Where you coming from?'

'I'm going,' I said. 'To Cowpertown.'

'Y'are?' He lit a cigarette and dangled it in the corner of his mouth.

'To the M. A. Horne Hospital. I cut my foot, and I have a friend there who's an intern. He'll fix it for me.'

'You sure looked hagged out. Hop in. I'll drive you into Cowpertown, as far as LeNoir Street, and maybe you can get another hitch from there. I have a Saturday job at Diceman's Diner, so I can't take you any further. I'll be sacked if I'm not there in time for the breakfast crowd.'

So that's why he was up. I got in beside him. I had no choice. I hoped he'd go on enjoying the sound of his own voice. He was, I was pretty sure, one of the guys who'd

killed the tortoise. But I needed the ride into Cowpertown. I'd never make it on foot.

'Kate sure is pretty,' he said.

After a pause, I agreed. 'Yah.'

'You don't look like her.' He flicked ashes out the
window.

'We can't all be that lucky,' I said.

He looked at me instead of the road. 'Hey, how'd you
cut your foot?' He glanced down. The cut had broken
open, and blood was seeping through the bandage. It
probably looked a lot worse than it was.

'On a shell,' I said, 'a broken shell.'

'Why, you poor little thing.' He took his hand off the
steering wheel and patted my thigh. 'Hurt much?'

'Some.' I'd just as soon he kept his hands on the wheel
and his attention on the road.

'I got a good first-aid kit. Want me to fix it up for
you?'

'No, thanks. My friend at the hospital will take care
of it.'

His hand reached for my thigh again, rhythmically
patting. I stood it as long as I could, then pulled away.

'What's the matter?' His hand came down hard, and
I winced.

'I told you. My foot hurts.'

'Why don't you let me make it feel better?' He tossed
his cigarette out the window.

'It's my foot that hurts, not my thigh.'

'You don't like Straw, hunh?'

I remembered his face, full of lust for killing, as he
battered the tortoise. No, I didn't like him. 'I don't know
you very well.'

'Well, now,' he drawled, 'maybe Kate's right after
all.'

'About what?' I should have kept my mouth shut.

'You.'

If I knew one thing, it was that Kate hadn't talked to Straw about me. He'd never been one of her dates. He'd never come home with her for dinner. He wasn't her type. But he came from Mulletville, and he dated Mulletville girls. I pushed away from him as far as possible.

'So what's Kate's cousin doing at this end of the island?'

I didn't answer.

'You've been at Beau Allaire, haven't you?'

I looked down at the blood drying rustily on Ursula's bandage.

'We know all about those dames at Beau Allaire, and what they do. You've been with them. You're like the way they are, and that's why you don't like me.'

'Let me out,' I said.

He jammed on the brake, throwing me forward. 'You really want to get out?'

'Yes.'

'Don't have an attack. I'll get you to LeNoir Street.' He stepped on the gas pedal, and his hand came at me again, and I pulled away. 'What's the matter, honey? You really don't like Straw?'

What arrogance. This guy thought every girl in school was after him.

'You like dames, is that it? Can't make it with a guy?'

I shut my eyes, clamped my lips closed. He kept his foot on the gas pedal. The car rocked as he whizzed around a curve with a screech of tires. I didn't care if it turned over.

I opened my eyes as I felt the car slow down and we drove through the outskirts of Cowpertown, then onto LeNoir Street with its post office and banks and stores. Again he slammed on the brakes. 'Here we are.'

'Thanks.'

'I feel real sorry for Kate. She's a nice girl. Norm—'

I opened the door and jumped out, and the pain shot sharply from my foot through my body into my head, sending yellow flashes across my eyes.

Straw drove off with another rubber-smelling screech.

I was still a long way from M. A. Horne, which was at the farther end of LeNoir Street, a good three or four miles, too far to walk on a bleeding foot. I stumbled along, not knowing what to do, until I saw a phone booth.

I would call Renny.

I was jerked back into the present as I heard a sliding of sand and stones. Omio came leaping down from the top of the hill, wearing bathing trunks and a short terry jacket.

I couldn't stand Straw's hands on me, but I had liked Omio's arms around me as I cried under the old tree.

The door opened, and Omio greeted Vee by handing her a flashlight. "You may need it to warn drivers of our presence."

"Thanks, Omio, what a good idea. Half the drivers here are crazy and drive these windy roads as though they were the Los Angeles Freeway. And cars drive English-fashion, on the left, when they're not in the middle of the road, so we'll walk on the right."

She led us along the path which ran below the balconies of the dorm, and there was the tree I had fled to, and now that my eyes were not blinded by tears I could see how beautiful it was. "What is it?"

"A fig sycamore. I don't know how old it is, but hundreds of years. It's the most beautiful tree I've ever seen, and I keep trying to write poems about it, but thus far they elude me."

The moonlight turned trees and branches to silver. "Full moon, day after tomorrow," Omio said.

Vee started downhill. "Careful. It's rocky and rough, and we don't want any sprained ankles."

Below the monastery complex we came out on a road that ran through the lower part of the village. There were a few shops, closed for the night; what looked like a small bank; a taverna, with people sitting outside, laughing and talking. Music came from within, and light spilled out onto the road.

"Osia Theola is on its way to becoming a resort," Vee said, "since the old resort towns, like Famagusta, are now Turkish. If I were a millionaire I'd buy Osia Theola and save it from the tourists—as well as the Turks; it's anybody's guess as to who's the most destructive."

I said, recalling Max's teaching, "Poor Cyprus. It's always being taken over and ruled by somebody. The Italians were here before the Turks, and the Turks before the English, and now in the north the Turks have come again."

"That's the way of the world," Omio said. "Baki has always been prey to stronger, less peaceable peoples. Now there are more Australians and English than Bakians."

"And yet England," Vee said, "was overrun by Vikings and Normans. The Picts and Angles and indigenous inhabitants were ruthlessly wiped out. Genocide isn't new to this century."

We turned off the main village street onto a dirt road which ran past more tavernas, narrowed to a path cutting through walls of high grasses, and turned sharply at a boatyard. The sea was on our right. "Not far, now,"

Vee said, "and we'll come to a good place to bathe, beyond the village, but before the hotel, where it's too
crowded for my liking. I've found an unused bit of
beach. There's a wide band of stones between the sea
and the sand, and I've been trying to move them aside
to make a path to the water, but they keep washing
back."

"You've been here awhile?" Omio asked.

"For a week, resting. Doctor's orders, and orders I
was happy to comply with. I've slept and swum and
worked on my new novel with no interruptions or outside pressures."

So she *was* writing a novel. I wished I dared to ask
her what it was about.

Omio and I followed the path she had made through
the stones. I slipped and almost turned my ankle, but
Omio caught me. The stones were not very big, and they
were rounded from water, but they were still uncomfortable to step on. Although the cut on my foot had
healed, the stone near the laundry umbrella had reminded me that there was further healing needed, and
it seemed that I could feel the skin stretching around the
scar as I stepped into the water.

Omio dropped down and swam out, cleanly, barely
tossing up spray. Vee and I followed. The water was
cool, not cold, just right for getting cooled off. The sky
was misty with stars.

"Don't go too far out," Vee called. "Krhis is right
about the undertow. This is one of the safest places,
better than the beach up at the hotel."

Omio was a superb swimmer, like most island people,
but he turned around and came back toward us, then
veered off and swam parallel to the land, up toward the

lights of the hotel. I would have liked to swim with him, but thought it would not be courteous to Vee, who swam well but not quite as well as I did, since I've been in and out of water all my life.

She stood inside the stones, shaking water out of her ears. "Good thing we've both got drip-dry hair."

Omio had turned again and was swimming back. "He's a nice lad," Vee said. "I'm glad he's here early. You'll enjoy him. He's been through a lot, and he holds no bitterness. You'll find that's true of most of the delegates. I suspect Norine will fill you in on some of their histories. It's probably one of the most varied groups we'll ever encounter, geographically, physically, every way."

Omio had swum back to us and was running through the shallow water with great leaps, splashing silver spray.

"What energy!" Vee exclaimed. "Why can't you bottle it and give some to me? Come on, kids, we'd better go on back. Breakfast's at seven-thirty and we all need our sleep."

I felt comfortably cool after the swim, but the walk back to the dormitory building was all uphill, and I was sweating again by the time we reached the monastery. At Beau Allaire, Max has a white coquina ramp going over a jungle of Spanish bayonets and crape myrtle, down to the beach. At home we run along our cypress ramp over the sand dunes and across a lovely long stretch of beach. At Osia Theola we were going to have to work for our swim.

Norine was waiting at the dormitory building, waving to us.

"Polly," she said, "I have a phone message for you."

My heart thumped. "For me?"

"Yes. While you were swimming, some young man called. Zachary Gray. You know him?"

I hadn't told Norine who the flowers were from. "Yes."

"He wanted to make sure you'd arrived safely. He said to give you his love, and he'll call again."

"Oh—thanks." I could not help being pleased, and showing it. Then I said good night to Vee and Omio, thanked Norine again, and we all went to our rooms. I took a lukewarm bath and lay back in the tub, dazzled by Zachary's flowers, by his call.

The bedroom was hot. I lit the mosquito coil and opened the shutters and lay down on the bed to read for a while. At home there are screens everywhere, and windows open to catch the breeze. Max had told me that when she and M.A. were growing up at Beau Allaire, not many people had screens, and they slept under white gauze mosquito nets. A mosquito net would not be a bad idea at Osia Theola.

The coil went out without my realizing it, and instantly I was attacked by invisible, soundless insects. I slapped at them, struck a match, and relit the coil. Realized I was going to have to close the shutters. I was bitten on the legs, the arms, the face.

I slammed the shutters closed. Scratched my legs. Rubbed my eye. Could feel it hot and itchy. I remembered Renny telling me that the vector, the biting insect which put Trypanozomas into the bloodstream and ultimately the heart, frequently enters the body with its lethal poison by biting the corner of the eyelid. I had a moment of utter panic.

Nonsense, Polly. You come from a family of scientists. Use your mind. Chagas' and Netson's diseases are endemic in South America, not in Cyprus. They don't exist in Cyprus.

I rubbed my eyelid again. Looked in the mirror. The lid was red and puffy. Absurd. But I felt infected.

Idiot. Renny would have warned me if there was any Netson's in Greece or Cyprus. Max would never have arranged the trip. Ursula would not have allowed it. Daddy wouldn't even have considered it. There are plenty of biting bugs at home, nasty red bugs, shrilling mosquitoes, no-see-um bugs which bite and the bites puff up like the one on my eyelid and get red and feverish but are unimportant. That's the kind of insect these Cyprus bugs were, just like the Benne Seed no-see-ums, itchy and horrid but not dangerous. Nobody would have a conference center where insects were a threat to life.

My heart began to beat less fearfully.

But it was hot. My sheet was wet. The fan was blowing a warm draft over me, doing no more than recirculating hot air. I put down my book and turned out the light; even the filament of the light bulb added to the heat of the room.

The coil burned slowly, its end barely glowing, so that I knew it was still lit. I was not being bitten anymore. I turned on my stomach, spread-eagled. The cool waters of the Mediterranean seemed eons ago; I was bathed in perspiration.

And I wanted Renny to sit by me on the bed and reassure me, tell me I needn't worry about the bite on my eyelid.

How do you feel when you know that an insect bite on the corner of your eyelid means death to your heart? What a funny little muscle to hold life and death in its pumping.

But this wasn't that kind of insect, that kind of bite.

I wanted to run to Renny, the way I had run when I fled Beau Allaire.

I called the hospital. 'I'd like to speak to Dr. Queron Renier, please. It's an emergency.'

'Who is calling, please?' The operator had my most unfavorite kind of Southern accent, nasal and whiny.

'Well—could you just say it's Polly?'

'Just a minute, hon. I don't know if he's in.'

Of course he was in. He'd be in his quarters or on the floor. I waited. The nasal voice came again. 'He's not answering. May I leave him a message?'

I looked at the number of the phone in the booth, gave it to the voice on the other end of the line. 'Please . . . please try to find him. Please, it's urgent,' I said. I could not control the trembling of my voice.

I would have to wait for Renny to call.

Suppose, for some reason, he wasn't at the hospital? How long should I wait? And what then? I leaned against the wall of the phone booth and I wasn't sure how long I could stand up.

The part of LeNoir Street where Straw had left me was mostly shops. A few dusty palmetto trees drooped in the morning sun. My breath fogged the glass of the phone booth, and I opened the door. A few people walked by. A few stores opened. I waited. Waited.

Half an hour.

I couldn't stay in the phone booth all day.

I would have to go somewhere, do something. The night before, I had wanted to go home. Not now. I couldn't go home.

I crouched over, as though I had cramps, and heard a funny noise, like an animal's, and looked around to see what was making the noise, and it was coming from me. I pushed my hand against my mouth and it stopped.

Oh, Renny. Renny, help.

The phone was silent. I had been there for an hour. The street was waking up.

I had to go somewhere and there was nowhere to go. My foot throbbed, and blood continued to seep through the bandage. Numbly, not even thinking, I started away from the phone. I was a few yards down the street when it rang.

I rushed back.

Grabbed the phone off the hook. 'Hello?'

'Polly?'

'Oh, Renny, Renny—'

'Where are you? What's wrong?'

I heard myself wailing. 'My foot's cut, and I'm bleeding all over the phone-booth floor—'

Renny's voice was sharp. 'Polly. Calm down. Tell me where you are, and what's wrong.'

'I'm in a phone booth on LeNoir Street near the post office. Can you come for me, oh, please, Renny, please—'

'*Where* on LeNoir Street? Polly, don't get hysterical, this isn't like you.'

I looked around. 'Two blocks south of the post office. I'm right by a hearing-aid place. I'm bleeding—'

'All right,' Renny said. 'I've just finished making early rounds. I'll be there in ten minutes.'

I gave a sob, but there were no tears with it; it was so dry it hurt my throat. 'Hurry—please—'

The ten minutes I waited for Renny seemed longer than the hour before the phone rang. He drove up in his old green car, and I stumbled out of the booth. He hurried around to open the car door for me, and I almost fell in.

'Let me see that foot.'

I leaned back against the shabby seat. Stuck my foot out at him.

'Who bandaged it for you?'

'Ursula Heschel.'

'Polly, what happened?'

'I cut it on a shell.'

His fingers worked the bandage free. 'That's a nasty cut. How did you get here?'

'I walked partway, then I got a hitch.'

'A hitch?'

'Renny.' My voice was heavy. 'Hitching's a federal offense in my family. But I couldn't walk.'

'No, Polly, you couldn't.' He opened the glove compartment and rummaged among maps and dark glasses and a can opener and pulled out an Ace bandage. 'This will do until I can get you to the hospital and dress your foot. Then I'll take you home.'

Now the tears came, spurting out, as sudden as a summer storm. 'No, no, Renny, no, I don't want to go home, I can't go home, no—' I was being incoherent and hysterical and I have never in my life been incoherent or hysterical.

Renny shut the glove compartment, took my foot and wrapped it in the Ace bandage, then shut the door and went around to the driver's seat. He got in and sat down, waiting for me to get under control. 'Polly, what happened?'

I shook my head, and again that awful animal noise came out of me, but this time it flowed out with tears, and it was easier to stop.

Renny started the car.

'Renny, I don't want anybody to see me. Some of the doctors know Daddy—'

'I have no place to take you except the hospital,' Renny said. 'We'll go in through Emergency.' He drove in silence along LeNoir Street. The shops gave way to houses, at first close together, then set back from the street, larger and farther apart. The street curved around to the hospital driveway. He drove to the back. Opened the door for me. 'Try not to put too much weight on that foot.'

We went in through the Emergency entrance. There were only a few people in the waiting room, and the nurse at the desk was sipping from a Styrofoam cup. Renny greeted her, saying that he was taking a patient to have her foot bandaged. I don't think she even looked up from her magazine.

'It was a heavy night in Emergency.' Renny led me into one of the examining cubicles. 'It's all quiet now.'

'Are you on Emergency rotation?'

'No. Urology. Word gets round in a small hospital. How did you cut your foot?'

'I told you. On a broken shell.'

'Where?'

'Max's driveway.'

'When?'

'Last night.'

'Where were you going?' He was bathing my foot, holding it in a bowl of water, pink from my blood.

'I was running.'

'Where?' He swabbed the cut with disinfectant and I cried out. 'Where, Polly?'

'Away.'

His strong fingers held my foot, holding the cut so that the bleeding stopped. 'This was last night?'

'Yes.'

'Did you go home?'

'No. No. I couldn't. Then I got up early to—to come to you.'

Renny pressed a gauze pad against the cut, then taped it. 'You'll have to stay off that foot today.'

'All right.'

He was perched on a small white stool, keeping his hand around my foot. 'I do have to take you home, you know.'

'No. No!' My voice rose.

'Shhh,' he said. 'Unless you can give me a good reason, a real reason not to, I'll have to take you home or call your parents to come get you.'

'No.' This time I kept my voice low. 'I can't. I can't talk to them.'

He stood up, put his hands on my shoulders, looked into my eyes. 'You'd better tell me whatever it was that happened.'

'I can't.' I leaned toward him so that I could press my face against his white coat. Renny had been to our house once when Max and Ursula were there for dinner. He knew Max that way, and as an outpatient. I could not tell him.

'You were with Max and Ursula?'

'With Max, so she wouldn't be alone while Urs was in Charleston.'

'Oh, Polly—' He sighed. 'When did Ursula come in on this?'

'While I was running away from—she was driving home from Charleston. Oh, Renny, Max was drunk. She was in terrible pain and she was drunk. I've never seen anybody drunk that way. She didn't really know what she was—'

His arms came tightly around me. I didn't have to

tell him any more. And then he asked me who'd picked
me up to drive me to Cowpertown, and I told him about
Straw and his ugly insinuations.

'The creep,' Renny murmured, 'the crude creep.' His
arms were protecting, reassuring. 'The first thing you
need is some sleep. I'm going to call a friend of mine,
one of the nurses here. She's on duty now, but I'll get
her key. Wait.'

'Don't tell her.'

'Shhh. I won't tell her anything.'

'Don't tell anybody—not Mother or Daddy—'

'I won't tell anybody.' He shut the door of the exam-
ing cubicle behind him.

While he was gone I lay back on the black examining
table, which was too short for me. It was covered with
white paper that crinkled if I moved, so I lay still. I was
half asleep when Renny came back.

'All right, Polly, let's go.'

He led me along a back corridor, down some stairs,
and out a side door. We got back in the car and drove
to one of the streets around the hospital which had once
been a street of rich people in big houses and was now
funeral parlors and rooming houses. He pulled up in
front of a Greek revival house with heavy white columns
and none of the airy grace of Beau Allaire. We went up
the steps to a side verandah, and Renny opened the screen
door, then took a key and opened the inner door. He led
me through a small living room and out onto a screened
porch where there was a double bed, a green wicker
chair and stool, a cherry chest, completely out of place
with the rest of the porch furniture, with a few drawers
pulled half open.

'Nell wasn't exactly expecting company.' Renny
pulled down the white Marseilles bedspread.

A small, cold part of my mind was wondering who

Nell was, and why Renny was so familiar with her. He was rummaging through one of the open drawers.

I sat down.

He turned to me, holding out a shorty nightgown. 'Get undressed and put this on.' He flicked a switch, and the ceiling fan started to turn. In the hospital it had been cool. 'Some of the apartments have air-conditioning,' he said, 'but Nell sleeps out here half the year. I'll be back in five minutes.'

I undressed, put on Nell's nightgown, and got into bed. The floor of the sleeping porch was painted green, the wooden ceiling was green, and the green of a huge magnolia tree pressed against the screen. With the fan moving the air, it gave the effect of coolness.

Renny came in with a mug. 'Chicken broth,' he said. 'I don't want to give you any caffeine or anything cold.'

I put my hands around the mug. It must have been well in the nineties outdoors, but my hands were cold, and the warmth of the mug felt good.

'I have to get back to the hospital.' He sounded reluctant. 'Polly, I don't know what to do. You've had a bad shock. I think I should call your parents.'

'No. I don't want them to know.'

'You're not going to tell them?'

'No,' I repeated, 'I don't want them to know.'

Renny sat on the edge of the bed beside me. 'You're going to have to go home sometime.'

'They think I'm with Max and Ursula. I was to call Mother when I was ready to go home.'

'Will you still do that?'

'I don't know. Not yet.'

He got up and walked to the door, then turned back. 'When Max and Ursula find you gone and realize you aren't coming back, won't they call your parents?'

I sat up in bed, put my head on my knees. That had not occurred to me. 'Would they?'

'Likely.'

'But what would they say?'

'They might just want to know if your parents know where you are.'

'Will you call them?' I asked. But then they would know that Renny knew. And Max would have to see Renny when she went into Cowpertown for blood tests . . .

I got out of bed and followed Renny. 'I'll call.'

He nodded, pointing toward a desk in the corner of the rather drab room. On it, among a clutter of mugs and a coffeepot and a bowl of lilies, was a phone. Renny asked, 'Do you want me to go?'

'No. Stay. Please.' I dialed. —Don't let it be Max who answers. Don't let it be Nettie or Ovid. Let it be Urs.

It was. I said, 'Ursula, this is Polly. I just want you to know I'm all right. I'm with a friend, not at home, so don't call home, please. I need to sleep. I'm very tired. Goodbye.' I spoke quickly, not giving her time to say anything, though in the background, behind my words, I heard, 'Thank God. Where are you? I need to see you, to talk.' —No, Ursula. You don't need to see me. There's nothing to say. Go to Max.

I put the phone down and went back out to the porch.

Renny leaned against the doorframe. 'I get off at five. I'll come to you then. I'm sorry, Polly, so sorry—' He bent down and kissed me on the cheek.

I slept. Woke, with my eye itching. Rubbed it. Felt hot. The sheet was wet. I opened my eyes. Mostly my right eye. The left was swollen nearly closed.

I was in Cyprus, and I'd been bitten on the eyelid. I turned on the light, got up, and stared in the wavery mirror. It looked as though someone had socked a fist into my eye.

There was no Netson's in Cyprus. Anyhow, it was only my eyelid that was inflamed. No conjunctivitis.

I got back into bed. My room at home wasn't even half the size of this one, but it was all mine. After my roommate came, it would be very different. So I got out of bed, opened the shutters, and stepped out onto the balcony. The insects drove me back into the room before I could appreciate the loveliness of the night. I curled up, pulling the sheet just over my toes, and slept.

I woke to someone walking up and down the corridor, ringing a bell. Norine, I guessed, though there was only the staff, Omio, and me, to rouse. There was going to be no oversleeping at this conference.

I met Vee as I came out my door. "Polly, what on earth has happened to you?"

"The no-see-um bugs got me."

She scratched her arm. "Me, too, though not in as sensitive a place. Did you use the bug coil?"

"Yes, but for a while I tried to keep the shutters open to catch the breeze. Believe me, I shut them fast."

She leaned over to look at my eye. "I think one got you on a vein, right there at the corner of your lid. Does it hurt?"

"No, it's just uncomfortable."

"It *is* a temporary affliction, if that's any comfort; it'll go away in a day or so. The bugs are much worse in this humid heat than they were last week." She scratched again, bending down to her ankle. "Do you have a can of spray in your room?"

"No, just the coil."

"I'll find you some for this evening. It helps if you spray the shutters. Not so many of the little horrors get through the slats."

We walked the rose-lined path to the dining area of the cloister. The sun was already uncomfortably hot. Norine exclaimed over my eye and said she'd give me some witch-hazel pads to help bring the swelling down.

For breakfast there were packets of instant coffee in a wicker basket, and a big pitcher of hot milk. A platter of eggs was brought in by Tullia. There was a loaf of bread still warm from the oven, a big bowl of jam, and a smallish pat of butter each. I wondered how much refrigeration they had in the kitchen, which was simply the enclosed end of the cloister.

While we were still eating, the bells in the tower began to ring, and we could see people coming in through the gates to go to church. A young woman was carrying a baby in a long white dress; a man in a dark suit, face flushed with heat, had his arm about her. They were followed by a group of beaming people.

"A baptism!" Vee cried in delight.

As the people went into the church, most of them turned to stare at us sitting around the breakfast table.

Omio's delighted laugh pealed out. "Wait till the rest of the delegates arrive!"

Bashemath said in her solemn way, "We are already a circus for them."

Vee, Frank, and I were the only Caucasians. Krhis was Indian, Norine Oriental, Bashemath and Millie were African, and Omio was—I wasn't sure—Micronesian?

Omio wore a brightly patterned garment that was something between a kilt and a loincloth, and an ordinary cotton T-shirt. "At home, in the old days, we wouldn't have worn the shirt," he explained to me. He reached out one long finger, pale at the tip, and touched my inflamed eyelid. "Poor Polly, when we go swimming this evening, lo, the salt water will be good for it."

Norine passed the warm milk. "After breakfast, Polly, I'd like you to help me in the office. And I have the medicine chest with the witch hazel there."

Bashemath said, "You have the papers I want duplicated?"

Norine nodded. "And I showed Polly how to use the mimeo."

When we got to the office, Norine took a bottle of witch hazel from a tiny cooler. She rummaged in drawers until she found a gauze pad, which she soaked with the cold witch hazel. "Hold it to your eye."

I had forgotten my eyelid at breakfast. Now I was very aware of the itching and swelling. It was so inflamed that the witch-hazel pad warmed up quickly, and Norine wet it again. It felt marvelously soothing, and I thanked her.

"Any time you get a chance during the day, wet the pad and hold it to your eye, okeydokey? Now, are you ready?" She pointed at the typewriter.

"I'm afraid I'll be very slow."

Norine was busily looking through some files. "That is all right as long as you are accurate."

I sat down at the typewriter and typed, very carefully, a series of forms of poetry, lines of iambic pentameter, tetrameter, trochaic and anapestic measures. There were examples of meters, everything explained in the simplest way possible. Somehow or other I managed to make a passable stencil.

Norine looked at it, and nodded. "Okeydokey, now run it off."

I managed that, too, though I ended up with purple ink on my fingers and somehow or other got a purple streak down one leg.

"You can type Bashemath's stencil this afternoon," Norine said. "If you try to do too much at once, you begin to make mistakes." She indicated a wooden file box filled with cards. We were to check over the names and addresses of each delegate, and assign them rooms in the dormitory building, trying to choose suitable roommates for each.

"I have already picked your roommate, as I told you," Norine said, "because she is the youngest woman delegate—not yet thirty."

Not yet thirty sounded quite old to me.

"It is best if we put people of different languages together. That way they'll have to speak English. Here, you see, we will not put Andres, from Brazil, with Gershom, from Angola, because they would be tempted to speak Portuguese. Andres can room with Nigel from Bombay."

Norine did most of the choosing, and I stuffed blue folders for everybody, marking their names and room numbers on the cover.

When we had finished, Norine soaked the gauze pad in witch hazel again, and I was ready for it.

"You like Omio?" she asked.

"Very much."

"He has great talent. And the Bakian affectionateness. You are acquainted with peoples of different races and colors?"

"Reasonably. We lived on an island off the south coast of Portugal when I was a child, and we were friends with the Gaeans. And I spent a month in Venezuela and saw a good bit of the Quiztanos."

"Omio speaks better English than some of the other

delegates, and has no small estimation of himself. Bashemath is an interesting person, a fine educator. There was big trouble for her when she left home for her first conference. While she was gone, her husband's friends urged him to go back to the old ways and take another wife. When she got home, the other woman was putting Bashemath's own children to bed. But you have seen Bashemath. The other woman did not stay long."

I had seen Bashemath. "It must have been awful for her."

"It was. She is required at her university to attend a certain number of conferences, but after that she did not leave home again for two years."

Norine was something of a gossip. And I listened. I listened avidly. Was I being like Xan and Kate listening to the Mulletville girls? Not entirely. Norine relished her stories, but she was not being vicious.

Now she laughed her rather tinny laugh. "Bashemath could certainly frighten me away if she wanted to. She is a real warrior. Now Millie is quite different. She is a dear person, is Milcah Adah. She, too, has been through much grief. All her family died during an epidemic. Millie nursed them, buried them, and by some fluke did not get ill herself. She nursed children who had been taken to the hospital, and it was discovered what a fine storyteller she is. A rare person, if a little sentimental. Here, let me soak that pad again."

The cool pad felt so good I would have liked to pat it all over me.

When I took it away from my eye, Norine peered at me. "The swelling is going down. Are you thirsty?"

"Parched." At home there's always lemonade and iced tea in the fridge.

She went again to her little cooler, pulled out a bottle

of ginger ale, got two paper cups from the file cabinet. The fizzy coolness helped my thirst but did nothing to dry my sticky clothes. Even my feet were sweaty, and my wet sandal straps had made stained marks across my foot.

"We'll work on the table assignments now," Norine said. "We like to rotate the seating, so that people can get to know each other, and also to prevent cliques from forming. A conference experience like this can produce intense friendships."

We put numbers in a small wooden box for the delegates to draw. "This heat wave is absurd, positively absurd," Norine said. "It's a good thing many of our delegates come from hot climates. I think Vee feels the heat more than the rest of us, and she's prone to headaches if she's overstressed. You have read her books?"

"I love them."

"She is a fine writer. And it takes her mind off her husband."

What did she mean? "Is he alive?"

"Unfortunately." She looked at me. "This is of course in confidence, Polly."

"Okay," I said uncertainly.

"He is French, Henri Porcher. There was an American grandfather, I believe, from one of those inbred Southern families, who late in life married a distant cousin in Paris, a singer. There was a latent strain of insanity, violent insanity, in the Porchers. Until ten years ago, Henri seemed free of it. But then he got an encephalitis virus, which evidently triggered it, and he has been institutionalized ever since."

"Oh—how awful—"

"He is in a hospital in Switzerland, and Vee is able to be with us because her sister-in-law spells her. Henri is very dependent on Vee, and if she visits him daily he is less violent. Poor man, he is like a wild animal. I suppose, legally, Vee could divorce him, but Vee being Vee, of course she won't. Krhis says that in his own irrational way Henri still loves her. She is brave. Now"—Norine was brisk efficiency again—"we have done a good morning's work."

"I know," I agreed. I was already learning much from the staff.

At lunch we were served by the younger woman, Sophonisba. Omio whispered to me, "Look at her gold tooth. It's a status symbol."

Millie entertained us with stories, a few from her native Cameroon, others from different countries, and had us all in stitches. When Bashemath was really amused, her laughter was a deep booming. Frank had a hearty, contagious laugh. Even Krhis was shaking with laughter.

"The delegates have a treat in store," he said at the end of the meal. "Now, my dears, it is siesta time, and it is so hot—104° in Nicosia, and not that much cooler here—we will take the afternoon off, and have our meeting after the evening meal instead. I think that will be more comfortable for us all."

I walked with Millie along the pebbled path that led to the dormitory building. "You were terrific," I said.

She smiled. "When we are listening to stories, then it is the story center of the brain which is functioning, and the pain center is less active. I go into the children's wards of hospitals, where there are children in great pain. When I am telling them stories they laugh and they cry and in truth their pain is less. Mine, too." Again she smiled at me, and then at two old men with long hoses who were watering the flowers, and who smiled back, nodding and bobbing, looking curiously at Millie and me and the others coming along behind us.

I turned on the fan in my room, and I think it did help a little. I changed the water for Zachary's flowers, then stretched out on the bed with a book, and got up to a gentle knock. It was Vee, with a can of bug spray. "I got this for you from Norine. There's supposed to be some in each room."

"Oh, thank you."

"See you anon," Vee said, and went to her room.

I finished making the beds on the first floor, and did three rooms on the second floor, then decided to go back to my room for a nap.

I left the shutters wide open, and while sunlight streamed in, so did the breeze from the sea. Whatever the stinging insects were, they weren't bad during sunlight. I sprawled out on the bed and slept.

When I woke up I could hear snoring from the room on the other side of me, not Vee's, Millie's. I got up and went into the hall, and all the doors were closed. I walked softly in my crepe-soled sandals, out into the brilliant sunlight. Just walking along the path made me perspire. I went into the office and typed the stencil for Bashemath, suggestions about teaching small children to read and write. When I had finished, sweat was stinging my eyes, trickling down my legs. I went into the compound and the sun blasted at me like a furnace.

The church bells were quiet, but the doors were open, leading into darkness. I slipped in, standing in the back until my eyes adjusted to the shadows. The light filtered in gently, touching an icon here, a statue of the Virgin there. I sat on one of the stone steps leading down into the nave.

There was a screen covered with icons dividing the

main body of the church from the sanctuary. A little old man was polishing candlesticks, and when he turned and saw me his face lit up with a smile as though he had been expecting me. He came up to me.

"Come, little," he said, "come, *despina*," and led me down the steps into the church and to a wooden seat hollowed with age. I sat and watched him as he puttered about. He took a sprig of green from a stand in front of a statue, a flower from a vase before an icon, picking here and there, until he had a tiny bouquet, which he handed me, beaming.

"*Epharisto*." I was a little embarrassed. I hoped it was all right for him to give me flowers taken from icons and statues.

"*Parakalo*, little, *parakalo, kyria*."

I held the bouquet to my nose, and it was pungent and lemony-smelling.

He pointed to a statue which I had thought was a Virgin and child, but as I looked more closely I saw that the child wore a crown and carried a cross like a scepter, and that the woman was wearing red velvet. The old man spoke in Greek, and I thought he was telling me that this was Blessed Theola and her vision of Christ.

He beamed on me again and pointed to the lower section of the church. "Cave. Eight hundred, eighteen hundred old, *kyria*." He switched back to Greek, and I kept nodding at him, catching words and phrases about Theola and truth, and he gestured urgently toward the cave.

I followed him and stood in the entrance to the cave, peering into darkness. Was it here that Theola gave people the truth about themselves? Max had said that Theola was gentle and did not give people more than they could bear.

I stood there, and the only truth to come to me was that I was still in the darkness of confusion, about myself, and everybody. I allowed Zachary Gray, whom I had known only a few days, to be complicated and contradictory. Why couldn't I allow it in anybody else? Why couldn't I allow it in myself?

"*Kyria? Despina?*" The old man was looking at me anxiously.

"*Epharisto.*" I smiled at him and turned away from the cave and returned to the wooden seat he had first offered me.

"*Parakalo.*" He picked up a candlestick and polishing rag. I sat there for quite a long while, holding the little bouquet to my face. There was something healing about the pungent smell. Then the bells began to ring, so I got up and left quickly, waving goodbye and thanks to the old man, and wandered across the courtyard to the cloister.

Omio was there before me, in the refectory section, sitting at a table and writing in a notebook, with another book beside him. He looked up and beckoned to me. "I promised I'd show you this." He pointed to the big notebook and pulled out a chair for me, watching me while I leafed through the pages.

He had set down in this book the stories of his people, first in Bakian, then in English. The stories were lavishly and beautifully illustrated in bright watercolors. Many of his paintings and sketches reminded me of Max's notebooks. Max would love this book of Omio's.

"Why does this man have so many wives?" I looked up from a story of a man with seventeen wives.

He laughed. "Seventeen is, lo, excessive, is it not? But to have more than one wife was the old way. On Baki there used to be many more women than men, so the kindest thing to do with all the extra women was to marry them. Every Bakian woman had a family to care for, and to be cared for by. My grandmother was, lo, my grandfather's fifth wife, and the most beautiful. The children—there were many—thought of each other as whole brothers and sisters. If a woman did not have enough milk after childbirth, there was always another to suckle the baby." He smiled his merry smile.

"We were lucky on Baki." He put his hand down on the book, his long forefinger with the delicate pink nail pointing to a picture of a baby being held by a white man in a dog collar. "In some places the missionaries made the men get rid of all but one of their wives. Do you think Jesus would have wanted that?"

I shook my head. "It doesn't show much concern for the leftover wives."

"In Baki, the missionaries who came to us were warm of heart, and said only that when the children grew up, each, like my father, like me, should have one wife only. And this made reason because, with, lo, the new medicines they brought us, fewer male children died, and there were no longer many women needing men. They —the missionaries—wanted the women to cover their breasts, but they said little to those who went around as usual. They believed that, as time went on, we would move into their ways."

"Did you?"

He smiled. "We are still moving. The missionaries who came to Baki understood that differences need not separate. But they were followed by others, the military people, for instance, and their families. Some of their ways were good ways. But there were ways, too, which we did not understand."

There was a tightness in his face which I had not seen before. "Tell me—"

Omio looked at me with his dark eyes, which were usually so merry but now were simply dark, the pupil hardly darker than the iris. "I'm not sure you will understand."

"I can try."

"Our ways are so different."

"Please."

"On this far island of Baki there came, lo, many Australian and many English people. We felt very fortunate when my father got a job working in the big military hotel they built. These people called themselves Christian, you understand."

I did not.

"Although many people, my family included, welcomed them, they did not think they had to treat us as they treated each other. When my father displeased them in any way, they beat him. One time they beat him so that he bled on his back, and then salt was rubbed into him. My mother bathed him and bathed him, making more blood to come to wash away the salt, and then took him down to the sea because the salt in seawater is healing. But I heard his screams."

I looked down at the open page to hide my horror; he had painted birds and butterflies, vivid and happy. "How could you be Christian, then?"

He put his hand down on mine. "Oh, I think we could be. I think we were Christian, lo, long before the missionaries came, although we did not know to call it so. We knew only that the maker of the great whale came to us and was part of our lives, and the missionaries called this person who loved and cared for us by the name of Jesus. And we were glad to have a name for the part of the maker we had not known by name before." He turned the page, and there was a painting of the statue which had become so familiar to me at

Max's, the stone carving of the man laughing in sheer delight.

If Max had ever told me that the statue was Bakian, I had forgotten. Seeing it in Omio's book was like the slap of a rough ocean wave. I had last seen the statue in Max's arms as she ran down the stairs after me.

Omio said, "The missionaries who were our friends called it the Laughing Christ. Some of the others called it a heathen idol."

"Oh—Omio . . ." From Omio's painting it was evident that the actual statue was much larger than Max's copy, but the loving delight was the same. Had Max put the statue back on the landing? I looked at the joyous face and pressed my hand against my mouth to stifle a sob.

I hardly heard Omio. I was hearing, seeing, Max.

He said, "My father told me we must learn to love such people, because they must be sick in their minds, and only love could heal such sickness. When people have great power, lo, they become very sick, and must be loved as we love those who are dying. It was not easy, my Polly, after I had seen my father's back and heard his screams."

Suddenly he put his hand under my chin and looked hard into my eyes. I could not hide my confusion and pain. "My Polly," he said gently, "let us not hold on to past wounds. You don't have to bear it with me. I see you entering into the hurt of others, and I love you for it, but you must try not to carry too much."

His words echoed Max's the night she told me about her father, and the echo almost undid me.

He went on. "I do not think it is love if it is too easy. Have you not yet lived long enough to need to love someone who is not easy to love? Surely you have known people who have done wrong things and need to be healed."

I bowed my head and a tear dropped onto the page. Quickly I took a tissue from my pocket and blotted it, where it had fallen on the foot of the Laughing Christ. I looked up and saw Bashemath and Millie walking toward us. I could not speak to them. I ran to one of the open arches and jumped down, ran blindly to the shadows of the fig sycamore.

I could hear Omio running after me, but I could not see him for the blinding tears. His arms went around me.

"You are not crying about my father." I blew my nose, shaking my head. "What is causing your tears?"

I could not tell him. I wiped them away with the palms of my hands.

"Who has hurt you?" he asked. When I did not answer, but shook my head again, he kissed both my eyelids, the still slightly puffy one first, then the other.

Renny had kissed my eyelids, too. Young Doctor Renier, with his stethoscope and white jacket and all-American face, couldn't have been more different from Omio, and yet they were alike in their experience, and my nonexperience.

When I woke up in the green shade of the sleeping porch of Nell, the nurse, she was sitting looking at me. 'I'm home only for a few minutes,' she said. 'I hope I didn't frighten you.'

'No.' A mockingbird was singing sweetly in the magnolia tree.

'I just need to get a few things. I'm doing a double shift, covering for a friend. Renny asked me to fix you some more broth. Here it is, donax soup. It'll cure all ills.'

'Thank you.' Even in my state of shock I was impressed by Nell's offering of donax soup. The tiny shells are no longer easy to find, so it was a real gift. 'Thank you, a lot.'

'Renny'll be back a little after five. He's a good man. He'll be a good doctor, but that doesn't make a good man. Renny's good.'

'I know.'

She stood looking down at me. 'You're just a child.'

I moved my head negatively against the pillow. 'Not now.'

'Whatever it is, whoever it was, it'll pass, you'll get over it. People have bad things happen but they survive.' She turned away from me, took some things out of one of her drawers. 'You'll be okay?'

'Yes. Thanks for taking me in.'

'Make yourself at home. Wander about the place. There isn't much to it. But you'll be here when Renny gets back?' She was afraid I was going to run away. But I'd already run away. There wasn't any place else to run.

'I'll be here.'

After she left I managed to drink the donax soup with its delicate ocean flavor. At first I thought I was going to throw up, but I didn't, and I got it all down. For some reason that seemed important, if only for Nell's generosity in giving me such a rare delicacy. Then I wandered around a little. There was only the large sleeping porch, and a living room with a couch, where she probably slept in winter, and a kitchen and bath. It was obvious that Nell rented it furnished.

I went back to the porch. To bed. Nell's bed.

Nell had given me donax soup, something special. Renny, too, always gave to me. He didn't take. Straw wanted to take. Max—

I started to cry, but crying was exhausting, and I fell into sleep in the middle of a sob. I woke up as I heard Renny letting himself in, hurrying to the porch.

'Did you sleep?'

'Yes.'

'Nell make you some broth?'

'Donax soup. That was really nice of her.'

'Nell's a nice person. A good nurse.' He perched on the bed beside me. 'I want to take you home, Polly.'

'No. Not yet. I need to—I'm too confused, Renny. I can't see my parents till—'

He stroked my hair back from my forehead. 'Why are you confused, Polly? Tell me.'

'Straw—' I said, knowing that I was incoherent, but not knowing how to make sense. 'He killed a tortoise, with some other guys, and he liked doing it—'

'Polly, honey, what's that got to do with it?'

'If you try to *take* love, it's as bad as—as bad as that.'

'Don't let someone like that creep upset you.'

'It's just that—he tried to *take*—and it doesn't work that way—it has to be given—'

'Hush,' he said, 'hush. Yes, it has to be given.' And he kissed my eyelids again, then my lips, the way he did when he cut the motor on the boat when we'd been together. And the kiss continued on past the point where he usually broke off. Then, slowly, he pulled away.

I groped for him, as though I were blind. 'Renny, please, please—' My lips touched his.

And he was kissing me again, and slipping the shorty nightgown over my head. His strong and gentle hands began to stroke me, his hands, his lips, his tongue.

Gentle. Not frightening. Knowing what he was doing. I felt my nipples rise, and it startled me.

'Shhh,' Renny whispered. 'Shhh, it's all right, don't worry, just relax and listen to your body.'

He was slow, rhythmic, gentle, moving down my
    body, down . . .
and I was nothing but my body
there was a sharp brief pain
brief
and then a sweet spasm went through me
and I seemed to rise into the air
no more pain
just the sweetness
the incredible
oh, the
and then Renny, panting
I pressed him hard against me.

He kissed my eyelids in the darkness, under the fig
sycamore. "We'd better go back to the others," he said.
Omio said.

Bashemath and Millie were drinking tea, sitting at the
table. I hoped I didn't look as though I'd been crying.
Norine came toward me. "Where were you, Polly?" she
accused. "That same young man phoned you again, and
I couldn't find you."

Bashemath said, in her calm, deep voice, "She doesn't
have to tell you whenever she goes for a walk, Norine."

"Well, you missed him once more," Norine said to
me.

"Is he going to call again?" I asked.

"He didn't say."

I wasn't sure whether I wanted him to or not. This

world of Osia Theola was a completely different world from Athens, and Zachary seemed alien to it. Still, I was glad he had called. I was glad he had sent flowers.

"Tea, Norine?" Millie asked. "Polly?"

"No, thank you," Norine said. "I have work to do."

"Do you need me?" I asked. "I've typed Bashemath's stencil. Shall I run it off?"

"Not now, Polly. I'm going over some of my lectures."

"Then I'd love some tea," I said.

Norine trotted across the dusty compound to the office, and Bashemath got a mug, and Millie poured me tea from the large pot on the table.

Millie said, "There are some hot peppers by the dormitory building. I've picked a few, to add to the dinner tonight. This food is good, but not overly seasoned."

Bashemath spoke, following her own train of thought. "Do not let Norine bother you with her sharp ways. She has a heart of gold."

"She doesn't bother me," I replied. "And I'm here to work."

"But not to be overworked."

"Oh, I'm not, and I like work."

Omio drained his mug. "We're not likely to have another free afternoon. How about a swim? Or is it too hot?"

"Much too hot," Bashemath said.

"I don't swim. I'm afraid of crocodiles," Millie said. Omio laughed. "But this is Cyprus, not Cameroon."

"Nevertheless," Millie said firmly, "no. Thank you."

"I'd love a swim," I said.

"Let's meet under the fig sycamore." Omio smiled at me.

❀

He was there, waiting for me, and we started down-hill. "Polly, forgive me."

"For what?"

"I have given you, lo, a romantic picture of Baki. It is not only the Christians there who have done bad things. If the missionaries were not overly concerned about whether or not the women covered themselves, it was because they were more concerned about the black magic, the witchcraft. Using hateful, hurting magic was as bad as beating a man and rubbing salt in the wounds. Worse. It could kill. We Bakians and the Christians were alike, some good people, turning the heart to love, others wicked, turning to greed and power."

He was holding my hand, swinging it, as we walked. I said, "I guess everybody's like that." And then I asked, "Does your Laughing Christ always laugh?"

His hand squeezed mine. "It is said that in time of great disaster tears fall from his eyes. My great-grand-father is supposed to have seen him cry before a tidal wave which killed many of our people. I have seen only the laughter, and there have been bad things in Baki. But if I ever saw him cry, I think I would be very afraid."

Did the statue on Max's landing ever weep?

We left the houses of the village and moved quietly along the path protected by high walls of grasses plumed with pale fronds, bleached by the fierce sun. And then we came to a tiny pasture I hadn't noticed the night before in the dark. In the pasture were the most beautiful little goats I'd ever seen, with soft, silky hair, and long, drooping ears. We stopped and admired them. They looked at us with great, startled eyes, then went back to grazing.

When we reached the place which Vee had tried to clear of stones, Omio sat down in the water and began to throw stones far up on the shore, to make the path wider. I joined him, throwing the rounded stones as far as possible.

"If we keep at this a little every day," Omio said, "we will keep the path open. I think Vee has tender feet. She is a poet."

That seemed rather a non sequitur, but I thought it likely that Vee did have tender feet, or she wouldn't have bothered to move the stones. My cut foot was not that tough, either. I was glad of the path.

When we had finished throwing what Omio decided were enough stones, he said, "Last night you held back because of Vee, and that was nice of you. But I think you swim well. Let's race." And he splashed into the water and threw himself under a breaker.

I followed. I have learned that it is not a good idea for a girl to beat a man in a race, even though I think that's stupid. However, I did not have to hold back with Omio. It was all I could do to keep up with him.

"How do you come to swim so well?" he asked while we were splashing into shore. The sun was low on the horizon; evening came early to Cyprus; and the sky was flushed with a lovely light.

"I've lived on islands most of my life. We swim a lot."

Omio took my hand, and we walked on up the beach. "You are promised?" he asked.

"What?"

"You have a boyfriend? A special one?"

"No."

"In Baki, by your age, a woman is at least promised."

"In my country I'm considered too young. At least my parents would certainly think so."

Omio swung my hand. "It's time we went home." He gave me his shining smile. "It is home, isn't it?"

Yes. Already the monastery was home.

After the evening meal, with the dark closing in, Krhis said that we would stay in the cloister for the staff meeting instead of going to the upper room. He had each of the staff members talk a little bit about what they planned to do. Bashemath expected to have everything ready for a book fair, posters and all, by the first weekend. Millie hoped they'd be telling their own stories. Frank talked about the hope for small presses, and then, at his urging, Millie sang for us, and then Norine suggested that Omio do one of the Bakian dances.

Without embarrassment, Omio stood up and stripped off his T-shirt, kicked off his sandals. Then he moved into a dance which started with his entire body undulating in slow rhythm. Then the tempo accelerated until Krhis began to clap, joined by Frank, then Millie and Norine. Then Omio squatted low to the ground, with one leg, then the other, stretching out, somewhat like Russian Cossack dances, but much more quickly, incredibly quickly, and then he rose, rose, until he was leaping high into the air, fingers stretching him taller, higher . . .

Then the clapping began to come more slowly, winding him down. He was glistening with sweat, breathing in short, panting gasps, and the clapping changed from being an accompaniment to the dance, to applause.

"Lo, now we must sing *Saranam*." His voice was breathless, and he looked to Millie, who started singing.

> *In the midst of foes I cry to thee,*
> *From the ends of earth, wherever I may be,*
> *My strength in helplessness, O answer me,*
> *Saranam, saranam, saranam.*

> *Make my heart to grow as great as thine,*
> *So through my hurt your love may shine,*
> *My love be yours, your love be mine,*
> *Saranam, saranam, saranam.*

"What does it mean, 'saranam'?" I asked.

"Refuge," Norine said.

"God's richest blessing," Millie added.

Krhis said, "There is no English equivalent."

Frank laughed. "There doesn't need to be. Saranam says it all, loving, giving, caring."

Omio said, "I think it is like a Bakian word which means that love does not judge."

Vee added, "Love is not love which alters when it alteration finds."

"What's that?" Bashemath asked.

"Shakespeare, from one of the sonnets."

"Shakespeare?" Millie asked.

"Sonnets?" asked Bashemath.

Suddenly I realized that things I'd taken for granted, as part of my background, were unknown to people of other cultures.

"Shakespeare is probably our greatest writer in the English language," Vee said, "and the sonnet is a form of poetry. I'll talk about it in one of the workshops. I even hope to have people writing sonnets."

Another thing I realized was how little I knew about Vee. I knew from her poems and novels that she had loved, and passionately. Because of Norine I knew she had an insane husband. There were a few chinks my imagination could fill in, but I realized something else that evening. I realized I was too young to understand much that had happened in the lives of these people who had quickly become my friends.

We finished the lemonade, which was tart and lovely, and Krhis sent us off to bed. I walked across the compound with Omio and Vee.

"Too late for a swim," she said. "Ah, well, we'll make time tomorrow."

"Too bad Frank can't come with us," I said.

Vee nodded. "He does swim at home, in a pool. He misses it."

"Lo, he is a kind man, is Frank," Omio said.

"Yes," Vee agreed. "I wonder if someone who has never suffered, known loss and pain, is capable of true kindness?"

Omio took my hand. "We find much true kindness here in Osia Theola."

I watered Zachary's flowers, which were thirsty in this heat, then wrote in my school journal till my eyes drooped with sleep. Got into bed and turned out the light. Could smell the punky odor of the mosquito coil. Could smell the bug repellent I'd sprayed on the shutters. My eye was still itchy, so I guessed closing the shutters was worth it. Under my door I could see a line of yellow from the hall, where the light burned all night. A faint glow filtered through the shutters, and I longed to be able to open them to the sky and the night birds and the sound of the sea. I turned on my stomach. My pillow was hot, so I pushed it onto the floor. I thought of Omio coming to find me under the fig-sycamore tree, and I felt his lips brushing my eyelids.

I woke up in a puddle of sweat. I could not hear the dull whir of the fan. There was no line of light under the door. Because the power tended to go out on Benne Seed whenever all the development people ran their air-conditioners, I guessed that the power in the monastery maybe had gone off because all the fans were on. I peered at the travel alarm. Ten past three.

I got up and drew open one shutter just enough so that I could slip out on the balcony. The sky was filled with stars. There were no lights on in the village. So the power was off there, too. No one was stirring. Except the mosquitoes.

I withdrew and got back into my damp bed. I could hear Millie snoring, and her snore was so different from her glorious voice that it made me giggle. Millie looked as though she should have a baby in her arms. Norine had said that all Millie's family had died. Children, too?

I would have liked to have Millie come in and sit by me and stroke my hair back from my forehead and sing to me, one of the verses from *Saranam*, maybe.

But I was not Millie's child.

And I wasn't a child anymore. It felt lonely.

❀

Mother came in to me the night Renny brought me home, and sat on the bed by me, reaching her hand out to smooth my hair. 'Renny didn't tell me how you cut your foot.'

'I was running barefoot on Max's driveway, like an idiot. It was lucky Renny dropped by.' That was the story I'd cooked up and sold to Renny.

'Why would Renny have dropped by?'

'He's Max's doctor, peripherally. He assists Netson.' That would hold water if she checked it out.

'But you're upset about something other than your foot.'

Usually I could tell anything to Mother. I told her when that gross kid exposed himself to me while we were standing in line at the school cafeteria. Something smooth and slightly damp touched my hand and I turned, and there he was, sticking himself out at me. It was nasty, and I felt dirty, but it didn't really have anything to do with me, or even that stupid boy. And Mother could tell me that the same thing had happened to her, and she had felt like me, dirty, and wanting to take a bath.

But this wasn't something outside me that essentially didn't have anything to do with me. And I couldn't say a word.

Mother didn't try to use a can opener on me the way some mothers might. She just sat by me, stroking my hair, waiting. But I didn't speak. I closed my eyes. When she thought I was asleep, she left.

Renny, in a way, provided a smoke screen.

He called first thing in the morning, saying that he

was coming over to Benne Seed to check my foot. Daddy could perfectly well have checked my foot. Mother could have checked my foot. It didn't need a doctor. But Renny came, midmorning, and Mother brought him into the living room, where I was sitting in the comfortable leather chair with my foot up on the footstool. The rest of the kids were swimming, and they'd evidently been told not to bug me, because they'd pretty well left me alone, even Xan and Kate.

Mother brought Renny and me some iced tea, then left us, saying she was in the middle of baking bread. Unlike Ursula, Mother did not bake bread often, and it was usually a sign that she was disturbed.

As soon as she had gone, Renny wanted to know where I was in my menstrual cycle, and was relieved when I told him I was just over my period. Then he was full of rather incoherent apologies. He rebandaged my foot, saying that it was healing nicely. 'Nell sends her best—' He sounded awkward.

'What about Nell?' I asked.

'Nell's a good friend.' He sounded surprised. 'She's engaged to one of the male nurses, and they're both friends of mine.'

Why did that make me feel better about Nell? And a little ashamed about having asked Renny.

He put my foot down on the stool. 'Did you think I was sleeping with Nell?'

'I didn't know.'

'What with the general promiscuity in Cowpertown —and other places—I can hardly be surprised that it crossed your mind. However, Polly, if I had been, I wouldn't have taken you there. I don't sleep around. I'm a Renier. My relationship with Jacinta was not celibate. But I'm a lot older than you. Sweet Polly, what happened between us mustn't happen again. It mustn't happen with you at all, not with me, not with anybody, until you're older and ready to make a real commitment.'

'I'm not planning to sleep around, either,' I said stiffly.

He studied my bandaged foot. 'It's hard to remember you're only sixteen, you seem so much older in so many ways—' He let his breath out gustily. 'Polly, you're very attractive. Don't you know I've plain lusted after you all summer? And yesterday it got the better of me, because—'

'You didn't seduce me, Renny. I wanted it.' —And no, I had no idea you lusted after me. No idea at all.

'I wanted it, too. But I shouldn't have.'

I looked down at his hand, lying on the stool near my foot, and shoulds and shouldn'ts meant nothing at all.

Renny took our empty glasses and put them on the table. He was being very Renier.

'Renny. Stop. I'm glad what happened happened with you. But I'm—' I choked up.

'Oh, Polly honey, I'm sorry. I know you're hurting. I'm sorry.'

Max was there between us, but neither of us mentioned her name.

Daddy came in to me that evening after I was ready for bed. 'Foot feeling better?'

'It's fine. Renny checked it this morning.'

'Mother told me. Polly, is something wrong between you and Renny?'

'No. Renny's a good friend.'

'Are you sure?'

'Sure.'

'What about you and Max?'

'What about me and Max?'

'Mother said Max called today and you wouldn't come to the phone.'

'Renny said I shouldn't walk on my foot.'

'Was that the only reason?'

'Daddy, I was getting too dependent on Max.'

'What made you realize it?'

'Renny . . .'

'Max is a dying woman. You can't just drop her like a hot coal.'

'Daddy, I was like a kid, idolizing Max. It wasn't good.'

'No, Polly, idolatry's never good. But Max and Ursula have been a good influence on you. You've been doing admirably in school, and you've been particularly pleasant to have around the house. I wish Xan did his jobs in the lab as diligently as you do yours. Did anything happen to make you decide you were too dependent on Max?' He was looking at me, not his daddy-look, but diagnostically, trying to see through what I was saying to what was really wrong. But he didn't see.

'It was just time.'

'Did anything happen to upset you when you stayed at Beau Allaire?'

'Max drank too much.'

'Was she in pain?'

'Yes.'

'Why didn't you call me?'

'I don't know—'

'People with too much alcohol in them are always unpleasant, though to a certain extent it's understandable with Max. How much too much did she have?'

'Daddy, she was *drunk*.'

'It's not good to idolize people, Pol, you're right. I don't condone Max's drinking, but you have to allow even the people you most admire to be complex and contradictory like everybody else. The more interesting somebody is, the more complex.'

'Sure.'

'You don't have to like it, honey, but you do have to understand it.'

'Okay.'

Daddy stood up. 'All right, Polly. I'm sorry Max showed you her clay feet. If you want to talk about it further, remember, Mother and I are right here.'

'Yes. I'm glad. Thanks.'

He left, and in a few minutes I heard a knock on my door. Xan's knock.

I didn't want to talk to him. So I just let him knock.

The soft knocking on my door roused me. I got out of bed and opened the door onto darkness.

"It's Millie," came her gentle voice, with a slight tremor. "My fan's off—I think the power's out—"

She followed me into the room, holding my arm, and then sat on the first bed. "Do you think something's wrong?"

Millie was obviously afraid, so I said, reassuringly, "It's just a power failure."

"You don't think it's some kind of emergency?"

"No, Millie, I think it's okay." Suddenly I realized that while a power outage was to me a sign of poor electricity, to Millie it could mean that a power plant had been bombed, it could mean a military coup, an

attack on civilians— "I'll go check." I got up and slipped
out onto the balcony. Nothing but normal night sounds.
But Cyprus was an island of many emergencies, of
being overrun by Italians, Turks, British, and, within
the memory of everybody there, the Turks again. Millie
came from a world of emergencies, of small countries
fighting to get out from under the domination of foreign
powers. I understood why she would be so afraid that
she would fumble through the darkness to make contact
with someone in the next room.

I went back in. "Everything's okay. All quiet. I'm
sure it's just the power going off because it's so hot and
everybody's got fans on, and probably air-conditioners
at the hotel."

"Thanks, Polly dear. Thanks. I'll go back to bed
now."

I lit a match and helped her back to her room, standing in the doorway until I heard her bed creak and she
called good night. I went back to bed, but there was no
sound from Millie's room, no comfortable snoring. I
wondered what she was remembering.

I got up early enough to finish making the beds, and
then I still had time to go into the church for a few
minutes before breakfast. I went deep into the interior,
to the dark entrance of the cave.

A shadow moved, and I turned to see Vee coming
toward me. "I always drop in when the doors are open,"
she said. "It's a very special place." I nodded. "Osia
Theola is indeed kind in what she lets us know about
ourselves. She tells me that I am stronger than I think
I am. I've bought a little icon of her to take home. There

are some nice ones in that little shop up the hill." We were silent for a while. Then Vee asked gently, "What does Theola tell you?"

"She warms the cold place in my heart," I said. "She's helping the ice to thaw."

"But you have a loving heart, Polly, that's one of the first things I noticed about you. I'm glad Theola's making you realize it." She laughed a little wistfully. "Some people would call this the rankest superstition. But is it? What happens in a place does leave its imprint. Even today the sites of the concentration camps have a bone-chilling cold, no matter how hot the day. Osia Theola left love here, and we can catch it from her."

The ancient sacristan came up to us then, with two tiny bouquets. He, too, must have picked up the largeness of love from Blessed Theola, because he warmed us with it.

We left the candlelit church and went to breakfast.

I had been right about the power failure. Krhis announced that the power had gone off largely because of the air-conditioning at the hotel and that the power company promised to have it back on by noon.

Tullia served us fresh, hot bread, her toothless smile lavished on us as though we were her honored guests. Sophonisba brought us eggs, smiling so that her front gold tooth reflected the light.

I was sitting with my back to the monastery grounds, facing the sea, so I did not see anyone coming until I noticed people's heads turning, and I turned, too, and there was Zachary.

"Found you at last, Polly," he said, coming up the steps. He smiled at the tableful of what must have seemed to him very strange people. "I'm Zachary Gray, a friend of Polly's," he said. "I got here last night, just in time for the blackout at the hotel. I wonder if I could steal Polly for lunch today?"

"Oh, no, Zach—" I protested. "I have work to do."

Krhis looked at Norine, who looked at me, then said, "I'll need Polly in the office for a while this morning, but there's no reason she can't be free by eleven. And we won't need her again till two."

"That's fine," Zachary said. "I'll be back for you at eleven."

"Won't you stay and have a cup of coffee?" Krhis suggested.

"No, thanks. I've some things to do back at the hotel. I'm off to Mykonos tomorrow, so this is my only chance to see Polly till I meet her plane in Athens."

At that, Omio gave Zachary a sharp look. I did not think they would get on. Zachary represented a good many things Omio was fighting, and while somebody like Sandy could see this clearly and still get along courteously with Zachary, I was not sure about Omio.

"I'll rent a sailboat or a kayak for us," Zachary called as he jumped down the steps. "Nice to have seen all of you."

"Very good-looking," Millie said.

"He is the young man who has kept calling?" Norine accused rather than asked.

"Yes." And who sent me flowers. And made me feel special. I was excited to see him, and yet he seemed a slightly discordant note in this place and with these people. But I didn't wish he hadn't come.

"An old friend?" Norine asked.

"No, I met him while I was in Athens."

"You want to go out with him?" Bashemath asked.

"Well—he was very kind to me in Athens."

"It'll be a kind of culture shock," Vee said, "leaving the monastery and going to—oh, another world, with the beach full of topless bathers, and people sitting around the pool drinking and ignoring the real, unchlorinated water."

"If he takes you swimming," Omio said severely, "don't go out too far. And don't be late."

"I won't be," I said. "I'll have to be back at two to help Norine."

"And then, later, we'll have our swim," Vee said.

Zachary picked me up promptly at eleven, in a rented car.

"Do you have your bathing suit?"

"I can get it."

"Do, and hurry. I've made our reservations for lunch at one, and I thought we'd have a swim and a sail first."

He'd rented a cabana for me to dress in and suggested that we swim in the pool.

"No, thanks. I don't like chlorine and I do like salt water."

"All those rough waves—" But we went in the ocean. Zachary swam moderately well. He did the strokes correctly, but he had no stamina. After a few minutes he splashed into shore. I followed him, and started to tell him a little about the conference staff, but it was obvious that he wasn't interested in the people or the worlds they came from.

"Do your parents know this mixed kind of group you're with?"

"Of course."

He headed toward the pier. "I've rented us a kayak. All the sailboats were taken, okay?"

"Sure, a kayak's fine." Anything would have been fine with me, even a rowboat. I could still hardly believe that Zachary had come all this way to see me.

The kayak was waiting at the little landing dock. Zachary and the attendant helped me in, and Zachary sat behind, holding the double paddle used for this little play boat. The attendant said something in Greek that I could not quite understand, but I think he was warning us to be careful not to go beyond the white ropes strung from red buoys which enclosed a sizable section of water.

"You're a help to me, Polly," Zachary said. "You help me think clearly. I'd predicated my life on being a corporate lawyer. If I don't want that, what do I want? I couldn't be a doctor, I faint at the sight of blood. Listen, Red—" He splashed with the paddle instead of feathering. "I talked with my pop on the phone, and he knows your aunt and uncle."

"He does!"

Zachary nodded. "Not personally. Reputation. He says they're dangerous."

"They're not—"

"Hey, hold it, don't rock the boat, you'll have us in the soup."

"Sorry." My jerky movement had set the little craft rocking, but it stabilized quickly. "Sandy and Rhea—"

"Don't you see, Pop has to think that way? Megabucks is the only game he knows, and people who care about people get in his way. If you want to put a highway through a village, you can't be concerned about the people in the village whose homes are going to be destroyed."

"Is that your world?" I asked. "Do you really want that?"

"No, Polly, I don't. That's why I wanted to be with you today. I'm glad Dragon Lady gave you at least three hours off." He put the paddle across the thwarts and we drifted gently. "I wanted to tell you that I've decided to stop puddling around Europe. I'm flying home—after we've had our reunion in Athens airport—and I'm going back to college."

"That's wonderful!" Then I looked around us at the softly slapping water. "We're outside the white ropes."

"That's okay. I went way out this morning. And the sailboats all go out." He pointed to half a dozen colorful sails. "I'll paddle us back in a minute. Right now I need to talk. The problem is, Polly, I'm going back to college, but I'm not sure I still want to be a lawyer and take over Pop's world."

"Sandy and Rhea are lawyers," I reminded him.

"I'm not sure I'd have the guts to do what they're doing. I'm learning that I do have limitations."

"Sure," I said, "we all do, but given the chance, we can go beyond our limitations."

"Do I want to? At least, do I want to put my life on the line? People like your uncle and aunt are in danger, do you realize that? People like my pop, particularly those with even more money and power than my pop, are pretty ruthless about wiping out people who get in the way. They look down on lawyers who care about human life as stupid sentimentalists."

"Rhea and Sandy aren't sentimental!" I didn't like this conversation. I looked around and all I could see was water and a couple of sailboats in the distance. The tide, I thought, was going out, and we'd drifted rapidly. "Zachary," I said, "I don't see the hotel."

He looked around. "Okay, we'll go back." He picked up the paddle. "The thing is, Polly, you've really made a difference in the way I think about things. I've never been close to my pop, never loved him, but I thought his way of life was a realistic one and that I had every right to inherit power and prestige. But here he is, middle-aged, with ulcers, not happy, and not knowing how to do anything but make bigger and bigger deals. I don't think that's what I want to look forward to."

"I'm glad, Zach, very glad." I didn't think I could take much credit for his decision. It must have been under the surface all the time, waiting to break through. But I was glad it had.

He went on. "I want to thank you, Polly. I'm not sure what I'm going to do with my life, but you've turned it completely around." He rested the paddle again and bent forward to kiss me. It stopped being just a kiss and began to be more, and suddenly I wasn't sure how much I believed of all he'd just said. He drew back slightly, breathed, "Oh, Polly, come—" He put his hand behind my head to draw me closer.

"No, Zach—" The boat started rocking violently.

"Watch it!" And suddenly we were in the water. We came up sputtering. I grabbed at the kayak as it began to slip away from us.

"Now look what you've done!" he shouted.

I didn't answer. He was thrashing about, tiring himself. "Here!" I called. "Here! Hold on!"

He grabbed at the overturned kayak and managed to get a grip. If it had been a canoe, I could have turned it over and got in. It's not so easy with an overturned kayak. "Tread water for a minute," I said, "and let me try to right the kayak." Without saying anything, he let go, and I got under the gunwales and pushed, kicking as hard as I could, and to my relief the little play boat was light enough so that I could flip it over. The paddle was gone. "Do you think you can climb back in?" I asked.

"I doubt it. I'm not the athletic type. Do you want to try? Then maybe you can pull me in. I'll hold on and try to keep it level for you."

Even without the paddle, we'd be better off in the boat. Zachary's stamina was not going to last long. But when I tried to pull myself up over the gunwales, Zachary lost his grip. "Zach! Hold on!"

He splashed back to the kayak, and grabbed at the side, almost overturning it again. This was not going to work. I looked around for the sailboats, but although I saw a couple, they weren't in hailing distance, and they were too far off for anybody to notice us. We couldn't stay in the water for several hours till Norine missed me and someone came to look for us.

Zachary realized this, too. "If I let go and dog-paddle again, do you think you can get in without my help?"

"I'll try." I didn't say it would be easier without his 'help.' I was almost in the kayak when suddenly he grabbed at it and I lost my balance and slid back into the water. Fortunately, the boat did not overturn again. But the little boat was made for the quiet waters around the dock, within the boundaries of the ropes, not for the open sea. I didn't think Zachary knew much about boats. Left to myself, I could have managed to clamber in without overturning it, but Zachary was in a silent panic, and whatever I did, he was going to undo by grasping at the sides, or letting go and risk being swept away by the undertow.

"I can't see the hotel," he said. I'd already told him that.

"Listen, Zach." My voice was urgent. "Let me try once more to climb in. Tread water, but make sure you don't drift away."

"I'll try."

He let go and began to dog-paddle. I put one hand on either gunwale for balance and had almost heaved myself in when I heard him cry out. He had already drifted two lengths of the boat. I dropped back in the water, still holding the kayak with one hand, because it would be madness to lose it, and kicked as strongly as I could in his direction. "Zachary! Swim! Try to swim toward me!" The distance between us began to widen, and I could see that he was floundering, moving arms and legs aimlessly and futilely. I was going to have to let the kayak go in order to get him, and then what? We could never make it back to the kayak together; he simply didn't swim well enough. And we certainly couldn't even think of trying to make it to shore against the tide.

I wasn't ready to die.

But I couldn't save myself and let Zachary drown.

Why not? If I didn't save myself, we'd both drown, and what good would that do?

"Polly—"

"Don't thrash, Zachary," I shouted. "I'm coming." I let go of the kayak.

"Polly!"

I had one arm around Zachary and was kicking to keep afloat. He was pulling me down. I couldn't go on holding both of us up for much longer.

"*Polly!*"

It wasn't Zachary calling me. Zachary was an exhausted, dead weight.

"Polly!"

"Here!" I shouted. "Here, Omio, here!"

"Keep calling, so I don't lose you."

"Here! Here, Omio, here!"

And suddenly I saw a rowboat, a lovely, solid rowboat, with Omio at the oars. He saw us and pulled the boat to us with strong, sure strokes.

"Get Zachary in first," I said.

Omio rested the oars, reached out one strong arm, then both, as he realized that Zachary could do little to help himself. Somehow or other, Omio pulling, me pushing, we managed to get him into the rowboat. Then Omio's hands were stretched down to me, and with his help I heaved myself up, and flopped into the bottom of the boat, panting. "The kayak—" I whispered.

"Forget it," Omio said fiercely. Then he turned to Zachary. He let out a long stream of invective in Bakian. If I had thought Bashemath's anger could be terrifying, I was not prepared for Omio's.

"I'll pay for the kayak," Zachary said.

"And could you have paid for Polly's life? Do you know if I had been five minutes later you'd both have been dead? Would you have made everything right by paying for the funeral?" He was an avenging angel in his anger.

I was still gasping for breath. "How did you—how did you know?"

"I was worried. And Vee said she smelled danger, and told Frank, and he went with us to the hotel, and we were told you'd gone out in a kayak. But there weren't any kayaks in the roped-in area. So Frank suggested I take the rowboat. He and Vee will be waiting for us." He was rowing with strong, smooth strokes. Even so, it seemed a long time before we could see shore and the

hotel. "Where did you think you were going?" Omio
asked Zachary.

Some of Zachary's confidence had returned, though his
face was pallid. "I was thinking of emigrating to Syria
with Polly. It was farther than I realized."

"It is not funny." Omio still sounded enraged.

"Oh, come on," Zachary said. And then, with one of
his lightning switches, "I was an arrogant fool, and I'm
beyond apology."

"I would not have any harm come to Polly," Omio
said.

Vee and Frank were waiting at the landing dock, their
faces lighting in relief as they saw us.

Omio drew the rowboat skillfully up to the dock, and
the attendant helped me out.

"Thank God you're safe," Vee said.

"What happened?" Frank asked.

Zachary spoke swiftly, before Omio could say anything. "I misjudged the tide and lost my bearings."

Omio burst out, "And lost the kayak. Polly was holding him up in the open sea. They couldn't have lasted
much longer."

I discovered that I was trembling. Frank put out a
hand to steady me.

"We'll take you home," Omio said.

"Polly is having lunch with me," Zachary said.

Omio leapt onto the dock. "Polly is not going anywhere with you."

For a second I thought he and Zachary were going to
get into a fight. Frank stepped between them, and I said,
"I think I'm too tired to eat. I'm going to get my clothes
on." And I walked away from them, went to the cabana,
and changed. I was still very shaky.

When I had my dress back on, sandals on my feet, I

returned to the hotel, where they were sitting at one of the terrace tables, waiting. The three men rose as I approached. Zachary said, "Polly, please forgive me for having been such a monstrous fool."

Frank stopped his apologies. "Polly's exhausted, and we need to get her to bed."

Zachary did not argue. "I'll call you, Polly, if you're willing to speak to me again. I'll never be such a chauvinist idiot—"

"It's okay, Zachary," I said.

Frank borrowed Zachary's rented car to drive us home, and I was grateful. I wasn't at all sure my wobbly legs would have made it. Of course we'd missed lunch, but everybody was still in the refectory. Norine looked up in surprise.

"Omio and Frank will explain," Vee said. "I want to get Polly to her room and into bed."

Without saying anything, and somehow inconspicuous despite her great height, Bashemath fell into step beside us.

"There was a near-catastrophe," Vee said. "Polly needs a hot bath and bed."

"It won't be a very hot bath," Bashemath said.

"Even lukewarm would be heavenly."

When we got to the room, the fan was whirring, so the power was back on. "Go along," Vee said to me. "I'll tell Bashemath what happened."

The water was at least warm, and felt wonderful, and I lay back and relaxed for a long time, almost dozing once or twice, till my twitching muscles let go their panic tightness. Then it occurred to me that Vee and

Bashemath might be waiting, so I got out and dried myself and put on my nightgown.

Only Bashemath was in the room. "Vee's gone to see about getting some hot soup for you."

I sat, facing her dignified presence. "Omio saved my life."

"And Vee and Frank. It was Vee who had the knowing that there was something wrong, and Frank who had the wisdom to take her seriously."

"How did Vee know?"

"Vee is a poet. Sometimes poets still have the ancient knowings."

I was grateful to Vee, to Frank. "But, Bashemath," I said, "it was Omio who came with the boat and got us out of the water. I was tiring—we were almost drowning—I couldn't have held on much longer."

"But you had left the little boat and were holding up this strange young man—"

"What else could I do?"

"What else?" She turned to answer a knock. Norine came in, carrying a kettle of something which smelled delicious. Millie followed with bowls, and Frank with spoons. Omio and Vee came in together. Norine set the kettle down on the empty desk.

"Get into bed, Polly. We will spoil you this afternoon, okeydokey? You and your rescuers will have some of this good soup Tullia has prepared, and then you will sleep. Someone will bring you tea, and you can come to the afternoon meeting, okeydokey?"

"Very okeydokey," I said. Every bone and muscle ached, but I was so full of the love of these people I had not even met a few days ago that it didn't matter. Norine ladled out a rich soup full of vegetables and fish, and Vee and Frank and Omio and I ate. I was ravenously hungry. Back at the hotel, I had thought I would never want to eat again.

Norine noticed Zachary's flowers, which were drooping despite my ministrations. "These are completely wilted. Do you want me to throw them out for you?"

It seemed like throwing Zachary out, but Norine didn't know that, and it didn't make much sense to keep dead flowers, so I told her to go ahead.

When we'd finished eating, everybody stood up to leave, except Millie, who came and sat by me. "I will give Polly a back rub. She will sleep better. Roll over, little one." I hardly heard the others leave. Millie's hands were strong yet tender, and she seemed to know which muscles I had strained.

When I was half asleep, Millie drew the sheet up over me, and then started to sing, not *Saranam*, or any of the songs she'd sung to the group with her miraculous voice, but a song with an odd, minor melody, and words I didn't understand but which weren't unlike Gaean.

And I realized that she was singing to me as her baby, that for this moment I *was* Millie's baby—perhaps one of the children she had lost—and I was lapped in her love.

When I woke up she was gone, and my muscles were no longer tense, but the scar on my foot was pulling painfully. Why?

Renny had come to look at my foot again on Sunday. He called on Monday after school, though he didn't come over because I said my foot was fine, and he called again on Tuesday. When Xan yelled to me on Wednesday, 'Hey, Pol, telephone, I think it's Renny again,' I said, 'Look, if you keep calling they'll know something's wrong.'

'Something *is* wrong.'

'Okay, but I don't want them worried.'

'Aren't they?'

'I guess, but they don't know what about, and I don't want them to know.'

It was that evening Sandy called from Washington and said it just happened that he had to go down to Cape Canaveral to see someone and he'd drop off at Benne Seed on the way if we'd meet his plane in Charleston on Friday. This is the kind of thing Sandy does, so nobody thought anything about it. We were accustomed to having him or Rhea drop in on us from all kinds of places.

But when we were alone together, which wasn't until Saturday afternoon, he said, 'I need some exercise. Let's go walk on the beach.'

We took our sandals off and splashed along the water's edge. He said, 'Max called me.'

'Max?' I, too, had simply taken Sandy's coming for granted.

'She told me to come, because you needed me.'

We had splashed a little farther into the water, and an unexpected wave wet Sandy's rolled-up pants, so we turned toward the dunes. Finally I asked, 'Why did she say that?'

'She told me what happened. Do you want to talk about it?'

I was not prepared to have Sandy know. I was not prepared for him to have come to Benne Seed because Max had called him. 'You won't say anything to Mother or Daddy?'

'You haven't said anything?'

'No.'

'Are you going to?'

'No.'

'Are you trying to protect them?'

I didn't know who I was trying to protect.

'Polly, you've had a lot of responsibility, helping your mother with the little ones, helping your father in the lab, doing all kinds of jobs most kids your age haven't had to do. You're very mature for your age in many ways—'

'And very immature in others,' I finished for him. 'Please, Sandy, I don't want you to say anything to Mother and Daddy.'

He looked at me for a long time. At last I let my eyes drop. 'All right.' He turned toward a large sand dune, climbed partly up it, and sat down in a tangle of scuppernong grapevines. 'I think I'd just as soon not say anything to them about it myself. The problem is, Polly, you made Max into a god.'

'I know that.'

'Can't you let her be a little human?'

I didn't answer.

'Are you being fair to Max?'

Sandy, like Ursula, was considering Max and not me. 'Was Max being fair to me?'

'No. But two wrongs never make a right.'

'What am I doing wrong?' Did he somehow know about Renny?

But he said, 'It's not what you're doing wrong. It's what you're not doing. Max wants to talk to you.'

I shook my head and looked into the vines as though looking for the dark fruit of the scuppernongs.

'Polly.' He waited till I looked at him. 'Max is dying.'

I nodded, again dropping my glance.

'Perhaps you're too young,' he said, as though to himself. 'Too overwhelmed. You need time. But I'm not sure there's enough time.' I did not answer. He slid down from the dune, and I followed him back to the water's edge. 'Your mother is inviting Max and Ursula to dinner tonight. It's the natural thing to do, since we've been friends for years and I haven't been here since Christmas.'

'I don't want them to come.'

'I understand that. And I don't know whether or not they will come.'

I got up and headed for the house. I could not see Max. I could not. I'd have to get out of it somehow.

But when I got home Mother was on the phone. It was Urs saying Max wasn't feeling well. Sandy took the Land-Rover and went over to Beau Allaire. Renny called to ask me to go out for pizza. He was able to borrow a boat, so we went, as usual, to Petros', and sat in our usual booth. Max was between us. What had happened on Nell's green sleeping porch was between us.

'Polly, I don't want you to get the idea that making love is a casual, one-time thing.'

'It wasn't casual, it was wonderful.'

He put his hand over mine. 'I'm glad it was wonderful. For me, too. If my parents knew what happened between us, they'd think I should ask you to marry me, but that wouldn't be a good idea. I have a lot more studying to do, and so do you. You're much too young. But, Polly, please don't let—'

I stopped him. 'Renny, don't worry about me. I'm not going to make a habit of throwing myself at guys. How often do I have to tell you? Please get off your guilt trip.'

Our pizza was put before us, steaming and bubbly with cheese and anchovies and peppers. 'Renny the

Square. That's me. But the Reniers believe that there *is* right and wrong, and a world without restraints is going down the drain.'

'Hey, Renny, I do have restraints.'

'What?'

'My family. My parents. And'—my voice was very low—'Max.'

'Max!'

'Max acted without restraints.'

'Okay,' Renny said. 'I'm glad you see it that way.'

I didn't know whether to hit or hug him. 'Maybe I acted without restraints with you, but I still thank you.'

He cut the pizza and put a slice on my plate. 'Oh, Polly, I don't know what to say.'

'Don't say anything. And don't let it spoil our being good friends.'

But everything was changed. He couldn't even talk about his pet South American diseases without our both thinking of Max.

'When you get back from Cyprus,' he said, 'you'll have had a million new experiences, and you'll have been separated by all that space and time—'

'I'll write you postcards,' I said.

In the boat on the way back to the Island he cut the motor as usual and bent to kiss me, then stopped.

'Why?' I asked.

He held me so tightly that it hurt. 'Not tonight, Pol. I'm not sure I could hold back.'

And he was right, Renny was right. He had wakened my body.

And Omio had saved that wakened body. I had been

attracted to Omio from the very first evening. But now it was more, much more.

I lay there, half awake, thinking about Omio, when he knocked on my door and came in with a glass of iced tea.

I sat up. "Oh, Omio, thank you, thank you."

"It's only cold tea," he said.

"Not the tea. *Me*. My life. If it hadn't been for you, I'd be in a watery grave. I nearly was."

He put my glass down on the table between the beds and took my hands. "It was Frank, and Vee, as much as I, who saved you, Polly, but it has made you—lo, a part of me, a part of my own life."

"I'll always be grateful."

He was fierce. "I do not need gratitude. I do not want it. This is not our way." He smiled. "But we are friends forever in the mind of God, so I have brought you something." And he handed me the painting of the Laughing Christ from his notebook.

"But you can't take a page out of your book!" I protested.

"I will paste in another after I am home. I want you to have this so that you will always remember me."

"I would always remember you, no matter what."

"Lo, we need something we can touch or see," Omio said.

I wasn't sure how I felt about the painting of the Laughing Christ. Omio had no way of knowing that it could remind me of anybody except himself. I looked at it, and saw a double image, the face of sheer joy and Max carrying the statue, her face distorted with whiskey and fear.

"What is it?" Omio asked.

"Nothing."

"I have hurt you."

"No—no—it's not you at all."

"That young man, that Zachary?"

I shook my head. "Not Zachary. Omio—if I take this, I need to give you something, and I don't have anything."

"A picture of yourself? A snapshot?"

"I don't go around carrying pictures of myself. Well —I do have my school ID card, but it's an awful picture like most ID cards."

"But I may have it?"

"Sure, if you want it." Actually, it wasn't that bad a picture, or I wouldn't have dreamed of giving it to him. I got up and went to the desk and took it from my school notebook. I handed the picture to him.

He smiled. "Yes. That's my Polly." He opened his wallet. "You won't need it when you get back to school?"

"I can get another." It was all I had to give to Omio, and I wanted him to have something of me.

"Good, then, I will put it here, next to—" And he indicated a snapshot of a blond, fair-skinned girl with curly golden hair. On her lap was a dark-skinned baby boy, with a surprising mop of that fair hair.

"Who are they?" I asked curiously.

He looked surprised. "My wife and baby. When I married a girl who was born in England, I knew that I had truly forgiven, all the way deep in my heart, what had been done to my father."

My lips felt the way they do when the dentist has pumped them full of novocaine. "I didn't know you were married."

His eyes widened. "But, my Polly, I showed you my pictures that first night."

"No."

"How could I not? I showed them to Krhis, I know. Our little one was born since I last saw Krhis, and is named after him."

I got up and took the picture of the Laughing Christ to my desk and propped it up. But now I saw no laughter in the face, no joy. "Norine will be wanting me," I said. "I've got to get dressed."

"Polly, you really did not know that I have a wife?"

I shook my head.

"Why does it make such a difference?"

I shrugged. "It doesn't."

He put one hand lightly on my shoulder. "I am married to one wife, and I will be true to her. But that does not mean that no one else can touch my soul."

"No," I said. "Please go, Omio. I have to dress."

He dropped his hand. "To deny friendship is unlove." And he left.

Why was I making such a big deal out of Omio's not telling me he was married? He thought I knew. He wasn't trying to keep anything from me. He truly thought I knew. And why should it matter, anyhow? We'd be together for three weeks, and then Omio would go back to Baki, and I'd go back to Benne Seed, and maybe we'd write a couple of times, and that would be that.

But Omio had kissed my eyelids under the fig-sycamore tree. Omio had pulled me out of the sea. Yet, despite my own imaginings of his kisses, his touch, I knew that Omio had never kissed me as Renny had kissed me in the boat on the way back to Benne Seed. Omio knew restraints.

We were in Osia Theola. Theola's love, and her perception of truth, were restraints. Krhis was a restraint.

I worked in the office with Norine for the rest of the afternoon. If I seemed preoccupied or upset, she put it down to the accident with Zachary. She kept me busy with the ancient mimeograph machine, and I did my best to run off stencils without getting completely covered with purple ink in the process.

"I hope Frank is not getting too fond of Vee." She frowned.

"Does he know? About her husband?"

"She does not make it a secret. Neither does she talk about it."

"Well—at least they can be friends." As I could be friends with Omio. To deny friendship is unlove, he had said.

Norine's hands slowed down as she was feeding paper into the machine. "Without friends, we would not survive."

And I knew nothing about what had hurt Norine.

The phone rang, and she answered it in her usual brisk manner. "I'll see," I heard her say. "She may not wish to speak with you." She turned to me, her hand over the mouthpiece. "It is that young man who has caused so much trouble. You don't have to speak to him." She shook her head.

But I moved toward the phone. "I think I'd better. He's got to be feeling terrible."

Maybe my concern over Zachary's feeling was, under all the circumstances, inconsistent of me.

❀

He was, indeed, contrite, and I had it in me to be sorry for him, and agreed to meet him in Athens between flights.

Norine had left me alone, saying that she had to speak to Sophonisba and Tullia.

"Hey, Pol, you know I'm really sorry, don't you?" he asked. "I mean, I know it was my fault we went in the soup, not yours."

"It's okay," I said, and that was all I could think of to say to Zachary. The funny thing was, it *was* okay. I could let Zachary be the way he was and it didn't really bother me.

Was it because I didn't really care about him that much? He'd been terrific while I was in Athens; I'd had fun with him; he'd done marvels for my ego. But despite his talk about our chemistry being so great, it really wasn't. He didn't do things to my pheromones the way Renny did. Or Omio. I was going to be able to say a casual goodbye to Zachary, whether on Cyprus or in Athens airport; it wasn't going to make a ragged scar in my life.

I liked him, but I didn't love him. And that was very confusing, because I certainly hadn't sorted out what love is.

"Hey, are you there?" he asked. The phone was crackling as though we were talking long-distance.

"I'm right here. But I have work to do, Zach."

"But is everything okay with us? I haven't ruined it all?"

"No," I said. "It was an accident."

"So you don't mind if I meet your plane in Athens?"

"No, I don't mind a bit. It will be fun."

"Can you sound a little more enthusiastic?"

"Sure, Zach, I'm still kind of tired."

"I'm just grateful that you're not dumping me," he said. "See you in Athens."

I hung up and went back to the recalcitrant mimeograph machine, getting even more ink on myself. I didn't notice when Krhis came into the office until he spoke.

"Polly?"

I looked up from the machine and wiped my inky fingers on a rag. "Oh, Krhis. Hello."

"You are doing a good job, Polly, being very helpful."

"Thank you. I'm loving every minute of it."

"Despite your accident with the kayak?"

"Thanks to Omio—and Vee and Frank—nothing terrible happened."

"Norine is afraid we're working you too hard."

"Oh, no! I was afraid I wasn't working hard enough!"

"I am glad indeed that Max arranged for you to come to us."

I fiddled with the machine, spilling more ink.

"Polly, whenever I mention Max, you withdraw. Is something wrong?"

"Yes," I said, "but since Max didn't tell you—"

"What is it? Would you be betraying a confidence by telling me?"

I blurted out, "Max is dying. Maybe I am betraying a confidence, but oh, Krhis, she's afraid, and maybe you could pray for her—"

I could see a shadow of grief cross his face. "I will pray."

"She has an awful South American disease, transmitted by an insect bite. It affects the heart, and it's slow and painful. And lethal." I managed to keep my voice level.

He accepted without question what I said. "I'm glad you told me." He took my hands and looked into my eyes. "I think Maxa would be glad, too."

"I'm glad you know," I said. "Oh, Krhis, I'm very glad you know."

He squeezed my hands gently. "You are covered with ink. Go back to the dormitory, where there is warm water to wash it off."

I nodded. Left.

Krhis's prayers would not save Max's life. But they were nevertheless very important.

Omio came up to me as I walked along the path with the roses.

"I'm inky." I held out my purple hands. "Don't touch me."

"My Polly, you have been beaten, and you are still bleeding, and, lo, I have rubbed salt in your wounds."

I shook my head. Tears rushed to my eyes. "I'm being very silly."

"Is it that Zachary? Has it something to do with him?"

"No!"

"But you have been hurt. When I gave you my picture of the Laughing Christ, I hurt you. If you do not want to keep it, I will not be offended."

"No. Please. I want to keep it."

"Lo, I am glad then, of that. Before you came to Cyprus, someone hurt you?"

"Yes. But I'm not thinking straight about that, either."

"Are we still friends?"

"Of course." I closed my eyes, and the slanting rays of the sun made dancing dots behind my eyelids. "I don't know what's the matter. It doesn't have anything to do with you."

"Doesn't it? That does not make me happy." His fingers lightly touched mine. "We of Baki are still close to the old ways. It was always understood that it was possible to love more than one person at a time, without dishonor."

I nodded, looking at our shadows, which were lengthening on the hot ground.

"And," he said, "Jesus was more forgiving to those who made mistakes in love than to those who judged each other harshly and were cold of heart."

"Your picture"—I tried to speak over the lump in my throat—"of the Laughing Christ will not let me forget that. Omio, I do have to go wash off all this ink."

"And then we will meet Vee under our fig-sycamore tree. She is ready to go swimming."

I got most of the ink off before going to the tree, where Omio and Vee waited.

"Sure you're up to it?" Vee asked me.

"Sure. I had a good nap this afternoon." And my foot no longer hurt me.

When the water came in view, Omio stopped us. "Look!" he exclaimed. The moon rose above the water, waxing full and beneficent, while on the other horizon the great orb of golden sun slid down into the darkness behind the sea's horizon. I had never before seen the end of day and the beginning of night greet each other. We were caught in the loveliness between the two.

"Oh—joy!" Vee breathed.

Above us the sky was a tent of blues and violets and greens, with just a touch of rose, and we were enclosed in it. We walked slowly until we got to the path Omio and I had made through the encircling ring of stones.

"What a splendid job," Vee said. She bent down to the stones and searched until she had found four small round white ones. She put them in the pocket of her terry robe. "One for each of us. And one for Frank. Whenever there is a full moon we will hold our moon stones and think of Osia Theola, and the rising of the moon and the setting of the sun. Now, children, you go ahead and race."

"Just one quick one," I said. We swam parallel to the shore, and I could tell that Omio was constantly checking me.

"I'm a good swimmer, Omio, you don't have to worry."

He swam beside me. "If you were not a good swimmer, lo, you would by now be washed up on some strange shore, and that—young man with you." He used a Bakian word I did not understand, but I knew it was not complimentary. He went on. "I do not want him meeting you in the airport. I, too, have time between planes. I will stay with you to take care of you. If you will let me."

I did not answer that. I tried to turn it into a joke. "He can't take me kayaking in Athens airport."

"He is not good for you," Omio said. "He wants too much. He is someone who takes. He does not give."

Those words were an echo of something, but at that moment I could not remember what.

"We'd better swim back to Vee," I said, and we turned toward shore.

When we got back to her, Omio asked, "Will we be able to have our afternoon swim tomorrow, when the delegates are all here?"

"We'll manage," Vee said. "We need the exercise. Don't worry about it now. We have today to rejoice in, and this moment of sheer loveliness."

"Don't you have a saying?" Omio asked. "That we should live every day as though we were going to die tomorrow and as though we were going to live forever?"

"It's an old adage," Vee said, "but a good one. Let's have another swim."

The water was caressing as I swam, this time with Vee. The sunset was deepening, and Omio called out and pointed, and we saw great bursts of lightning zagging behind clouds which were all the way across the Mediterranean.

"Shouldn't we get out?" I asked. "Isn't it dangerous?"

Vee reassured me. "It's all right. The storm is over in Lebanon and Syria, so far off we can't even hear the thunder."

But we swam for only a few minutes longer, then turned into shore. Vee put on her robe and pulled two of the stones out of the pocket, giving one to Omio, one to me. Moon stones.

We walked slowly through the steamy evening, up the sand and stones of the hill, pausing to say good night to the little goats. Omio leaned over the fence, and one of the goats came and nibbled on his fingers, and he stroked the soft ears. Then we walked on. Omio did not take my hand.

❀

After dinner we stayed in the cloister. Krhis said that a bus would meet the first load of delegates in the early morning. There would be delegates coming in on three different planes. And our lives would change radically as we were joined by thirty or more different people from all over the world except behind the Iron Curtain.

"But you will be amazed at how quickly you come to know them," Krhis said, "how soon they will seem like family, as we are family around this table."

"But there will be four or more tables," Norine said, wiping her face. The breeze was hot, the air so heavy it was tangible.

"This heat has got to break soon," Krhis said, "and then I will insist on swimming at the scheduled time, Vee, please, in the middle of the day."

Vee put her hands together, bowing. "Yes, master."

Then we sang for a while, ending with *Saranam*.

> *For those who've gone, for those who stay,*
> *For those to come, following the Way,*
> *Be guest and guide both night and day,*
> *Saranam, saranam, saranam.*

Omio walked with me back to the dormitory and down the length of the long hall to my room. My room alone for this one last night. As I turned to open the door, he took my hands. "Would you want never to have had these days together, before everybody comes, never to have become friends?"

"Of course not. It's been marvelous."

"Isn't it still marvelous? It will go on being marvelous when lo, we are a large instead of a small family."

Omio had never promised me anything except friendship, and that was still his offering to me. The intensity of the experience with the kayak was part of that friendship. I had been greedy, grasping. Everything Renny had warned me of I had fallen for, if not actually, at least potentially. I felt small and chastened.

Chaste. Chastened.

Omio looked at me questioningly.

"It's still marvelous," I said.

Would I want never to have met Max? Never to have had my horizons expanded? Would I truly want to eradicate all of the good times because of one terrible time? Yes, it was terrible, Max insane with alcohol and pain and fear. But would I wipe out all the rest of it for that moment of dementia?

If I wanted Max as goddess, as idol, then, yes, I would have to destroy it. But not if I wanted Max as a human being, a vibrant, perceptive human being, who saw potential in me that I hardly dared dream of. Not if I wanted Max as she was, brilliant but flawed. Perhaps the greater the brilliance, the darker the flaw.

And what about Ursula? Surely Ursula had given me the best, with open generosity, not threatened by Max's love of me.

Why was I able to feel compassion for Zachary, who was selfish, who belonged to a world of power and corruption, and who had nearly killed me? Why didn't I want to wipe Zachary out?

And now I knew that I no longer wanted to wipe Max out. To wipe Max out was to wipe out part of myself.

"Good night, my Polly," Omio said.

I got ready for bed and worked on my school journal.

I was in the middle of a sentence when there was a great flash of lightning, coming through the slats in the shutters, followed immediately by thunder, and the heat-breaking storm struck.

I closed my notebook. This was not the kind of violence one could write through.

There was a knock on my door and Millie came in. "You all right, Polly?"

"Yah, fine. This is going to break the heat."

"You're not afraid?"

"No."

"Would you like me to stay with you for a few minutes, till the worst is over? These storms never last long." Millie was nervous over man-made power failure, but not of a storm caused by nature. She had come to me, not because she was afraid, but because she thought I might be. "Yes, please, Millie," I said.

The lights went out.

Millie reached over and took my hand.

"Ahoy!" We heard Frank's voice outside, and he came in with a flashlight and a handful of stubby candles.

"Krhis has these for all of us." He came in, and we saw that Vee and Bashemath were with him. He lit candles for us, placing them on desks and chests of drawers. In a moment Norine came in and Vee beckoned her to join her on the spare bed.

Millie began to sing, her voice unwavering through the crashing of the thunder. Khris came and stood in the doorway, looking at us with his gentle smile, and Norine pulled him in and Omio offered him one of the desk chairs.

"All of us sing," Millie ordered, and we sang until

the storm was over, and cool air came in, even through the cracks of the shutters. Bashemath stood up and yawned, and said good night.

"Yes, it is time," Krhis said. "Tomorrow will be a busy day."

Frank held out his hands to Vee. Omio left with them.

Krhis stood looking down on me sitting on the bed. "Bless you, Polly. Good night."

I felt somehow as though at last I had been allowed past the outer gates of Epidaurus, and into the sacred precincts.

Millie stood and stretched. "Good night, little one. It's cooler."

"Much. We may even need our blankets."

"You'd better not open the shutters, anyhow. Did you light your bug coil?"

"I will."

Millie bent down and kissed me, then went to her room.

I lit the coil, blew out the candle which remained. The darkness was lifted by the lightness in the air.

I was suddenly wide awake, because the power had come back on and the lights in my room were bright. I got up and turned them off, pushed the shutters open to a lovely cool breeze. Through the wall I could hear Millie snoring—safe, comfortable snores.

I slipped outside and the breeze was fresh, not burdened with moisture. I was not attacked by insects. The full moon was low in the sky, streaked by swiftly moving clouds. The storm in Osia Theola was over, but in those troubled lands across from us the electrical storm was still playing.

"Polly—"

I looked over the balcony and saw Omio.

"You're awake—"

"I was sound asleep," I said, "but when the power came on, my lights woke me."

"Come and sit on the wall by the fig sycamore for a while."

The stones hurt my bare feet, but I made it to the crumbling remnant of wall and sat looking at the moon sliding below the horizon. Omio sat beside me, and when I shivered in the cool breeze he drew me to him to keep me warm.

Whatever it was I had silently been demanding of Omio I was no longer demanding. I was happy sitting beside him, watching the night sky. I loved him, but I loved him as a friend, as I loved Max as a friend. The clean feeling of love blew through me with the breeze. I sighed with a joyful kind of relief.

Omio's arm tightened about me. "Is everything all right with us, Polly?"

"Everything is fine. I'm sorry I was such an idiot."

"It was not Omio," he said. "It was whoever hurt you."

"I was very confused."

"And now?"

"It's okay," I said wonderingly. "It's all right!"

"We are true, good friends?"

"True, good friends."

He kissed me, gently, on the cheek, and we climbed back up to the balconies, and he waited until I was in the room, drawing the shutters not quite closed.

I slept and dreamed. I went into the church and Osia Theola's cave. Inside the cave my littlest brother and sister, Johnny and Rosy, were blowing bubbles, and the bubbles with their iridescent colors illumined the darkness of the cave. Then I saw that each bubble was filled with stars, with galaxies, countless galaxies; each bubble was an island universe.

The cave was gone, the little ones were gone, and all I could see was the loveliness of the bubbles, universes glowing softly with the life of all creation.

And then I saw a hand, and all the bubbles were in the hand, which was holding them, tenderly, lovingly.

And in the dream I understood that this was Blessed Theola's vision of love.

I woke up even earlier than usual, feeling rested and refreshed. I dressed and hurried out into the clear air. The sun was warm, not hot; the day sparkled. Nobody was about, not even the old men eternally watering the roses.

I thought I heard sounds in the direction of the church, and moved across the compound. There was an early-morning service going on, and I stood in the doorway, watching the people standing quietly, their heads covered. I listened to the Byzantine chanting of the priest.

I felt a presence behind me, and it was Krhis.

We turned away from the church together. "Krhis, would it be possible for me to make an overseas call?"

"We can try." He did not sound surprised.

We went to the office, and he dialed several times, spoke to three different operators, finally gave the phone to me and left me alone. I gave the operator the number. There was a long, blank pause, and then the sound of distant ringing. And then a voice. "Hello?"

"Urs—"

"Yes, who is it?"

I had no idea what time it was at home. It didn't matter. "Urs, it's Polly. Max—may I speak to Max?"

Ursula's voice sounded hollow, with an echo following it. "Just a moment, child." . . . *moment, child.* The echo came faintly.

I waited. Waited.

And then Max's voice. "Polly?" . . . *Polly?*

"Max, I love you. I just wanted to call and tell you I love you—" I stopped because I could hear my own voice distantly echoing back what I had said.

"Oh, Polly, forgive me—"

"Me, too, forgive me, too—"

Forgive . . . forgive echoed back.

"I'm so glad you called" . . . *you called.*

"I love you, Max, I love you" . . . *love you.* "I have so much to tell you—" But before the echo had a chance to repeat my words the connection was cut and the phone went dead.

It was all right. I had said what I needed to say.

Krhis was waiting outside. He didn't ask me who I had needed to phone so suddenly. We walked slowly across the compound to the refectory part of the cloister. The cold place within me that had frozen and constricted my heart was gone. My heart was like a lotus, and in that little space there was room enough for Osia Theola, for all of Cyprus. For all the stars in all of the galaxies. For all those bubbles which were island universes.

In the cloister everybody was gathering for breakfast.

"Polly!" Norine called. "We will be very busy today. All the delegates must come into the office, and we will check them off and give them their blue folders and room assignments . . ."

She paused for breath and Omio took my hand and pulled me to the chair next to his.

"Saranam," he said.

It's the summer of 1946, and Elizabeth has just been offered her dream job—to apprentice at a theatre. Now she's one step closer to becoming a real actress. But too quickly Elizabeth begins to learn the harsh realities of life and love in the theatre.

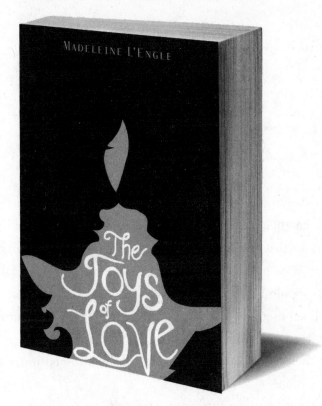

Turn the page to read an excerpt from

The Joys of Love
by Madeleine L'Engle.

That day in Mr. Price's office in New York, Elizabeth thought now, had been the turning point of her whole life. If it had not been for that day last spring, none of the summer—working in the theatre, getting to know Kurt, beginning a completely new life—would have been possible.

Even then she had been aware of it. Sitting in the anteroom of Mr. Price's office, she had thought, How strange to know that the whole course of my life can be changed today in this dingy office.

But it was true. It was so frighteningly true that her hands had felt cold with fear and her heart had beat so fast that for a moment she was afraid that she might faint in the hot stuffiness of the little room. Although it was an unseasonably hot April day, steam hissed in the radiator, and there was no window in the anteroom. Even the office door to the main hallway was closed.

Because she had not been able to sit still another moment, she went over to the receptionist. "My appointment with Mr. Price was at one o'clock and it's after two now," she said.

"Yeah?" The receptionist looked at her with a hot, annoyed face.

"I mean—he's still going to see me, isn't he?"

"You've got an appointment card, haven't you?"

"Yes."

"Okay, then, relax. Sit down. Though why you want to see him I don't know. I'm sure he doesn't want to see you."

Elizabeth sat down again. She felt miserable and young and more than snubbed. She looked at her feet because she was afraid that if she looked at the others waiting in the room she would find scorn in their faces.

"Don't let it get to you," the girl next to her said. "I've just been in an office where the receptionist was nice enough to say 'Thank you for coming in' after she told me the cast was all set. They're not all like the sourpuss here. Though with the second-rate theatre Price is running, I don't know why we're all hanging around here like a lot of trained seals waiting for him to throw us a fish."

The door to the hall opened and a young man entered. The moment he came in, a slight, pleasant smile on his face, Elizabeth saw that there was something different about him, that he was not like anybody else in the room. And then she realized what the difference was: he was the only one who was not nervous.

He walked over to the receptionist's desk and said, "Hi, Sadie, how's my duck today?" He had a slight accent.

The sour face was surprisingly pretty when it smiled. "Oh, dying of the heat, Mr. Canitz. Otherwise I guess I'll survive. You want to see Mr. Price?"

"If he's not too busy."

"Oh, he always has time to see you, Mr. Canitz. Go right in."

The young man smiled his pleasant smile at the room full of hot, nervous people, and opened the door to Mr. Price's office. Elizabeth looked in quickly and saw that it was very like the anteroom, except that it had a large open window and a brief, welcome gust of cool air blew in at her. Mr. Price was sitting at his desk talking to a young woman with blond hair, and he waved his hand genially at Mr. Canitz. "Oh, come in, Kurt. I want you to meet this young lady."

Then the door shut and heat settled back over the room.

"If I had any sense," the girl next to Elizabeth said, "I'd leave this hellhole and go home. And so would you."

"Home," Elizabeth found herself answering, "is the last place I'd go."

"Well, then, I guess you have a point in hanging around. Why don't they at least open the door into the hall?" She appealed to Sadie. "Couldn't you turn off the heat or something?"

"No, I can't," the receptionist snapped. "The radiator's broken. And I'm just as hot as you are. Hotter. If you don't like it here, why don't you leave? I tell you, he isn't going to hire anybody else. He's got the whole season set. You're wasting your time."

The girl turned back to Elizabeth. "That's the way people get ulcers. People with vile natures always get ulcers. If I stay here much longer, I'll get ulcers, too."

"But is it true?" Elizabeth asked.

"What?"

"That he has the whole season set."

"Of course it isn't true. She only said it because she's in a vile mood. What's your name? I'm Jane Gardiner."

"I'm Elizabeth Jerrold."

"Listen, I don't mean to butt in," Jane said, "but don't be nervous. You're practically making the bench shake. After all, the world isn't going to end if Price doesn't give you a job. Nothing's that important."

"But it is," Elizabeth said. "For me it is."

The door to the office opened again and Kurt Canitz and the blond woman came out. Mr. Canitz had his arm protectively about her, and he ushered her gallantly to the door and said goodbye. Then he sat down and smiled at Sadie and looked slowly around the anteroom. His eyes rested on Jane, on Elizabeth, on a little man in a bowler hat. Sadie picked up a stack of cards and called out, "Gardiner."

Jane rose. "That's me. Well, this is only the fifteenth office I've been in today. What've I got to lose?"

Elizabeth watched her as she walked swiftly into the office, shutting the door firmly behind her. Yes, Jane was obviously a person who knew her way around theatrical offices. She had a certain nervous excitement, like every actor waiting to hear about a job, but it was controlled, made into an asset; it gave a shine to her brown eyes, a spring to her step. Elizabeth felt that Jane was dressed correctly, too. She wore a pleated navy blue skirt and a little red jacket. Her hair was very fair, a soft ash blond, and on her head she wore a small red beret. Elizabeth felt forlorn in the other girl's absence, and suddenly foolish. She herself wore a simple blue denim skirt and white blouse, and she felt that she belonged much more on a college campus than she did in a theatrical office on Forty-second Street in New York. If someone as desirable as Jane had been in fifteen offices that day and still did not have a job, then what was Elizabeth thinking of when she was letting everything in the world depend on whether or not Mr. J. P. Price took her into his summer theatre company?

But Mr. Price was Elizabeth's only hope after her twenty letters of inquiry to summer-stock companies. Many of the managers had sent back form letters that offered her opportunities to apprentice—but at a two- or three-hundred-dollar tuition fee. Mr. Price had simply sent her a card telling her to be at his office at one o'clock, April 14, and he would see her then.

Elizabeth looked around at the dingy anteroom; the buff-colored walls were cracked and some of the cracks were partially covered with signed photographs of actors and actresses of whom she had never heard. There were no familiar names like Judith Anderson, Katharine Cornell, Eva Le Gallienne, Ethel Barrymore. The air smelled like stale cigar smoke from the little man in the bowler hat who sat stolidly on a folding chair and surrounded himself with a cloud of heavy fumes.

Elizabeth noticed Kurt Canitz was writing busily in a small notebook. He looked up and stared directly at her for several seconds, then scribbled something else in the notebook, tore off the page and gave it to Sadie with a radiant smile, and left.

Elizabeth wondered what his connection with the theatre was. Was he an actor, a director, perhaps a producer? Certainly he was connected with Mr. Price's summer company.

Again the door of the office opened and Jane came out. She grinned at Elizabeth.

"Did you get a job?" Elizabeth asked eagerly.

"Well, not exactly the job I went in for, but at this point it'll do. I'm going as an apprentice, which I swore after last summer I'd never do again, but this time at least it's a scholarship."

"Oh, I'm so glad!" Elizabeth exclaimed. "That's wonderful!"

"Thanks," Jane said. "Good luck to you, too."

Sadie was looking at her cards. "Jerrold," she called.

Elizabeth stood up.

Jane took her hand. "Good luck," she said again. "Good luck, *really*. I hope I'll see you there."

"Thanks," Elizabeth answered, and went into the office.

"Well, what can I do for you?" Mr. Price asked, looking Elizabeth up and down until she flinched.

"You can give me a job," Elizabeth said, and was surprised at how calm her voice sounded.

"And what kind of a job are you looking for, my dear?"

"A job in your summer theatre. As an actress." Elizabeth felt that her voice sounded flat and colorless; anxiety had wiped out its usual resonance.

"And what experience have you had? What parts have you played?"

Elizabeth ignored the first part of his question. "I've played

Lady Macbeth and Ophelia and I've played Hilda Wangel in *The Master Builder* and Sudermann's *Magda*, and the Sphinx in Cocteau's *The Infernal Machine*."

"A bit on the heavy side, wouldn't you say?" Mr. Price asked her. "And aren't you rather young for Lady Macbeth or Magda? How about something more—recent—and perhaps a little gayer?"

"Well—I've played Blanche in *Streetcar*—oh, I know that's not very gay, but it's recent—and—and—I've done some Chekhov one-acts. They're not very recent but they're gay—"

"And where did you get all this magnificent experience?" Mr. Price asked her. "Why, after all this, have I never heard of you?"

"At college," Elizabeth said, looking down at her feet.

"My dear young lady." Mr. Price sounded half bored, half amused. "Perhaps you do not realize, but I am running a professional theatre. I am sure you were very charming and very highly acclaimed at college, but I am really not contemplating producing *Macbeth* or *Magda* or even *The Infernal Machine*. So what do I have to offer you?"

"All I want," Elizabeth said desperately, "is—*anything*."

"Anything what?"

"Maids, walk-ons, working in the box office. Anything."

"I take a certain number of apprentices," Mr. Price said. "They take classes from the company actors. We use the star system. We do a new play every week and the company professionals rehearse all week in bit parts. Then the star arrives on Sunday. The stars have one rehearsal with the company before the show. Although one or two of them will direct the plays they are starring in, and those actors will be there longer. If I can, I use the apprentices in at least one walk-on part during the summer. The fee is three hundred dollars."

Elizabeth shook her head. When she spoke her voice trembled. "I—borrowed the money to come to New York to see you today. I—I—"

"And I suppose if I didn't give you a job you'll jump off the Empire State Building? Or into the Hudson River? Or perhaps the East River would suit you better."

"That's not funny," Elizabeth said with a sudden flare of anger. "Would you really laugh if you were responsible for someone's death?"

"If you did anything so foolish as to kill yourself, I wouldn't be responsible. You would." Mr. Price's voice was calm and reasonable.

"As it happens," Elizabeth said, anger still directing her words, "I agree with you. And I do not approve of suicide under any conditions. However, a weaker character in my circumstances might."

Mr. Price smiled. "Are your circumstances so very particular?"

"To me they are. You never know what people's circumstances are."

"Perhaps I can guess some of yours. You go to a good college and major in drama. Your family has a thoroughly adequate income."

"Wrong," Elizabeth said. "I go to a good college but I major in chemistry and I am on scholarship and I have no parents. I was president of the Dramatic Association and took some theatre courses in Theatre Workshop at school. I graduate later this spring."

"I stand corrected."

Elizabeth looked at him, tried to smile, and said, "And now, since you haven't a job to offer me, I'll say goodbye and go throw myself under a Fifth Avenue bus."

The door to the office opened and Sadie thrust her head in. "Say, Mr. Price, I almost forgot. Mr. Canitz left me a note to give you."

Mr. Price read the note and handed it to Elizabeth. Kurt Canitz had written, "Give the tall girl with glasses a scholarship. I have a hunch about her."

Mr. Price looked at Elizabeth. "You are tall—rather tall for an actress, incidentally—and you wear glasses, so I assume Kurt means you. By the way, how does it happen that you don't take off your glasses for an interview?"

"I forgot," Elizabeth said. "I don't always wear them, but I really can't see well without them. I never wear them onstage, of course."

"I suppose I'll have to answer to Kurt if I don't at least have you read for me. All right. Read for me."

"If you like me, will you give me a scholarship?" Elizabeth asked.

"I'm known for—shall we kindly call it being shrewd?— about money, but as far as the theatre is concerned I also have a conscience," Mr. Price said. "I collect as many three-hundred-dollar tuitions from the apprentices as I can. If a girl can afford it, why shouldn't I take it? However, if I think a kid has possi-bilities, and they can't afford the tuition, I give them a scholarship for the summer and I work her—or him, as the case may be—like a dog. There are usually two scholarships for young men and two for women. I have both my men set and one of my women. You might possibly fit the other scholarship. The apprentices and most of the resident company live at a cottage a few blocks from the theatre. Of course the scholarship apprentices pay twenty dollars a week for room and board. Could you manage that?"

"I'll have to," Elizabeth said.

"I have a feeling that you are a hard worker," Mr. Price told her. "Also, believe it or not, I have a healthy regard for Kurt Canitz's hunches—and also for his dollars, which help finance the theatre. More of a respect for his hunches and his dollars than I have for his acting, I might add, though I could pick a worse director. Okay, now read something for me." He picked up a dog-eared copy of *The Voice of the Turtle*. "This is pretty much a classic in its own way," he said. "Maybe you won't feel too much above it."

Elizabeth stood up. "Mr. Price, I know you're laughing at me, and I know you have a perfect right to. Maybe the parts I've played are silly. I didn't do them because I expected to repeat my college triumphs on Broadway, but because they're parts anyone who really cares about being an actress ought to study, and because it was my one real opportunity to work on them—until I'm an established actress and can really do them if I want to. I have learned a lot from them that I can apply to anything I do."

"Pretty sure of yourself, aren't you?" Mr. Price asked.

"No. But I have to talk as though I were."

Mr. Price sighed. "Darling Miss Jerrold—it is Jerrold, isn't it?—there are so many like you. So many who believe in themselves as potential great ones—and many who don't have the handicap of being tall and wearing glasses—so many who have real talent. Do you know that with ten young women of equal talent only one of them can possibly succeed?"

"I'm willing to risk it," Elizabeth said.

Mr. Price sighed again. "All right. Read for me."

"What shall I read?" Elizabeth took the book from him.

"Just hunt for a longish passage. One of Sally's. Are you familiar with the play?"

"We did it in college. I directed it, though; I didn't act in it."

"Good. That means you ought to know it pretty well but you won't be giving me a rehash of an old performance. Found something?"

"Yes. Here's a speech of Sally's." Elizabeth read the speech slowly, not trying to force a quick characterization. She made her voice low and pleasant, her words clear and well-defined, but she felt that she was failing thoroughly, that Mr. Price expected a performance. When she had finished the speech she said, "I'm sorry it was so bad. I can't plunge into a character right away."

"No, and you had sense enough not to try," Mr. Price told her, and for the first time his smile was for her and not at her. "One of the greatest banes of my existence is the radio actor who gives a magnificent first reading and then deteriorates until his performance is thoroughly mediocre. Each time I cast a show I say that I won't be fooled, and each time I am fooled.

Okay, Miss Jerrold. If you want to come under the terms I've outlined—as a scholarship apprentice—you may."

Elizabeth sat down abruptly. "Yes. I want to," she said, and her voice sounded as though Mr. Price had punched her in the stomach.

"Good. Give Sadie your address and she will drop you a line about trains and when to arrive and so forth. Also I will have her send you a note confirming all this so that once you get back to that good college of yours you won't worry about my forgetting you. Goodbye, Miss Jerrold. I'll look forward to seeing you at the end of June, and you, in the meanwhile, may look forward to a summer of hard work."

"Yes. Thank you," Elizabeth said, still sounding winded.

Mr. Price smiled at her again. "And one more thing. I hope you realize that I am offering you this opportunity not because of your reading, which, as you were aware, was barely adequate, but because of Mr. Canitz's hunch and my own whim. The theatre is not a reasonable place. You may as well learn that now." He held out his hand to her.

Elizabeth shook it and then, after giving Sadie her address, left the office. She almost missed Jane Gardiner, who was standing in the dim hallway leaning against a fire extinguisher.

"Hello, how'd you make out?" Jane asked her. "Thought I'd wait and see."

"I've got a scholarship," Elizabeth told her, beaming, and very pleased at Jane's friendly interest.

"Oh, good, I'm awfully glad. Look, let's go have a cup of coffee at the Automat to celebrate."

Elizabeth hesitated, then said, "I don't think I want any coffee, but I'd love to come while you have yours."

"Fine."

They went down in the elevator, both smiling with a vague and dreamy happiness at the prospect of the summer ahead of them. And to Elizabeth New York was no longer frightening but suddenly full of excitement and glamour, and the starkness of the Automat was vested in glory because Elizabeth Jerrold and Jane Gardiner were going there and perhaps one day other struggling young actresses would say, "Do you know, the great and famous Elizabeth Jerrold and Jane Gardiner used to come here!"

Elizabeth sat down at one of the tables and waited until Jane came back with two cups of coffee. "Just thought you might have changed your mind," she said casually. "If you don't want it, I'll drink it. Or, if you're broke or something at the moment—and heaven knows almost everybody in the theatre is—you can pay me back sometime."

"But that's just the trouble. I probably can't," Elizabeth said. Her voice sounded rather desperate.

Jane looked at her with friendly curiosity, then said lightly, "What's a cup of coffee between friends? Anyhow, I was referring to the golden future when we're both rich and famous and have our names in lights. Look, let's get to know each other. I'll give you my autobiography and you can give me yours. Though as for me, I'm a lot more exciting than my autobiography."

Elizabeth laughed. "Me, too."

"I'm just a damn good actress," Jane said. "How about you?"

"I'm a damn good actress, too."

"Good. Now we know the most important thing about each other. As for the unimportant details, I was born in New York and I've lived here most of my life. My father teaches higher mathematics at Columbia and I can't count up to ten. Neither can my mother, who is terribly beautiful but has never made me feel like an ugly duckling. I graduated from Columbia against my will and on my parents' insistence, though they're both very nice about my wanting to be an actress, and last winter I went to the American Academy of Dramatic Arts and fell madly in love with a great young actor named John Peter Toller who also—and for this I got down on my knees and begged and it's why I took this scholarship rather than a job anywhere else though I *did* honestly and truly *try* to get a job; I told you I'd been to dozens of other offices today—anyhow where was I? Oh, yes, John Peter has a scholarship with Price this summer, too. He's been away for two weeks visiting his parents and during these fourteen days my life has been blighted. I feel as though I'm not breathing when I'm out of his presence. He's the oxygen in my air, the sun in my universe, the staff of my life. From this you may gather that he means a great deal to me, but please don't tell him because he knows it far too well already. Now tell me about you."

A sober, rather sad look came over Elizabeth's face. Then she said lightly, "There isn't much to tell. My parents are dead and when I'm not in college in Northampton, I live with my aunt in Virginia. She doesn't approve of the theatre. I graduate this year. As for men, I'm footloose and fancy-free, and I've no idea of letting an emotional entanglement hamper my career."

Jane laughed. "Now if that doesn't sound like a college student. *My* emotional entanglement, if you want to call it that, hasn't hampered my career a bit. It's helped it. I know more about life and humanity and understanding and compassion and knowledge—and therefore about acting too—since I've known my darling John Peter than I ever dreamed of knowing before. Just you wait, my girl. You'll see." Jane pushed back her chair. "I've got to dash now, I promised my mother that I'd meet her. Maybe we'll room together this summer. I do hope so. Anyhow, I'll be seeing you at the end of June."

"Right," Elizabeth said. "Good luck till then."

"And good luck to you, too."

They shook hands. Elizabeth watched Jane walk swiftly out of the Automat, erect, graceful, assured, and somehow more alive than anyone else in the restaurant. Elizabeth realized that Jane was probably well in advance of her as an actress, and then thought happily, But I'll learn! Now I'm being given my chance to really learn with a professional company!

READ ALL OF THE CONTINUING ADVENTURES OF POLY O'KEEFE AND HER FRIENDS

The Arm of the Starfish

Adam Eddington is spending the summer in Portugal working for the world-famous Dr. O'Keefe. But when he meets a beautiful girl named Kali Cutter, he becomes involved in a battle between good and evil. Knowledge that could affect the future of the human race is at stake, and Adam doesn't know which side is good, and which side is evil. Then Dr. O'Keefe's daughter, Poly is kidnapped. Adam better pick a side soon, before kidnapping escalates to murder.

978-0-312-67488-5 • $9.99 US/$10.99 Can

Dragons in the Waters

Simon Renier is on an ocean voyage to Venezuela with his cousin Forsyth, a man he's never met before, who may not be altogether trustworthy. Then Forsyth is murdered and everyone on board is a suspect. Simon and his newfound friends, Poly and Charles O'Keefe, are determined to track down the murderer, but will they succeed before they land? Or will the murderer escape into the jungles of Venezuela?

978-0-312-67442-7 • $9.99 US/$10.99 Can

A House Like a Lotus

Polly O'Keefe is excited about taking her first trip alone to work at a conference on the island of Cyprus. During a stopover in Athens, she meets Zachary Gray, a wealthy and handsome young man who shows her the sights. Polly enjoys their fleeting friendship, but she's also eager to get to work. Then Zachary shows up at the conference and tries to persuade her to skip out on her responsibilities. But his reckless behavior and desire to impress her might end up getting both of them killed.

978-0-312-54798-1 • $9.99 US/$10.99 Can

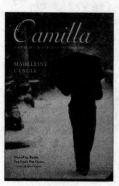

THE AUSTIN FAMILY CHRONICLES
Available from Square Fish

From Madeleine L'Engle, author of the bestselling classic,
Newbery Medal winner *A Wrinkle in Time*,
comes a beloved family series, The Austin Family Chronicles

ISBN: 978-0-312-37931-5
$6.99 US/$7.99 Can

ISBN: 978-0-312-37932-2
$7.99 US/$8.99 Can.

ISBN: 978-0-312-37933-9
$7.99 US/$8.99 Can.

These five novels feature Vicky Austin and her family as
they grow together through the joys and sorrows of daily life.

ISBN: 978-0-312-37935-3
$6.99 US/$7.99 Can

ISBN: 978-0-312-37934-6
$7.99 US/$8.99 Can.

SQUARE FISH
WWW.SQUAREFISHBOOKS.COM
AVAILABLE WHEREVER BOOKS ARE SOLD